Deeply moving. In lyrical prose, Anne de Graaf weaves a tapestry of chilling suspense interlaced with bright threads of love and faith. Africa comes alive as the plight of the child soldier brings aching tears and, ultimately, a vision of hope."

CATHERINE PALMER
best-selling author of *The Happy Room*

"Using language and intelligence, Anne de Graaf masterfully transports her readers to the places our hearts need to go. She challenges us to expand our borders and think more globally as we vicariously experience the struggles of the less fortunate through her. And all this within a page-turning adventure that holds the reader **spellbound.** What more could you ask?"

MELODY CARLSON
author of *Looking for Cassandra Jane*

"*Anne de Graaf writes with* **emotional power** that grips my heart even as it opens my eyes and illuminates my spirit. Anne has invested precious seeds of her life in *Into the Nevernight,* and we are all richer for her efforts. Not to be missed."

ANGELA E. HUNT
author of *The Shadow Women*

"With sophisticated style, Anne de Graaf takes readers to a deep place of hope as they journey *Into the Nevernight*. Her characters: Miriam, Owen, and Simba mdogo are unforgettable. The extent of her research is evident. The result is that readers are transported to another place where they are given new eyes to see the *unflinching beauty* found in truth."

ROBIN JONES GUNN
best-selling, award-winning author of the Glenbrooke series

"It's all here—foreign intrigue, romance, suspense, danger, vulnerable children, compassion, and love. Anne de Graaf goes for the heart—yours—and touches it at many levels. Discover with her the irony of peace in places of war, light in the darkness of conflict. Discover hope and a God who cares and touches people at unexpected times and places of life. Based on actual stories of children the author has interviewed, *Into the Nevernight* **will take you places you've never been before.** You'll be glad you went."

TERRY MADISON
President/CEO, Open Doors USA

into the
nevernight

THE CHILDREN'S VOICES SERIES
BOOK ONE

into the

nevernight

ANNE DE GRAAF

Tyndale House Publishers, Inc., Wheaton, Illinois

Visit Tyndale's exciting Web site at www.tyndale.com

Learn more about this author and book at annedegraaf.com and thechildrensvoices.com

Into the Nevernight

Edited by Anne Christian Buchanan and Dan Elliott

Designed by Kelly Bennema and Luke Daab

Published in association with the literary agency of Alive Communications, Inc., 7680 Goddard Street, Suite 200, Colorado Springs, CO 80920.

Library of Congress Cataloging-in-Publication Data

De Graaf, Anne.
   Into the nevernight / Anne de Graaf.
      p. cm. — (The children's voices series ; bk. 1)
T.p. verso.
ISBN 0-8423-5289-9
1. Africa—Fiction.   I. Title.   II. Series.
PS3554.E11155 158 2003
813'.54—dc21   2003001365

Printed in the United States of America

08   07   06   05   04   03
 9   8   7   6   5   4   3   2   1

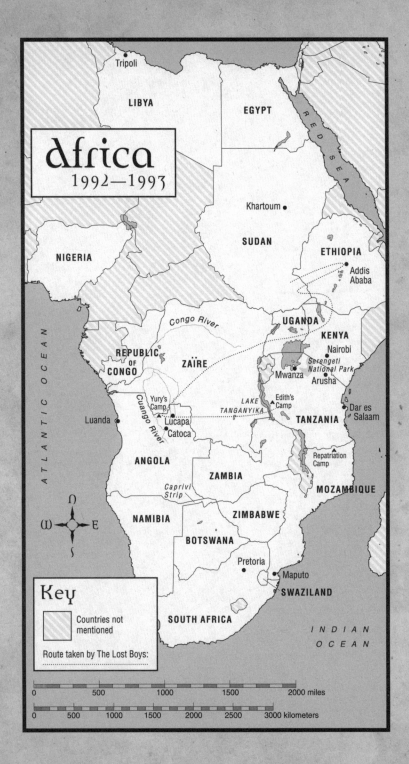

There will be no more night.
They will not need the light of a lamp or the light of the sun,
for the Lord God will give them light.
And they will reign for ever and ever.

—Revelation 22:5, NIV

Usiku hautakuwako tena,
wala hawatahitaji mwanga wa taa au wa jua,
maana Bwana Mungu atawaangazia,
nao watatawala milele na milele.

—*Habari Njema kwa watu wote*, Kiswahili cha Kisasa
***Good News for Modern Man*,** Today's Kiswahili Version

To Erik

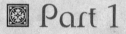 # Part 1

I could not know, would not know. I could not know how Africa would touch me, bend me, remold my heart, grant me hope . . . and change my child, giving me another.

Sometimes there is a place you do not know about, but it is still there, outside your knowing. When you reach this place you change, and you wonder how you could possibly have lived without the knowledge of it inside you. It is as a third dimension to a flat two, color to black and white, a sixth sense to a mere five.

For some, such places may be in their minds, milestones of healing, memory, revelation. For others, as it is for me, this place has physical, geographical characteristics. I can point to it on a twirling globe, rest my finger over the spot on a map, close my eyes, and I am back there again, seeing as ravenously as a near-blind woman, reveling in the assurance that only in darkness can I sense the parallel dimension.

Before, I just barely missed, barely caught glimpses of it. Now I know it is there and it has redeemed the rest. For everything I see now is through eyes that could not see before, ears that did not hear, and a heart that would not understand. . . .

# Chapter 1

Miriam's own laughter woke her.

"Tell me." Owen's voice. She opened her eyes and saw him leaning over her. She reached out an arm and slid it under his broad chest, his warmth all around her now.

"Tell me the joke, what it is you're dreaming of."

She smiled, surprised to be off the beach, the place her mind had stranded her. "I . . . I don't know the joke."

A woman walking on a distant shore, the roaring surf a cadence to her soul. The familiar dream image still lingered in her mind, but the laughter . . . she had no idea where the laughter came from. And now, in the real world of her Owen and the sun and a sea breeze blowing the cotton curtains, the questions clanged, an echoing bell that bridged her conscious world with the unconscious, the sound itself an ancient cry.

Was *she* the woman in her dream? Which shore was it? From where did the sun shine this time? Over which shoulder? Which way did she head? The woman's shadow haunted Miriam. In her dream the sun forged its image sometimes from left and sometimes from right, the pounding waves on opposite sides. Did the woman walk toward the east or west?

"You're dreaming again."

She focused on his glorious face, a trail of battles fought and won, his eyes adoring her. "I am. You're right. Sorry."

"Come here."

Later that morning Miriam followed the twisted beach path down from their condo on the north side of Kauai. Both hands were full of handles and straps—she carried her son's little backpack with his sketchpad and pencils and her own bag of legal journals slung across one arm. Miriam was determined on these last few days of their vacation to at least skim through most of them. That way she wouldn't have to admit she had hauled them all the way here from San Francisco for nothing.

At the turn in the path she paused, shifting her snorkel and mask to the other hand so she could shade her eyes. There, just beyond the reef, near the corner of the cliff to the right, she could make out her husband and son, their backs bobbing up and down with the waves. She knew Martin's hand rested on Owen's back. All week the three of them had been swimming to the same spot together, going out to meet the sea turtles. The gardener had told Owen about the spot, and Martin had dubbed it their very own secret cove, since no one else swam there.

The Hawaiian vacation had been Owen's way of making up for the year's many long absences. His latest negotiation assignment had meant empty weeks every time he flew back and forth to Africa. And before that, the failed Irish deal had drained him more than either of them was willing to admit. He needed—they needed—this time away together.

Miriam hurried down the rest of the hill, leaves bigger than two hands brushing her cheek. At the bottom, she dropped her things and waded into the warm water, white sand between her toes. She spat into her mask, swished water around inside, slipped it over the curls covering her ears, and slid into the sea.

Martin saw it first. "Look, Dad—my backpack." And then he caught sight of his mother's sandals in the sand. "Dad?" He turned around to see his father emerging from the water, shaking his head like a grizzly bear.

"What is it, Martin?" But he wasn't even looking at the beach.

"It's Mom. She's still out there." Martin kept his snorkel on since he could see better through the prescription glass and turned around to face the horizon. Here on the beach the waves were quiet, but out there they pounded onto the reef. The tide had fallen while they snorkeled. During their swim back, Martin had noticed how narrow the passage through the coral had become. In some of the places his father led him through, it had barely missed scraping his stomach.

Now he could see the dark shapes rising between the waves like boulders. He knew they could hurt a person. And he knew something else— that the lower tide would give the waves more strength. If Mom had gone out to their secret cove, the waves now could dash her against the rocks at the base of the cliff. This was the reason he and Dad had headed back when they did.

Martin shook his head. He suddenly knew, knew for certain, that his mother was not safe. He knew it because he felt his heart beating faster and he yelled as loud as he could, "Dad!"

His father had already turned around and was lumbering back toward the reef, his flippered feet sending up little geysers with every step. The lower tide meant the waves out by his father made more noise, and if he had heard Martin, he gave no sign. Martin screamed again, "Dad! I'm coming too!"

This time his father turned around. He yelled something back, then held up his hand, palm toward Martin. Tears clouded Martin's snorkel mask, but he still saw his father's hand telling him to stop, then pointing at the shore. Martin understood he was to stay on the beach. But he didn't want to. The breakers thundered out at the reef. How would his dad ever get through to the other side? The passage through the coral would be gone by now.

Martin watched his father dive into the surf. He could see him battling the undercurrent. He yelled again and felt torn in two. "Dad, please!"

Martin could think of one thing only: What if he lost both his parents out there? He cried out one more time, his seven-year-old voice breaking on the beach, "Wait for me! Dad! Come back!"

Miriam relaxed to the rhythm of the sights below her, the booming surf a distant music. She felt the rhythm of water across her back, her calves, and thought, *There must be a song, a song to which the trees and waves and light and breeze all move. A score, a beat in time. They dance. But I don't hear it.*

She swam, swam and saw. A whole new world, another planet, a fourth dimension. Coral reef, butterfly fishes yellow with black stripes and spots. Colors she never knew existed before Owen took her snorkeling for the first time last week. She saw striped wrasses, sunlight never standing still; two unicorn fish, bigger, smaller, spotted; zebras—all moving in time to the same current, the seaweed swaying.

Owen's voice came back to her, *"Don't push against the waves, swim with them."* So, moving, back and forth, up and down with the swell, forward and back, back and forward, she made her way toward the breakers on the reef. She followed the route he had pointed out to her the first day, a way between the coral that would bring her to the opening in the ridge. There she would have to swim hard to get through the waves. Miriam remembered the directions: turn right, swim parallel to the reef with the open sea on her left until she reached the outcrop. At the bottom of the cliff swam the sea turtles that had entertained them all week. Owen and Martin would be surprised when she joined them out there.

The waves still carried her up and forward and down and back as she moved toward the reef. Miriam thought, *I see the fish dancing to this score, a meter I don't know. And I try to match their movements. This kaleidoscope of color, symphony of movement. And still, somehow, a stillness. A time apart.*

That, in so many ways, was what this vacation had become—a stolen season, their place of peace. Here they had rediscovered the time to sit and listen to Martin's many stories, the space to share silence. Like last night, when Miriam had joined Owen on the lanai, their balcony overlooking waves and palms, and together they'd watched the moonlit beach, the light carving its way through water and sky, moon looking down, clouds a halo around stars, light from sandy point to sandy point. And then this morning from the same vantage point, they had watched in silence the swell, the wave movements, the surf on the sand, hearing the under-roar, the break of water. Owen had pointed, and together they'd seen the shadow of a school of fish pass across the seafloor.

"Like a cloud's shadow," Miriam had said.

"No, like God's hand across the surface of the earth."

Miriam had heard the longing in his voice. This was what Miriam loved most about her husband, his poet's heart for peace.

Owen summoned all his great strength to throw his body through the breakers. Again and again they pitched him backward, but he swam with all the might he could squeeze out of his arms and legs, chin on his chest, battering the wall of water again and again.

He thought only of Miriam. If the island crosscurrents pulled at him with such a deadly grip, how could *she* possibly fight them? Though a fair swimmer, she was slight and slender—not much muscle on her bones to power against the current.

But she was strong. Owen pushed against the panic by focusing on this quality in her. It was a different kind of strength, like a stubborn root. And it came from so deep within her that she herself had trouble seeing it. Whenever he tried to describe what he saw in her, she would look away and change the subject. Yet even in those moments he could glimpse the determination, the enduring brightness that shone in the depths of her.

My own rare jewel. Miriam's father, Ben, had called her that. Ben Vree, the diamond cutter, who had likened his only daughter to a diamond of deep and subtle brilliance. It was the reason Miriam's father agreed to design their engagement ring using a black diamond. Owen's idea.

Owen raised his head for the hundredth time to survey the water's surface, hoping for some sign of Miriam in the swell. His Miriam, his own precious gem, with multicolored facets he had only just started to catch sight of in their eight years together. *Too short!* "Miriam!" he cried out loud.

The sound of her name summoned her image. He grabbed on to it as if holding her in his mind would somehow keep her safe. Even as he battled the waves, he heard her gentle voice, saw the soft smile, round eyes the color of mahogany but flecked with tiny splinters of blue, dark chestnut curls framing her face, smelling like the sea. He sensed her gentle spirit, somewhere near. He prayed with every stroke that God would keep her afloat.

Owen inspected the horizon but saw nothing, no one. Then he

turned toward the line of waves that cut him off from seeing the shore. Here he thought he heard another voice, an answer to his own.

Saltwater streamed into her snorkel just as Miriam inhaled. It burned her throat, and she threw her head up and back so she could spit it out. Only then did she see the height of the waves around her. Miriam thought of the full moon the night before, remembered it meant extreme tides. She realized now was the time of day for low tide and stronger undercurrents. Miriam had to tread water hard to keep her arms above the surface and blow the water out of the snorkel.

She kicked full force to keep afloat and felt her foot hit knife-sharp coral. She cried out as pain seared up her leg, the coral's threat now exposed. The current sucked her closer to the reef. Miriam looked down through the clear green water and saw a wisp of red begin to wind away from her feet.

She gasped and brought her knees up to her chin to keep them off the coral, then used her arms to turn herself around, then around again, trying to get her bearings. With the waves so high, she could only guess the beach was to her right. That meant she had to swim just a little farther to get through the breakers, hit calmer water, then head for the cliff, which should be straight ahead. She figured she must have veered out of the passage through the coral to be in such a shallow place, where the reef almost hit the surface. Miriam glanced downward again, and this time shock ran up her spine as she watched blood billowing like a mushroom cloud around her ankles and a shape moving somewhere below.

Chapter 2

Me, I write this from the future, from a place in time where I can write, and can read, and am safe in the knowledge that I will not die in the dust tonight.

You have asked me to write this story, to tell on paper what happened to me, what I did—to do this for my own sake. I don't want to, but I will write it for you. You have told me that none of it is my fault, but what I have done is so terrible, I cannot help but feel it was my fault. You will not allow me to say such things. So I do so only on this paper, in this green leather-bound notebook you gave me so I can take the questions out of my head finally and make them hold still.

How can God forgive me?

Who am I?

Where am I?

This last question is the easier one so I will answer it first. And the answer is very good indeed.

Where I am now, I sit on a chair made of wood, at a table also made of wood. I am in a place I think God must have forgotten to take back to heaven with Him. Books all around me, walls made of books. Believe me now.

There are no books on the ceiling or floor. On my first night here, when I did not know better, I checked. The man who built this place, he made extra walls just to hold the books. There are twenty-six rows of these book walls. I counted them.

I work here. Well, I do not call it work—not like carrying millet or jerry cans of water or bending over in the sun all day planting maize. What I mean is, they pay me to find homes for these books.

Each evening after my classes I come here, and a cart of books is waiting for me. I take them around, between the walls, and find the right place for each of them. The books, they tell me where they belong by a name on their covers or a number on the sticker on their spines. When I have finished, I go to a place in the back where seats and tables are one and a high wall surrounds each space, and I open my own books to mirror their messages in my mind.

You have brought me here to this place, and my young, old-man's heart is happy. Why must I leave this place where light shines even at night and go to the place where I can tell this story? For this is what you have asked me—to return, to search the darkness yet again for that small boy, his eyes clenched closed, hands clasped before one eye as he learns to pray.

Chapter 3

Martin dove into the water. He would not be left alone. His father had said he was a good swimmer. He would just go back out through the route they had taken coming in. All these thoughts ran through his mind. *I can do it!*

But after only a few strokes he was tired, and again the tears fogged up the inside of his mask. He couldn't see the coral he feared, and that made it even worse. He stopped, treading water, looking around, but he had completely lost sight of his father. "Dad!" he cried. But no answer came, only the sound of pounding surf.

He slowly headed for the shore. It was no use. Then he realized he should go for help. He pulled off the flippers and mask, remembering that his glasses were back in the condo. It didn't matter. He knew the way. Martin started running up the steep hill, the pebbles biting into his soles. He ran, and the tears kept falling over his face, but he didn't care. He had to help his father save his mother. Had to.

At the curve in the hill he stopped to catch his breath. He leaned forward, panting, and rested his hands on his knees, then looked behind him, back out to sea. Beyond the reef, near the cliff, he thought he saw her. Some shape was out there, moving on the waves, but he couldn't see clearly enough to know for sure. "Mom!" He screamed and waved but knew she could not hear him. Martin held up his open hand, palm down to shade his eyes. "Mom! Mom!"

He wasn't even sure it was her. Why didn't anyone come down the path to help him? Martin squinted his eyes. As he tried to focus, his eyes too weak, he thought he saw two things. There was his mother's blue swimsuit in the waves just beyond the cliff. And there was another shape, larger, swimming toward his mother. Something sticking up . . .

Martin whirled and raced to the top of the hill. On the lawn between the row of condos and the parking lot, he began to yell, "Help! Someone help me, please!"

He held his breath so he could hear better, but only the sounds of the trade winds in the palms answered his cries. Martin ran up the ramp to their condo and tried the door. Locked! He should have known. He needed to call 911 or get his glasses or something!

"Can I help you?"

He turned around and saw the gardener. "Yes . . . my mom is in trouble . . . out there . . . and my dad went out to be with her, to save her and I'm not sure, but I think there's a—I think I saw a. . . ." He could not say the word. If he said it, he would make it real, give it a shape and form. The word lodged in his throat and refused to budge. Instead he pointed toward the sea. "Sh-she's out there!"

But the gardener was just nodding his head. Martin moved closer to look at the man's face. "Do you have a key to our condo?"

"I can get one. Listen, your parents are good swimmers. I'm sure they'll be fine. And we rarely have sharks on this side of the island. Are you locked out, then? I'll help you. Follow me."

She did not even know it was there. Not until she looked down.

Miriam had managed to pull herself out of the surf in the direction of the open sea beyond and to veer toward the cliff, but only at the price of sheer exhaustion. Her mask rode on her forehead so that every few strokes she could twist herself around and try to get her bearings. She alternated between this little dance and floating on her back to rest or sidestroking toward the sea cliff. But now that she came closer, she knew she dared not go in too far. For some reason, the waves were crashing against the rocks even harder than usual. And the current was stronger than she ever remembered it.

She looked longingly at the boulders at the base of the cliff. They called to her to reach their sides and climb onto their round shoulders, from where she might be able to scramble up the hill. She could even see the condo now from where she swam. So close, yet the power of the waves warned her against trying.

Her muscles threatened to cramp, and Miriam knew they would never get her back through the surf. Her chances of finding the gap in the coral leading back to their beach were a million to one. She was certainly too tired to swim along the coast to the next beach. All she could do now was wait—wait until she regained enough strength to swim back . . . or until help came.

Stay away from the cliff, away from the coral. Miriam muttered this plan under her breath, spitting out saltwater, though deep inside, she knew she was fooling herself. It was not so simple. For every time she rested on her back, trying to slow her panting and distance the hyperventilation, the current would sweep her toward shore. Then she would find herself both closer to the cliff's boulders and hovering above more outcroppings of coral. The second time it grazed her foot, she screamed.

Panic rose in Miriam. Panic and blood. *Low tide*—the realization gave logic to why it all had gone so wrong. Miriam fought the panic, but it still forced her into a cringing fetal position, knees tight under her chin, so that the next time, the coral cut her knee.

Blood all around her now. In an open sea. *I'll never survive out here!* A change in the water color below caught her eye. Miriam looked down but could not focus through the choppy movement bouncing up at her face. Taking a deep breath, because she could not tread water with the coral so close, Miriam submerged her mouth as her hands went up to pull the mask down over her eyes and then pull her hair off her forehead and out of the mask. She quickly positioned the snorkel into her mouth and pushed all the air from her lungs to blow the water out the pipe.

Miriam looked down and saw the coral jump up at her, felt an electric shock of recognition that it really did grow so close, within arm's length. She blinked twice, took a deep breath, and exhaled slowly. *"Relax."* Owen's voice. *"Face the fear—that way you can see it better."*

Miriam struggled to open herself to the world below, the moving colors replacing the murky surface that had confused her a moment earlier. She stretched flat to swim over the coral, her floating body now not even scraping its top. The calm sway of underwater plants caught her in its rhythm. She began to swim with her arms, not daring to kick because of the coral, again toward the open sea.

Only when Miriam looked down to the right did she see a shadow as long as her legs. It slid toward what looked like a cave, just beyond her line of vision, and slipped inside.

Owen swam parallel to the shore, heading for the cliff. He kept his mask over his eyes and his chin on his chest, and he timed his breathing to match every three strokes. He had caught sight of Miriam once he cleared the breakers. Still near the cliff, but too close. He knew where to go, but he had to get there quickly. So he focused all his energy on the crawl strokes, making each kick, each dig of his arm pull him as close as possible toward his wife.

Owen tried to clear his mind. *Stroke, stroke, stroke, breathe.* His eyes wide open, the colors and shapes on the seafloor beneath him rushed by like a silent movie.

Miriam froze, arms forward and bent at the elbows, her body bobbing with the waves. Saltwater stung her cuts. She hoped the flow of blood had ceased, but she didn't dare look. She felt a sharp pain in her side, a pressure in her chest, and slowly released the air bursting in her lungs. She cocked her head and saw how the ocean bottom receded into a narrow gully. The figure had disappeared. Rocks fell away beneath Miriam as she swam forward. Brown gave way to dark green, then light teal and gray. She felt like a plane flying higher as the sea bottom dropped, almost out of sight, below her.

A part of the cliff bottom broke away and swam straight for Miriam. She froze again, held her breath, then sagged in relief as she recognized a sea turtle circling beneath her feet. She watched it dive low, then slowly swam after it as the coral dropped behind like a bad dream. Once, the yard-long creature circled around beneath her, flippers waving gracefully as it flew in slow motion through the water. Miriam could count the mossy patches along the edge of its shell. Eyes centered in a scaly face gazed without expression in her direction.

The next time Miriam looked up, the cliff stood far to her right. She had caught a different current and now swam much farther out to sea than she had ever been. She knew this was very deep water—she could no longer even see the bottom. But she reveled in the absence of coral as she stretched her legs downward, wiggling her toes, working out the cramp in her thigh.

Something smooth and wet bumped against her shoulder. Miriam gasped, whirled, choked on saltwater, then cried out.

"I found you," Owen said.

He held her tight, so tight she could hardly breathe.

Echoing her thoughts, Owen said, "We were afraid we would lose you."

His words brought a nervous laugh of recognition to Miriam's mouth. "I knew you'd come," she said as he held her, their legs treading water now to the same, silent tune.

Chapter 4

Owen remained at her side during the long swim back, holding her hand lightly as they kicked their way back to shore, arms at their sides. When they reached what was left of the narrow passage through the coral and Miriam felt her overtired muscles tighten in fear, he swam in front of her, so all she had to do was blindly follow his flippers.

At the beach they staggered onto the sand. She could hardly stand. Once she caught her breath, Miriam said, "Owen, where is Martin?" She watched her husband look up, then back out at the sea, as if he had just heard the echo of a cry.

"He was calling after me," Owen mumbled.

Miriam didn't want to say the words, didn't want to give this thought a place in her mind. So instead she asked, "What was he calling?"

"That I should wait for him." Owen took a few steps toward the water as if he meant to go back out.

Miriam felt her stomach muscles cramp. *No.* Instinctively, she joined him in looking out to sea.

"Who are you looking for?"

The voice took them both by surprise. Miriam whirled and saw a man with Asian features smiling at them. He stood where there had been only the shadow of palm branches a few seconds earlier.

Miriam opened her mouth to answer, but nothing came out. Instead, she felt tears running down her cheeks. *No, not Martin.*

"Why are you crying? Who are you looking for?" he repeated, now looking concerned.

Owen stepped forward. "Our son. He's a boy of seven, light hair, eyes like my own. He usually wears glasses, but I'll bet he was wearing his snorkel mask when he left here. You're the gardener, aren't you?"

Miriam watched this dialogue as if from a distance, too exhausted to participate. Owen's presence reassured her. He towered over the gardener, his blue gray eyes dark and shining with concern, shoulders hunched forward. He spoke in even tones, moving his hands like a magician's. *If anyone can take control of a situation, it's Owen.* She told herself that. She told herself twice.

The gardener smiled again, "He's safe. Look." He pointed toward the top of the cliff. Miriam heard the child's voice before she saw him. Martin called to them both from the lanai. She found their veranda among the others and saw his little figure waving with both hands, calling out, hooting as his arms waved back and forth.

Back in the condo, Miriam held on to Martin and wondered if the tremors running up her arms came from her muscles or his. "What is it, Martin?" she asked.

"I was so afraid of. . . ."

"Of what, son?" She felt Owen's arms around her again, around them both. Now she could kneel down onto the pale aqua carpet and find the courage to look into Martin's eyes, risking the pain she knew waited there.

"Nothing."

"Martin, you won't lose us." Miriam heard Owen make the promise. She watched Martin nod and felt thankful for Owen's willingness to read the boy's thoughts. Miriam stood and headed for the kitchen.

Then she heard Martin say, "Dad?" and the alarm in his voice caused her to whirl around. She wondered at the stare of surprise crawling across Owen's face.

He caught his breath, gasping. "My chest burns." He rubbed a fist against the skin, massaging the spot, but it seemed only to grow worse.

Miriam watched her husband, a large man with reddish blond hair, slightly balding, a man in blue and red swim trunks, watched in the stopped moment as a face that no longer looked like her Owen's turned red, the mouth twisted in pain and incomprehension. He tilted his head, reached for a nonexistent wall, and slowly, slowly crashed to the floor.

Chapter 5

Before I write anything else, I must write down these words: God has blessed me indeed. Fine words, these.

So, where am I? First I was in the dark, and now I am in the light. Thanks to you, I am safe. In this new country, no crocodiles swim in the lakes. Here women wear trousers. Sometimes chicken soup has not even the tiniest bit of meat in it. Here, there are so many cars, so many houses. Here I can control the warmth of the sun inside my room by means of a small box on the wall. Here I eat three times a day instead of once or not at all. The next time you visit, I will show you how I can vacuum. I am so happy. Here, there are no scorpions, no malaria. My days here are as full with classes and work as they were empty before. But you will not hear me complain of this fullness, for I am young, and this is the moment to grab my chance.

Still, bread does not taste like bread here. And meat does not taste like meat. What is this hamburger? Also, I am ashamed of some of the things I hear students say to the professors. And I will not approach a girl here! No! Some are bold enough to speak to me, but then I run away because these must be bad girls. Yes, you will say now that girls are different here, and it is another culture. But me, I know that an honorable woman should behave more modestly.

Some mornings my mind is so heavy in bed, it says, "Stay here!" And I do. Yes, there are times when I have trouble getting out of bed to work at my jobs or go to classes.

In this place, I am the janitor, the one unloading luggage or inspecting briefcases at an airport. I am the taxi driver, a waiter, a boy shining shoes in the hotel lobby. I am a librarian's assistant.

Do you see the men and women in these places? Do you see them now, busing tables, making your bed, helping you back out of a parking place? Now see their shadow selves, what they were, what they could have become. Shall I introduce them, the brothers and sisters like myself, so you can give them a kind word, a touch, or smile on them as God has smiled? These are the members of our family who have been given a second life, who will not die in the dust tonight.

Do you see where I am? Do you see my story? What do you see?

Chapter 6

Miriam listened to the pilot tell them the altitude and thought how easy it had been to change their tickets. Owen's diplomatic passport had its advantages. She could not even remember packing their things or how they had gotten to the airport. One small flight to the main island, and now this four-hour one back to San Francisco.

It was the middle of the night and she should sleep, but she felt too restless. The hum of the plane engines had not put Martin to sleep either. She could hear him chattering to the woman beside him, a friendly grandmother type. He had just explained the contents of his backpack and now sat telling his life story, it seemed. Miriam eavesdropped on his banter, smiling at how easily he had forgotten the afternoon's fear.

"My name? I'm Martin O'Neill. . . . I was born in 1985, so I'm seven. . . . My father makes peace, and my mother finds out stuff. . . . I'm in second grade now. I'm learning how to write cursive. But I already read sixth-grade books. Mom says I learned how to read when I was five. She says they didn't teach me. I was just doing it. . . . I like to draw. . . . I want a dog, but Mom says it wouldn't be fair to the dog since we live in the city and go on trips. What I *really* want is a computer. . . . I have two best friends, Pete and Matt. Pete's dad is my soccer coach. The three of us put together our Hot Wheels tracks and made a huge racetrack on our basement floor. . . . My favorite movie is *Jurassic Park*."

"Martin, why don't you try sleeping now?" Miriam smiled at the woman on the other side of her son. "Thank you for putting up with him."

"Excuse me? I couldn't hear you."

When Miriam repeated herself, careful to speak up, the woman responded, "No problem. He's a good boy. A little excited, but no doubt a good boy."

"Yes." Miriam ran out of words as Martin laid his head on the pillow on her lap. Within a few moments he grew heavy with sleep. She ran her fingers along his temple, smoothing his hair, the red almost all bleached now, but still there to remind her of Owen's own hue. Tawny freckles spilled across the bridge of Martin's nose, a path of bread crumbs leading to his eyes. She carefully slipped the glasses off, noticing how much smaller his eyes looked without them. She managed to do this and place the glasses in her breast pocket without waking him.

Miriam felt watched, looked up and smiled again at the lady, who nodded and finally looked back down at her magazine. Miriam turned to Owen on her right, a dog-eared green paperback in his hand.

"What are you reading?" Miriam asked carefully. She knew he'd only grow impatient if she fussed over him. But try as she might to relax, she could not stop going back over the events of that day.

The paramedics had arrived at the condo in five minutes' time. By then Owen was conscious. They said hitting his head on the coffee table had probably knocked him out. But he had also suffered a minor heart attack, a fact confirmed by the equipment in the ambulance and again at the hospital.

"We've run a battery of tests but can't find any residual damage," the doctor had told them when he finally returned to where they sat. "Luckily, the episode was very, very minor. Since you've clearly stabilized and there don't seem to be any further symptoms, I suggest you get home as soon as possible so you can receive care from your own physician. Sometimes people your size don't do well in this heat. It's just an added factor."

Sitting there in the plane, Miriam still felt the relief. The change of plans had cut their vacation short by only a few days. Leaving on a weekday had proved no problem. All this, Miriam left unsaid. Instead she ran her hand over his arm, up and down, reassuring herself that he was really beside her.

Owen looked up in response to her question. "Something written in the mid-fifties, a collection of African writing called *African Voices*. Listen to this: 'For when we were caught by the English, we were glad. But when I thought about my home, I cried. But still, because slavery up the country is a very hard life, and because we do not know about God there—yet we know Him, but because we cannot worship Him well—and perhaps because the Europeans do not sell people, for these reasons we were glad.'"

Miriam blinked. "A slave?"

"Yes. Amazing really. A boy wrote this in the 1880s. He was captured from a slave ship off the east coast of Africa. A British cruiser rescued him and others like him, then took him to a school on Zanzibar. This one made it. And he wrote down his story. 'Yet we know Him.' Can you imagine the implications?"

Miriam shook her head, leaning over Owen's side to see the book better. "How does it start?"

Owen said, "What I read you was the ending. Listen. 'Since I left my own land, and, indeed, since I was born, I never saw or knew my mother.'"

Miriam pursed her lips, wondering if she really wanted to hear this. Owen stopped and closed the book. "You know, I would dearly love to take you there one day."

"Where? To Zanzibar? We just went on vacation. Do you think we could survive another?"

They both smiled then, and Miriam realized it was the first time she had seen him relax since her swim. He picked up her hand and started stroking her fingers, one at a time. Neither of them seemed willing to discuss the day's fears. Instead Owen said, "No, to Africa. The light is like no place I've ever been. Amber light, you know, something similar to what we see in the autumn. And the colors—it's like you've been walking around all your life with a filter over your eyes, and then, when you land in Africa, even as you descend the stairs from the plane, a whole new spectrum opens up before you. The colors jump out and grab your very soul."

Miriam laughed. "Oh, I love you," she whispered.

He continued, his voice breathless. "And the children. Now, even if the light and the colors weren't enough, the children—they're gorgeous. Clever too. When those kids smile, you want to give them the world."

Miriam remembered where it was that she had seen a nation full of beautiful children before. "Even more beautiful than the Irish?" She thought of the bright hair, the freckles, the startling green eyes that so often had welcomed her to that island on their honeymoon.

"Even more gorgeous than myself." Owen brought her hand to his lips.

After the film, Owen glanced beside him and raised the armrest to ease Miriam's head onto his shoulder. As he listened to her soft breathing, Owen sighed and shook his head slightly. How close had he really come?

He had heard that Christians in China would ask the question, "Is this the day?" They didn't mean *Is this the day a government agent infiltrates my house group and I am arrested for my faith?* or *Is this the day others will torture me in prison?* Their question was: *Is this the day I get to come safely home, into Jesus' arms?*

When the muscles around his own heart had tightened, Owen hadn't even had time to wonder. Only now, when the danger had passed and the three of them sat together in the plane's still darkness, did he have the chance to ask himself, *How close to heaven did I really come?* Torn now between profound gratitude and deep longing, Owen bowed his head.

When he reopened his eyes, Owen realized how often he flew alone, sharing the seat beside him with a laptop or a stranger. Then he sighed again. During his eight years of married life, he still had not found a way to reconcile his guilt over the time he spent away from his family. By definition, an international negotiator traveled. It was part of the job. But after the breakdown in the Irish talks last year, Owen had felt driven to compensate for his failure. Perhaps he had pushed it too hard in Mozambique, he thought now. Was that what his heart had been telling him?

Or maybe he shouldn't have taken on Mozambique in the first place. With its bleak history of three decades of war, it was not exactly the best place for a peacemaker to make an impression. But Owen loved to take risks. That was part of what made him a valuable negotiator. The very difficulty of the Mozambique peace deal had attracted him at a time when he needed a personal compensation for all that had gone wrong in Ireland.

Certainly no one else had wanted to take on Mozambique. And Owen had made enough of a name for himself around the world to be able to pick and choose most of his assignments. Although he usually worked as a negotiator for the U.S. State Department, he easily obtained a leave of absence to work as an international negotiator under the banner of the United Nations.

Owen smiled at that thought. "International negotiator" sounded too complicated for what he did, what he loved to do. Really all he did was get people talking. Bringing people together—that was what gave Owen energy.

"What motivates you?" a reporter had asked him in one of the few interviews he ever gave—his usual policy was to stay out of the headlines. He had answered then what he still felt now. What he longed for more than anything else was peace—a lasting peace in places where conflict had ripped societies apart. Places like the land of his birth—where he had failed so spectacularly only a year ago. He frowned now, remembering.

One of his worst professional fears had always been to negotiate for someone's hidden agenda. And that was exactly what had happened last year with the Irish talks in London. Thinking that peace was at last in sight, he had even gone against his better judgment and brought the IRA to the table, only to learn they had no intention of compromise and would never surrender their arms. And then to have the talks break down because they were able to bring up his father's and sister's involvement in the IRA . . . that was the clincher. The fact that he had cut all ties with his family years ago and devoted his life to the pursuit of peace had meant nothing to any of them.

Lesson learned. Never again would he negotiate with personal enemies. Unfortunately, you couldn't have a career like Owen's without making enemies—even in his home office.

Owen knew the State Department cut him a certain amount of slack because he was a naturalized citizen. Having two passports had its advantages, and he could get away with more than most because of his track record. But the fact remained that his outspoken views against what he called "enemy-of-our-enemy politics" had earned him some powerful opposition of his own—even long before the Irish talks.

He had a reputation as the negotiator who refused to compromise when it came to switching sides. He smiled wryly. Perhaps he should have just quietly declined to get involved in whatever the latest set of side-switching politics might be. Instead, he had often condemned the very basis of the policy that revolved around befriending whichever country happened to be the enemy of the worst enemy of the day. In any given year that could be Noriega—to keep the communists in line—or, as in 1980, the Islamic zealots in Afghanistan—to keep the Soviets in line. America had put Saddam Hussein into power to keep Iran in line during the hostage crisis. Then last year's Gulf War, when Saddam became the enemy, had catapulted Iran into the friend's seat.

Owen knew the process wouldn't end there. He would have liked nothing better than to be put out of a job. No wars, no need for negotiations and negotiators. But though he might be naïve enough to work for lasting peace, he was not stupid enough to think wealth and power would ever stop being the motivating factors behind world events. The power brokers of the world, the movers and shakers behind the TV politicians—*they* couldn't care less about a lasting peace. In fact, they usually found it in their interests to keep the conflicts fueled and firing. Again and again, Owen had seen peace talks run aground on that reality. Arms was good business these days, oil and diamonds even better. Major powers tended to change sides every twenty years or so, and those changes guaranteed a market for war— and a job for negotiators.

After the Irish talks, he had begun to wonder if the time had come to give it up and go on the lecture circuit once again. Or maybe he would actually start writing the book he'd been talking about for ages. The truth was, a man could fight a losing battle—even a vitally important one—for only so long.

But then came Mozambique.

Negotiating for peace in that strife-torn land had demanded most of his time and energy for the past several months. But what was happening there now was enough to convince him to keep going a little longer. That country, its people, its history, its responses in favor of a lasting peace, had thrown all the theories and graphs and projections right out the window.

The peace hadn't happened yet, but it was coming. He could see it on the horizon, could almost taste it. A firm framework stood in place. With the negotiations in their final stages, he even felt confident enough to leave the talks and take his family on this much-needed family vacation.

What was happening right now in Mozambique was nothing short of a miracle from heaven. And Owen, more than most, knew how rare that was in a world obsessed with enemies and enemies' enemies.

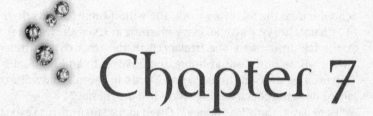 # Chapter 7

Miriam slid the van door shut and picked up the last of the bags, then started up the steps to their front door. She paused to breathe in the air coming off the bay. She took great pleasure in watching Owen bend down and snap an old yellow rose off one of the bushes standing guard along the front of the house. His heart attack seemed as far away as the tropics.

"Here, let me help you with that." Owen came down the stairs and took the suitcases from her. She bit her tongue to keep from telling him to take it easy.

Miriam could hear the phone ringing inside the open door and caught a glimpse of Martin dashing across the doorway to grab the receiver. As they entered the house, she smiled at her son's enthusiastic voice. "Hello. Martin O'Neill speaking. . . . Hi! . . . Yeah, okay. No problem. . . . Yeah, just now. . . . Okay, bye."

Miriam shut the door behind them. "Well?" Owen asked. He was leafing through the stack of letters on the table in the entryway. The pile there was thanks to Miriam's best friend, Sue, who had kept an eye on the house for them while they were away, watering the plants and bringing in the mail. Miriam crossed to the kitchen and opened the fridge. Sure enough, Sue had even thought to stock it. Miriam made a mental note to call and make a dinner date to thank her friend once she had tamed the dirty laundry threatening to reproduce inside their suitcases.

She heard Martin answer Owen as she returned to the front hall. "That was Coach Anderson. He said we have a soccer game tomorrow and could you guys drive. I said yeah." He grinned.

Owen looked over at Miriam and rolled his eyes. "Welcome home."

School started the following week, and with it came the bass rhythm of Miriam's heavy schedule. Every morning at seven she left for work at the law firm where she freelanced in the research department. Owen, whose office was at home, took Martin to and from school. That evening she came home to find Martin in Owen's study. She collapsed onto the couch and sighed. "Give me Hawaii."

"Hard day at the office, honey?" Owen looked up from his keyboard and smiled.

Miriam nodded. "Martin, how was your first day of second grade?"

"Okay, but there's these dumb girls who talk all the time, so the teacher made us stay after."

Miriam shot a glance at Owen, who continued typing very fast with only his two index fingers. "Dumb girls?" she asked.

"Totally," Martin answered, giving the globe a vicious spin that almost knocked it over.

"And did these dumb girls maybe say something about you during all their talking?" Miriam asked.

Now Owen looked up and nodded at her. The world spun so fast it looked like it might fly right off its axis. "Martin?"

"No. Well . . . a little . . . yeah. They just don't know how to draw."

"I see," Miriam said.

Martin jumped up and grabbed the small box of colored thumbtacks that always sat on a corner of Owen's desk. He climbed onto the wheeled stepladder and skated over to the far wall with the giant map of the world. Without a word he placed his finger on California, then dragged it across the Pacific until it hit Hawaii, then Kauai. He stuck a pin on the spot. "There, Dad. Now you've been there too. Hey, Mom,

Dad and I are making tacos for tonight. I'm going to go call Matt." And he shot out the door.

Miriam looked at the scattered path of pins on the map. "He wears me out, and I just got home. Can you follow what he's talking about?" She leaned over to ease her pumps off.

"Oh yeah." Owen grinned at her. "Totally."

On Wednesday night Miriam went upstairs to put Martin to bed and found him bouncing high enough to touch the ceiling. "Martin, you'll break the bed. Come on, give your old mother a break."

He laughed and waved an empty pajama sleeve in her face. "I'm the one-armed monster, coming to take you away." He tucked under his bottom lip and stuck his front teeth out at her.

"I've never seen a monster in rocket-man pajamas before. What happened to your arm, one-armed monster?"

"I ate it!" He bounced over to her and growled. Miriam grabbed Martin and flipped him down onto the bed. They tickled each other until Miriam had to yell for him to stop. Laughing and out of breath, she ran down the checklist. "Did you brush those lovely teeth, Dracula?"

"Of courrrrse." He crinkled his nose up as if he were going to bite her neck.

"Done your reading and your homework?"

He nodded. "And I took my bath. I was *seriously* dirty."

She smiled. "Okay, then it's lights out."

"What about prayers?" Martin asked.

Miriam knew this was just his usual attempt to delay. She felt beat. How could it be only the middle of the week? "Okay," she told him. "You say them this time."

"No, *you* say them."

"All right. Close your eyes," Miriam said, then repeated the "Now I lay me down to sleep" prayer.

"But I want the Dungeon and Dragon prayer," Martin said when she finished.

"What's that?"

"Dad says it all the time."

"Well, Dad can say it next—"

"Did I hear my name mentioned?" Owen stuck his head into the bedroom.

"Yay!" Martin clapped his hands.

"Oh, I just had him ready to go to sleep." She gave Owen a disapproving look, which he ignored.

"He'll go to sleep now, won't you? I just came by to give him a good-night kiss."

"Dad, can you pray with me? Mom's prayers aren't the same."

Miriam frowned, thinking she didn't need this right now.

"Mom's prayers *are* the same," Owen said.

"No, go ahead," she said. "I want to hear this Dungeon and Dragon prayer. I thought that was the name of that computer game you're always asking for." Miriam stood up to make room on the bed for Owen and went over to stand by the wall, her arms folded.

"Well, it's just a prayer, a collect actually, from the Church of Ireland's service of Evening Prayer. I liked it as a kid—my ma said it for me at bedtimes when I was Martin's age—and I thought Martin might like it too. So, close your eyes. 'Lighten our darkness, Lord, we pray; and in your mercy defend us from all perils and dangers of this night; for the love of your only Son, our Savior Jesus Christ.'"

Before Owen could say the word, Martin shouted, "Amen! And now the vision song."

Owen said, "No, we don't have time for that now."

"What's the vision song?" Miriam asked.

"It's actually just an old Irish hymn from the eighth century. 'Be Thou My Vision.'"

"Oh," she said. "I think I've heard that one."

"Sure you have. We sing it at church. But not tonight."

"Then do the blessing," Martin begged. "The blessing."

"What did you do, teach him the whole *Common Book of Prayer*?" Miriam asked.

Owen looked embarrassed. "Just my favorites, that's all. *The Book of Common Prayer*. All right, close your eyes again now." Owen's hand covered the top of Martin's head. 'The Lord bless you and watch over you; the Lord make his face shine upon you and be gracious to you; the Lord look kindly on you and give you peace; and the blessing of God Almighty, the Father, the Son, and the Holy Spirit, remain with you always.'"

Again Martin shouted, "Amen!"

Owen looked over at Miriam, who just nodded. "Well, you're right," she said. "I could never pray like that."

Martin held out his arms and Owen hugged him. Then it was Miriam's turn. Finally, she turned out the light.

Downstairs, as she bent over to load the dishwasher, Miriam heard Owen come in and ask, "Uh, was that okay? You looked upset when I came into Martin's bedroom. Are you mad about something?"

She straightened up, asking herself the same thing. Her hand went to her lower back and rubbed a muscle. She shook her head. "No, I don't think so. I was just thinking while I watched you with Martin."

"And that thought would be . . . ?"

"Nothing. Just . . . don't you think you overdo it a little? Oh, never mind. Come on, let's get the kitchen done."

Owen gave Miriam one of his looks, but she ignored it.

"Can I have a glass of water?" They both turned at the sound of Martin's voice. He stood in the kitchen door, rubbing his eyes as if he'd just woken up.

Miriam sighed, but before she could say anything, Owen held up his hand. "I'll take care of it. Come on, young man. Stop faking it. Off to bed, and I mean it." He reached for a glass from the cupboard as Martin scurried back up the stairs.

When Owen came back downstairs, he found Miriam stretched out on the couch. He hoped she was in a better mood than earlier.

"I must be crazy," she said. "But you know how I've been thinking we could have another child?"

He sat down and pulled her legs onto his lap, then started massaging her feet. He liked the sound of her little sighs. "You were saying?"

"Yes. Another child. And you said we should wait and pray. Well, I've waited, and I'm still thinking maybe we could do it. What do you think?"

"I'd love nothing more, Miriam. You know that. But I'm concerned about you. You work hard, and you love your work. You're excellent at what you do, and you want to become even better. But you work hard at being a mother too, and you're hard on yourself. I don't mind that you want to work later these days when I'm home. I enjoy the extra time with Martin. But it's already a lot to juggle, and you push yourself. So sure, I'd be behind you, whatever you decide. I say go for it, but you're already saying it's so hard. What would it be like with two little ones?"

"If I knew I could count on you being home like you are now, it would make a difference," Miriam said.

Owen felt the familiar tightening of his own muscles. The words pushed their way out of his mouth, despite the response he knew awaited. "I can't promise that. You know I can't."

"And I'm not allowed to ask you, am I?" Miriam stood up and walked away.

Sunday afternoon after church Martin skipped between his parents, glad he could talk them into going for a walk on the beach. He'd brought his ball. His dad drew a line in the sand and then started asking all the people going by, skaters and kite flyers and other walkers, if they wanted to play.

Martin hopped up and down on one foot, then the other, listening to his dad make people actually turn and listen to him. "Would you care to partake in a game of one of the finest sports ever invented?"

"We don't know him," Martin said to them. His mom shook her head. But people laughed, and, sure enough, soon they had two teams of strangers organized on opposite sides.

Dad walked up and down the dividing line, tossing the ball into the air and laying his Irish accent on thick. "Let it never be said that American football is not a great sport. Ah, but this one, it's greater by far. Have ye never heard of Gaelic football, then? No? Well, today the good St. Patrick is smiling down on all of us."

The rest of the afternoon Martin, his mom, and at least twenty other San Franciscans spent rolling in the sand as Dad coached them all on the finer points of Gaelic football. His mom called it "a cross between the more barbaric side of American football, rugby, and mud wrestling." When the game was over, Martin heard several people actually exchange phone numbers. He liked the way his dad could get people together and everybody got to be friends.

Martin held on tightly to his father's hand during the good-byes. He smiled at everyone, pleased that he had more sand on his legs and arms than they did.

The last man to leave wore glasses like Martin's. He had played really badly and forgotten he could touch the ball with his hands. Now he went up to Martin's mom. "I know you," he said.

Martin looked at his dad, who also was wondering, so they walked over to eavesdrop. Mom straightened up from trying to brush the sand off her knees and gave the guy her lawyer smile. "You do?"

"You do?" Dad asked. They all laughed.

"I mean, we do *now*, Abe, but did we before this afternoon?" Mom asked.

Martin let go of his dad's hand and started dragging his big toe through the sand. He drew lines all around and in between the three grown-ups.

"Aren't you the chess lady?"

Martin looked up at his mother and watched her blush. He stopped. "Mom, you're a chess lady?"

"Yeah, Martin," said the man she'd called Abe. "She probably doesn't know we call her that, but there's a group of us who hang out playing chess in the park. Your mom comes by sometimes at lunchtime, and the guys say no one has beaten her yet. I haven't gotten up the nerve to challenge her. But I've watched her play, and she's vicious, man."

Mom laughed at the surprised look his dad gave her. "I knew you were good," Dad said. "She's beaten me often enough," he said to Abe and Martin. "But I didn't know you had a following." He put his arm around her waist.

"She's teaching me to play chess," Martin said proudly.

"Would everyone please stop talking about me like I'm not here," Mom said.

Abe turned to Martin. "Well, you're lucky, then, because I could use your mom as a teacher. My chess is even worse than my Gaelic football." Martin liked it when everyone thought this was funny, but his mom still looked embarrassed.

After Abe left, Martin said to both his parents, "Let's go for a walk." When they agreed and held both his hands, then swung him high, Martin thought maybe now would be a good time to ask for an ice cream.

On Monday evening after getting home from work, Miriam picked up the ringing phone before the answering machine got it. She heard a distant crackling and then a deep voice say, "Madam, please. I wish to speak to Mr. Owen O'Neill. My name is Marcos Duarte, and I am calling from Maputo. It is quite early on Tuesday morning here, and I have tried all night to get through."

Owen emerged from his library office next to the living room as she said, "Just a moment." Miriam nodded at Owen. "It's for you. Do you want to take it here, or should I transfer it to your office phone?"

"I'll take it here. Why?"

Before she could answer, he had crossed the room. She mouthed *Mozam-bique* and handed him the phone. Then she sat down on the couch to wait, hoping she had guessed wrong but knowing what the call meant. Just when she had started getting used to Owen's being home again, started leaning on his presence and even taking it for granted, he would be leaving again. Miriam eavesdropped shamelessly, knowing if Owen wanted privacy he would have taken the call in his office.

"Yes. Yes, Marcos, I understand. . . .Well, we can certainly work on that. . . . What? Do you think that would be in everyone's best interests? . . . Oh, I see. Well, I can try. . . . Of course. . . . Why is that? . . . Tell me, what changed your mind? . . . Ah."

Owen listened for quite a while then, nodding and saying "I see, yes," every few moments as he scribbled in the small notepad he always carried in his pocket. Finally he laughed. "No, no, it's no problem at all. . . . I understand. . . . Yes, certainly I will. . . . You know I always do. Listen, how is your son? I heard he was due to get out of the hospital last week? . . . Oh, very good. Party at home then. . . . Yes. Right. Well, was there anything else? . . . Fine. . . . Yes. Thank you. Good-bye." He hung up and kept writing.

"So why did you lie?" she asked him quietly.

He grimaced. "What do you mean?"

"You told him it was no problem."

Chapter 8

Owen heard her say the words he didn't dare voice.

"You're going back."

He looked away, part of him still trying to figure out what hadn't been said during the phone conversation. "I have to."

"And you can't wait to do it, so maybe you weren't lying."

Owen hated that this would hurt her. He tried to make light of it by switching into his lecture voice. "Lying is for short-term negotiation results. For peace, there must be a foundation of trust. I may not trust them, but they must trust me."

"I know, the imperative of trust," Miriam said softly. "I've heard it before, remember?" She sighed. "I knew it was too good to be true."

Her words cut Owen to the quick, but he tried to mask their effect. He could hardly blame her for being disappointed. So often he had asked for her understanding, and now he had to do it again.

Miriam said, "I'm sorry, Owen. It's just . . . hard to accept. That you're going to be gone again so soon."

"I know," he said. "But surely you understand. There's been a breakdown in the talks, but I still think the situation is salvageable. I still think we can get that—"

"Lasting peace?" Her tone mimicked his own, only slightly laced with sarcasm. But it was enough.

He swallowed, aching at the bitterness in her voice. "Miriam, I don't feel I have the right to ask this of you again, but I know we're close—"

"You mean you and me?"

He coughed. "No, I meant, we're so close to peace. Please, you have to let me go."

"Owen, you know it's not a question of my letting you go. You're free to come and go for your work. We both give that to each other."

"I'm just so afraid. . . ."

She looked up now for the first time and made eye contact. "What? What are you afraid of?" She asked the question softly.

As if the answer had always been in him, Owen said, "I'm afraid of having a war on my conscience. What I mean is, what if I don't go back and the talks never get back on track? I'd never forgive myself for not trying."

❖ ❖ ❖

Miriam stood and turned her back on him, hands on her hips. Had she really expected he would say he was afraid for their relationship? No. How could her petty needs ever measure up against the threat of war?

"Yes, 'what if,'" she said, almost to herself. "Well, what if you have a . . . I mean, what about your health? Do you really think it's such a good idea to travel so soon after having a heart attack?"

"When I had my checkup with Joe, he said as long as I didn't stay up all night or try to run a marathon, I'd be fine. Come on, Miriam. It's not as bad as all that."

Silence hung between them for long minutes. Finally Miriam swallowed. "All right, Owen. We'll manage. We always do." Saying it tore Miriam in two. Yes, this was the life they both had chosen. Yes, she had married him in full knowledge of what his dream required. But somehow, now that they had a child and she had her job, the daily doing of the dream had become difficult. Increasingly difficult, the more he was gone. The many exotic vacations were well and good, but they couldn't just live from vacation to vacation. And this latest fear about his heart didn't help.

To make things worse, she didn't feel like letting Owen near enough to comfort her. Not at that moment anyway.

As he took a step toward her, Miriam grabbed her keys and ran out of the house toward their van. *I just feel so tired . . . and alone,* she thought as she fastened her seat belt and turned the ignition key. A voice inside her said that it was her own fault, that she was the one putting distance between them. She ignored it and turned on the radio as she started down the steep hill in front of their house.

Before long she found herself parking in another part of the city. No restored homes here, just boarded-up shop fronts and walls embroidered with graffiti. Miriam got out, locked the van, then fumbled with her keys as she walked the half block to a storefront.

She stooped to unlock the padlock at the base of the metal protective grill, then heaved the grill upward. It clanged all the way to the top, where a faded sign hung: Vree Jewelry and Watches. The kids at school had always teased her about her dad's advertising "free" jewelry and watches.

Miriam glanced once at the evening sky, clouds laced in gold, and did a mental check, relieved that tonight Martin would sleep over at Pete's. Then she stepped inside the store.

The old smells of oil and floor wax welcomed her first. She turned on the lights and was greeted next by the sight of her father's workbench. Then the display cabinets, the curtained-off stairway, his desk at the back, the giant green safe, its door now swung wide open to tell the world that here hid nothing worth stealing.

Miriam locked the door behind her and made sure the curtains were closed all the way. Then she reached for the broom. For the next hour she swept and dusted the counters, the cash register, the empty display cases. As she worked her way around the store, she let her mind escape into the past. She was a child too big to be sitting on her father's lap but doing it anyway, diamond dust sparkling on the leather apron spread before her.

"Look, Miriam. Look through the loupe and see what I'm talking about. Can you count the fractures in this stone?"

Miriam knew her father was more than just a jeweler. He was a trained diamond cutter, what they called a cleaver. She looked and saw. "Three."

He corrected her. "Look again. *See.*"

Her mother entered the shop from the stairway that connected the store with their home upstairs. She felt her father's arm and stomach muscles tighten, an edge enter his voice. *"Ja, wat is er?"* They still spoke Dutch with each other. Miriam understood every word, but she only spoke it when she sensed tension in the home, as if the sound of their native language might serve as balm to her parents' raw discomfort.

Her mother ignored his question and said to Miriam, "Have you done your homework? Did you do the chores I asked you?"

"Yes, Mama." At age ten, her jobs were to sweep and dust.

"Then go upstairs. Your father has work to do."

Miriam looked at her father's face, so near her own. A fleeting shadow passed through his eyes, then his words. "Listen to your mother now. Off you go."

Miriam slid off his lap and stood in the center of the store, shiny objects all around her. She looked from one disapproving parent to the other and felt their fighting was somehow her fault, that her mother could have had a happier life if Miriam were not there. This was the unspoken message, the message always blinking in her mother's eyes.

Miriam's parents finally divorced when she was in college. She had tried to keep them together—as a child by being good, as a teenager by suggesting compromises until her mother told her to mind her own business. When she was accepted at an out-of-state college, she had felt she should decline the scholarship because she thought she could somehow keep her parents together by staying home.

Sue was the one who had told her that idea was crazy. If her parents were going to get divorced, they would do so with or without her.

And they had. Without her.

Sue! The thought of her friend brought Miriam back to the present. She fumbled in her purse for the small black leather day planner. Business cards fell out of one flap as she dropped it on the floor. She stuffed these back in the pocket with phone messages waiting to be answered and flipped it open to that week and Monday's entry: *7 P.M. Sue at Guido's.*

She glanced at her watch. Fifteen minutes to get across town.

She'd be late, but not too late.

Sue always waited.

Chapter 9

The next question: Who am I? But to answer this, again I must speak of "where."

A child is born in the world. But what is this world but many smaller places?

So I say, a child is born in Africa. But this, too, is not one place, for Africa is made up of many countries, and in each country there are many regions, and in each region many tribes, many villages, many clans, many families. So, what is Africa? How to describe this place?

A child is born in Sudan. Ah, you think, this is a place now finally, a place with a name. But again, I have tricked you early in the story. What is Sudan? Sudan is the largest country in Africa. The Northern Sudan, geographically speaking, is predominantly populated by Muslims and Arabised people. The majority of the population in southern Sudan is predominantly Christian and African. Sudan is governed by Arabs, and in some regions in southern Sudan people are captured, then sold as slaves by these Arabs. In southern Sudan, people are driven from their homes and used as fodder for a war that has lasted many decades, a war you will find in no history book.

But I am getting ahead of myself, and I know some of this because I work in a library, so in some ways that is not fair. You will really wonder, can I trust this narrator?

Back to the story. A child is born in Sudan. A child is born in the South of Sudan. A child is born to the Dinka Bor tribe, in a village on the River Bahr el Jebel. This life of the village, it was solid and stable—a splendid, noble, and grand life in all ways, also authentic. There is a Dinka word, payam, meaning "safe harbor." That is the meaning of this village. A child is born into a clan, a family. A child is born.

This child, he is very blessed. He has two parents. His father is wise and respected. He does not say much, but when he does, everyone listens. The boy's mother is a storyteller, so she can take people out of the place where they sit and help them see into the faraway distance. "What do you see?" she asks us so we can feel the story around us. "Listen to the story very carefully and pay attention. What do you hear? What do you smell?"

This child, he tends goats. He rises early each morning, and his mother is already cooking food for him to eat. His father comes home once every month or two because he works somewhere else.

When he comes home, he brings gifts for the boy
and his younger sisters. There are three sisters.
He is the eldest, of course. Three sisters would be
enough to help his mother with gathering water
and washing clothes and cooking.

These three sisters have names.

This boy has a name.

I know what they look like. I see the boy's
village, his home, his parents. The sun shines.
Flowers color the bush. His goats are fat and
return to the stable in a straight line every evening. Into this family, in a village near a river in
southern Sudan, in Africa, in the world, before his
sisters come, this child is born.

Chapter 10

Miriam took all the shortcuts she knew, but late rush-hour traffic kept her from reaching the restaurant before half past seven. All the way across the city, she tried to silence the ragged whispers of her parents' fights. A part of her desperately hoped that she and Owen didn't sound that way to Martin.

Miriam drove past the restaurant, looking for a parking place. Through the window she saw her friend waiting for her. Sue was staring outside, but she did not see Miriam.

Inside the restaurant, the smell of garlic mingled with oregano, and the intimate ambience of small tables and candlelight embraced her. Miriam smiled when her friend stood and walked to greet her. The sight of straight, blue-black hair swaying down past her waist caused both men and women to watch Sue long after she had passed their tables.

"Hey," Sue said, reaching over to squeeze her hand, "you had me worried." Miriam squeezed back, then followed her to the table in the back.

"Is that a silk skirt you have on?" Miriam asked as they sat down.

Sue nodded. "You're not going to say anything about the fact that it's lime green?" She smiled, and Miriam felt herself turning toward the warmth like a sun-starved flower.

"No, the color suits you," Miriam said. She gazed at her friend—the olive skin, tiny hands, slim wrists. "Listen, I wanted to thank you for watching the house."

Sue's eyes narrowed. "Yeah, right. Correct me if I'm wrong, but there's more to this dinner than one of us saying thank you. So come on. Tell me."

Sue's directness caused tears to well in Miriam's eyes. *Am I that transparent?* She blinked them away. "No, really. I mean, when I called you it really was for a girls' night out. But this afternoon, that sort of changed." She paused, but Sue said nothing. "Owen has to go back to Mozambique."

Sue nodded. "And?"

"And . . . I went back to my dad's place and was thinking."

"About?" Sue ran her fingers over the embroidered butterflies on the table linen.

"About us . . . and my parents and when I was Martin's age. I don't know. Everything. Who I am. Where I am in my life. Whatever. I don't know. . . ." Miriam listened to her own voice trail off and wondered what in the world she was trying to say. "Well, I guess as always, we're not going to talk about the weather."

Sue laughed, the sound releasing the knot in Miriam's shoulders. "When do we ever?"

The waitress appeared, and they ordered, Miriam going for three courses while Sue settled for a main course only.

When Sue shook her head, it was Miriam's turn to laugh. "What? Can't a woman eat a healthy meal? I can't help it if I like good food. Must be my metabolism. I'm always on the go."

"You still only need six hours of sleep a night? That used to drive me crazy when we roomed together. I was so jealous."

Miriam sighed. "Yeah, but nowadays it's a rare night when I don't wake up in a sweat, disoriented. I know what you're thinking—don't say it. It's *not* the change of life, or whatever they're calling it these days."

"Hey, we're only thirty-seven."

"My point exactly."

"Well, what do you do when you wake up like that?"

Miriam thought about it. "I guess I just stay awake and do some work or go watch Martin sleep and sit in the rocking chair in his room with a book until I nod off for a few hours. I don't know. . . ."

Sue said, "Listen, while you're thinking about all the stuff you don't know tonight, I have a favor to ask. I really wish you'd consider coming down to the legal co-op office once a week. We're *really* short-handed."

"Ah, Sue, when are you going to stop this? You know I don't have the time."

"And I do? Come on, Miriam. *Make* the time. You're a freelancer—you work on a contract basis. Schedule the time in."

Miriam shook her head. "Look, with Owen leaving again, there's just no way. I'll be lucky to get the work done I've taken on, let alone do more. Plus, I'll be the one driving Martin everywhere. And don't forget soccer practice. Never mind the cooking and the laundry and the house."

"Just one afternoon a week, Miriam. You could help with wills and contracts or do research for small nonprofits or something. You could do it. You're just not *willing* to do it."

Miriam grimaced. "Maybe you're right. Maybe I think one do-gooder in the family is enough. All I know is, my hands and heart are full with the job and my family. I'm sorry. No."

They were quiet for a few moments, not in an uncomfortable sort of way. Miriam knew Sue did not take offense at her honesty. She and Sue had been friends since high school, when Sue's parents broke with tradition and sent her to a school outside Chinatown. They had stayed close ever since, even in law school. Miriam sometimes thought Sue knew her better than Owen did.

Then Sue broke the silence and said tentatively, "You know, I didn't ask you to build an argument. Obviously, it's your decision." Miriam shot her a look and Sue held up her hands, palms facing outward. "But listen, don't you think there's something else going on here?"

"I don't know what you're talking about."

"I'm talking about how you hold yourself back. Like you're terrified that someone will notice you or expect too much."

"What's to notice?" Miriam asked. "I'm just . . . well, ordinary." Miriam had always thought it was one of life's paradoxes that she, the plain one, had found a husband, and Sue, the exotic beauty, was still single.

"Oh, you're far from ordinary. You're just good at blending in. Exhibit A: the basic black lawyer ensemble. Why not be bold and branch out into gray or taupe?"

Miriam frowned, looking down at her dark suit and white blouse. "Hey, this is navy blue."

Sue said, "I rest my case. So, what *are* you working on these days?"

"Right now I'm doing research for a case about international fishing rights." She paused. "Listen, Sue, I know I'm being difficult. Humor me though?"

Sue wasn't looking at her.

"What? What are you thinking?"

Sue pursed her lips and leaned forward. "You hate conflict, and you dread loss. You always have."

"No I don't." The words were out of Miriam's mouth before she could stop them. "No, really. I don't. Well, not as much as I used to. I'm a lot more mature now."

Sue said, "I didn't say you weren't. Yes, you're more mature than I am, that's for sure. No, I was talking about something else."

"Okay, Owen says I'm too sensitive, but I sometimes pick up on things even he misses. I watch people and read them. I was thinking tonight how I could always tell when my parents had had another fight. When I came home from school, I'd feel the tension and make up some excuse to go to your house. And now I think of Martin. . . ."

Sue shifted her position, leaning back as if once again her point had just been proven. "And your parents?"

"What about them?"

"Well, what about why you still hold on to your dad's store seventeen years after the accident?"

Owen looked around the kitchen. He had put together a gourmet meal, and the pots and pans stacked all over the counters were evidence. Parsley stems laced both cutting boards, onion skins lurked in dark corners around the kitchen, and the two sinks brimmed over with encrusted measuring cups and the mixing bowl.

Only now that the sauce had reached its prime, bathed gently in the steam of the *au bain marie*, did he remember he would be dining alone that night. He sighed and went around lighting the candles in the entryway and the living room anyway. The flames reflected nicely off the old oak floors, the brass and glass. He liked the classic, straight lines and the warmth of his home. But tonight he missed the two most important elements, his son and his wife.

Owen looked at his watch again. Miriam was with Sue. He rechecked the calendar on the fridge. And Martin was spending the night with Pete.

He turned on the stereo, putting in the Dvořák CD, then went to his study and called their pastor to cancel the meetings he'd set up the previous week for the committees he headed. They'd have to get along without him . . . again. He only hoped Miriam would continue going to church and taking Martin. During his last trip, she'd stopped altogether.

Owen thought of all he loved about Miriam—her honesty, her quiet passion, her intensity of purpose. The drawback was the way they sometimes argued. As they had this evening. He hated it when they left each other without feeling close. But surely she could understand that he *had* to go. Especially now, when peace was a true possibility.

Peace. It was everything he stood for. Miriam knew that about him, surely had accepted it by now. God's own peace in people's hearts, so the nations would know peace. In those stuffy hotel rooms in Mozambique, he had smelled it, touched it, been privileged to help birth it into the world. He couldn't turn his back on that now.

Owen grabbed a pile of folders and dumped them on the couch. Tonight after dinner would be a good time to finish the preparations for his trip. The empty house would actually be an advantage. He'd make it nice though, so when Miriam did come home, he'd be free and could spend the rest of the evening with her. And now his leftovers would provide her with at least one dinner in the fridge, so she wouldn't have to cook. Owen leaned over the hearth and turned on the switch to allow the gas into the fireplace, then lit it, careful to place the screen in front. He would never get used to the repetitive flames—"Not a real fire," he often said to Miriam. Not a peat fire with its acrid smell and living flames, like back in Ireland, back home. *The sea is wide. . . .*

Owen began humming the song gently as he returned to the kitchen and checked his sauce. Then he peeked at the fish poaching in the oven. It still needed another few minutes, so he started cleaning the kitchen. As he worked his way through the stacks of pans, he thought he heard the phone in his study ring.

Owen reached for the dishtowel, and in his haste, knocked over a

glass. It bounced off the edge of the counter. He reached out and
caught the glass, but it had already broken, and its other half shattered
at his feet. He looked down at his right hand and saw the stem of a
glass. And then, on the white tiles at his feet, the falling drops of
blood.

Chapter 11

". . . after the accident."

At the sound of Sue's last words, the restaurant table melted away, and Miriam saw their undergraduate dorm room, the gold shag carpet she could not take her eyes off of when she got the phone call about her parents. Her father had picked up her mother after some doctor's appointment—he still did things like that, even after the divorce. A truck had jackknifed on the Bay Bridge in a storm. Her parents had died in the traffic pileup that followed.

That gold carpet, the yellow phone, Sue's hand on hers . . . as it was now. Miriam looked up at her friend. She did not want to go back to that dark place, and she could not understand why Sue was asking her to.

"Miriam, I'm sorry. I didn't mean it that way. I have no right. Okay . . . where's a safe subject? Why don't you tell me about Martin. How's my godson?"

Relieved that Sue had backed off, Miriam sighed and shivered—as if someone had walked over her grave, Owen would have said. But she knew it was nothing but the shadow of the past.

"Ah, Martin. He's wonderful. I worry a little, though. Friday he came home and told me about some bully at school. I called his new teacher, and evidently Martin's been standing up for the underdog. The kids listen because he's tall. A big boy like his dad. Owen's Irish genes."

Sue leaned forward again, her voice a bare whisper. "And how are you and Owen these days?"

A memory of her fight with Owen ran through her mind. She pulled at her hair and heard her voice admitting, "Owen's work worries me. It . . . it's harder than it used to be. And it's not just the separations. I mean, those are hard, but we're used to them. But sometimes he can't even tell me what he's working on, and that's when I worry most. Certain projects mean we have a car parked on the hill outside the front door, bodyguards. But Owen insists that's just American paranoia. He really is a legend in his time, despite the stalemated Irish talks. They were cursed from the start—that's what he says anyway. . . ."

Miriam realized she was rambling. "Ah, Sue, you know I love that man more than life itself. And that love—his and mine and Martin's—it's what I live for. I don't know what I'd do if I ever lost them. And I hate it when we fight. I hate the added distance it puts between us—even when I'm the one that starts the fight.

"I just want to have it all, I suppose. I want the perfect marriage. I want to be the best mother, always there for my son. *And* I want more work, and more time to do better research for the clients I have, even though right now I can barely manage the work I have. The uncertainty of freelancing is nerve-wracking, but I know I couldn't manage full-time work at a firm. And . . . there's still this part of me that wants more, maybe even another child, while another part just wants to keep everything the way it is. Am I making sense? Is that asking so much?"

Her friend shook her head, and Miriam watched the raven wave of hair break and catch the light. Sue said, "It's asking a lot, especially the way you ask it. But listen, about Owen's trip—what are we talking about? A few weeks, a month? Just make sure it's a romantic good-bye this time. Otherwise you'll be kicking yourself like you did last time."

Martin could smell Pete's mother as she leaned over and unbuckled his seat belt. She smelled like bacon. "There you go," she said. "We're sorry it didn't work out this time, Martin. But with Pete running a fe-ver, I don't want to take the chance you might get sick too. Pete needs to sleep tonight to get better, okay?"

Martin nodded. "Yeah, that's fine. No problem. I hope he can play in the game on Saturday." Pete's mom was double-parked, so she waited in the car, the engine idling, while Martin climbed the steps, holding his sleeping bag under one arm and backpack under the other. He looked in the front window and saw lights on, faded light—*from the fireplace*, he realized. He looked closer and saw candles lit, but he couldn't see his mom and dad. But he knew they were home, be-cause Pete's mom had called. *They're probably in the kitchen.*

Martin tried the front door, but it was locked. He started to ring the doorbell but then he remembered his key. Mom always liked for him to have a key, just in case. He fished it out of his backpack and un-locked the door, stepping into the light of the empty entryway. He dropped his backpack and sleeping bag on the floor, then stepped back out and waved until Pete's mom had pulled away from the curb and headed down the hill.

Martin closed the door and locked it. Then he heard his parents' voices coming from the living room.

"Even when we're apart, we're together." His dad's voice.

"You can't always be taking us on vacation to make up for every-thing."

"Sure, I travel a lot, but you've always understood in the past. I *do* want us to have more time together, but when I think about the qual-ity of relationship we share, the quantity becomes less important. I'm a twice-blessed man, with a wife who loves me, and my son."

Dad's leaving again? Martin kicked at his lumpy sleeping bag. That meant he'd miss the game Saturday. *He always misses my games.* Mar-tin left his backpack and sleeping bag on the floor and walked toward their voices in the living room.

"Ah, Miriam," his dad was saying, "you know I have no choice here. People in the UN know me, and I've saved enough politicians behind the scenes for them to be thankful. But after all that went wrong last year in Ireland, I need Mozambique to be a success. And that godfor-saken country needs me too."

"It has to be you. It's always about you, isn't it? There's no other ne-gotiator who can do the impossible like you."

Martin cringed at his mother's tone. She hardly ever said stuff loud like that. And when she did, it usually meant he was in trouble or would be soon. Martin backed up slowly, returned to the entryway, opened and slammed the door hard, then called out, "Mom? Dad? I'm home."

He headed for the living room, talking every step of the way. "Pete threw up twice—that's why his mom had to bring me home. But we watched a video first, which is why I'm this late. Sure hope he can play on Saturday—"

His parents stood on opposite sides of the living room, both staring at him. They looked so far away from each other. He moved to the middle of the room and looked from one to the other. "You guys okay?"

It was like his voice had broken some law that told them to stay put. They both moved toward him, and toward each other.

"We're fine, Martin," Mom said.

"Son, I have to leave again in the morning for Africa, I'm afraid."

"I know," Martin said.

"What?"

"I mean, oh no," Martin hurried to say. "You'll miss my game." And then he could have bit his tongue because he saw his mother shoot one of her looks at Dad.

"Yes, I'm afraid I will, and I'm sorry for it. But there'll be other games, right? Come here and give your ol' Da' a hug. Our Martin. Pray for me, right?"

Martin nodded and looked over his father's shoulder at his mother turning her back on both of them.

Chapter 12

This child, he became a Christian because of his sister's sandals.

His eldest sister, one year younger than he, told him, "Brother, I have been dreaming of wearing sandals."

He laughed. "Sandals?"

"Yes. With heels."

He looked up at his sister. He was older, but she was taller. And if he looked at her through the eyes of another boy, she might have been pretty. But sandals? Wasn't it enough that he and his sisters each had one pair of shoes, this thanks to their father who worked hard in the city and came home only once every month or two?

"I have prayed to God for these sandals for a very long time."

"Sister, this cannot be good, praying for sandals."

She looked down.

"What did you pray?"

She blinked at him, so this boy, he had to repeat himself, even as he was thinking his father was right: there is no understanding the mind of a woman. But he did what his father did and leaned forward, nodding. Sure enough, the sister began to talk again.

"I'm not sure if this was a good thing. But I prayed, 'Our Father, if You are real, then You know what I need even better than my own father. If You bring me sandals, I will believe in You, not because of my parents or my village, but because of You and me.' Was this a good prayer, Elder Brother?"

This boy, he was thinking no, but he did not say the word. He could not bear the wide-open eyes of wondering he saw in his sister's face. So he nodded instead. And she smiled.

That weekend, their father came home from the city, and oh yes, he had a pair of sandals for this sister. Dark blue, with straps across the toes. And heels. She changed color when she saw them and began to cry foolishly. The boy, he felt as if someone had tied his feet to the ground. Right there, he lowered his eyes and prayed, "Father, if You know this small thing about my younger sister, then You know big things about me. I believe in You, not because of all our parents have taught us, but because of You and me."

This boy began to think about what he wanted badly, like his sister had wanted the sandals. So he prayed, "Please, Father, let me go to school."

He prayed this every morning when he woke up
and every night before he fell asleep.

It was a strange thing. For this boy should have
gone to school earlier. He was old enough. Perhaps there was no school nearby. Perhaps there
were no teachers. He knew no children in his village who went to school, so it was not as if he
knew what he was asking for. Still, he wanted to
go to school very much indeed.

In his village there are trees and huts with
pointed, thatched roofs. Women grind grain with a
tall, smooth branch, pounding it inside a high-sided
wooden bowl—like a drum with no skin cover. They
sing to the rhythm of this pounding.

The traditional dress of a Dinka man might be
red and blue and green, with a long shield and
an armband with a feather. The mothers carry their
babies at their sides, under one arm, wrapped in
a bag or pouch made of the dried, leatherlike skin
of goats or sheep.

On Sundays, this boy's father sometimes leads
prayers while his mother leads the singing. Her
voice is deep and rich, and everyone begins to
sway and clap, one hand on top of the other,
another hand on top—back and forth, left, right,
shuffle, clap.

When this boy returns from taking care of his
father's goats, there is still much work to do until
dinner is finally finished and people begin to rest
from the day. Then, after dinner, in the dark, if he
is under ten, he sometimes sits at the feet of his
mother or of a very old woman in the village and
listens to stories of brave men and wise men. If he

is older, he sits by the men to listen to the stories. This is the time when he is often told, "Listen well. What do you hear?" It is his job to remember these stories.

I have drawn pictures of this place. The trees around the village have flowers or fruit. There is plenty of firewood, plenty of food, plenty of water.

Perhaps the reason this boy does not go to school is a war.

Chapter 13

"I pray for you both whenever I see the moon."

Miriam had waited for Owen to say those words, as he always did before he left on a trip. But this time she heard them only in her mind as she lay in bed replaying the evening's conversation.

So much for Sue's advice. Miriam knew she had blown it. Their last night together should have been tender and romantic. Instead, it had turned into another fight. Why hadn't she just kept her mouth closed?

Miriam turned over, turned over again, punched the pillow into a different shape, hoping for sleep but too frustrated to succumb. She had promised herself last time that she would let him go with a smile on her face. But how could she, when she faced weeks and maybe months of doing everything herself and missing him on top of it? She already felt the loneliness, even with Owen asleep at her side. She told herself she couldn't complain. She *shouldn't* complain.

"Mom! Dad! Mom, help!" Martin's terrified cries cut into Miriam's thoughts. She bolted out of bed and ran down the hall, flipping on the light in Martin's room. He sat in bed, hugging himself as the tears squirted out of his tightly shut eyes.

"Sweetie, Martin, it's all right. Honey, it's just a dream." She sat down on the edge of his bed and took him into her arms. Was he still asleep? "Martin? Wake up. It's just a dream." The rock-hard back relaxed, and he crumpled into her arms, still sobbing.

"What was it?" she whispered. "Do you want to tell me what you dreamed?"

He mumbled into her shoulder. She sniffed his hair and then pulled back enough to cup his face in her hands. "What did you say?"

"I dunno." He squinted against the light. She got up to turn it off, but he said, "No. I need the light."

"Why, Martin? What was it?"

"I dunno. Mom, stay with me tonight?"

It's our last night together, Miriam thought. Oh, well, Owen would be up at four for his early flight. She'd hear him and get up with him and try to make everything right. They'd talk it out then, and she'd apologize. Besides, Owen was asleep now, and once that happened, nothing woke him. Miriam brushed her fingers through Martin's bangs, then ran the back of her hand across his cheek. "Sure, honey. Scoot over." She slipped between the sheets and laid her head on his dinosaur pillow, wrapping one arm around his waist so he could feel her warmth. "I'm right here," she whispered.

When Miriam woke, it was to the touch of someone shaking her shoulder and whispering, "I'll be off now."

She thought three things: *Who is leaving? Where am I? No!* Then she opened her eyes and wanted to say, *Oh, Owen, I was going to get up with you.* Instead, the words that came out of her mouth were, "You're leaving us again."

"Miriam, I . . ." He leaned over and kissed her, then kissed Martin's head on her shoulder. Then he frowned in that way that made him look his age, all the wrinkles deepening. "We will see each other soon. It won't be as long as last time, I promise. Maybe . . . maybe if it takes longer than a week, maybe afterwards, we can even fix it so you can come over. We could take Martin out of school, go on safari. I could make this up to you, like. . . ." He hesitated.

The words flew out of Miriam's mouth, sounding more sarcastic than she meant them to: "Like Hawaii? Another trip of a lifetime?"

Owen grimaced. "Try to arrange your schedule so you can get some time off again. I'll send for you as soon as I can." And he was gone.

When Owen called later that week, neither of them mentioned their arguments. Instead, it seemed to Miriam that they both tried to make up for the way they had parted. She forced herself to say kind things to Owen, tender words of encouragement to compensate for her lack of support before he left. But when Owen brought up the possible trip to Africa, Miriam ran out of such words.

"What about my work?" she asked, still waiting for him to show more interest in how she was spending her days.

"You can take a break."

"I took a break just a few weeks ago. I'll lose clients if I keep this up."

"We don't need the money."

"No, but I need the clients."

And so they went, round and round the real issue of trying to find more balance in their lives. *I just feel so lonely without him,* Miriam thought after hanging up. But why did a similar loneliness seem to haunt her even when Owen *wasn't* gone?

Owen's few weeks became four. She deliberately accepted a major case that doubled her workload in the span of those weeks. The project involved a so-called "price of life" insurance case, which was essentially a matter of assigning monetary value to individual lives. The case had become a nasty tangle of definitions, with children in minority groups awarded the lowest position. It was an altogether depressing job, but Miriam threw herself into it—partly to make the days slip by more quickly, and partly to make up for arriving an hour later than usual each morning after taking Martin to school.

She had an arrangement with Matt's mom to pick up Martin after school, and the boys didn't mind playing together on Matt's computer for a few hours. On Wednesdays Martin went to Pete's house and then to soccer practice. But Miriam still had to be there to pick up Martin from the field, and every day after she brought him home, she had to cook dinner, help him with homework, make sure he still did his reading, even if he was reading four years above his grade level, put him to bed, do the laundry, and still try to get in some professional reading of her own.

Saturday mornings Miriam felt like she got a breather as she sat in the bleachers enjoying the autumn sunshine and cheering for

Martin's soccer team together with the other parents. But then it was always a race to get Martin home and showered in time for his Saturday afternoon art lessons at the community center. While he was learning to draw, Miriam did the grocery shopping for the week. The other housework rarely got done. Sometimes she could nag Martin into doing a little vacuuming, but it didn't happen often.

Every time Miriam climbed the front steps to their house, she tried to take a few moments to tend Owen's roses. As she snapped off the dead blooms, careful to avoid the thorns, Miriam thought how pleased Owen would be to see one last crop of color before the winter.

The worst part of those weeks apart from Owen came at night. Martin's bad dreams continued to plague him. In fact, they became a regular feature in their nightly lives. And Miriam couldn't even count on the moon to remind her of Owen's prayers on those nights when she lost sleep comforting her son. Even when she remembered to look for it, autumn fog kept its light from her.

One night, a little over a month after Owen had left, Martin's voice sliced through Miriam's sleep with a hysterical edge. Miriam stumbled to his room and turned on the light but found Martin's bed empty. Instantly awake, she called his name.

"Mom?"

Miriam whirled, then realized the sound came from near her feet. She knelt on the carpet and peered under his bed. Martin's eyes shone back at her. He blinked.

Miriam said, "Sweetie, come out of there. Did you have another bad dream?" At the same time she shook her head, wondering what on earth had brought this on. *Did he sleepwalk? Is he still asleep?*

Martin crawled out and curled up on her lap like a kitten, adjusting his position a couple of times until he stopped moving, all the time watching Miriam's face and saying nothing. She didn't know if she should wake him or say anything that might upset him further. She pulled the pillow and blankets down off the bed and wrapped them around herself and Martin.

She held him, feeling his body relax in her arms. After a few moments his eyes closed. Miriam was trying to stand with him and get them both into the bed when Martin suddenly gasped and cried out. "Dad! Dad!"

Miriam nearly dropped him. Martin struggled in her arms as they both fell onto the bed. He tried to crawl away from her, and she shook him. "Martin, you have to wake up now. It's just a bad dream. Come on." She had never seen him like this before.

Martin woke. She could tell the difference from his previous state by the way his eyes darted around the room. "Tell me your dream so it will go away," she said.

He moved his head slowly back and forth. "I don't know. . . . I don't remember."

"You called out for your dad."

He continued to shake his head, then sat up straighter.

"You remember something?" she asked.

"Mom, we have to go see Dad." He took her hand in both of his and tugged on it.

"What? Now?"

He looked around the room and at his clock and seemed to realize for the first time that it was the middle of the night. "No," he said slowly, "but soon. Matt got time off when his parents took him to Europe. You have to. We have to. Dad needs us." Then, as suddenly as he had awakened, Martin fell back asleep.

But Miriam could not. She sat in the chair by Martin's bed, struggling to shake the spell of urgency his words had cast upon her.

The next morning Owen called. Miriam tried not to link his call with Martin's dream. She listened to him talk about the final preparations for a peace celebration in Maputo. He had pulled it off, after all. The treaty he had helped forge had finally been signed in Rome.

"I need to stay here for the festivities," Owen told her. "Then I'll be home by the end of October."

Miriam could tell he was trying hard not to say something that might annoy her. Their last calls had not ended well. Each time he had pleaded with her to make the arrangements necessary for yet another vacation, this time one in Africa, and each time she had responded angrily. It seemed now he had given up on his idea and was bending over backward to appease her. Miriam could almost see Owen thinking about how to bring peace back into their relationship. The distance must wear on him even worse than it did on her, she realized. She had their home and friends and Martin. He was alone, with only his work to keep him going.

As they had all night, Martin's insistent words came back to her. Miriam heard herself blurting out, "I don't think so."

"What?" Owen said from the other side of the world, static humming around his voice.

"I said, I don't think so. You won't be home by the end of October."

There was a short silence.

"And where will I be then? Do you know something I don't?"

The tension, the striving, the worry of their separation, Martin's furrowed brow and cries at night, and his inexplicable tears all spelled out one message to Miriam. She saw it clearly now for the first time. Her heart turned over at the sound of Owen's willingness to go where she wanted in the conversation. Was it really that easy? Just not put distance between them, and they could be close again?

"We're coming to you," she said. "I changed my mind." *Had a change of heart*, she thought.

Again the silence, then Miriam could hear Owen smiling through his voice. "Have you now? But what about your job? The insurance case?"

Now he shows interest, she thought. "I'll work something out."

"Martin's school?"

Miriam thought fast. "He's only in second grade. Matt got time off when they went to Europe." She smiled at her use of Martin's words. "Besides, I miss you. And this is sort of a dream of yours, our being together in Africa. Isn't it?"

"Aye, 'tis."

Now she laughed out loud. He only laid on the Irish when he wanted to snap her out of a bad mood. "So you win again, Mr. Negotiator. I'll make the arrangements."

"Miriam, we both win."

After she hung up, Miriam thought of her latest contract. She'd have to work nights to complete the necessary research, but it was doable. She only had a few more points to research, and the case would be wrapped up.

She wondered again why she had done what she did. When Martin came home from school that afternoon and overheard Miriam speaking to Owen's travel agent, his look of unabashed delight handed her the only answer worth having.

So a month and a half after her last flight, Miriam found herself on another plane, headed east this time, away from the islands where she had first sensed that something new and raw had begun.

Miriam had envisioned the week following their return home from

Hawaii as the second bead on a strange new strand. Her swim that last day around the coral had been the first—or maybe it had been that dream of walking on the beach. And perhaps these last five weeks had merely tied a knot in the string, marking a space between then and what now lay ahead.

What is this new thing taking shape just beyond the periphery of my sight, its form like no other treasure I have seen? Miriam had the thought but did not understand its meaning.

On this plane, after refueling in Frankfurt, with only Martin beside her now, Miriam realized she felt the same as when Owen's eyes first fell on her, the same as when she found out Martin grew inside her, and yet again when he was born. Turning points of tremendous anticipation, milestones of mystery.

Miriam shook her head. What was it? What was she *not* seeing?

She watched Martin draw in his sketchpad, saw it was some sort of building, then recognized the air-traffic control tower at home. *No, what I'm seeing is not a pattern,* she thought. *It's a maze, and I cannot see what's ahead.* This was Miriam's last thought before falling asleep.

The plane circled a place eleven time zones ahead of her home. Once they landed and stopped taxiing, a staircase rolled up to the cabin door. Miriam stepped outside and paused at the top of the stairs. She smelled dry grass and jet fuel. She raised her face and looked past the runways to the empty fields surrounding the airport. She saw the mist rising off the grasses like islands of smoke between the flat-topped trees in the distance.

"Come on, Mom." Martin tugged at her. "People are waiting behind us."

Miriam nodded.

A man from the airlines smiled at them both. *"Karibu,"* he told them. "Welcome to Kenya."

Miriam smiled self-consciously and grabbed Martin's hand as they descended the metal staircase together. Her eyes took in the disorder on the ground, the carts of luggage being unloaded by young men, the forlorn building with *Nairobi Airport Arrivals* over the door. Despite the early-morning air, a strange warmth rose up to greet her as she neared the ground.

She wondered again at the wide sky, a twist of pinks and purples. Then suddenly a ball of light rolled over the horizon and landed on the plumb line of her vision.

Miriam had the most overwhelming sensation of having arrived somewhere she had always been destined to see, destined to be.

A place that had waited for her all her life.

Filled with hope for no reason, Miriam thought, *This, then, is Africa.*

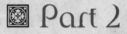 # Part 2

Looking back, I see the vacation in Hawaii as the portal.

It granted me access to a borderland where loss loomed at every twist in the path. Through its opening, my own greater vulnerability reached out, pulling me into a place of raw fear, and raw hope I had never known before.

The season following Hawaii, the events themselves, formed a string of small pearls in my mind, translucent beads I could later worry over and over and over in that dark place of confinement. There the memories dangled, a single strand of all that remained, like rare gems on a rosary. . . .

Chapter 14

Yury Gennady Falin ran a sweaty hand through his blond hair. From where he sat on the veranda of Nairobi's oldest and finest hotel, the twenty people surrounding him in rattan chairs pulled up to round tables felt like a crowd. He had deliberately chosen the corner table so he could see who approached. He would never have picked this place, but the Libyan business contact he was due to meet in half an hour had a taste for fine things—fine hotels, fine cars.

Yury watched the small brunette reappear. She wore a short, sleeveless dress and a single string of pearls around her neck. Good pearls, from the look of them. He noted the security agents standing casually by the steps leading to the entrance. Yes, the clientele here could wear any jewelry they wished and not have to worry about theft. Yury glanced back to the woman's table and thought that his client could keep his hotels and cars; he himself preferred fine women.

Curious. She sat with a young boy, obviously her son. And who were they waiting for? Ah, if the look on her face said anything, that was the lucky man.

Yury noticed he was not the only one to stare at the couple lingering in each other's embrace. Other heads were turning at tables around the veranda. She was American—that much he had heard—

but her husband did not speak loudly enough for Yury to catch the accent.

"I see you have already noted our reason for meeting."

Yury masked his annoyance at being taken by surprise by quickly scraping his chair back, away from the table. The man sat down opposite him and turned around to stare with the rest of the guests at the dark-haired woman's family. He wore a custom-made suit. *London tailor,* Yury guessed. But he had seen El-Fatih in turban and flowing, dust-covered robes, the grime encrusted in the lines on his face. The first time they met, he had looked very different indeed. But then, so had Yury back—when was it? More than ten years ago.

El-Fatih's voice interrupted Yury's thoughts. "Yes, there is no doubt—he is the man. I brought a photo, but I see it will not be necessary. They have been very accommodating, meeting in the open like this. I knew the date and place but could not know if they would show themselves."

Yury watched El-Fatih pull out his gold lighter and hold the newspaper clipping over the ashtray as he set it on fire. He glimpsed the image of the woman's husband before the flames licked it clean. Last to go was the headline: ". . . Breaks Impasse among Renamo Leaders."

The tall North African leaned so far forward Yury could smell his stale breath. "I was watching your interest. He is the one we are interested in. What you do with the rest of the package is your business."

Yury knew full well whom "we" referred to: a huge conglomerate of Western governments and multinational corporations who could not work in the open. He listened as El-Fatih began to talk in heated sentences about the terms of their agreement. Yury hated meeting in the open to discuss these details. But as El-Fatih had pointed out when they agreed on the location, sometimes the more public the place, the better. Yury already knew what he would and would not agree to. He watched El-Fatih's hairy hands move up and down in time with his words. "This peace in Mozambique is a threat to the people controlling arms supplies for my other foreign interests."

Yury decided to add yet another characteristic to the list of things he didn't like about El-Fatih. He talked too much. Yury did not need to hear yet again of El-Fatih's drug interests in Afghanistan, the diamonds in Angola, or the oil fields there and in Sudan. Yury had profited for years as the man's partner in the field. And he certainly didn't need a lecture about what peace could do and how it could be sabotaged. This was Yury's business—arms smuggling, diamond running, training small, crack mercenary troops to perpetuate wars that enabled his clients to continue turning immense profits. He knew far better than the now soft and spoiled man sitting opposite him how to support whichever side would throw a region into the greatest anarchy.

Yury raised his square chin, knowing this would stretch his cheekbones, the arrogant posture adding to his height. He narrowed icy blue eyes as if seeing right through El-Fatih.

This, then, was what Yury viewed as his only human quality, that he understood and saw the bigger picture. He accepted that it was all just a game of risk and manipulation. That thrill was what brought him back time and time again for more. Only the scale differed.

Some played with nations. But Yury played with people and, when he had the chance, with women. Preferably fine women.

⊠ ⊠ ⊠

Miriam stared out of the jeep, her eyes soaking up the sight of golden grass washed in amber African light. She opened herself to the strange beauty of the place, here and now, as Owen had taught her. A land so different from what she had known, and yet so quickly a part of her.

She watched the curiously shaped trees out the car window and counted the days. Only two weeks since she and Martin had boarded the plane that brought them from San Francisco to Nairobi, where Owen had gone to meet them from Mozambique. Less than that since they all left the hotel in Nairobi and began a cross-country trek through South Africa and the surrounding countries. Only two weeks so far, yet this trip across southern Africa had given them so much already.

Owen had done it again. She shared his fulfillment that the Mozambique deal had worked. The hallmarks of Owen's skill, his patience and dedication, had proven their worth in Rome earlier that month, when those who had been enemies for thirty years had finally signed for peace.

Miriam glanced at her husband now. How did he manage it?

Owen sighed, and she realized he must be bored with the long drive from the lodge to Victoria Falls, along—what was it called again? She glanced at the map lying open on the dashboard. Caprivi Strip, just below the very center of Africa, a thin piece of Namibia wedged between Angola, Zambia, Botswana, and Zimbabwe. The drive to Vic Falls, just across the border in Zimbabwe, would take them at least half the day.

Miriam traced the route they had taken on their trip so far, crisscrossing through sub-Saharan Africa. She held the memories up to the light, each image precious after all the time she and Owen had spent apart.

The stars—every night she had shared great joy at learning, together with Martin, at Owen's side, the names of the Southern Hemisphere constellations. The photo safaris, or game drives, as their guides called them, when Martin cried out with excitement at each major sighting. And Miriam's own personal favorite, the sundowner cruises at sunset along rivers where they watched elephants showering each other with their trunks and staring back at them.

In Botswana, when they toured a diamond mine in Jwaneng, Miriam had listened to the guide boast of the relative peace and prosperity his country enjoyed, especially as compared to other diamond-rich nations on the continent, whose histories were plagued with endless conflict.

At the end of the tour, the guide had chased away a group of children standing by the entrance to the office. One of them had tugged on Miriam's sleeve and said something to her, his eyes pleading. The guide's harsh tone scattered the children like a flock of birds.

"What did he say?" Owen asked. Miriam watched his eyes follow the children as they ran away. She glanced at Martin, but he was already following the guide inside the air-conditioned office.

"He was just begging," Miriam said.

The guide closed the door behind them. "Yes, this is true. These children are everywhere. They were asking you if you had any pens, ballpoint pens for school. Please sit down." He motioned to the chairs in front of a long table and headed for a dark green safe in the corner of the room.

Miriam watched the guide reach into the safe and felt the familiar tug of childhood memory. He pulled out a white envelope tucked in among a shoe box full of brown ones, then placed a velvet-covered piece of cardboard before them and sprinkled down the stones.

"Oh, Mom, look! Real diamonds!" Martin's eyes lit up.

Miriam looked out the window at the deep pit, a crater in the flat savanna. Hills rose in the distance, topped by a field of small clouds that rested all on the same level, as if on an unseen hand that dangled them just beyond her reach.

"Perhaps you would like to see them through the loupe," the guide offered.

Miriam watched the thickset man lean over her son. He removed the orange hard hat, and she saw the sweat marks left by the helmet on his brow. An uneven mustache wove its way around his mouth. His big hands engulfed Martin's small, pale ones as he showed Martin how to hold the loupe with one hand, then positioned a stone with the tweezers for Martin to view. His other hand steadied Martin by covering his small shoulder.

She felt Owen's hands on her waist as he leaned forward from his position directly behind her in the cramped office. The moment hung as quiet as the clouds. To Miriam it felt the same as when she'd followed the turtle in Hawaii, as when Martin woke her the night before Owen left, as when she emerged from the plane—as if the whole earth had paused to take a deep breath. The air reverberated with a message she felt should have told her something, but it drummed a rhythm she could not read.

"You try," Owen said, pushing her forward slightly.

She looked at him over her shoulder and saw his eyes light up with humor. She smiled and shook her head. He just wanted to show her off as the diamond cutter's daughter.

The guide straightened as Owen pressed Miriam to sit down. Martin handed her the loupe. She took it in her right hand, closing the index finger and thumb around the handle. She grasped it by the small handle that was screwed onto one of the eight sides. With her left hand she picked up the tweezers and quickly shuffled through the pile of stones until she found one of the smaller ones. She brought this to her other hand so the fingertips met, and she peered down.

"Madam has chosen a fine stone."

Martin said, "But it's not as big as the one I had."

Miriam leaned toward her son. "Look, Martin. Count the fissures. See the color? It's more white than the yellowish one you had. Look again and *see* the difference. The size isn't everything. Color and clarity count even more." She stood and gave the astonished guide a smile. Owen was chuckling softly. When no one was looking, she gave him a quick kick.

In that office, her father's words came back to Miriam as if he had whispered them to her in the still air. The years melted away with the feel of the loupe between her fingers again. She had spent so many hours of her childhood listening to her father tell her the same words, watching him cut the stones, hearing him talk of their values.

It was for him that Miriam had kept her maiden name *Vree*. "Pronounce it the Dutch way, like *afraid*," she told everyone, "but without the *a* and *d*." And it was for him that she introduced Martin on this trip to the secret world of reading the stones.

Earlier in their trip, before Botswana, her parents' Dutch language had helped Miriam get her own family out of danger. It had happened in South Africa, very late at night, when she and Owen misjudged the distances and got turned around, ending up in a township. Miriam had watched angry faces follow them as Owen drove down one street, then had to back up and try another. He had told her then to pray for their safety. On that night of dark stares, because she could read a language similar to Afrikaans, they had been able to follow the signs until they found their way back to the highway.

The next day, it had been a relief to cross into little Swaziland, where everyone seemed somehow related to the king. People there had touched her on the arm and looked her in the eye and let her take photos of their children. When they had doubled back through South Africa, they'd toured the wine country and headed along what was called the Garden Route. Owen had even tried to ride an ostrich at a ranch where the birds were being raised for their meat, but the poor beast had never stood a chance.

Now, in the car, Miriam laughed out loud.

"What?" Owen turned to look at her as the jeep hit yet another pothole.

"You and that ostrich," she said, glancing at him.

His sea-gray eyes caught hers, and the chuckles erupted, filling the cab of the jeep. "I am rather stout, am I not?" he asked, patting his chest.

Miriam's eyes took in his jeans, creased from sitting too long, dust outlining the folds around his thighs, as solid as tree trunks. Perspiration stains streaked his khaki shirt. She mimicked his accent. "You are indeed."

"I thought we agreed to forget about that unfortunate situation," he growled.

She smiled at his reference to their term for political crises. "Well, it had the potential for an international incident, that's for sure," she said.

"So tell me about that leopard this morning. What did he sound like?" Owen asked. "Not that I'm trying to change the subject." Again, Miriam looked out the window and thought back to that morning, the leopard's panting and growls as he padded past their hut.

"Owen?" she whispered into the shadows when the leopard's grunt awakened her. It was very early, what her husband liked to call the wee small hours of the morning.

His soft snoring continued. Miriam reached out a hand in his direction and felt his arm, the stubble on his cheek. He did not move.

Miriam sat up straight and hugged her knees to her chest, moving her feet in their soft bed. She held her breath. The expensive lodge where they were staying had posted a guard near their hut. She reminded herself of this—and of the fact that he carried a gun.

Another guttural growl, this time closer. She turned her face toward Martin's room, the door just beyond the closet.

No sound. He slept as soundly as his father.

Miriam waited, listening, the window screens the only thing between her and the African night. She heard nothing but birds.

Finally she lay back down at Owen's solid side and slept again, her last sight the dim shadows of the high bedposts decked in sheer mosquito netting that rose above her like angel wings.

Chapter 15

This child I have just described, I have thought about him very often. This child, he is not me, yet I know his story as if it were my own. Please don't stop reading! You think, see, he is lying, playing with my trust in the story. But this is not true. Listen!

This child's story was a false story. These are lies I have told myself. I wrap them around me at night like a blanket of blindness, wishing and willing it all to be so. They are the stories of other children I have heard, other children I wish I were. I stole the details from the stories of my brothers and sisters I met on the journey. I stole the best parts of their stories and made them part of my own imaginary dream.

Oh! That was painful to admit!

Now I will describe the beauty of Africa. I

should love the darkness best. At night the hot sun cannot blind me. It is cooler, and sometimes a breeze washes my face. I am less thirsty. Best of all, stars stretch over me like a blanket I can hide under, and enemies cannot find me. At night Africa sounds like a great beast, turning over, groaning, stretching, settling in. From the insects to the elephants, we all rest. For me, the blanket of lies I told is not real. Only the darkness remains.

Now then, this is part of the story I was wishing to make up.

Who am I?

You are wondering, but will he tell the truth this time? For this boy, he is taking me on a twisted path. The path is one I choose because it protects me from facing too much truth too soon.

But here is a little piece of truth now. Trust me?

Who am I? All right.

I was born in Sudan. This makes sense when I see pictures of others from the Dinka tribe in the southern parts of that nation. I see my chin and eyes and ears on their faces sometimes.

But—and this is what is so hard to write down now—I remember nothing of my homeland. So instead, I tell everyone I am from East Africa. And this is true. I grew up in the desert of Ethiopia, on the plains of Uganda, between the foothills of Kenya, and across the savanna of Tanzania. How could such a thing be?

Instead of Arabic or a Sudanese local language, Kiswahili is my native tongue—the language that spans East Africa. But I write this now for you in English, so you will be proud of me, yet spiced

with Kiswahili so you will hear the soft rustle of
tall grass and the call of the cicada as you
become one with my story.

I have many names, but I am one person only.
Do not become confused if you hear several voices.
I am the only one telling this story. Perhaps the
different voices are because of so many native languages I have heard along the way, plus the English and Portuguese my elder brothers and sisters
learned in their schools before they joined me on
this journey. Did you know there are over six thousand languages spoken in Africa? I only know perhaps ten of these, so I have still much to learn.
Sometimes their voices may join my own.

Now, my name.

A name is an important thing. In my culture, a
name is a prophecy, a mother's wish, a chronicle
of events, a curse. You told me to find out about
Sudan. You said, "To know where you are going,
you must know where you have come from."

So I have learned that in Sudan the naming of
a child has a special ceremony. It depends on the
particular village, for this varies from Dinka tribe to
tribe, and whether this takes place in the country-
side or a town. In some places in the South of
Sudan, the naming of a girl takes place three days
after birth. A boy is named four days after birth.
The father of the child kills a lamb at sunrise. He
says, "By the name of God I am going to call my
boy or girl. . . ." And then he says the name. This
naming day is called Simayah. And all the child's
relatives, friends, and neighbors spend that day
celebrating with the family. Sometimes the mutton

is sent to these families. Parents can choose any name they wish.

The name a person bears is sometimes a key to understanding who he is deep down, in the dark and light places of his soul. This is especially true with nicknames and praise names. In my culture a name is worth more than any other possession, for this one thing will survive his death. Even the poorest man has a name that lives on after he dies.

So now you see how very poor I was as a child, for I did not have a name. I did not have my own name. Instead I had many, too many—all mine, and none mine.

I will give you a list of all my names and the places in my life where they became mine. The names are like signposts. When you hear them, you will see the course of my journey better.

Also, that I have so many names will tell you how filled with sorrow my heart is. I belong nowhere, come from nowhere, and where do I go now?

In this beginning place, then, I am Mamboleo, "Temporary Thing."

Chapter 16

Miriam did not see the glint of sun on metal nor the bloodshot eyes following their progress along the asphalt road in Namibia. If she had been staring out the right side, Miriam might have seen the men, might have caught a glimpse of metal shimmering in sunlight, might have sensed their presence, might have warned her family.

Instead, she was looking left, letting her thoughts wander, feeling the rhythm of the car, looking out into a sky of pure, clean blue. *Hemelsblau,* her mother would have called it. "Heaven's blue."

She leaned a little out the window, raising her face to catch the sun. Here, on one of the few asphalt roads they had traveled on, no dust clouded around the jeep. Instead, the smell of dry grass followed her as it had since she landed on the vast continent.

Her eyes narrowed and caught the reflection in the mirror mounted on the door. The wind whipped strands of hair across her face. She took off her sunglasses and saw tired brown eyes looking back, the skin below, lighter half-moons rising above the darker cheeks. *How can I feel so at peace and look so awful?* She rubbed her eyes and then traced the wrinkles with her fingers. They encircled the edges of her eyes, pulled at the corners of her mouth, and furrowed across her forehead. Her hands looked old too, creased. Owen always said they gave her away because they never held still.

Miriam let her thoughts gallop far away, back to her home on what seemed like another planet. Since coming here, that home seemed far out of reach. Here, impossible things happened.

Just yesterday evening, before she heard the leopard, Owen had brought up the subject of having a second child. Before, the discussions had always ended with her having to bear the responsibility of deciding. But something about last night had felt different, as if they were discussing a real possibility of them *both* making the decision.

They'd already been over and over all the pros and cons. She had spent the last seven years trying to balance her responsibilities as wife and mother with the demands of being a young lawyer. When it became obvious she could not continue working on staff in a firm that took overtime for granted, she'd gone into freelance work. And because she had chosen for a family, it felt like her career had gone nowhere.

"I still think you don't understand," she said now. It sounded harsher than she meant it to.

Owen glanced at her and frowned. "What? About the leopard?"

"No, about the job thing. What we were talking about last night." She loved the openness this prolonged time together had fostered between them. Now she no longer needed to guard her words, waiting for a time when Owen could listen, was rested and at her side. He was right to ask her to come here. She was right to come.

"Of course I understand," he said. "You want more in your career. I say go for it. But you won't do it. And there are plenty of reasons why you don't, some of them fair. But there's one very good reason why you should."

Miriam smiled, remembering how Sue sometimes teased her about trying to debate with a professional negotiator. "I know what you're saying," she countered, "but I don't think I can. Really. It's a physical impossibility to put in more hours than I've been working." *And raise a family,* she thought.

"Don't you want to know what that good reason is?" Owen asked. When she didn't answer, he said, "It's what you *want*. That's why."

Miriam stifled a sarcastic laugh. What she *wanted?* What she wanted was a career in international arbitrage, researching for people like Owen. But that would require going back to work full time, and getting back into a firm would be just one step down the road. It was a road that seemed longer and longer every time she thought of the years already wasted—well, not wasted, but certainly gone. And what would happen if they had that second child? She did want another child, a little brother or sister for Martin. She thought she did anyway. At least talking about it last night had felt good.

The trouble is, I want it all, she admitted to herself. But the years had escaped her, gone, like grains of sand spilling between her fingers.

I'm being ridiculous. Miriam brought herself up short. There they were, together, having the vacation of a lifetime, and she was obsessing about all the things she didn't have. This resentment was the very thing the trip had healed. But now she had gone and spoiled the mood again.

"What we need to figure out," Owen was saying, "is what we can change to make it all possible. What it would take."

"Help," Miriam mumbled.

"So, we'll get help. Help with the housework, help to take care of Martin. Now that he's going to school full time, that makes a difference. Am I missing anything? Help for the baby, if the time comes. Help to handle your husband maybe?"

"Don't try any of that Irish charm on me," Miriam started to say sternly, but she knew he knew he was doing just that. And it was working. In that way of his, Owen had waved his wand and caused the tiny thread of tension to dissipate. Miriam shook her head. "You're good," she muttered, but she still felt relieved. She didn't want to complain. Not today, not here.

"Am I now?" He reached over and took her hand in his, a bear paw with fingers. Miriam saw the love in his dazzling eyes, felt their one-heart of eight years, then gazed back outside.

The weighty color resting on acacia treetops, flat from the burdened beauty of such a horizon—this place mesmerized Miriam. She felt relaxed and safe and fulfilled as all around a splendor shone. The spell seeped into her sigh. "So strange, that this place could exist. I mean, it's existed all along, and I didn't know about it. That sounds self-centered. I mean something else, I think. Was it waiting for me?"

"You talk in poetry."

"I get carried away sometimes." Miriam rested a hand on Owen's back. It didn't matter how many years they had been married.

Whenever his smile and dancing gray eyes fell on her gently as now, they still raised goose bumps on her arms.

When Owen's large form entered a room, he never failed to dominate it. She had seen it happen time and again, no matter the country or the culture. It wasn't his size, but the charm he exuded, humble and hopeful, that way he had of calming emotions. Owen's charisma could charge a group so powerfully, he had made a career of getting enemies to talk with one another.

She ran her hand over his broad shoulders, massaging away the tension she felt there. Then, still using her fingers, she combed his hair the way he liked it.

"Still some hair up there?" he asked, not taking his eyes off the road.

"A little," she teased. "Not bad for forty-seven."

Owen felt every year of his age but managed to chuckle. "And you're not bad for thirty-seven." He didn't mind the ten years between them, was proud even to have a young wife as smart as Miriam. *If* they went through with this and tried for a second child, they would have to do it soon.

Enough said, he thought. But still, to have a little girl like Miriam herself, to see what she was like as a child . . .

Owen smiled. Better not to belabor the point. So he said, "Now, about your description of this fine day. Haven't I told you all along? We're both in the wrong line of business. I'm a gypsy, and you're a poet."

"Are we now?"

His eyebrows furrowed in mock concern. "Sure, you wouldn't be makin' fun of a poor Irishman's brogue now, would ya? And yes, we are indeed." His light tone belied the stress of the last months. Only now, after two weeks of vacation, was it beginning to seep out of his system. Miriam's fingers on his back muscles felt like warm balm. And having her and young Martin at his side again made him feel whole. He made a mental note to accept only negotiation assignments in the future that kept him where he could have his family near. And then he tried to forget how often he had made—and broken—that same promise.

Thankful for the paved road empty of traffic, Owen hung his left wrist over the steering wheel and allowed himself to revel in the great hope that this time he might have pulled it off. Never mind his personal past. In his business, the worst of all possible defeats were the ones, as in Mozambique, when the civilian population paid the highest price.

The amazing thing about this latest deal in Mozambique was watching the decades-old conflict disintegrate once they had managed to eliminate all outside involvement. The people wanted peace; they had chosen peace. After the signing in Rome between the president, Joaquim Chissano, and the head of the Renamo opposition movement, Alfonso Dhaklama, Owen had flown back to Mozambique one last time. There he had joined in the celebrations in the country's capital, Maputo, and that was just before Miriam and Martin had flown to Nairobi to join him.

"Rome, Nairobi, Maputo—it all has an exotic ring to it, doesn't it?" Owen asked, reaching up to squeeze Miriam's hand. "Come to think of it, I probably *am* a gypsy."

Martin listened to his parents in the front of the jeep. He had been asleep but woke up when they started talking. He liked the sound of their voices, heard something that felt like a hug in their tones. They all belonged together, and Martin didn't like it that his father was gone from home so much. Well, he didn't mind that much really, but his mom didn't like it, and Martin didn't like *that*.

It didn't matter now though, because they were having a great time on safari in Africa. Martin especially liked all the animals—the kinds that were only in zoos at home. He recited the names of the big five to himself again: *lion, water buffalo, elephant*. . . .

"Hey, Dad, which animals are numbers four and five again? Not giraffe, or is it?"

His mother turned and smiled at him. "Where's your book, Martin? It will say." He'd rather his father told him, but Martin didn't mind an excuse to haul his backpack off the floor and dump its contents onto the seat so he could check his treasures again. That's what his dad called the stuff—"his treasures."

He put the pens back in their box, set the Walkman and tapes to the side, and placed the little box that opened into a miniature magnetic chess set next to him. Then he picked up his book. On the inside flap was a chart with pictures of different animals and little squares to mark with an *X* when he had sighted the animal.

"Oh, and leopard—that's another one. I can mark it now because of you, Mom." Martin paused, then asked, "So, did you really hear the leopard this morning?"

He saw the back of her head nod. "What is it with you two?" she asked. "No one believes me."

Martin said, "Yes, I do."

At breakfast that morning at the lodge, he had been eating pineapple when she said, "I heard something this morning when it was still dark." Two waiters had been dishing up thick slices of bacon and eggs dripping in butter.

The game guide said, "Madam has good ears. Yes, we were visited by a leopard. We heard him enter the river from the other side and cross. A great splash. I have never seen leopard swim before. Very amazing sight." Martin remembered how the guide had opened his left hand wide, fingers spread like a sunflower.

"*Chui,*" Martin now said out loud, opening and closing his fist, trying to talk low, in the deep voice of the guide.

"What's that, Martin?" his mother asked.

"*Chui* is Kiswahili for leopard. And it *is* one of the big five. Look, Mom."

Martin ran his finger down the list as his mother turned around. He fumbled with the book and dropped it, leaned over to pick it up and find the page again. Only then did he hear a sound he had never known before in his young life, a sound he would never forget.

He heard his mother cry out in fear.

Chapter 17

The tank reflected the sun's glare in a single shaft of light. Miriam had turned around to look at Martin when the flash just past Owen's shoulder caught her eye. She saw trees, the bush that had replaced the grassland, and then movement. It was probably only a second later, but she would later remember the events as a series of images—seeing the flash of light, recognizing it came from a surface camouflaged with leaves and branches—then seeing the netting, understanding it covered a tank, noting the movement of men, focusing on the color of their hands, the same as the long guns they held.

Miriam saw many men dressed in parts of uniforms. And she wondered why this detail should stand out so, but it did. She saw that some had caps, others had khaki shirts of different patterns, a few had black boots, one or two walked barefoot. But that tank rolling along just behind them onto the highway—that made everything clear.

Miriam did not see their faces. Or perhaps she did not look. Later she would think about that too. After the split second it took for the shock of recognition to wear off, she jerked on Owen's hand and cried, "Turn the jeep around! Look!"

When Owen looked behind them, Miriam knew he saw it too—the tank emerging from the bush, catching up with them, turning in front of their jeep, slowing. Owen braked and swung the jeep in an arc, just avoiding a collision. They ran off the road and into the bush, the car out of control until a tree rose up before them.

"Mom!" Miriam heard Martin scream. She reached back and tried to grab on to him just as the jeep crashed to a halt.

When she looked up again, it was into the red-veined eyes of a man pointing a rifle through the other window, at Owen's head.

She felt with her hand what must have been Martin's leg. He lay with his legs jammed under their seat, his pillow and the contents of his small backpack piled on top of him. The colored pens and his water bottle lay scattered across the seat and on the floor, the sketchbook folded over his head like a small fort. And he was breathing; Miriam could feel as much. But why did he remain so still, so quiet? She told herself maybe this was better.

She twisted back toward the front and saw Owen only then raising his head from where he had hit it against the steering wheel. A thin line of blood ran across one cheek. She caught his eye and read his thoughts as clearly as if she could hear his voice—the same words he had used with Martin during the last minor earthquake back at home: *Be calm. Think!*

Miriam swallowed her terror as bitter bile. She looked down, rubbing her neck, trying not to stare at the men who had gathered around the shattered jeep, men who stared at her.

"Anything broken?" Owen whispered. Miriam shook her head no.

The rifle angled sharply upward, and its butt smashed into Owen's ribs. Miriam cried out his name and lunged for him. Hands pulled her out the door. She saw Owen roll onto the ground. Black boots kicked his big body as if it were nothing but a log. Her knees buckled. Four hands grabbed her and kept her upright. Miriam's only thought clear as a bell: *Martin, no sound.*

All of this was what she saw and heard. But at the same time, part of Miriam staggered, gasped, retreated, insisted, *No!* Where was the family vacation of just a few short moments ago? Who were these men? What did they want? Why? Where were the other vehicles on this road? The questions trickled down Miriam's mind like the blood on Owen's face, slow and thick.

A man emerged from under a tree. He carried himself like a leader. He gave orders in a language Miriam could not understand. Four hands dragged Owen upward, and he hung heavily, pulling his captors forward with his weight. The lumbering tank rolled to a stop as five men scrambled to cover it with the net full of leaves.

Miriam glanced back at the road. What sign had they left? A door had opened and closed. Over there they had breathed in safety; here her family panted in desperate danger. Was the difference between then and now, here and there, marked only by those circular skid marks she saw? Was there really no other sign that anything out of the ordinary might be happening just a few short meters from the asphalt?

Miriam looked up.

She saw eight sets of eyes still staring, unblinking. She felt small. She felt soft and weak and female in her shorts and a sleeveless top. She saw herself in their eyes and swallowed, thankful that they answered to some sort of authority, that they were not a wild mob. Or at least she hoped this was so.

Owen groaned. The eyes pivoted from her onto him. The two men heaved him in Miriam's direction and, as he stumbled, she bent forward to help him stand. At that moment, she realized he was stronger than he looked. As she leaned toward him, Owen mumbled under his breath, "If what I try next does not work, then I will cause a distraction. You take Martin and run back to the highway. There are bound to be cars passing by."

"I won't leave you," Miriam whispered. *Cannot. Will never*, she thought.

He looked up and caught her in one of his slate-eyed grips. "You will not look back," he ordered.

Miriam stood, sweat drenching her sides. Her tongue tasted the dust on her lips. She looked around, trying to see. That direction back to the highway. The jeep a good five paces back and to the left of where she stood. She thought, *Still no sound from Martin. I can do this*.

Guns bristled all around them. The black-blue metal swung casually from hand to hand, hanging, pointing toward the grass, toward her and Owen. Many guns—the circle of soldiers seemed a crowd. She calmed herself by counting them. Fourteen in all. But some of the soldiers held two guns. Miriam narrowed her focus and saw old, Russian-made Kalashnikovs. AK-47s.

Owen began to talk. *No one watching me now,* she thought, and slowly started backing toward the jeep.

He spoke in Portuguese, which she now recognized because he

spoke more slowly than the soldiers. The language made Miriam realize the soldiers must be Angolan. Yes, she had read about the rebel forces, but none had been reported this far south. Still there were rumors that Namibia was being drawn into the conflict that had torn Angola and other surrounding countries to shreds. *For the oil and for the diamonds.* The thought came to Miriam, and she set it aside.

Owen spoke to the soldiers, and Miriam watched their faces, knowing she must focus, must see, must think. *We'll be all right.* She willed the words to give her courage. Owen would be offering them a bribe. She saw him reach for his back hip pocket as the rifle tips lifted a few inches. At the same time, Miriam took another three steps toward the jeep, casually resting one hand on the jerry can strapped onto the spare. Only one soldier even glanced at her. She turned and looked behind her at the group, smiling a little. The rest all moved closer to Owen as he drew out his wallet.

Miriam could see part of Martin. She undid the jerry can as if she wanted to get some water. Owen was passing out bills. She leaned forward and whispered, "Martin, are you all right?"

She lifted the edge of his backpack and saw the red T-shirt, little arms in the sleeves, but his face remained covered by the sketchpad. His glasses lay on the floor, broken. Among all the clutter she could see his one pudgy palm upturned. She placed her fingertips on his wrist and felt the pulse, strong and sure.

Miriam gingerly lifted the sketchpad and saw to her relief that Martin had only a small bump on his forehead. He seemed only unconscious, not seriously injured. She had to fight the urge to cry out and gather him into her arms and wake them both up from this dust-choked, sweaty nightmare.

Owen's instructions still rang in her ears. But instead, on impulse, Miriam let the sketchpad softly cover her son again, this time so no part of him showed. Then she turned and raised the jerry can to her lips. Before lowering it, she saw one of the men coming toward her.

She moved away from the jeep and hoped he had not seen her speak to Martin. Owen's voice became louder. Miriam looked over, as did the soldier coming toward her. Owen thrust a fistful of *pula,* the Botswanian currency, in the others' faces, and now for the first time Miriam heard the one in charge speak in flawless English, but with a French accent.

"Nice that you offer us your money. But we are after something of much greater value."

Owen coughed, holding his side. "Fine. You outnumber us. What do you want?"

"It seems we have what we want," the leader said. He nodded, first at Miriam and then at Owen. The two men locked gazes. Miriam saw that this man wore a complete uniform. His boots shone.

In the next second, Owen bent and rammed a shoulder right into the leader's middle. His tackle took everyone by surprise. Miriam knew Owen could move amazingly fast for a man his size. Perhaps she could buy him some time by creating a diversion of her own. Grabbing the idea that suddenly had formed in her mind, Miriam ran, telling herself that Martin was safer undiscovered. She veered to the left and sprinted through the swath of broken brush the jeep had cut when it careened that way less than a half hour earlier.

Miriam ran, thinking about the roots and logs she could not trip over. "A car will come by," she gasped out loud. "I know it." She ran and heard herself making little crying noises, the same sounds that could wake her from a dream.

Then Miriam looked back. Owen lay on the ground, pinned down by three men. She slowed enough to hear Owen shout, as if he could see her, "Run!"

She turned, trying to force away the image of what must be happening behind her. And Martin! She could not leave him behind.

"Miriam, go! Run!" Owen's words pushed her forward, and Miriam concentrated on that saving strip of pavement shimmering just beyond the trees. When she felt its smoothness under her feet, Miriam swerved right and started down the highway. Only then did she realize what an easy target she made on the open stretch. Unless a car happened by at just the right moment, she stood a good chance of being shot down.

Miriam thought she heard Owen call again after her, but she could not understand him. She ran on.

Miriam looked up, moaning for a car. Instead, where a few seconds earlier there had been only an open stretch of road, she now saw more soldiers, another group, waiting, laughing. Where had they come from? Two stood smoking, but three shot their rifles straight at Miriam. Bits of roadway bounced up a meter in front of her. Miriam looked down and watched the ground as it rose up and pulled her somewhere else.

Chapter 18

Me, I cannot tell you many details from the start of my journey. I was in school. I spent many nights there. Kind women took care of me and other children. We slept in a big room and all wore the same clothes. This was a dormitory. I know that now, now that I have gone to school and have learned enough to know how to write these words:

"And the truth will set you free."

I think I was seven. I might have been six. I have been captured twice.

The first time was then, as a too small, small boy. I am an oldie man now. The kind women of that place who wore crosses around their necks would not recognize me.

This is what I remember.

I sat up in bed and rubbed my eyes. These were the loud noises we had heard all week. Shooting.

Guns shooting. Men shooting guns. The loud noises came closer. Some of the other boys were crying. I was not. Then many lights, more cries.

Dark, then lights. Yanked out of bed by hands, big hands. Put on my clothes, no shoes. "My shoes!" I cried, and the hands hit me across the mouth. I tasted blood. My blood!

Okay, so now I will tell you what happened next. I can tell you this is not easy for me to write. Is it also so hard for you to read? Does your heart pound now like mine?

The truth is not always good. I mean, it can be an ugly animal. But now I will call it out and shoot it down.

We were all crying now, all us little ones. I did not feel little. But I remember how big the soldiers were—I had to look way up at their faces—and I remember many tears. We little ones were tied together with one rope. In a row we had to walk, one behind the other. This was the beginning of my walking career. I am very good at it now. Then though, my mind did not know what thought to settle on. All I knew was the pain in my feet, the rope tugging at my hands, the fear in my heart.

One of the kind women who took care of us ran after the soldiers. Her hand brushed my cheek as she passed us. She stood small in front of a commander, her hands on her hips, her voice first angry, then clever. We stopped and listened. She was offering him money, bargaining for the little girls. When I heard this, I was very sorry for being a boy.

She paid the soldier, and I held my breath

because even at that age I knew sometimes big people do not keep their word. He did, though. The money would pay for one hundred of the little girls.

The kind woman began walking down the line of tied-up children, where I was. She counted the girls out loud to a hundred and kept counting! I had been counting with her under my breath, but at one hundred I let go of counting because this meant I could hope. When she reached number one hundred nine, the soldier, this commander, walked over and took out his panga, then cut the rope between girl number one hundred nine and one hundred ten. He yelled something I did not understand, and all one hundred nine of the little girls ran to the kind woman and they ran back to our school.

Without me.

I will always remember that kind woman. I wanted her to touch my cheek again. She was also the one who taught us about praying. She wore a cloth over her hair and a string of small round stones around her waist. These stones made a sound like dry leaves in autumn, so we always knew when she would appear from around a corner.

But now I will take you back to that night. When I looked at the little girl who was now the first in the girls' line because she was number one hundred and ten, I thought this: "Ah, little sister, I know how you feel." Her face showed that my first prayer should be for her.

That was how they captured me the first time.

The second time I was captured, the soldiers

scarred me. Not my face, but my back and arms and legs. Both times I became a slave, just as if they had paid a price for me, for I bear the marks of a bought boy.

In these places, then, my name is Knumbe, "Sold Person."

I have heard there are tribes who wound the faces of their babies so that their children show scars. This goes back to a time when certain other tribes conquered and sold them to the Arabs as slaves. For this reason they learned to cut open their babies' foreheads, cheeks, and noses. The scarring made their children into unsalable goods.

For at least one such tribe, in their language the same word means both "ugly" and "free."

Now I am very ugly.

Chapter 19

"A child is a strange thing." Yury Falin looked at the group of new recruits in front of him and wondered at the blank faces staring his way. They were hardly older than the ones he was teaching them to command, and they seemed to have no idea why they were there. *They'll wake up soon enough.*

"Most children will obey blindly. So use this. Tell them whatever it takes. Tell them they are protected by magic, give them a pouch to hang around their necks as a talisman—they'll believe you. I've sent scores of these younger soldiers into frontline battle, and I can tell you, they fight more courageously than most grown men."

Without warning, Yury swung his rifle off his shoulder and, in one motion, sprayed the air above their heads with bullets. The two men on the left dove for the ground; the others only covered their heads.

"Did you get that, Joseph?" Yury nodded at the small man with shoulders like a wrestler's who stood just behind him and to the left.

Joseph grinned. "Yes, Commandant." He wrote down the names of the two slapping the dust off their new uniforms and climbing back onto the half-log benches.

Yury smiled and continued his lecture. "And use the prize of having their own weapon. The boys will covet the power it gives them, the ability to be in authority over the other boys. In these parts, the price of a light automatic weapon like the old AK-47 is one chicken. Although there may sometimes be a shortage of military personnel in the various conflicts you'll be involved in, remember that there are always plenty of guns and plenty of children."

An hour later Yury's jeep careened onto the nearby airstrip and skidded to a stop. A cloud of red dust engulfed them. Joseph jumped out and ran toward a copse of trees. Yury climbed out of the vehicle and took the duffel bag out from under the seat. He slung it over one shoulder and jogged toward the edge of the airstrip.

Joseph had already hauled the camouflage netting off the small Cessna and bundled it into a pile. Together he and Yury removed the blocks at the base of the wheels, then Yury unlocked the pilot's-side door and threw his gear inside.

Joseph stood with his face turned upward. Yury joined him, both men sweating under the sun. For a few moments they said nothing. Then Yury nodded. "Right. We only have a window of half an hour before more patrols fly over. Lucky for us our government friends keep to a tight schedule. Some days they're here, and some days they're not. But I'm not going to take a chance." He turned to Joseph and tipped back his hat.

"I topped off the fuel," Joseph said.

Yury stretched his right arm out to shake hands with his foreman. "You'll be all right? Taking care of everything at camp?"

Joseph nodded. "Yes."

Still Yury hesitated, shading his eyes and watching the sky.

"Not so glad to go?" Joseph asked.

Yury smiled without answering. Joseph knew him well. Yury belonged out in the bush—the men, the warfare, the troops, the intrigue. He could not stomach the restrictions of so-called civilization. Out here he could breathe and do as he pleased. Having so recently returned from Nairobi, he didn't look forward to another city trip, this time to Harare. "So how do you think this latest group will turn out?" he asked, purposely changing the subject.

Joseph moved his hand from side to side. "So-so. One or two will not make it past the first week."

"Right." The two men shook hands a second time, and Yury climbed into the pilot's seat for his trip to Zimbabwe. He called down to Joseph, "I'll see you there," and waved as he started the motor. He ran a quick flight check and taxied out to the center of the strip. And then the small plane was charging down the dirt track and tipping its nose above the treetops.

As the ground fell away from him, Yury felt himself relax. He scanned the sky one last time for air traffic, then settled into his seat and pulled the maps out of the under-seat pocket.

He hadn't slept much the night before and needed to be sharp. El-Fatih always had interesting ventures for him, but this one promised to pay extremely well. He'd take the usual precautions. And he'd have to get to the bottom of what had happened to the antiaircraft missile launchers he had ordered. His troops needed them desperately to ward off the combat helicopters he expected to swoop down from the surrounding hills any moment now. With the money for this job, he might see if he could find a few more helis, but with infrared jammers at the ends of the blades. The latest in weapons technology, together with his knowledge and provision of technical assistance in the field, was what helped Yury maintain an edge among his competitors.

He thought of what Joseph would face back at camp. The last group was headed toward a probable 70 percent mortality rate. It was always that way, Yury thought, especially when they had so many young ones. But then he only got the best to train, so anyone could imagine what the rest were like.

Yury himself had been fifteen when he joined the Soviet army. No Young Pioneers meetings for him. He had waited a long time to escape the state orphanage on the outskirts of Leningrad where he had grown up. At fifteen he'd known he could pass for seventeen and had gone to sign up. The incentive was simple, at least back then, before 1989, when the Soviet states could still be called a union. The army had not only fed him better than the orphanage but had also trained him and paid him.

In the military, for the first time in his life Yury had felt at home. He'd discovered that his sort—lethal, quiet, strong, distrustful—did very well in the army. He liked weapons and believed in action. He had no problem with the rules and discipline. That was nothing compared with the orphanage regime. And he fought dirtier than any of the boys in his barracks, so they all left him alone.

Yury had already been a military man for thirteen years when they sent him to Afghanistan—when was it?—twelve years ago, back in 1980. He'd sworn then that if he ever survived that wretched place, he'd become his own boss, use everything he had learned to train others for war and grow rich in the process.

And so Yury had ended up in Africa—and discovered where he truly belonged. His rivals might enjoy their posh Moscow *dachas* with their fake blondes, but Yury preferred the bush. He had traveled the world, and there still was nowhere better for making an illegal, secret fortune than Africa. Here he could enjoy his freedom while keeping tabs on all his various business ventures. His diamond territory wasn't the fastest expanding area in central Africa for nothing.

No, his influence was expanding because he was known for making deals on the spot with the men directly involved. He thrilled to the constant game of shifting shadows—the ever-present possibility that today's ally might put a bounty on his head tomorrow. He loved the challenge of staying one step ahead of everyone else. Just this week, he had moved into territory that previously belonged to the Lebanese mafia.

Well, he'd soon find out how effectively his new troops could fight. He well knew the value of young soldiers. *They obey and are fearless, as I was.*

▩ ▩ ▩

A humming sound. Miriam was being thrown from one side of something hard to the other side. She smelled blood and tasted gritty dust. Her mouth hurt, lips burned. She could not move the muscles of her lower face.

Miriam opened her eyes and found herself inside what felt like the back of a truck, a bag over her head, duct tape across her mouth. Her hands flew upward and felt the sack, tied with a multitude of knots around her neck, felt the tape through the sack. Terror tightened its grip. She now understood that she was beyond the reach of any car driving past.

Miriam put out her arms and began to feel her way along the floor of the vehicle. Felt sand, dirt, bits of metal, more rope, and then a foot. Her hands fluttered up the body, feeling a familiar shirt, his chin. Her fingertips brushed against clotted blood around the eyes. She held a finger under his nose. Owen breathed.

And only then did Miriam allow herself to remember Martin. What she felt she could not explain in terms of mere loss. It was something much more. *What have they done with you?* Frantically she searched the rest of the truck, willing her hands to find yet another foot and at the same time wishing, hardly daring to hope, that he might have escaped.

Her hands found nothing.

Miriam tried to dam the thought of Martin wandering alone in the bush, hyenas hunting him, the same stinking beasts who had invaded their camp on safari, their half-dead witches' cackles waking them in the false dawn. *No, stop it!* Miriam refused to allow herself to imagine these things. A part of her began to realize, to get a premonition, that her mind might prove the greater enemy in this new dimension of danger she had stumbled into. *Martin! Let him be safe. Please.*

The truck turned several times, so abruptly it threw Miriam from one side to the other. Then it slowed and stopped. She heard men's voices very near, felt their hands, and cried out as they dragged her and Owen from the truck and threw them into some place with a door. She knew that much because she heard the door shut and a metal bar fall into place. Miriam felt the rope around her neck that had held the bag in place. Hands had cut it before the men left them. Miriam pulled off the bag now, breathing deeply, and saw Owen lying beside her. She saw his nose beaten in, both eyes swollen closed. But at least his chest was rising and falling in ragged rhythm.

And now Miriam began to wait, her thoughts refusing to leave her in peace. She waited and thought of home, as if summoning a place of sanity might make the present lunacy disappear. She thought of their house, the bay window in the breakfast nook, Martin's bedroom, the street in Chinatown where Sue lived, the shops they liked to visit together—she grabbed on to any image that might ground her. As she sat beside her breathing husband, Miriam hoped with all her heart that in reminding herself that she actually came from that other place, she could somehow calm the heaving seas that had tossed her from there to here.

Miriam must have dozed off. Filtered light threw long shadows when Owen finally regained consciousness, and she woke to his one word, "Martin?"

She had dreaded this moment, known the telling would tear her apart. She saw her tears fall in the dust as, sobbing, she admitted, "I left him in the car. I left him behind."

And then Owen, her brave husband, said the words she did not dare: "He is alive."

They held each other in the fading light, her deep grief etched by fear. "I saw him alive, with my own eyes." Miriam said it so softly she could hardly hear herself.

Chapter 20

Me, I will write down here one of the poems I have carried in my head. I do not remember the first time I had such a thought poem; it was just there.

Of my peace, of my peace, the peace I seek,
In time of war I die lonely, on the edge of a road,
More isolated than a shipwreck,
In the middle of a lake, forgotten by all,
Remembered by no one, no one to wipe my tears,
Crying, covered by the sweat of death.

There was no peace—this is why people ran away from Sudan. Refugee children do not have a country. We do not have a home. Often we no longer even have a family, except for the larger group our smaller group may join. We are children without a childhood. There are many things I do not understand. Why must a child run like this? In danger, exhausted, miserable, and scared every step of the way. It is a bad thing to be hungry, day after day.

Now, when I think back on those days of waking up with a lion in my belly and going to sleep feeling worse, I bow my head in thanks to our Lord Jesus, that He has brought me here where I can eat and live in peace. This is a very great miracle, and I am so grateful sometimes I cannot swallow.

You have asked me to write everything I remember. But this is a strange thing—many things I do not remember. Of the first time I was captured, I only remember being taken away on the night when I wished I were a little girl. After that, my next memory is of the walking, but my hands are not tied, and big boys are telling me to get up and walk on. So yes, I know this means I escaped, but I have no memory of this first escape or of what happened after the first night they tied me up and I was six.

Or seven.

Only the hyenas who stalked our group know how much time went by when I followed behind big boys and we were not tied up anymore. This is what I know: we walked at night because during the day the sun is hot. My feet burned. So we walked at night, and then I did not have to think so often, "I want water. I want water." It was very bad for me to rest too long under a tree. I told myself many times: I can die if I give up. The lion will kill me; wild animals will kill me if I stay behind and say I don't want to do this walking. I don't want to run; I just want to sit. Then the lion will kill me.

But me, I was not so scared because I was with many big boys. When the lion came, we yelled very loud, and then the lion, he did not kill us.

So we walked some more. We ate dirt. We ate leaves. The big boys said, "Go this way. Go that way." But me, I know God showed us the way.

You remember?

I think this because I have God, and He says to me, "Go this way." Just imagine—without God I could go that way, any way, and where do I go? Worse, where would my journey end?

Something else that is important: I know I cannot just leave a person who must sit down. So I pinch him and yell that he must get up. This thing the big boys did for me. And now I do it because of God. He says to me, "Don't leave this person behind. This person, he is life."

You asked many times how I kept going. I was not strong, but when I saw a smaller boy than me walking, I said to myself, "See that small boy? He is walking." So I walked too.

Often stories helped because then we told stories about going to get food and how we would be happy somewhere, someday. Stories about now, I think, and these stories made us happy, and it is easier to walk when you are happy. I want to learn in a way that will help me tell stories that make people happy. Do you think this is possible? When I hear stories about Sudan, this also makes me happy. It is a place I want to go back to, when it can be my home. Perhaps.

Don't ask me why these things happened to me, why I am a refugee. How could I know? I say, ask the big people why. What do you think?

I remember many days when I was not feeling good. I just walked. You asked about seeing people dying. I think you don't know what it is to see many dying. They die of hunger. Even my friend who walked by my side most days, he died. No water is worse, but no food is very bad. When I saw my friend dying, I still kept walking. I think sometimes I can help, and then sometimes I cannot. I am talking again about life. If I had stayed with my friend, I would also be dead. What could I do? He refused to go with me. I am sorry for this and keep walking, walking, walking.

On this long trip with the big boys, I call myself Nsami, "One Who Moves a Lot."

Chapter 21

Martin woke to the distant sound of gunshots. He felt all twisted up, outside and inside. He pushed his sketchbook off his head and felt the light before he opened his eyes and saw it. Bright sun, right on his face. Instead of sitting up, he decided to stay put, lying on the jeep floor. It was darker there, and farther away from those sounds. Besides, his head hurt.

Martin's hand felt broken glass. He looked to his left and saw the mangled remains of his glasses. Mom would be mad.

"Mom? Dad?" He closed his eyes and listened. He heard nothing close by, only engines being revved up and pulling away. Then birds and crickets. He felt hot and thirsty.

When he could not stand the heat in the baking jeep any longer, he sat up. He looked around but still saw no one. Martin climbed into the driver's seat, where his father should have been sitting. The door stood wide open. He held the steering wheel in both hands and looked up. He saw the shattered windshield and cried out at the sight of dried blood, clotted and streaked like a painted sign pointing right at him.

The sound of his own cry brought back that of his mother's, the last thing Martin remembered before the accident. His mother's cry of fear—he had heard that. Then his father had veered the jeep off the road, and he didn't remember anything else after that. Where were his parents?

Martin called out hesitantly; then he yelled as loud as he could. "Mom! Dad!" He listened but heard only a soft stirring in the tall grass. He climbed out his father's door and stood leaning against the jeep's hot metal shell. He felt dizzy. Martin's hand went to his forehead, and he felt a lump. He swallowed and tried again. "Dad? Mom?"

Martin gulped back the tears. *I'm alone out here.* If they had been thrown from the jeep, he thought he would be able to see that. Instead he saw signs of—he didn't know what. Martin walked over and nearly tripped over the pile of fresh-turned dirt. He squatted down to peer closer. It looked like a bulldozer had been through the clearing.

Martin called one more time, "Help! Anyone! Mom! Dad!"

He turned around slowly in a circle, taking in the forms of trees, the tangled undergrowth. Without his glasses, he couldn't see well into the distance, but he remembered there were plains beyond the road.

A truck roared past.

"Hey!" Martin walked toward the road, then broke into a run, his legs pumping, the flat road looming bigger the nearer he came. Just before he reached the edge, another huge semi rumbled past, this time carrying a load of long tree trunks.

Martin stood at the highway, bent over, his hands on his knees, trying to catch his breath. He remembered again how thirsty he felt and licked his lips. Then he heard more gunshots. He looked to the right and squinted at what looked like an army truck coming toward him. He could see arms waving and guns in the hands. He took five steps backward until the bush hid him. Martin crouched as he walked, moving away from the scene of the accident, but parallel with the road.

The truck was slowing down. Martin moved faster, trying to put as much distance as possible between himself and the truckload of cheering soldiers. They were shouting now and shooting some more. *Who are they?* he wondered. *What do they want? Did they see the accident?* But he never thought to approach them. Some held green wine bottles, and they made so much noise he felt afraid. He told himself he should stay near the road but stay hidden from *them*.

A sudden explosion shook the ground, and Martin fell at the base of a huge, gray tree. He looked up and saw branches, strong limbs sticking out like stairs. He scrambled up the trunk until he was high enough to just see over the bushes in the direction of the crashed jeep. Flames and smoke rose from the place he thought it was. *They burned our car?* Martin wondered how they knew the car was there. Had they seen the accident?

All the time he thought these things, Martin was trying not to think of the other thing. But his hands shook. He saw that when he shaded his eyes to look at the burning jeep.

He swiveled around so he could see the highway. It stretched like a strip of sea across the landscape, with flatland on the opposite side of it and undergrowth and trees on his side. If he looked ahead down the road, he could see a blur of green where trees grew on both sides. If he looked the way he and his parents had just traveled, he could see where the plains appeared on both sides. So this was sort of a cross point between the wooded area and the savanna.

Martin climbed down and stood at the base of the tree and waited. After the truckload of soldiers clattered past, he returned to the highway. He didn't know what else to do. If he stayed in the trees, some snake or a lion might find him. On the paved road, there was a chance his parents might find him.

As Martin walked, he began to cry. He knew it was silly, but he didn't care. He had never felt so hot and thirsty and scared before. Now he couldn't even return to the jeep to get his stuff or look for water or food in the back. That idea had come to him only after the men blew up their car. Now it was too late. All alone, Martin knew his parents must be looking for him, must be somewhere, must be alive.

Now he could not quiet the voice; the other thing would not leave him. Martin hated being alone, and he hated his fear.

The fear is everywhere. It follows you into sleep. It slams you down when you wake and try to stand. It stalks you, hunts, haunts, taunts.

The thoughts flung themselves back and forth in Miriam's mind, back and forth, back and forth, banging hard against the limits of what she knew as possible, the borders of her consciousness. Short images, cutoff experiences, amputated appearances. *What is happening to me?*

Miriam memorized their cell. The wooden door wore an old coat of paint, light blue. Nails stuck out at odd angles, their backs broken. Two hinges, a crossbar running diagonally from the top left corner to the bottom right. She drank in these details and counted them—the nails, the nail holes, the bricks along the bottom layer of walls, the ridges in the corrugated-iron roof, the waves per sheet.

Wire mesh covered the one window, the mesh size too large to keep the mosquitoes out. At dusk the insects rushed in as a cloud, descended on Miriam and Owen's still form, biting through their cotton clothing, devouring bare skin so that, after that first night, Miriam felt welts on top of welts. She lay on top of Owen to protect him, trying to summon the presence of mind to banish thoughts of malaria, remembering only how she had packed their pills into her beauty case back at the lodge.

Beauty case? A ridiculous concept here. Miriam shook her head and forced herself to focus. *Who are these men?* This question rammed her consciousness. Terrorists just randomly kidnapping tourists? Was it really just a matter of her family being in the wrong place at the wrong time?

During their second night in the very dark space, Miriam caught sight of a mouse scuttling underneath the door, its tiny form silhouetted in the moonlight. Miriam watched this with Owen breathing beneath her, her thoughts now only of him and their son.

Chapter 22

Yury cursed Joseph under his breath. He should have been more thorough and checked the jeep. In the next breath, Yury cursed himself. He should have communicated to Joseph that there were three in the party. If Yury himself had not seen the family back in Nairobi, even he would not have known about the boy.

They had already blown up the jeep by the time Yury reached the scene. He stared at the smoking vehicle, the charred grass, and guessed his men had passed through less than an hour earlier. There was no telling where the child was, but he must be near. *Or burned alive.* Yury poked through the remains of the jeep and saw nothing that resembled human remains. *Still . . .*

Finding the boy would be a tremendous advantage. A secret treasure like that, hidden away, would persuade O'Neill to see things the way of El-Fatih. If the wife wasn't enough, the son certainly would be.

Yury had been watching the side of the road as he approached the site but had seen nobody. He could only imagine what the boy must be feeling at the moment. *Abandoned.* Yury reached up and rubbed the side of his head, trying to ward off another headache.

When he glanced up again, he thought, *Ah.* Only a hundred meters farther up, a small boy stumbled across the road. Yury dashed back to his own four-by-four vehicle, threw it in gear, and charged back up the tarmac. He let the boy stagger in his direction a few moments longer, then slowed to a halt beside him.

Yury looked in his rearview mirror and cursed under his breath to see an approaching Pajero with the insignia of a major tour operator on its hood. He pushed open the door on the passenger side. The boy was so exhausted that he collapsed as soon as Yury sprang out and grabbed him.

The Pajero slowed, and a game guide asked, "Everything all right?"

Yury greeted him in Shona, and the man smiled and responded. Then he asked, "You need some help?"

"No. He's my son, a little delirious. We're on our way to the hospital at Vic Falls now. I shouldn't have let him get out of the car, but he needed to go. I think he's just dehydrated—nothing serious."

"You need water?"

"No, I've got plenty."

"Well, keep him out of the sun. They'll probably put him on a drip, and he'll be fine in a day or so."

Yury nodded and lifted the boy into the passenger seat. He thanked the man and headed east.

Martin could not breathe. Where had everyone gone? He felt his legs wearing out as he veered in and out of the bush. Finally he just stayed on the road, hoping for someone to come by. And somebody did.

A blue jeep slowed down, then stopped. The man who got out didn't look like those soldiers. He was quiet and smiled and wrapped his arms around Martin just before the shaking in his legs made him black out.

When he opened his eyes, he sat safe in the man's car.

"My parents . . . we were in a car accident. I don't know. . . ." Martin's voice sounded so distant to his own ears. He coughed.

The man said, "It's all right. I know where they are. I came back here looking for you. Here, drink some water." He pulled a plastic bottle out of the backseat and handed it to Martin. Martin spilled all over himself as he guzzled the liquid down. The man had a funny accent.

"You know my parents?" Martin asked.

"I know right where they are. Shall I take you there?"

The third night Miriam spent yelling at rats while Owen lay beside her. She saw the forms moving around the cell, circling closer, felt their touch on her leg as she slept, woke to a movement near her face.

On the fourth night she knew why they came back. When the guards threw in their bread, hard and dark with mold, crumbs fell in the dust. Miriam wondered if the guards purposely spread those crumbs over the cell when tossing the bread, for once the rats had eaten the crumbs, they left.

By then, Miriam was longing for two things: clean water and Owen to regain consciousness. He did come to, but only off and on. Then they talked, but Miriam heard what he did not say better than what he said. Owen cautioned her to whisper so the guards would not hear them.

He fell in and out of fever, sweating so that Miriam worried about dehydration. What little water the guards gave them smelled like something stale, from a river. All the warnings in the guidebook seemed absurd in these surroundings. The advice to drink only bottled water faded in Miriam's need to slake her own raging thirst and care for Owen's.

Miriam spent most of that first week watching the sun stripes crawl across the dusty floor. She watched alone because Owen still could not see; his eyes remained purple pulp shut tight. A great knot of grief bound Miriam's emotions. She watched and listened to Owen. She tried to memorize important details like the faces of the different guards who brought them the bread. She sensed she would die in this place. But because of Owen beside her, because her feelings could not move about, tied as they were to the tangled grief inside her, Miriam accepted each day, one at a time, on its own terms.

When he was awake, Owen often insisted they pray. Miriam bowed her head and listened to his voice but not his words. *My son is missing.* This was her chant, her mantra of mother's loss. *My son is missing.*

Owen called upon her to cultivate hope. "There are lessons you can learn in the dark better than in the light." He told her about Terry Waite, whose release he'd helped negotiate in Lebanon two years earlier. Miriam vaguely remembered meeting Waite in England once when she traveled with Owen. He, too, was well-known as a negotiator, a special envoy from the archbishop of Canterbury. He was famous for brokering the release of hostages held by Qaddafi in Libya. But then he himself had been taken hostage in Beirut and held captive for five years.

Five years was all Miriam could focus on when she thought about Terry Waite. But Owen was more interested in something Waite had said after his release. "He told me that God blessed him during that time. He gained a more intimate knowledge of who God is through the waiting. If we seek that now, it may ease the time. . . ."

Owen's voice trailed off, and Miriam felt glad he could not see her expression of disbelief as she thought, *I don't want to know God intimately. I want to be free and safe and back home with my husband and son.*

On that seventh day of captivity, Miriam worked to clean the scab and puss from Owen's eyes with cloth from her shirt. One remained closed, but one gray eye opened to look at her. His face near hers, he reached up to stroke her cheek. "Fitting that the first thing I see clearly is your beauty, my Miriam. I will never forgive myself for getting us into this. They told me to take a bodyguard on the trip, but I refused. You . . . our Martin . . ." Again the fading voice.

She helped him straighten up enough so they could sit together, leaning against the wall. "Hush. It's done. You have to get better. When we get out of here, we'll talk of these things." It was Miriam protecting him, but she knew *he* knew better.

"No. We'll talk of them now. We'll talk of it all now, because . . . Miriam, I should warn you, they will probably separate us."

The words thudded in her ears, stirring up small clouds of unrest. Miriam did not answer.

He took her hands in his, fixing on her with his one good eye. "It is the pattern in incidents like this. Then they can play us off each other."

"But why? Owen, who are these men? I heard the Portuguese. Do you mean they're not Angolans? Are they from Mozambique—after you because of the negotiations?"

He hesitated, then said, "No, I don't think so. But that first day, when they took us, the one who was kicking me said my name. They know who I am, all right."

Miriam realized as she said the words, "Then it's you they want."

"Yes, and whatever it is they want me to do, they'll have better luck if they separate us and can use you as . . . a threat against . . ."

Miriam saw he left the thought unfinished and supposed she under-stood why. She would be played with . . . she was expendable. She wanted to encourage him but didn't know what to say. And she wanted to be upset, to be filled with dread at the prospect of losing Owen and having to face the nightmare alone, but Miriam realized she felt numb. It was as if she stared out of some place where she could no longer feel for either of them. Had a part of her descended into a dark place, lost with Martin? Was she withdrawing, regrouping, trying to figure out how to function without the vital organ of her mother-love?

She heard Owen pray, "Lord, you've been giving me Scriptures. Thank you for their comfort. Thank you that this one eye is open. I pray for the protection of my Miriam. Lord, we are here in a frightful place. Deliver us. Free us. Protect our son. Keep us from further harm. Ward off disease. Increase our faith. We pray in your name, Jesus."

Then Owen's voice dropped to a low and solemn tone. " 'Although the Lord has given you bread of privation and water of oppression, he, your teacher, will no longer hide himself, but your eyes will behold your teacher. And your ears will hear a word behind you, "This is the way, walk in it," whenever you turn to the right or to the left.' "

It was like no prayer Miriam had ever heard Owen say before. Their church life back home, his own spiritual commitment, were very im-portant to him. She knew, for instance, that he prayed for each of the parties involved in whatever deal he was working on. He said it helped him to see the people as separate from the issues. He was a praying man.

Miriam tried to be like him—in so very many ways actually—but in her heart she knew she usually failed. Certainly at that moment, she had no prayers. Even so, Owen's words now had moved her as little else could in that place of dust and dismay.

She stared and asked softly, "What did you just say?"

"It's from Isaiah. I don't know where. A verse I memorized some-where. I've been remembering the strangest things."

He lay down, and she cradled his head on her lap, stroking his face. Even where the skin was undamaged, it looked dust-caked, worn, wrinkled. He could be sixty. She imagined she didn't look good, ei-ther.

Miriam repeated in a whisper, " 'Bread of privation and water of op-pression.' "

Chapter 23

The time dragged itself from sunrise, through red dust, into dreaded nights. Every day Owen prayed and Miriam listened, wishing vaguely she had it in her to pray as well. He recited Scriptures and sometimes Shakespeare.

"You Irish—what don't you memorize in school?" she asked and wondered that he had it in him to laugh.

At that point he was seeing a little better, though one eye remained closed. Half blind, then, her husband tried his best to teach her how to see so they could figure out where they had been taken—and where they might flee if the occasion arose. Again and again he had her describe the intricate details of their setting. He coached her in obtaining information indirectly from their guards, taught her to watch for a waning moon and note where the sun rose, observe the plant life, listen to the languages being spoken around them. He taught her some Portuguese. And he insisted on going over and over the fundamentals of his profession.

Even then, Miriam wondered why Owen thought it so necessary to teach her negotiation. He insisted on it though, explaining both the general principles and the tricks of the trade, including the knowledge of how to manipulate a conversation.

A n n e d e G r a a f

"Remember," he would say, "keep the people separate from the problem. When you are alone, focus on personal interests, not the position of weakness or power. Try to come up with options where both parties benefit. Play along; decide what you want; don't be a victim."

He stopped, and Miriam managed a grim smile. "That might be a little tricky."

"No, I mean it. You have it in you, Miriam. You can walk like a queen sometimes, and you can do it without appearing arrogant. You need to learn to summon it from deep inside you—that . . . authority. Call on God whenever you can as you talk to your captors. He'll give you the right words. Try to understand their interests, their motivation, both in general—what they stand for as a group—and, more important, their personal, individual motivation. Put yourself in their shoes. Try to imagine you want the same things. If it's to get me to do something, well, work with them. Don't worry about me; watch out for yourself. I won't be here to do it."

"I thought we didn't negotiate with terrorists."

"Ah, but we do. They just don't know it. Even if I say, 'We're not negotiating,' that's a form of negotiation. Look, you're trying to influence their decisions—that's what it all comes down to. The better your communication, the better your chances of having an impact on whoever is pulling the strings here. That's what I'll be trying to do on my end, develop a conduit of information. In the meantime, promise them whatever you can—anything to get out of here. If you can make them see that letting you go isn't giving in, that they can still get what they want, well then, you're halfway there. Aim for direct, personal dialogue—that's your best bet. Remember to always be making offers, and couch them in language that sounds attractive." He paused and Miriam saw his face fall. "I'm lecturing—listen to me. And who am I to tell you anything, when I've put my own family in such a spot?"

She could not bear to see the defeat drawing down his face. She picked up his hand and ran her fingers over his.

Owen said, almost to himself, "The worst is when you negotiate for flesh and blood."

Especially when it's your own flesh and blood? she wondered.

He straightened and said, "We may be running out of time. There's no room for my regrets."

Miriam marveled at how her husband managed to keep despair at bay.

"Remember to investigate all your options," he went on. "Patience is key. And again, above all, don't think in terms of being the victim. Never put yourself in that position. Always think in terms of conflict management. Wait, and then wait some more, until you see an opening."

"An opening for what?" she asked.

"You'll know, Miriam. You have it in you. You know how to think strategically—imagine it's a chess game. But you also have the gift of reading people, of seeing, of searching for peace and finding the right words. I've always said it. You will be, you *are*, a great negotiator, but you are blind to these abilities in yourself. You see the whole world except your own gifts. And yet that too can be a gift. Another reason you will do well is you know how to take a backseat. Egos only get in—"

"But hold on. I'm confused," Miriam said. "What is this about me becoming a negotiator? You mean like you? Oh no. I mean, I've talked about wanting to work my way into a firm where I could eventually work on some arbitrage cases, but that was *behind the scenes*. As a researcher . . ."

Owen took hold of Miriam's shoulders with his hands and turned her toward him. "What I'm saying is that *you'll need these abilities*. I mean here, now, soon. We were targeted, and I doubt that it was at random. They knew our names."

"Your name," she corrected him.

"They'll think you're just a helpless, unskilled wife. You can use that to your advantage. Be thinking all the time. They'll be expecting you to cave in. In other words, you can prove them wrong, Miriam."

"But who are *they?*" She wondered why he still would not tell her.

He lowered his voice. "We've heard them speaking Russian, together with Portuguese."

"And what are Russians doing down here?" she asked, hoping finally for some answers, something with a shape to fill in the blanks.

Owen was quiet for a moment, then said, "There was an intelligence rumor. The Lebanese mafia—they run the diamond smuggling out of countries like Angola and Zaïre, where there's very little rule of law. The rumor was that they're fighting their own war against Russian mafia factions who've been trying to move in and take over. Uh, Miriam . . ."

She looked at him.

"You should know, I've never been in Angola before. But I was asked to . . . well . . . assess the situation. For a colleague."

"On another assignment besides Mozambique?"

He nodded. "I can't tell you what it was or which countries it involved. For your own sake, because what you don't know, they can't use against you. Anyway, I declined. I hesitate even now to bring it up, except if anything should happen to me, I want you to know there was more at stake than one country's peace."

It was a favorite phrase from Owen's lectures. He had even used it when Miriam first heard him at the university. She remembered now. She felt him watching her as she remembered. "One country's peace" was the finish line, the goal worth reaching for above all else. He had said so—many times. So why was he saying now that there was something more? Miriam waited, but he turned away from her.

"Listen, Miriam. I'm probably grasping at straws here. None of these connections may even matter. What's important for you to do above all else is find out what they want, then decide what you must have. In this case, my love, it is *your life*. Do you hear me? At any cost, save your own life."

"You still think they'll take you away from me?" The look on his devastated face when he turned back to face her told Miriam what his words did not. She suddenly realized, now that she knew there was more at stake than an already agreed-upon peace treaty, that he too feared the future.

She scrambled to cover the dangerous silence. "Talk to me. Talk to me about what you did in Mozambique and at the Rome talks. . . . And this other job—were you *near* Angola? Is that what you meant?"

Owen shook his head, brought a finger to his lips, and said more definitely, "I declined." Then he changed the subject, began speaking softly of his recent work. Miriam watched him closely. Her hope was that he might indirectly tell her more about what was really going on. But she also hoped that talking about the work he loved would serve the more immediate purpose of keeping his mind off his pain and thirst and loss.

Our loss, Miriam remembered. Sometimes it took all her self-control to hold on to hope, to avoid imagining that the worst had happened to Martin. Again and again she pushed herself to believe her son had made it. Miriam fantasized every day, every night, that she heard him calling. Always she hoped, hoped so big it hurt, that Martin had gotten away from the jeep, that tourists had picked him up as he walked down the road and radioed that they had found a boy. Miriam willed the words *Martin is safe* into the muddled morass of darkheartedness that seemed to be her new wilderness.

She gazed at Owen and realized that as always he saw right through her. But he didn't call her on it. Their unspoken agreement was just to get through each day, moment by moment.

When he paused in his description of the Mozambique deal, Miriam said, "You told me you believe it could be a lasting peace." She used the words on purpose, knowing it was his negotiator dream phrase. "Why?" Miriam asked.

Owen nodded as if to say, "I'm in." She knew he knew the game they played. He said, "The Mozambicans themselves say there's no need for a truth and reconciliation commission like what they're setting up in South Africa. They buried their political and military differences virtually overnight. They say they're interested in planting seeds and not starting war tribunals to punish the guilty. This is real peace."

The word triggered a lone emotion Miriam had not felt for a very long time. It sounded faraway in her soul, like horns sounding across a distant wood, yet something in her now rose up to listen.

"In Mozambique's case," Owen was saying, "it was their colonial struggle against the Portuguese that first sparked the savage civil war. Frelimo forces began the war of independence against the Portuguese in '64. Then in 1975, after independence and being duly elected, Frelimo took charge of the government and set it up as a Marxist state. That's when a guerrilla movement called Renamo took up the conflict.

"Renamo was first set up by white Rhodesian officers because Frelimo opposed Rhodesia and apartheid South Africa. Later it was funded and supported with military advisers from South Africa and the U.S., who objected to Frelimo's Marxist orientation and its support from communist powers.

"The trouble was, all that outside involvement only further prolonged the conflict. The war raged for nearly three decades, fed by weapons from apartheid South Africa and America on one side, and Russia and China on the other, all involved in this skinny, poor country. And who paid the price? Innocent civilians—especially the children.

The conflict might have died a natural death if such an abundant supply of arms had not been made so readily available."

"How can a civil war die a natural death?" she asked.

"By undergoing exactly what we can witness now in Mozambique. After thirty years, can you imagine? There is hardly anyone left to fight a war except maybe the women and children. Remember in Europe? Twenty years had to go by between the two world wars in order for Germany to raise up a new generation of soldiers, cannon fodder. At some point the people stop caring about the cause because the cost is too great.

"And the Mozambicans have reached that point," he added. "They are fed up with war and just want it to stop. Refugees are spread throughout all the neighboring countries. Plus, with the Cold War supposedly over and Mandela's release from prison two years ago, the outside powers more or less lost interest, so the supply of arms dried up. The Mozambicans . . ." His voice trailed off.

"What?" she asked.

"Well, you know what I've said about their children. I was in a lift in the hotel in Maputo. A bellboy shared it with me. We were the only ones. He looked up and must have recognized who I was because he asked, 'Will there be peace, sir?' In English, not Portuguese, mind you, so this was a boy who had learned the language somewhere other than school, maybe even taught himself and practiced on the hotel guests."

"Well," Miriam asked, "what did you say to him?"

"I said I would do my best. He believed me. He smiled from here to heaven. If you ever see Mozambican children smile, it's something you'll carry with you for the rest of your life. There's something about the power of peace. . . ."

"Yes," she said, doing her best to smile for him, "I know."

That night, Owen pulled Miriam close. He ran his hand over hers and fingered the black diamond in her engagement ring. "I think you should take this off," he said. He said the words as though they pained him.

Her other hand flew to the ring. "But if they haven't taken it from me by now . . ."

"No, Miriam. It's too large, too noticeable. It's asking for trouble. Keep the wedding band, but give me the engagement ring. Here . . ." He gently slid both rings off her finger.

He reached down and yanked out a bootlace, ran it through the engagement ring, then tied the ends of the lace together and passed the loop over her head. Her head bowed before him moved Owen deeply. Then he took her left hand and slid the gold band back on. The gesture reminded him of flowers and friends and family all gathered that proud day he had stood by her side and sworn before God to love and cherish her, to protect her from evil.

Owen swallowed. His one open eye stung. "With this ring, I thee wed." His voice broke, and he pulled her downward. They lay sideways, her body folded into his, arms under their heads. He held her and felt the ring under the cotton of her shirt.

"What's the word again?" he asked. "The Greek word your father taught you about the diamond's hardness?"

He heard her sigh ever so softly, as if his question asked too much. But she answered him. *"Adamas.* The Greek word *diamond* stems from it. It means 'indomitable' or 'untamable.' "

"Right," Owen said, patting the stone one more time before moving his hand to cover hers.

Owen spoke to her in the darkness so she could not hear the other sounds—the hum of the mosquitoes and skittering of the rats and mysterious noises from outside their dusty cell. He wished his whispered words to wash over Miriam in cool waves of comfort. "My love, I know you are closing yourself off, and I just want you to know you are not alone. Sometimes there is a darkness, and it is like being put in the shadow of God's own hand. Be still there and listen. I ask myself now, for instance, where is my confidence? Is it placed in God? This is so crucial. The one thing we must know for ourselves is that God is real. He is always with us. With you."

"Even if you are not?" Miriam's words cut him to the quick, but he quickly told himself she had not meant them to hurt. He was the one who had warned they might be separated. She added quickly, as if she sensed the blow and wanted to make light of it, "You should have been a priest."

"That's what my mother always told me. Well, a vicar. Church of

Ireland, you know." He paused. "Miriam? I must ask you . . . is God real to you?"

She shifted her position to face him. A voice in Owen asked how he could ask such a thing in such a place. She shook her head slowly back and forth.

"You blame him for this and for Martin missing." It was more a statement than a question.

Again Miriam shook her head. "I don't blame anyone. It happened. You must stop blaming yourself, Owen. Stop referring to it as your failure. No, it's just that the God we prayed to back home, the one we worshiped on Sundays in our church with heating and electricity and friends around us—he can't be here."

"Why not?"

"Because . . . nothing else is, no one else is. I am . . . we are . . . so alone."

"No." It was all he could say. *No.*

The next time Owen heard Miriam's voice, it was morning. An unfamiliar form filled the sunlit doorway, and Owen woke to the sounds of English words pronounced with a Russian accent, ordering his wife to stand.

Chapter 24

Rough hands pulled her out of the cell, away from Owen, and forced her to follow as she stumbled blindly into the sunlight. It was the first time she had been allowed outside in eleven days—she had kept track by marking the brick beside the door's lower hinge—and now her eyes refused the sunshine. She felt hands on her upper arms, propelling her along, as her own hands covered her face and burning eyes. Miriam tried to focus on her feet, but she could not find even these. So she fell to her knees once and was pulled up.

The hands tugged her first left, then three times right, then left her standing alone. Miriam waited. She felt eyes upon her, probing eyes, and was glad for the red dust. If she looked anything like Owen, it covered her completely, filling every pore.

When she managed to peer out from under her hands, Miriam saw she had been left in shadow. Now, finally, her eyes began to adjust.

The man had thin blond hair. Drawn eyes rested on top of a chiseled face. His hands were stained, the nails bitten. He sat at a table made of tree trunks cut in half and drank vodka, liquid sweating down the small glass beside the bottle with Cyrillic letters on the label. Miriam's mind, loose with fear, wondered how he had made the ice. She watched him, lowering her hand and trying to gain eye contact, but the man would not let her. He reached for his sunglasses on the table and put them on as if afraid she might recognize him.

He rose and walked toward Miriam. He did not stop until he stood quite close. As he leaned forward, she could smell his sweat and see the light-colored stubble on his chin, even as she watched her own reflection in his glasses.

"Who are you?" Miriam's voice dropped off to barely a whisper.

He said, "I have been looking forward to this moment. I collect uncut diamonds. That is who I am." He pronounced the last three words in mimicry of her own tone.

A truck roared out of the camp, broke the tension. He straightened and moved around to stand behind Miriam. She heard his voice say, "You will do exactly as I say. Do you understand? Yes?" His accent pushed the word upward like the tail of a dog.

"You are Russian?" she said.

"Yes." Again the same word, but now with no tail. "Now, Joseph, what do you think? What shall we do with her now that her half-blind husband has been taken away?" He laughed.

Miriam whirled. *The truck!* She held her hands up to protect her eyes, trying too soon to focus on the distance. All she could see was a red cloud. The door to what looked like their cell stood open. Why hadn't she heard anything? Why hadn't Owen called out? Had they harmed him, beaten him again? "Where is he?" she moaned.

The man raised an eyebrow. "At least she has some courage. So, Joseph, do we have a use for her?" He watched her closely. Miriam swallowed, but the spit stayed lodged at the back of her throat. Her eyes traveled back and forth between the door to the cell, the last place she had seen the truck, and the face of this man, his features narrow and waiting, every muscle tense, readying himself to lunge. *For the kill?* Miriam wondered.

She started to shake. She could feel her heart pounding, her breath becoming shallow. "Owen?" She could not keep the word from wheezing out of her lungs, as if a great weight bore down upon her. It was the weight of unwanted truth, and she could not move, could not breathe, could not live under such a thing. Owen himself had warned her. But now that the moment had arrived, the shock rang through Miriam like a hammer striking iron. She turned her eyes to her captor without moving her neck.

He was still laughing at her. He rolled a cigarette and licked the paper closed. He spat a leaf of tobacco onto the dust between her feet.

Miriam stood like stone, feeling the tears run down her face and roll onto the ground. She watched him back, while another part of her listened for the retreating dull roar of the truck's motor, already long gone.

"You said?" he asked.

"Owen?" This time the word came out unhindered, in a rush of fear, like the wetness coursing down her cheeks.

"Yes. That was your Owen. He is gone." He lifted his chin and fit the cigarette between his lips, holding it with a thumb and forefinger. The man he had called Joseph moved in and lit it for him. They both watched Miriam shaking and crying.

She felt humiliated beneath their gazes.

Then the Russian reached out, cupping his hand around the back of her neck. At his touch she broke, began to struggle. He laughed. "What do you want?"

"My husband. I want Owen. Please don't take him away. Bring him back."

He spun her around until he held her from behind, both of her arms pinned with one of his. Miriam smelled the vodka on his breath as he leaned toward her ear. She could not move.

"You beg me? Maybe then."

Saying the word would get her nothing. Miriam knew that. But she also knew she could not survive in that place without Owen. "Please."

He began to laugh again. Miriam could feel his chest rise up and down against her back. Then he pushed her away from him, and she stumbled forward. Now she was no longer under the overhanging canvas, and the heat bore down onto her from above and below. She looked back at the two men, but the Russian did not look at her. "So you want her, Joseph?"

The other man laughed deeply. "She's not my type." Miriam recognized the French accent. She peered closer, glancing down at the gleaming boots, and recognized their kidnapper. Both men stepped near to Miriam and stood very close. She tried again to focus. They both wore light khaki uniforms with a camouflage print. But the blond man was much taller. For the first time she noticed his broad shoulders, his long legs.

"Which means she *is* my type," he said, "and that is the only reason

I can think of to keep her alive. After all, you must break camp, and I have business to attend to elsewhere."

He threw down each word individually. Miriam breathed hard, trying to think, trying to remember Owen's whispered words, the gifts he had given her. Gifts she only now was learning how to open.

Miriam swallowed. "May we speak alone?"

"For a beautiful woman, I would do this anywhere. Joseph?" He moved his right hand as if swiping at a fly, and the man moved away. Then he repeated, "You will do as I say. Everything I say."

Miriam felt her way slowly. "No. I . . . don't think so." He looked amused and she thought, *So, you enjoy this.* The fog of fear shifted slightly, and Miriam saw the game itself as something she could offer him. Perhaps.

"Do you know why you are here?" he asked.

She said nothing.

"Do you know where *here* is?" he demanded in a louder voice. "Do you even know which country you are in?" He lunged and jammed his face close to hers. "Very well. I cannot help you." In one motion, he reached behind him and pulled a pistol out of his belt. He slammed the cartridge in with the palm of one hand, then took the gun into both hands and held the warm metal tip against Miriam's forehead.

She did not move. *"He wants something from you. As long as you keep him from getting what he wants, he will allow you to live."* Owen's words. The fear Miriam felt now was different, not laced with panic. If Owen was gone, if they were going to kill him, then she would die too. Miriam said this to herself. Owen gone. *And Martin?*

Then Miriam saw it—a possible negotiating position. Like a trapped gazelle, she panted in fright, but she did not move.

In one swift movement, he lowered the gun. To her amazement he turned and started to walk away. Miriam's hand shot out before she could stop it. "Wait," she hissed. His wrist filled her palm. She could not close her fingers around it. Blond, wiry hairs sprang up between them. She saw herself as he did, grasping for something unseen.

"Wait?" He remained standing but did not turn around. "And why should I wait? Are you so desperate?"

The question caught her off guard. She nodded, their moment of confrontation still with them both. The places where he had touched Miriam burned. She would have bruises from his hands.

He said, "And what will you give me in your desperation? You know if you give me nothing, I will have you shot."

"And when I give you what you want, you will have me shot anyway."

"This is true. You are a smart American woman." His tone was mocking. "But I don't believe—"

"Diamonds." The idea flew into Miriam's head like a small bird, touching down, startled, unsure, but still there. She hurried on before it took flight again. "I know a great deal about diamonds. You mentioned how you collect them." She blurted out that her father was trained in Antwerp. "He was a Dutchman, a diamond cutter. And he taught me everything about assessing the stones. Antwerp," she repeated. "If you're in the diamond world, you'll know what that place means." Then on a wild hunch of daring, she added, "You can't find anyone with my knowledge in the bush."

She still did not know what she was doing as the words poured out of her mouth. A part of her took desperate risks in this conversation, but most of her just stood aghast beside a tree in Africa, watching, wondering at what she dared, how she managed to even continue such a gross charade. Yes, she knew a certain amount about stones. But without the proper tools—a good scale, a loupe—her knowledge would be extremely difficult to prove.

Again the chilling sound. When he stopped laughing, as abruptly as he had begun, the man whirled on his heel and leaned toward her. "You have no idea what you are saying. Your name?"

"Miriam Vree."

"Well, Miriam Vree." He exaggerated the "ray" sound. "What cannot be bought is given. Of course, I have been thinking. I can always take you with me."

He stood straighter and took her hand, bringing it to his lips. With the other hand he drew off his sunglasses. His eyes, the palest blue, shallow, fathomless, locked onto Miriam's. "You are meeting Yury Gennady Falin."

Martin listened carefully but could not understand any of the words the men around him were saying. The man who picked him up on the road had brought him to a plane, and Martin had fallen asleep during the flight. This he now regretted. He had wanted to watch the man fly the plane.

They landed in this place where there were a lot of soldiers. It wasn't a hotel, and there weren't any other tourists around.

"Where are we?" he asked the man.

"Listen, you are not allowed to ask questions. Is that understood?"

Martin stared at him. He had changed. He wasn't as nice as he'd been when he picked Martin up on the road. Martin knew he wasn't supposed to get in the car with a stranger, but he'd had no choice. Where else could he go? And now he'd gotten into a plane!

"Listen, uh, I just . . ."

He stopped short as the man started walking away from him. "Come."

Martin ran after him.

"What is your name?" the man asked.

"Martin O'Neill. What is yours?"

The man stopped and stared down at him. "You may call me Commandant. We are at what you Americans would call my boot camp for—"

Martin interrupted, "Camp? You said you would take me to my parents. Is this where they are?" He stopped as the man pulled the biggest pistol Martin had ever seen out of the back of his belt.

"No, your parents are not here."

Martin stopped walking and looked at the man. Now he knew for sure. This had all been a huge mistake. "But you said you were going to take me to my parents."

"I will, but it will take a few weeks to bring them here. Trust me, Martin. I will take good care of you. You like this gun?"

Martin nodded slowly, blinking back the tears. The man handed him the pistol, and Martin liked holding it, like he was on TV. It felt heavy in his hand, and he supported his wrist with his other hand.

"No, you hold it like this, with your palm cupping the hand to steady it." Martin liked it when the man leaned over him to show him. "If you are a good boy, you will get your own pistol. But first I will teach you how to handle a rifle, like a real soldier. Would you like that? You can learn these things while we wait for your parents. Will you be a good boy then?"

Martin felt embarrassed. This was much more than his parents would ever have let him do. He asked, "What kind of place is this?" He had noticed a group of boys around his age staring at him.

"I told you, like a boot camp. This is where children like you are trained to be soldiers. But you are different, so I will give you special treatment. Here, you can be like a general, in charge of your own group. I will give you your own cabin and very good food and lots of gifts, but then you must do as I say. Do you understand?"

"Oh yes." Martin could do this. He looked at the man who smiled at him and smiled back. "I mean, yes, Commandant."

Chapter 25

Me, what do I know? Even now it is hard to remember. But you told me to write it all down this one time, even what is not interesting. Would you have me write of every day over and over and over again? You said this will help heal me. I do not know. But I will write this story for you.

Where are we? I do not know. Walk, walk, walk, walk. Step after step after step. Okay, so now I know about maps, and I have seen how far we boys walked. Over two thousand kilometers. Watch this. That is the same as twelve hundred miles.

Now, after a very long time we knew we were walking in Ethiopia and not Sudan, because some people told us so. In this place, black dust coated us. It is hot and we drip with sweat and at the end of a day on the road, everyone in this place is encased in a thick, crusty armor of dirt. Between

dusk and dawn the roads are controlled by evil
men called shifts, who would rob us of everything
if we had anything.

In Ethiopia we also met good men who showed
us how to get fish and dry it. This was okay! I
could catch fish by the river. Life is God's gift
indeed. The Ethiopians, our fellow friends, they
rescued us. But everyone wanted to do it, and
this made a problem. In this place we are way too
many people and not enough fish.

I saw many strange things in my travels. Many
things I do not understand.

In Ethiopia I saw other Christians. I could tell
they were because they wore crosses around their
necks—strange, feather-thin, silver crosses.

In Ethiopia I starved. I woke up and felt the
sun's heat and knew it would be another day of no
food. How would I end this day? I wondered. One
fine day I drank bitter water squeezed out of an
antelope's intestines. The days ran one into another
in this way—sleeping and wondering. And always
the walking. We were not the only ones. I passed
people who headed for the big city Addis. They
hoped that in the city they might find food.

I saw these people sell everything. I saw what
they sold. They sold children like me. They sold
them to good people. In the villages outside
Addis, there lives a tribe of people who love children. This people wish for children, and when others come to them at the city gates with nothing,
they gladly buy the children and promise to feed
them and love them and give them a home.
Remember that these are things the children have

not had for some time. Otherwise their parents
would not have ever taken them on such a journey
away from their homes, their villages.

When I watched this, I wished I had parents
who would sell me into this place. You may wonder
now why I did not ask this tribe to take me in. But
I knew I must move on. I could not stop. Perhaps
a part of me knew that my two brothers waited for
me. So I moved on.

And outside the city gates I saw something even
more amazing. These same parents who had lost
all, now starving and naked, waited before the city
in a place where a vast array of stands stood. It
was a market where people who had next to nothing could sell that next and then have nothing.

What do you think were the last things these
people sold? Their children were gone. What did
they save until the very last? Their crosses. The
filigree crosses shining against the smooth skin
even Isaiah wrote about. I know that now because
I read it in my own Bible. So these crosses carried
by a people who had lost all—land, food, water,
children, clothing—the crosses were handed over
solemnly to the stand owners. And then they truly
had nothing left.

Now more people have joined our group. Or we
joined them. We are boys and girls and mothers
and fathers. No guns. One day we had to cross
a big river, the water high and fast-running after
the rains. Planes dropped bombs overhead. People
were screaming and children washed away like
sticks. We had to swim across. Many people
drowned then.

The ones who did not know how to swim said, "No. How do we know this is the right way?" We helped each other with strings and ropes. Some people stayed to learn how to swim and then try crossing. If you cannot swim, you die because the water goes over your head and you roll over and cannot breathe and die.

Here, it was a good thing to be a small, small boy. A nice man carried me on his shoulders, and I could see all these things happening around me like the bird in the sky. Still, the booming of artilleries and whizzing of bullets—these sounds remain intact in my brain.

Now, this is the good news. We made it to a place where people wanted to take care of us. This was my first camp, a refugee camp. In our first camp they did not have food, but they had peace. So I stayed with many others. The United Nations, he came, he saw us, he went to Geneva to find food, he came back. During these years in Ethiopia I did not feel bad anymore. I went to school and lived with four other boys. We sat under big trees and opened our minds. We had no paper yet, but wrote on the floor and counted sticks. Then the United Nations, he left, and we had to run. What could I do? It was not my home.

We children ran to another camp. Sometimes in these camps people asked me many questions. Not like you—you listened. But these question askers, they never came back to help. Always they go away. When we had to run, we had nothing and no one gave us anything and nobody came back to help. Some of us sustained boils on our bare soles.

I wrapped grass around my feet and this helped some. No food, no water. Indeed, I thought God might have forgotten us.

So again we children found another camp, but they only had enough food to give us one handful every week. The water was also dirty, and I was sick. Then the United Nations, he warned us that there was fighting further on, bombs going off and soldiers who might grab us. Then we were back in Sudan again and found another place where we could build a school and get books, but two months after this we had to run again.

This is how it goes. Running, then walking. More walking. The walking of the many. This is what happened: the United Nations, he was in Kenya but not Sudan, so now we headed for Kenya, but in major insecurity.

How much time went by? Me, I don't know. Maybe after another year of wandering like this I came to a refugee camp in Kenya. The people there were amazed at our little army. I call us little because we were children. But in numbers we were very large. I have since heard we numbered over twelve thousand. They still call us The Lost Boys.

I wanted to play football and thought about this while I was walking. And I wanted to go to school. Back to a school like we had in the very first camp in Ethiopia. There I had learned to read from some of the big boys. They said I was not so dumb. I hope so.

In Kenya every child or adult was given two cups of maize, a quarter cup of beans, and a jerry-can top full of oil. This should last a fortnight.

By this time, my mother and father are not even faces in my memory anymore. They would not know me either.

You know how sometimes people think about children like me—they don't laugh, how can they play? But of course we do. We're children! You know this thing about me, how dancing makes me happy. I close my eyes, and my head is happy. Sometimes I play the drum for others, but I prefer to dance.

And yet I have sadness too, always in my heart.

I, who have no name, wonder: does my mother call out my name at night? Does my father search, asking others for me by name? Do I not hear because I don't know what to listen for? Are there no cries in the dark with my name on them, no sighs in dreams about me?

Running like this, back and forth across Sudan, over Ethiopia, into Kenya, I am Mwatabu, "Child of Sorrow."

Chapter 26

Her strength surprised him. Yury had liked the feel of her hand around his wrist. He enjoyed noting how the thumb and forefinger could not span its width. She was just a woman, but he could not tell whether she was cunning or merely stupid. One thing was for sure. She was a fighter, and this kind of challenge Yury enjoyed.

It was like hunting for lion. Eighty percent waiting. Ten percent choosing the right place—waiting for a location where she would become vulnerable, like the lioness's water hole. And the last ten percent choosing the right time—waiting for the moments that confuse, when darkness becomes light during the vagueness preceding false dawn.

Yes, he would hunt her, this fine, proud woman with fire in her eyes.

Miriam fought the knowledge and dodged it about as well as she would dodge a bomb: *I am truly alone*. Her separation from Owen and Martin took on monster proportions. All she cared about, all she could hear, was her own heart's cry to be reunited with her family.

The man called Yury had locked her up in the cell again. She couldn't see signs of the camp packing up, but she could hear them. Many soldiers and jeeps came and went. There were lots of shouts, but through Miriam's little window, she couldn't keep track of any familiar faces.

She certainly didn't see the one called Joseph anymore. And this leader, Yury—he just left her to rot. Only the sun's rays radiating off the corrugated-iron roof, baking the cell like an oven, told her the time of day . . . day after day.

Miriam could no longer control the thoughts that mocked her conscious world. They battered her mind numb. Echoes of Owen surrounded her—his voice, some reddish hairs she found glowing in dust of the same color but a different shade. She summoned the memories of her life with Owen and Martin. Outside, her *there,* as opposed to inside, this *here.*

She moved into random time, remembering how often she had come home to a baby-sitter, had felt guilty about not spending more time with Martin. She remembered her parents' deaths, wondering if they saw her now; remembered her honeymoon in Ireland; smiled to remember how, a year later, Owen had made it to the hospital for Martin's birth by commandeering a helicopter at the city airport. Miriam thought of her baby, her Martin, the smell of his hair, his sweet milk breath and pudgy palms. His hands on her face as he asked his questions.

My son!

Miriam willed herself to recall, word for word, the conversations she and Owen had shared in this cell. She tried to train her mind as he had said she should—reciting, memorizing. More than just a game of concentration, this forcing her memory back and delving for details seemed to be a way of not losing herself. This, at least, Miriam had control over. Most of all, she hoped the sheer strength of her memories, the security and safety of her past, might prove powerful enough to banish the present.

A mountain of a man. That was Miriam's first impression of Owen O'Neill. She met him in law school while finishing her degree in international law. Sue was the one who invited her to hear the guest lecturer. "You should see this guy. He's built like a Viking and talks like a leprechaun."

So she sat in the lecture hall that afternoon, looking down from her tiered seat, another face in the darkness, and felt her skin begin to tingle. Miriam leaned forward, fascinated by his brogue, the movement of his eyes, but most of all by his words. The man spoke of hope, of making a difference in a world gone crazy with betrayal and broken promises.

"There is still such a thing as truth," he said. "Set your sights now, before some corporation or government has bought you out. Set your own limits, how far you are willing to go to achieve your personal goals. Then establish the ground rules—your rules—and determine to live by them.

"This willingness is crucial. Don't underestimate its power."

The fervor of his words stirred Miriam, reminding her of why she had majored in international relations as an undergraduate. All those many years ago, hadn't she wanted to make a difference? Had she already become so jaded by the process, the wearing down of new ideas among so many of the old, all needing to be memorized and regurgitated for the sake of a good grade? Nearly a decade had gone by since she'd been so excited, felt so young and hopeful. How could this middle-aged stranger from another land inspire her passion like this?

Afterward there was an invitation to the house of one of her professors for an informal get-together. Coffee and cake. "I'm going," she told Sue.

"You never go to these kinds of things."

Miriam shook her head, bemused. "I know. Who is he, anyway?"

"An international negotiator. Some hotshot from behind the scenes. A protégé of Kissinger or something like that. Supposedly he's kept the Western world free while leaping tall buildings in a single bound."

Miriam nodded. "Right. Glad I've got his story straight."

She looked at her friend, so petite and professional. Sue wore a gray business suit and a blue silk blouse, her straight black hair swept up and back in a twist. "You look nice. Should I change?" Miriam ran her hand self-consciously through her own brown tangles. She hadn't done anything different with her hair for years. It had something to do with staying a student for so long and pursuing a law degree. The thick curls rested a little longer than her shoulders, left to go their own unruly way. Miriam glanced in a window and saw her slim figure dressed in a short denim skirt and sleeveless black top, a questioning face, the wild hair.

"You look fine," Sue said. "Come on. There's the house. It *would* be clear on the other side of campus."

As they crossed the manicured lawn, Miriam thought about the professor hosting the event, her mentor. He was tenured, safe and secure. It was her own hope to achieve that security in the near future. A safe, quiet university campus in the Pacific Northwest somewhere, settled with a stable husband and a few kids, teaching maybe twenty hours a week. *Not such a bad life,* she thought with a wry grin.

Miriam remembered how, because of her parents, after they were killed in the accident a few years earlier, she had vowed that all she wanted was some peace. She thought of her mother's Dutch love of housekeeping, so often humming as she hung the bed quilts out the window to air, to their neighbors' amazement. Soft-spoken, Miriam's mother always did take great pride in their home. And her father, glasses perched on the edge of his nose, looking at Miriam over them and smiling whenever she came to him with good grades or a new design for the gems that passed through his hands every day.

Despite the tension that may have plagued her parents' personal relationship, a quiet life was all they had ever wanted, and it was good enough for Miriam. A life of research, writing books, and lecturing—that's what her dissertation would buy her, if she ever finished it.

As they entered the palatial house, Miriam heard the most amazing sound. Deep laughter, heartfelt, "from the toes," her father would have said. She left Sue talking to a few other friends in the entryway and made her way down the hall, drawn toward the booming voice.

"Ah, but, Winston, you've forgotten the first rule in every negotiation is to decide ahead of time what the objectives are and then dictate the level of acceptable loss."

Winston would be her professor. Nobody Miriam knew had ever called the esteemed, published, Nobel Laureate pride-of-the-university by his first name. Ever. She turned the corner and stood in the doorway.

The huge Irishman stood with his back to her. Other students milled around the room, chatting and holding coffee cups and motioning with their hands.

Miriam stared at the Levi's and the corduroy blazer patched at the elbows. She stepped forward. At exactly the same moment, the man whirled like a top.

Miriam froze. As he faced her, his hand dropped the coffee cup and saucer. He simply let them go, the fluid staining his shoes. Miriam watched them shatter on the floor, watched the spoon bounce, then looked up into eyes the color of swirled slate.

The noises in the room faded, and all she heard were his words. "Sweet heaven above. Winston, you've found me a wife."

Chapter 27

In her dream, Miriam could not reach the man whose arms held Martin in midair, yet she could see her son swallowing the terror like bait. Martin opened his mouth; she heard no sound. He struggled, kicked, fought.

"Martin!" Miriam yelled as loudly as she could.

Then, even as she watched, Martin bit his captor, and the man's fist flew, the back of his hand landing with a sickening thud against the child's temple. Martin's body went limp.

"No!" Miriam threw herself at them, heard bullets whistling past her cheek. But the man cast Martin's body over his shoulder and strode away from her in the direction of the bullets, walking boldly toward the snipers in arrogant confidence that he controlled their targeting. She never saw his face.

"No!" The wind snatched her scream from her. She struggled after them, but more bullets, this time from both sides, forced her down, down, to her knees, down to the ground. Down, her hands over her ears. Down, watching. Down, seeing the retreating figure and a child's half-body bouncing against the man's back.

Miriam crawled to the spot where she found drops of blood leading off in a direction the rain of bullets did not let her follow. In crawling to the spot, she had traveled a great distance, a mental shift from hope to despair. And with nothing but despair within her reach, during that journey, she changed.

Yury watched her curled up and whimpering in the dust. Had he done this to her? Reduced her in this way? Disgusted at himself, he quietly entered the cell and closed the door behind him. His goal had been to stalk, then bend her will to his, not break her. There was nothing less attractive than a victim. No challenge left.

Yury stooped low. He could not take his eyes off her. This Miriam. The red dust streaked her face like paint. But beneath the grime, he saw her sculpted beauty. Yes, despite the snarled hair and the hollows above her cheeks. A long neck, bowed shoulders, small frame. Beaten. "I may be too late," he mumbled to himself.

The sound woke her, and without a word she crawled toward him, then flew into his arms and began to weep. Yury knelt beside her, shocked at the feel of her body against his, the sobs shaking her back, the thinness of her form. *Her need for me.*

Then she said "Owen," and he realized she must still be half dreaming or delirious, must have taken him for her husband. It did not matter. The touch, her shape—it woke something deep inside Yury. He caught himself thinking, *I have never wanted a woman as I want this one.* Even the wanting was different.

He surprised himself with the fantasy that this time he would do it right. This time he would have her want him. In one swift moment his lust changed form so that more than anything else now, he wanted her to really need him, as she did now, during these precious moments between sleep and wakefulness.

Then it was over. Her body stiffened, and she gasped, then threw herself away from him. She crouched against the far wall, and Yury saw the hate before she could mask it. But even this told him something. She could wear masks. He would remember that for when she lied to him. For she would. And the fact that she hated was also good. It meant he had not broken her, that she could still feel passion.

He coughed, feigning embarrassment, and stood up. "Mistaken identity, perhaps?"

Her eyes narrowed like a cornered cat's, but she said nothing.

"You may hate me now, but I have it in my power to make your life much more agreeable. I will be honest with you. I am not happy with what I see here. We will be leaving soon, as I promised, together. But first, I want you to spend this morning trying not to feel like a prisoner. Joseph will bring you bottled water, some food—not too much to begin with—a chair. He will take you to a place where you can shower. We have clean clothes for you."

He approached her. *Those eyes! Dark, but with fragments of light like tanzanite stone, blue as a Crimean summer sky.* He bent down and took her hand, pulling her upward so that she stood. She broke his gaze and looked away. He placed a finger under her chin and brought it upward.

What he saw then did not surprise him. Her gratitude would be just the beginning.

Miriam had read that victims of kidnapping sometimes grew attached to their captors, even fell in love with them—it was a documented phenomenon—because of the total dependence.

Not me, she thought.

She knew how dependent she was. *He feeds me, he quenches my thirst, he decides when I may walk free, if I may live.* And yet she felt nothing but repulsion for her captor, this *Yury.* She thought of him as a beast, an animal, on exactly the same base level as some of the terrorists Owen had had to do business with.

But Owen had told her something about that—about the temptation to think of cruel and deadly men and women as inhuman. The very thought, Owen had said, can impede a successful negotiation.

To prove his point, he had described a case in Belgium concerning a pedophile. There was no question about the man's guilt. He had confessed to the torture and rape of at least ten children. Owen had been in Brussels on another case but heard from the colleague involved about the trouble they were having in getting information from the man. This friend asked Owen if he and his negotiating team would give it a try. So they sat down across the table from the murderer, but Owen's people had trouble right away with the discussion. Unable to maintain eye contact, they made repeated mistakes. Finally, Owen was forced to adjourn the session. When he got his team alone, he asked what was happening. One or two admitted that all they could think about were the heinous crimes the animal had committed.

And then Owen had said, "Think about what is at stake here. There are parents out there who still do not know where their children are, dead or alive. This man knows where some of these children are buried. That knowledge is our objective. You would jeopardize what little peace of mind the parents may still find in this case for your petty prejudices? If you can't see him as a human being, as someone who could just as easily be your brother-in-law, then I want you off my team!" It had been one of the few times Miriam had ever heard Owen admit he lost his temper.

"See the man, Miriam. See the man. Divide the person from the policy, the individual from the action." She could hear him still, saying it. *All right, my Owen. For you, I'll see Yury.*

Miriam reflected on these things as she stood under a bucket of sun-warmed water balanced on a board between two tree branches. A green tarp stretched around the trees, forming a circular enclosure, so only the monkey up to her left could see her. She breathed in the clean air, not dusty or stuffy or stinking of herself, but fresh and smelling of humus, the trees and plant life all around her.

The camp was quiet in the dry noonday heat. Miriam heard only the buzzing of flies. She twisted the valve that was stuck into a hole in the bucket's bottom and let the slow stream flow over her face—mouth closed, hands rubbing, soap lathering—through her hair, cleansing, cleaning, rinsing, disinfecting.

It felt as if more than dirt washed away as her senses came alive. A dullness fell away in the suds gathering in a puddle around her bare feet, unplugging her ears. Miriam heard the birds in the trees, the monkey's angry chatter. And in this place, released from her captivity only a few hours earlier, she vowed to stay alive, vowed to survive, vowed to see and hear all she could to save herself and be reunited with Owen and Martin. She must try to get back to Owen and Martin, must get her family back. Whatever it took.

Miriam wrapped her newfound resolve around her like her new clothes. She dressed, smelling the ironed fabric as she buttoned the shirt. The man called Joseph was waiting for her when she emerged from the trees. Without a word he led her to an airstrip, where Miriam saw a group of men gathered beside a small plane. She wondered if she could afford to trust what few instincts she might still possess. Yury had said she would be joining the group leaving the camp, and Miriam clung to that promise. Any escape was better than returning to the cell. She glanced upward and reveled in the sky above her, the vista of endless trees beyond the clearing, the sheer space of *outside*.

Then Miriam caught sight of Yury jogging toward the group from the opposite direction, a pack slung across one shoulder. It was the first time she had seen him since their humiliating encounter that morning. She flushed at the thought of how she had literally thrown herself at him. No doubt he would dream up something excruciating to make her suffer in front of these men.

Yury nodded at Miriam and opened the door opposite the pilot's seat, indicating she should enter. She climbed up the narrow ladder and read the words painted on the side of the plane: Cessna Caravan. Yury closed her door, then spoke in Russian to the men wearing sunglasses, men whose eyes seemed to undress her no matter how high she might button the light green cotton fatigues Joseph had given her to wear. These men wore black leather jackets despite the heat, and they began to clamber aboard through the rear doors. Miriam's own clothing was clean, with folds neatly pressed down the middle of the trouser legs and short sleeves. Buckled into the copilot's seat, Miriam enjoyed the sight of these creases and ran her dust-free palms over their soft surface. She could feel the eyes of the men on her as Yury walked around the front of the plane and entered after the others, slamming the back doors. The pilot joined Miriam in front, climbing in his door on the other side.

"I have more room to work if I sit back here." Yury leaned forward from his seat behind her and spoke in English for the first time since he'd arrived. As Miriam turned around, she counted the three additional rows of his men, all facing toward her. She felt very much a woman and very much Yury's woman in their eyes.

The plane took off and rocked from side to side. Miriam looked to her left and noticed the pilot's olive skin. He nodded in her direction. "You might want to fasten the shoulder harness as well as the seat belt." He sounded Greek or Italian. Miriam saw the straps he meant and reached over to click them into place and pull them tight.

"Perhaps I can help you." Yury's hand on hers, finishing the motion. She closed her eyes. *And so it starts*. Just how high would be the price he asked of her? At the risk of angering Yury, Miriam felt compelled to refer to their initial encounter and make clear what exactly she did have to offer.

"Listen," Miriam said, sounding braver than she felt. She leaned to look around her seat back, then said emphatically but not too loudly, "I'm selling you my diamond expertise and that's *all*. Understood?" In answer, his eyes shrank, and a thin smile stretched across his face as he leaned against his seat. It was as if they both knew she said the words just to hear them. The plane dipped again, and Miriam wondered how she dared say such things. What was this sudden courage?

She turned back around and watched the landscape unfold below, revealing round huts in villages scattered across the savanna, a patchwork quilt of brown on light brown squares. Every now and then a spot of red stood out, a herdsman with his cattle or goats—so many specks.

They cruised low, in and out of clouds. The land was there, then gone. Miriam remembered the last time she flew between "heaven and home." Martin's words. Miriam swallowed—hard. *No tears.* That prior flight had been as they came into Nairobi. The sunrise had bathed the sky in a thousand shades of pink and purple, then gold, the dark amber that is Africa, its grass, its light.

Miriam closed her eyes, remembering, then opened them again. If she kept looking out the window, she could almost forget her aloneness, the danger, the staring eyes behind. With the peace and beauty of clouds and color all around her, suspended between here and there, she remembered Owen's counsel and thought, *I should pray*.

Miriam did not want to believe in prayer. The hard knot of anger and loss, with betrayal melted all over it, still bound her. But as with so much of what she was doing that day, she thought she should do it for Owen. He had told her he always prayed before leaving on a trip— for travel mercies, for discernment, for spiritual wisdom. *Whatever that is.* She thought she should pray for his safety, for their continued courage, to be reunited someday soon with Martin. But she didn't. Perhaps she couldn't. Then she thought she should pray instead for sanity, for surely something in the way she woke up that morning had been a warning. Was she becoming "touched," as Owen would have called it?

Miriam gave up on prayer and resolved instead to keep alert, to focus better. But the motor's hum lulled her to sleep, the comfort of the airplane seat the first softness her back had known in more than two weeks.

Miriam woke with a start. She looked for the sun and saw they were flying southwest. She turned around to look at Yury, but he was deep in discussion with the man behind him. Miriam realized their voices were the reason she had awakened. They seemed to be arguing. When both men looked up and stared at her, she could guess about whom.

"Yes?" Yury frowned toward Miriam, but she refused to make a fool of herself again in front of the others. She swiveled back around to face the front, then noticed that the plane had begun its descent. Miriam looked at the scrub rising to meet them and saw something long and white in the distance. As they came closer, she recognized it as the shell of a plane—the fuselage and one wing. A few hundred meters to the left lay the other wing. One fuel truck waited at the airstrip, which was nothing but a cleared-out stretch of road in the midst of grassland and warped thornbushes.

The plane landed. No one but the pilot made a move. The truck rolled up, and the pilot opened his door and jumped down. Together with the driver he began the refueling procedure. When they had finished, the pilot returned to his seat, and the plane roared off again, this time headed straight toward the setting sun. No one said a word.

Just after dark they landed again. *I have no idea where I am,* Miriam thought. *No one, anywhere, knows where I am.*

She swallowed hard. Here even Owen's words could not stretch over her like the protective prayer they were meant to be.

Chapter 28

Martin wanted to draw. He had found some paper and a pen in one of the cupboards. He leaned in close to the paper and sat sketching a row of trees when Commandant entered.

"This is a girl's thing you do," he said. Commandant ripped the paper away from Martin, wadded it up into a ball, and threw it outside. Later, when Martin found it on the grass, he smoothed it out and put it under his mattress.

Another time Commandant told Martin, "Someday you will need to prove yourself, so pay attention to everything I teach you."

"In battle, you mean?" Martin asked.

"In a trial. If you do well, you will be rewarded."

Martin had seen the other boys in the camp. This was different than when he thought he had lost his parents. Here everything was different—the food, the weather, the languages, the color of the people's skin, the rules—all different.

At first his mind could not take it all in, so he had locked down, closing the windows to his soul, shutting the door to any contact whatsoever. He had stopped eating and stopped drinking and just lay on a dusty floor, feeling but not hearing the insects biting his face.

"Well, make him eat!"

He had heard Commandant's voice outside the window and known he must be very angry. This was in the beginning when Martin felt hot all the time. He had expected Commandant to hit him again, but he didn't. He came into the little house Martin got all to himself and picked Martin up. Then, instead of putting him to bed, he just held him while sitting in a chair, like Martin's mom used to do when he was sick. He sang to him, too, using words Martin had never heard before.

It wasn't that Martin had decided not to eat; he just didn't want to anymore. But after that, Martin felt better. "When will I see my parents?" he asked. "Are they okay?"

"They left you behind, but I will find them for you. You must be a good boy though. A good boy eats and drinks. Is this clear?"

Martin nodded. He wanted more than anything to see his parents. Commandant was powerful enough to find them. Martin knew this for sure.

Miriam climbed out of the plane, looked up, and staggered at the sight of the night sky. She threw her head backward, taking a few steps at a time, dizzy with the sheer mass of light above her, stars from one horizon to the next, a blanket of stars so close she almost felt the hum of energy.

"Welcome to the Kalahari." Yury stood behind her, his hands on her waist to steady her. "Botswana's San people say that at night in the Kalahari, you can hear the stars in song."

Miriam stepped out of his grasp.

"Come." Yury did not comment on her action. "It is time to go."

The group of men who had emerged at this second airstrip and stood along its periphery holding torches now finished unloading the cargo from hatches under the plane. Together with Miriam and the other passengers, they all climbed into three waiting vehicles and roared into the bush. The headlights cut a swath of light, glowing eyes watching at each turn.

When the convoy finally halted, Miriam saw a ring of tents surrounding a fire with a tree trunk sticking out of it. Yury brought Miriam over to one of the tents and said, "You can sleep in this one."

Then he said something in Russian to the man behind him carrying the bags. Yury's things went into the tent beside Miriam's.

Trying not to show her relief, she wanted to fill the silence and said the first thing she could think of. "These men all speak Russian?"

"Did you think we Russians gave Africa only the AK-47?" He laughed hollowly. "But I wonder about you, *Ms.* Vree. Your husband is so *gifted.*" He made the word sound like a poison. "What languages besides English do you speak? Or are you not as exotic as I thought?"

On instinct she told the truth. "Only Dutch. My parents, remember?"

Without missing a stroke, he switched to Afrikaans and asked if she would join him for dinner that night. "I will see to it that my business acquaintances do not interrupt us."

Miriam shook her head and answered in Dutch, "I don't think so. It's been a long day. I think I'll just go to sleep." Then, in order to avoid any argument, she turned and entered the tent, letting the flap down with a finality she hoped left no room for questioning.

She held her breath, but no one followed. Miriam admitted to herself she did not know what she would do if he did appear beside her cot in the middle of the night. He carried a weapon. These were his men. She looked around her tent, spotted a spare stake in a corner, and determined she would fight him with whatever means she could.

The gravel crunched outside her tent. She waited, then heard the zipper being opened in Yury's tent, then the zipper again as he shut the flap.

Miriam removed her boots but kept her clothes on. She ducked her head under the mosquito netting and slipped into the sleeping bag on her cot. Her fingers pulled on the leather lace around her neck. She turned the smooth roundness over and over in her fingers and ran the face of the stone up and down the inside of her palm. She glanced out the high mesh window at the starscape and thought, *What song is mine? I wonder.*

When Miriam closed her eyes, she imagined herself walking through the rooms of her house in San Francisco, counting the windows, until she fell asleep.

In the early morning, while it was still dark, Miriam rose from her cot and turned up the flame in the lantern. She looked around the tent and found her boots polished and standing by the door, a basin of clean water on a small table beside a cup of steaming tea. Someone had entered the tent and done so recently.

Miriam tried not to think what the day might bring, what she would be asked to do, or how she possibly could survive being held hostage inside a diamond-smuggling ring somewhere in the middle of Africa.

"One thing, one day." Owen's words.

As she emerged from the tent, Miriam saw Yury waiting by the fire. He kicked the last remnant of the tree trunk into the flames and nodded toward the east. Broad brush strokes of pink crisscrossed the entire horizon. Miriam's eyebrows rose. *You notice sunrises?*

"Good morning," Yury said. "Did you sleep well?"

She could not get used to the shift in their relationship, his new civility since . . . had it only been yesterday that he found her moaning in her sleep? She nodded and helped herself to the food on the table behind him: rice, a corn pancake, and instant coffee powder in a mug. She relished what seemed a gourmet variety of tastes compared to the moldy crusts she and Owen had been forced to eat for almost three weeks. Miriam turned to the cook for boiled water and was surprised to recognize Joseph. He grinned and said, *"Bonjour, madame,"* while pouring the steaming hot liquid into her tin cup. She noticed his huge hands.

"Joseph is an excellent cook and *askari,* a guard. Did he get the temperature of your water right? In your tent, I mean. I have assigned him to protect you. And, of course, in any way to meet your needs."

Miriam ignored his sharp laughter when he said that. What she thought more likely was Yury trusted Joseph and wanted him near her, near him. Then another thought occurred to her. *He wants me to know that Joseph saw me sleeping.* She straightened her shoulders and looked straight at Joseph. To her surprise, his dark eyes held her gaze. "Thank you, Joseph, for the tea—and for having my boots polished."

Joseph broke into a low rumble of a laugh and nodded at her, then bent over the cooking fire. She very much doubted that Yury's right-hand man had done the polishing himself. She had seen him command the men who kidnapped her family.

None of this seemed believable. Their landing in the middle of nowhere, Joseph acting as if he could speak only French, when she had heard him yesterday and on the road in Namibia sounding quite educated and intelligible in—

Her thoughts were interrupted by the arrival of the other guests.

"Ah, here are my colleagues," Yury said. "You will excuse me?" He walked over to join the men, and immediately a storm of yelling and hand motions erupted from the group. Miriam backed away, toward her tent, hoping to stay out of whatever was being argued, when all seven men turned as one and marched in her direction, eventually surrounding her.

"They insist I prove to them your worth," Yury said, holding his palms upward.

Miriam's eyes grew round. She shot a look at Joseph, who continued squatting by the fire, his back turned toward them. Miriam scanned the faces surrounding her, angry and impatient faces. Dark rings already had formed on their shirts under their arms. She took a deep breath and stared back at these men, sweating in the heat, wearing shoulder straps with pistols. *Is it Yury they don't trust?* Miriam wondered. Then, *What do they want me to do?*

Yury reached into his pocket. When his hand emerged, he held in his palm a jeweler's loupe. He shoved it at her. Understanding slowly dawned on Miriam as she accepted the warm glass. He led the group over to the table where the food was spread out with cheesecloth draped over it. He sat down and cleared a spot before him. Then he reached into the breast pocket of his vest and, with a flourish, pulled out a small pouch of black velvet. As he untied the strings and unfolded the fabric, in its center shone the light of translucent, uncut diamonds.

So this was how she was being put to the test. Miriam wished the sun were higher in the sky.

"Come. Sit." Yury nodded at the bench opposite him. The others crowded around them. The quick movement of a strange red-haired man who wanted to examine the gems himself was not too quick for Yury. In one motion he flipped a corner of the cloth over the stones. Without another glance at the man, Yury said to Miriam, "The light, it is not the best, is it?"

He's giving me an out, she thought. She glanced at the newly risen sun. "One of the butane lanterns will do," she said.

Yury raised an eyebrow at the others and called to Joseph to bring a lamp. Yury fished a pair of fine tweezers out of another pocket and laid it on the velvet. For the second time, he lifted the cloth and exposed the diamonds to the light. This time, with the lantern turned up as brightly as possible, the handful of stones quivered with energy.

Miriam fit the loupe against her eye and thought of her father. His voice, his words guided her now. She adopted her father's trick of blocking out the surrounding sounds and scents. The men and their breathing faded away as Miriam selected the largest stone and brought it up to the glass. Then she gasped and quickly glanced at Yury. He sat opposite her, the ends of his mouth twitching.

She cleared her throat, confident now, speaking of something she finally could claim as her own, a topic from *there* that fit into this *here*. Miriam's voice rose and fell in the same cadence as her teaching father's voice as she said, "I'm sure you gentlemen are familiar with the four Cs? Cut, carat, clarity, and color—those are the criteria for determining a diamond's worth. Mr. Falin may have mentioned that my father was a cutter trained in Antwerp. He passed this training on to me.

"What we have here is, I suspect, nothing less than river quality. You will certainly know that this means it has top-quality potential. No one can know for certain when a stone is uncut, of course. But from the bluish tint of the milky light, I am almost certain this stone, once it is cut and polished, will yield a near-flawless blue-white. That is, a diamond of the best quality. Those terms refer to the clarity and color. *Flawless* means 'loupe clean'; in America this is also referred to as IF, which stands for 'internally flawless.' And the color is judged from *D* to *Z*—with *D,* or 'colorless,' being the most sought after. That's your blue-white."

As she talked, Miriam had been quickly inspecting several more of the larger gems on the table between her and Yury. She paused, set the loupe and tweezers down, and looked up at the men leaning down toward her. "As far as I can judge, this entire package is nothing but the highest quality of uncut stones. In New York or Antwerp, such stones would be worth a fortune."

Yury said, "And so it is. So it is. Now, gentlemen, any more questions?" When they moved away, Miriam breathed a sigh of relief. Yury stood and with a sudden movement swept up the dark cloth and its precious contents, stuffing them into his trouser pocket like a pouch of broken seashells.

Chapter 29

Me, I think sometimes about this word refugee. In English, it is very like the word refuge. Before I knew better, I used to call the camp a "refuge camp." Not a bad name.

Okay, so I go to Jesus now for refuge. But His father and His mother fled with Him to Egypt. In the middle of the night. In fear of the soldiers. Just like me. A little child refugee.

See, a refugee is someone normal like you or me. A refugee is someone who must run away and leave everything behind.

Dry bones. There came a day during the walking when we entered a valley. A strange place, this valley held no wind, and no birds were singing. It was very still. As we walked, bare trees loomed up around us, trees like in the winter. There was a mist, and many things looked different then.

We turned a corner and came across a boneyard. This is a place the elephants return to. They
move with their feet the bones of other elephants
who have died, and they return to the place
again and again, shifting the bones of dead
elephants that belonged to their herd. Some say
they grieve.

As we grew closer to this boneyard, the quiet
fell on us like a blanket. And then we saw that
among the elephant bones lay human bones. The
skulls are easy to recognize, but there were not so
many of those. More smaller bones, legs and arms
and hands—these I could tell were from men.
Because there were little bones, even smaller,
I knew parts of children also lay here.

At night I wondered many things. Why were
there so few skulls? What terrible thing had happened to that village? Who had brought the bones
to the elephants' boneyard?

In this place where I am now, where I write
this, I have peace and food. You have helped me
reach this place. And here I read in God's holy
Word, in the book of Ezekiel, "Can these bones
live?" And I wonder.

Me, I wonder about this field of children's bones.

I have seen fields of living children, an army of
child-soldiers. Like Ezekiel, I have had a vision.
This is the truth! A holy man rested his hand on
my head during a dream. "Write the vision." Maybe
I could tell stories for the children in that field,
and also for the Lord, or about my comrades.

When telling a story, it is important to become
one with the story. You do not do this? Then you

have missed tasting a story. To make a story come alive, I must ask questions.

"What do you hear?" I ask.

And you are quiet and listen. Then you tell me you hear the gunshots coming closer.

"What is in your mouth?" I ask.

"Dust coats my teeth," you say.

"Where are you headed?"

"I am lost." See, now you are one with the story. You will never forget it because it has come alive for you. You have been to this place and know what it is like. You walk beside me now.

It is easy for me to dream of the future. This task you have asked of me, to turn one final time toward the past, to shine Jesus' light on all I did and was made to do, to carry His comfort with me—this is still a too-hard thing.

I was like a bundle of dry bones. And now I return with Jesus' forgiveness covering my guilt, flesh on dry bones, a valley full, coming to life now. I am grateful to God at this moment, who has kept me well. He is a good God; none is like Him. Bless His holy name.

The first time I heard English it was from some big boys who had joined our group during the walking. I ran after them and thought, "These are new sounds," so I tried them and they fit in my mouth. They taught me a few meanings and then a few more. Your language.

What is mine?

Right now, because I can call to a language, because I call words together into stories, because I call on God to heal hearts, I am Mwita, the "Caller."

Chapter 30

Yury smiled to himself. Her performance pleased him. The more he considered Miriam, in fact, the more he liked his latest quarry. His friends in Libya could do as they pleased with the husband. She was his prize.

Now she took her cue and stood up from the table as he did. He walked beside her, away from the group as their voices followed them, this time low and interested as they started in on their breakfasts. Someone told a joke, and they erupted in laughter.

Yury caught Joseph's eye and nodded slightly. Joseph smiled. She must have misunderstood, for then she approached Joseph. As Yury helped himself to more coffee, he heard her ask Joseph, "Aren't you trained for better things than to baby-sit me? You're more than just an askari, aren't you?"

"Some think this is so," Joseph answered, "and others do not. That is how he wishes to keep it."

Miriam lowered her voice. "Where do you come from?"

"Zaïre."

"That explains the French," Yury heard her say half under her breath. Again, he exchanged glances with Joseph, who started to fill a small basin of water from a jerry can.

"We have saved each other's lives," Joseph said. "Many times." Then he moved away.

Yury felt himself drawn toward her. There were not many who could get Joseph to talk about his and Yury's history. He picked up a mango off the table, sliced away the skin with a knife, and started eating it, the juice running through his fingers. When he'd finished, he threw the remainder of the fruit into a bucket and wiped his mouth with the back of his hand. He said brusquely, "You did well. Now, I have arranged for us to be alone the rest of the day. The others are going on an . . . excursion. You will come with me, yes?"

He strode purposefully away and climbed into one of the jeeps. Only then did he look back to see if she obeyed. He saw Miriam throw a desperate look at Joseph, who simply shrugged his shoulders and continued washing the pans he had used to make their breakfast. Yury called out, "You will come with me." This time it was not a question.

Miriam followed, but there was no mistaking her reluctance. It did not matter, Yury told himself. Once she entered the jeep, he drove them toward the airstrip.

"You must relax," Yury said to her, but her tense posture did not change. Without another word he parked the jeep, left the keys in the ignition, and led her toward the plane.

There, they locked stares, and then she looked down, followed him, and climbed in. He shut the door and came around into the pilot's seat and started the engine. Yury liked the woman's silence. He liked it that she could control her obvious fear. He nodded to himself.

Yury quickly prepared to take off, then roared the small plane's strong engine. He glanced at his passenger and was pleased to see her hands shake as she buckled the straps, this time remembering the shoulder harness. Neither of them spoke as the Cessna rolled forward, picked up speed, and then took off, arching upward.

"I think I owe you an explanation," he said when he had leveled out the plane and set his course. "It is not often that I just happen to be carrying uncut diamonds of the quality you examined today."

Miriam kept her eyes fixed on the horizon as he continued. "I will explain. One of the men you saw here had given them to me as a late payment the previous day. I mostly sell rough diamonds for other forms of payment. Only rarely do I receive diamonds back, and then only after I have returned from India."

"So I was lucky," Miriam said.

"Lucky in that you had an easy assessment. But I do not doubt your abilities." Yury set his face and stared straight ahead of them. "But I think you would agree with me after seeing these particular diamonds close up, the more transparent and pure a diamond is, the more delight and desire it incites."

Now he looked out his side window so Miriam could no longer read his face. Yury thrilled at the image of the Cessna's shadow flitting over the rippling sand dunes.

Yury said, "I agree with your assessment—well, more with the assessing criteria. And if you had asked me for scales to judge the carat, I would have had to oblige. But I have thought often about this. Tell me, do you agree? I believe that just because it is possible to categorize the stones, this should not mislead one into thinking that a diamond's true worth really can be set at a certain value." His voice dropped. "This is the mystery. The diamond's beauty and brilliance incite such intense emotions and real passion."

Yury stopped and shook his head, annoyed and embarrassed. Why did this woman bring out the weak emotion in him? But he swallowed and continued, "For centuries, really, there is no way to define it all. Some people say it is like a sickness, trading in diamonds. The diamond dust gets into your blood, and you cannot go too long without having them in your hands, under your eye, so to speak. A diamond's beauty is the beauty of light."

Miriam shook her head ever so slightly, and this caused Yury to laugh. Then he caught himself thinking something so outrageous it did not seem to come from his own mind.

He would show her something today that might win her heart. *If I can open her eyes so she sees me, who I really am, this time I may find—and keep—what I have sought so long.*

The thought flew unbidden into Yury's mind. This was not the man he knew himself to be. Did he even want a woman that way? He looked down at the ground to cover his confusion. What was this power she had over him? He caught himself saying things, and thinking them, in a way that left him feeling unprepared, open to attack. She distracted him, and in his line of work, a distraction could be an invitation to disaster and death. He knew, for he watched for this same weakness among his enemies.

Every one of those men this morning would give anything to catch

Yury with his guard down. They would leap at controlling the diamond fields he had in his territory.

But they wouldn't get a chance. Even with the woman distracting him, Yury felt confident of this, because he knew his strengths. Yury had control of the diamonds in his region because he didn't fly in and out like the others. He stayed in the field and saw to it personally that his business was run the way *he* wanted it. And whenever anyone stole from or cheated or lied to him, well, he had his own form of justice. *I am the best at what I do because I do it here. Africa has been generous to me.*

He banked the plane and smiled in anticipation of her reaction once they passed over the dunes up ahead.

Owen could not tell how far they took him from where he and Miriam had shared the cell. His last memory of her before that dreaded morning was of the night before, when he had held her close. During the next several days, as he pitched from one side of the truck to the other, Owen anchored his thoughts in what he knew for sure. He knew he was not alone. He prayed for his wife and son. He prayed for their protection. Owen knew it had been light when they took him and dark when he arrived. But then, he could have been driven in circles for a week and never known it.

They had thrown Owen into a cage made of rough-hewn sapling trunks and tied with water-shrunk leather. In the days that followed, Owen wracked his brain to figure out the motivation for their kidnapping. If he could discover this, he'd know what to offer his captors. It could have been only a random act, he thought—renegades preying on tourists. But then how did they know his name? And back and forth flew his thoughts yet again.

Other than this, he could think of little else than Miriam and Martin. During the day, he summoned every detail, every morsel of memory about them and savored them like chocolates.

But at night, with the sounds of the bush so restless around him, Owen could no longer resist the dark thoughts hovering at the back of his mind. Past failures, dreams denied, hopes dashed, most of all the desperate desires for his family—all whispered in the night. On good nights, he forced himself to face the past and try to silence these cries for those he'd loved and lost. On bad nights, he could only huddle as the memories buzzed around him.

He saw his father's face, open and passionate, then increasingly angry and bitter. His mother's quiet pain, her stoicism, her crumpled form as she lay at the bottom of the stairs that killed her. And Niamh. His sister with the flame-colored hair and temper to match, who fell in love with Owen's best friend, then turned. And let bitterness riddle her heart with empty wrath, hollow fantasies of revenge.

I work for peace all over the world, but it began at home, when I tried negotiating with my sister and Da'. I'm not afraid of a good shouting match, but at my house there wasn't a cup or plate that was safe.

Thinking of his sister, of his homeland, proved treacherous. For then Owen couldn't help remembering the last time he'd felt so trapped. That had been eight years earlier. And the cage had been of his own making, the borders of other countries his bars, a united Ireland the forbidden freedom.

The sea shone like glass that morning. Seagulls screamed as Owen stood on the cliff overlooking the beaches and returned Michael's stare. Inwardly he gave thanks for three things: that Miriam was still in their honeymoon cottage twenty paces back from the bluff, that she slept so soundly, and that he had no gun to match the one in this man's belt.

"I told you *never* to seek me out."

"Did you now?" The dark look, heavy brows, brooding eyes, fingers with the nails bitten down to the quick—all these familiar features rose up to face Owen and pull him down like quicksand. Their Michael, his countenance, all that he stood for, represented the one secret he had kept from his bride. The less she knew about his family's past, the connections cursed with betrayal, the safer she would be. It was what Owen had been working against, running from, bleeding for, ever since he'd left Ireland more than ten years earlier.

"You're a rare bird, you are, Owen. A Protestant from the south and a traitor to boot." The man hissed the word *traitor*. "They tell me you were named for himself, Owen Roe O'Neill, the man who lost to Cromwell and opened the door to the bloody English occupation we've had to endure these last seven centuries. They say he was a great chief, a great general. And also, unfortunately, a great loser. Like yourself."

"And you're one to talk," Owen answered him. "Recruited by the IRA in exchange for a car and a pension for your parents."

"That's right. Taking care of family—now that's a concept you wouldn't understand."

"Leave my family out of this," Owen said.

"Which part of the family might that be? The older brother killed by a drunk driver—or perhaps by my comrades? Or would it be your father, God rest his soul? Or your mother maybe?"

Owen recognized the old trick. He used it himself in his negotiations. Get personal, get the emotions working, get the opposing side to lose control. He braced himself mentally and replied, "I hate the evil hanging over this country, and I swore long ago I would do all I could to fight it. Since then I've discovered it's the same evil in other parts of the world, wherever innocent people suffer. I thank God for my mother. She taught me to pray for my enemies, to love them, taught me the ways of peace. She even hauled us to Mass as well as Church of Ireland services every Sunday."

"And she's been punished accordingly."

"She wasn't punished for attending church." Owen swallowed. After all the years, his mother's death still stained his heart with guilt.

As if he could read Owen's mind, Michael said, "But she's not the one you betrayed. It's your father who's turning in his grave. The son of a Republican commander—who would imagine you'd turn your back on us?"

The IRA had first approached him with a deal a decade earlier. Owen had refused to spoil the peace talks. And his mother had fallen down a flight of stairs and died. She'd already been a widow for five years.

A sudden thought strangled Owen's hold on sanity: *Miriam will be waking up. I have to get him away before she comes out.* He fought for control. Owen's training kicked in as he searched for ways to give Michael something he wanted.

He caught Michael watching him, and the insight that had made Owen famous among his colleagues threw up a red flag.

Michael said, "Here's the deal then. You leave Ireland and never come back, you and she both, and we'll leave you in peace. For the sake of your father."

"And why should I trust you?"

"Because I was your friend."

"Was," he said to the back of Michael's black leather jacket.

Michael looked over his shoulder at Owen. He spat on the purple blooming heather. "By the way, your sweet sister sends her regards. Sure you know, she's the one who sent me."

Owen thought on these things in the African night and grieved that he had never managed to reconcile with his sister. A year ago he had tried one more time for peace in Ireland, careful to stay in London where the talks were held. But again he had failed.

With the blood of family still ringing in his ears, the first Owen knew of Martin's proximity was when he woke up to the sound of his son's voice. He called out to him in the dark, "Martin! Is it you? Martin!"

Sobbing, the sounds of cries, then one word, "Dad?" The two found each other this way, Martin sticking his thin arms between the wooden bars of Owen's cage.

The realization slammed down on Owen that the sick mind directing this sad play would not accidentally place Owen where his son could find him.

Owen would pay a price, and the price would cost him dearly.

Chapter 31

I am sorry I don't remember some things. The first time I admitted that, you said you have known the same empty places in your mind where only echoes sound. I believe this is God's protection. I want to write now about something I do not like. I am panting like the impala when duma, the cheetah, has been chasing him. Maybe you have noticed that now I write in circles, not wanting to see what is before me.

Okay. A long journey this.

So I wandered some more and came to another camp. Then our refugee camp was raided by rebels, and many were killed. These deaths made others run mad in the camp. If you saw someone staggering, or falling down due to drinking, it means the person all of a sudden thought the rebels were back. I have witnessed these killings

by the rebels with my own eyes. The refugees
were extremely worried because what happened in
Sudan could happen in Kenya. This was the rebels'
work, killing people. This is the bad thing that
happened, killing refugees. We pray that war will
stop quickly. We also pray for their souls to rest
in peace.

There came a time when I stayed in another
camp. This camp was in Uganda. I know what you
are wondering. All this walking back and forth—
who can keep track of the countries? I was in
Kenya, and there we made huts in a village, and
we smashed cans to put on the roof so the sun
would shine on them and light dances. God stood
by me, and my father and mother were the school
I wanted to go to, there every day waiting to
teach and raise me up. I longed to belong in a
school. I looked up to and obeyed whatever school
asked of me. But then things became much worse
there, so I ran away from the camp in Kenya and
went to this place in Uganda. How I wandered in
despair and agony, looking for peace. A large
group of us boys went to Uganda. We did this
thing because there was no food and we were
hungry. We sought peace and security, but we also
wanted to go to school.

At this time of walking to Uganda from Kenya,
I was not one of the lucky ones, but many of the
boys in our big group carried books under their
arms. We did not have food, but they had books.
I did not know then what I know now, or I would
have found a way to take a book with me too. I
could still remember the refugee camp in Ethiopia,

where we boys lived in dormitories and were given education and security. This is what I prayed for.

In Uganda we had a good camp. Peace and food, and I could go to school again. This is the first place I heard God's Word. On that day I was like the child-soldier David who hears trees clapping their hands. I also learned that my way lies through Gethsemane, through the city gate, outside the camp. The way lies alone, and the pathway winds until there is no trace of a footstep left, only the voice, "Follow Me."

So finally I thought, "Okay, I will live." Here, I am Ambakisye, "God Is Merciful to Me."

Chapter 32

When Miriam heard him call her like a dog to heel, her feet seemed made of lead, and she caught herself counting the individual birdcalls coming from the trees, staring at the ant trails in the dust at her feet, memorizing the print left by Yury's boots. What was she doing here? When could she leave? What would be her fate?

As she entered the plane, she could not shake her sense of dread. It crashed over her now like an unexpected wave. *Who on earth is this man?* she thought, not daring to look at anything but her own hands as he spoke at her.

Miriam cursed her powerlessness even as she questioned her choices. In offering Yury her knowledge of diamonds, she had taken a path she had no way of altering. All she had wanted was a way out. Had she made a desperate situation even worse? *What do I do? How will I ever escape? Owen?* The questions would not be silenced, echoing between her thoughts like a death knell.

Once she settled in the copilot's seat, Miriam was very much aware of Yury, the movement of his hands as he checked the Global Positioning System navigator in front of her, the hair on the backs of his fingers as he brushed against her leg to reach the charts folded neatly under her seat. He consulted them as the small plane's motor roared and then, in one movement, threw them to the side and pulled the plane up and over the bare landscape.

Obviously, the Cessna had been refueled. He had access to multiple fuel dumps. Miriam added this to her cache of knowledge.

Owen's lessons about maintaining a dialogue came back to Miriam. "Why?" she asked Yury. "Why did you target my husband?" She dared not ask what his purpose was in keeping her.

Instead of answering her, Yury began to talk about diamonds. As she listened, Miriam did not want to admit his words sounded like her father's. As a girl, when she listened to her father's stories about the stones, Miriam had watched the fawn-colored *boezelaar* nailed to his workbench. As a trained diamond cutter and cleaver, he had used his boezelaar to collect all the chippings and diamond dust. Miriam had watched and waited for glimpses of the falling dust as her father taught her about the passion of the stones. Now, in a dimension she wished she could fall out of, she saw that same passion reflected in Yury. *And yet the two could not be more different.*

The plane continued soaring toward the west. The sun shone squarely behind them the entire trip, more than an hour of endless sand dunes—this was the Kalahari Desert, Miriam reminded herself. She tried to find some landmarks, thought she sighted a salt flat, but then. . . .

"The ocean!" Miriam gasped, and immediately regretted being so transparent.

"Of course." Yury raised his eyebrows. "You did not think we could keep on flying away from the sun indefinitely, did you? Do you know where we are now?"

Miriam thought for a moment. "Back in Namibia." As she said the words, her heart sank. *Of course.* Another part of her summoned the image of the map. On a dashboard in a jeep, her husband at her side laughing, her son sleeping safely . . . *no!*

Miriam would not go there. She must concentrate on this *now*. This present, this place, this *here*. With a tremendous shift of will she visualized the pages in the guidebook. *Ah yes.* She rammed the knowledge through her consciousness, leaving little room for anything else, reciting the facts to herself.

They were flying over the hundred-mile stretch of beach in Namibia that boasted one of the world's richest diamond sources as a marine deposit. Eons ago the diamonds found on these beaches were carried downriver toward the Atlantic. The larger diamonds sank to the ocean floor, while others were left at the shoreline.

"Very good," Yury answered her. "Behold, Miriam. The diamond-studded beaches of Namibia."

As the Cessna dove toward the surf, Miriam caught sight first of thousands of seals dotting the beach, then, to the left, the watchtowers in the dunes that looked like transplants from the old East Germany.

"Where *are* we?" Miriam mumbled.

Yury said, "You may choose, for all beach-mining operations on this coast look the same. From Walvis Bay southward you have Hottentot Bay, Lüderitz, Elizabeth Bay, Orangemund. Then south of the border in South Africa there's Alexander Bay, Port Nolloth, Kleinzee, and Lambert's Bay. We can be anywhere you wish to be, Miriam."

She caught the sarcasm in his voice as Yury brought the plane parallel with the coastline. Now she recognized the schools of fish moving like dark clouds underwater against the backdrop of a sandy bottom and, in a glimpse of memory, thought of that evening in Hawaii with Owen. Onshore, she saw men, groups of men ahead of them. Gunshots rang out, and Yury laughed his eerie laugh, always cut short like breath in a dying man.

It happened so fast that Miriam could only watch the events unfold like a play, even though she was the one onstage. She sensed this, a part of her witnessing her own reactions with the same hunger Yury's gaze reflected. "Look quickly now," he said. "They don't like us getting so close. See the square mounds of sand? They block off the sea and drain chunks of the beach, keeping the water at bay with those dikes, see? They're just mounds of sand covered with plastic. Then they sift through it. The largest diamonds from this area have been found resting on the surface, gifts from the sea. That's what they're looking for. But these men are watched constantly. Anyone caught pocketing even the smallest stone is shot and killed on the spot."

He paused, then added with a grin, "But some still manage."

They skimmed over the water, just outside the range of the rifles aiming at them from the towers. They flew so close, Miriam could see the sweat glistening on the faces turned their way, tired faces of men dressed in green plastic, standing knee-deep in brown-red sand, men paid to do nothing but search for diamonds under the sun.

Yury wagged his wings and roared off farther southward. Soon they came upon huge square pools of blue seawater walled off from the sea by broad dikes wide enough to accommodate two-way tractor traffic. From the air the squares of blue looked like submerged sapphires beside an endless surf. In the distance, Miriam could just make out a network of square, covered walkways. Yury explained that these connected the processing and polishing warehouses, factories set out like a child's game of blocks, the blue sky a backdrop for it all, the bluer sea below it.

With a smooth turn to the left, Yury brought them around, away from the towers and the beaches, pointed inland now.

"You like to play with people," Miriam said softly, finally daring to look him straight on.

He pursed his lips and said, "Perhaps. But not you. I trust you, and this is a strange thing. I have not believed anyone for a long time. Of course, you have noticed I am a man of power. I can have anything and *anyone* I please."

Miriam closed her eyes, as if not seeing would prevent this sick accident his low voice insisted on causing.

"But you I will not take," he was saying. "I decided this last night as I thought of you asleep in the tent, so close to my own. I will make you come to me of your own free will. I do not know your history, Miriam. Whether you are a woman who knows what men want. But you are here in my world now. And I can promise you the wealth of nations if you will *choose* to become mine."

Below her, Miriam saw only the wrinkled waves of sand breaking from dune to dune in the wind. But she felt as if she stood on a parapet, looking down on many kingdoms . . . and beside her, the devil himself.

Chapter 33

After the flight with Miriam along the Namibian coast, Yury steered them far north, refueling several times. He explained that he had finished his business with the Russian "colleagues," and Joseph would close the deal. "And since we did not bring any luggage with us, we have nothing to take away." That laugh again.

Miriam watched the sun, and her heart sank as she realized this time he was landing somewhere different, much farther north from where she last saw Owen.

"Where are we going?" Asking him had become merely a habit, an exercise in futility.

But now he surprised her by answering. "And you have not guessed by now? This surprises me. It's a beautiful country, Angola. Truly a land of opportunity."

Angola. The very name summoned broken images of civil war from the rare news documentary she had watched back home. In September, after their trip to Hawaii, she had seen reports of elections being held there. But soon afterward the brief reports stated the country had plunged hopelessly back into civil war.

In the days to come, Miriam wielded the only weapon she had against Yury's desire—her will. He wanted her to want him. Owen's voice in her thought to use this, her only bargaining chip, knowing that in some ways the challenge Yury had issued to himself would be her only guarantee of protection as she reentered the otherworld called Angola.

Miriam found herself in what appeared to be a more permanent camp than before, a small tent city ruled by Yury like a fiefdom. When she heard both Portuguese and French being spoken around her, Miriam deduced they had in fact flown so far north that they must be somewhere in a northern province of Angola, probably near the border with Zaïre.

The air was more humid, with dense green jungle surrounding the camp. Miriam could not be sure of her exact whereabouts, but she heard some of the men refer to the area and river near the camp as Cuango—not Congo, she was told, which was the former name of Zaïre and still the name of a country and a river farther north. When she asked Yury, he openly admitted the location was the site of some of the richest diamond deposits in all of Africa. Miriam soon understood that from this diamond camp, millions of dollars' worth of stones were being smuggled out through neighboring Zaïre and probably back to Antwerp.

The camp was very much a man's world. Miriam saw soldiers of all ages and shapes, their uniforms varied and tattered. And yet she noticed that the weapons they carried looked new, modern, lightweight, and sophisticated.

The eyes of these men followed her wherever she went. During her first week in the camp, Miriam had to make a conscious effort to shrug off the stares searing through her khaki uniform. But some word from Yury evidently kept her out-of-bounds, off-limits, relatively safe. The fact that he wanted her for himself meant she could walk around freely, though Joseph often tailed close behind her. Soon, out of necessity, she accepted her status and tried not even to notice the comments and glances in her direction.

Yury put Miriam to work immediately. She fell into a routine of assessing the many stones brought to the camp by local men, women, and children. During the days she worked under a canvas stretched between two baobab trees. Beside her stood another stand with a sign that read *Comptoir—D'achat de Diamant*. Diamonds Bought and Sold. Men smelling of the jungle came to her, emptying their pockets of stones. Only some were actually rough diamonds. And it was usually the least likely looking finders who brought her the best gems. Miriam never handled any actual cash. Instead, she wrote out the values on small slips of paper that could be cashed elsewhere in the camp.

Miriam soon figured out that the camp had two layers of residents: the mercenary soldiers, trained by former Soviet bodyguards Yury had picked up somewhere in his travels; and the diamond traders, whose business centered around Yury and his inner circle. Miriam tried to learn as much as she could about the more permanent faces. If the bits of information she picked up from odd conversations could be trusted, here murderers mixed with the mercenaries fighting on the side of the Unita rebel forces, who opposed the Angolan government.

Miriam remembered Owen telling her that in many ways Angola's story was similar to Mozambique's. She tried to remember the details. If you counted the guerilla war for independence from Portugal, war had gripped Angola since the late fifties. After independence in the seventies, though, a power struggle had dragged the country back into battle. Here it had been the Cuban-backed government forces against the Unita rebels. Unita was headed by a man named Jonas Savimbi. Miriam remembered the name because she had heard it mentioned in the camp. Unita had received much of their funding and arms from pro-apartheid South Africa and the U.S. But there the similarities between the two countries ended. Because of Angola's oil and diamonds, the motivation for prolonging the conflict was strong.

But the soldiers-in-training and the diamond traders were not the only people with business in Yury's camp. From time to time she also saw government officers from other West African countries, South African mercenary "dogs of war," and soldiers from opposition forces in Liberia, Zaïre, and Sierra Leone, all united under the common banner of a profitable anarchy. Whenever she asked Joseph to explain yet another foreign insignia or language, he complied.

Miriam gradually came to realize that she now lived in a country with practically no infrastructure, no rule of law, no law at all except that of men with guns. She made the mental effort to try to stop thinking about certain aspects of her past. Owen and concepts like peace belonged to another world, she told herself. If she was to survive here, she would need all her wits and wisdom. And that meant focusing on the *now*.

Yet she longed for Owen, longed for her husband's touch in her loneliness. At night she heard the men around her shuffling, coughing, moving in the darkness. She knew there were young girls in the camp. Sometimes she even heard their quiet weeping in the still of the night, and she could guess their fates.

Yury had made a point of placing her in a tent beside his own. Again. She appreciated the relative safety this granted her. It also meant she heard what happened in his tent every night—and she knew he could hear her every move.

And after each long night, there came yet another day when the Angolans came to her table under the twin baobab trees, spreading their diamonds for her to hold closely, peer at through the loupe, and assess. Many of the rough diamonds looked like nothing but shiny, smooth pebbles—blue, yellow-gold, dark brown, red, sandy, and yellow translucent stones. But their weight, carefully measured on the precision scale Yury had supplied her with, plus their shape and color, determined the price Miriam assessed for each individual diamond. She quickly learned that in several languages the term for inferior stones was *tchop tchop*.

Entire weeks passed during which Miriam did nothing but peer into the depths of diamonds presented to her. Some were already cut, but she never asked their origin, catching signs of feathers and fractures, damaged ribs and culet. Her worldview narrowed to focus on each stone's hidden facets.

These facets, then—color and a stone's inner fire—mirrored her own terror, doubts, and incredulous belief at what had happened to her world. This was what she searched for through the magnifying glass of her fear.

Until the day an Angolan boy said, *"Bom dia.* Good morning. Do you recognize me?"

Miriam looked up from her table, rolling the loupe over and over across her palm with one thumb. She signaled to the boy that he should wait a moment. Then she leaned back and whispered to the young man who brought her food and stood guard behind her chair every day. He acted as interpreter when it was necessary, and she asked now that he tell the others in line to back up some and not crowd so much around her workplace. This was not an uncommon request. Several times a day she had to ask the crowd of waiting people to give her more space.

Once they had more privacy, Miriam studied the face of the boy who had asked her the question. "Should I know you?" she asked. She did not recognize any familiar characteristics. She saw a pug nose, small ears, a tense smile. He had long arms and kept clicking his knife open and closed. There were others around who spoke Portuguese and English. Had she seen him before?

"Do you not remember my name? I have told you last week and the days before that."

Miriam pushed her hair out of her eyes and cursed the humid heat. Her forehead felt too warm against her hand. Was she flushed from a fever? It was so hard lately to keep track of time. And Yury had warned her if she made mistakes with the stones, she would end up in a cell again. This job was the only thing keeping her out in the open like this. That and his demented obsession with her. She looked at the boy again but could not push the image of Yury's impatient and threatening voice out of her mind. She dared not be caught talking about anything but the trade.

"I'm sorry," she mumbled, thinking the boy must be tricking her. She saw Yury walking toward them. She shook her head at the boy. "I don't know you. Next please!"

Miriam could see for herself that the diamond-smuggling trade out of countries like Angola and neighboring Zaïre and Liberia was nothing but a huge free-for-all. Here in Angola, the illegal smugglers were called *garimpeiros*. They found their diamonds in alluvial deposits—bending double with huge, flat pans, sifting through the yellow mud all day. Or sometimes they dug into certain hillsides and found their treasures between the clods and roots of trees. An entire network of men in charge of men, women, and children ran the various digging operations.

Miriam tried not to see where she had ended up, what she had become. And even when Yury admitted to her the dynamics of his Russian-mafia triangle of smuggling African diamonds into Antwerp through Luanda, the Angolan capital, Miriam hardly heard him.

"These wars in West Africa are ideal for our purposes. There is always a demand for professional soldiers, even though most of what we have to work with are unskilled teenagers. Still, you'd be surprised how well some of them take orders. They will do anything. And the AK-47 is simple to operate, a lightweight weapon easily carried by kids. Children are good fighters because they try to make a good impression. And they think it is just a game, which is why they are not easily frightened.

"I know from my own experience, for example, that children are very good in recon work. You can send them across enemy lines without anyone suspecting them because they are so young. Ah, and they are not afraid to take chances."

He sat opposite Miriam, the night's fire between them. In the last three weeks it had become their routine at the end of the day, his demand of her. Yury talked to Miriam as if she were a partner in his ventures. And Miriam watched the flames and tried to remember again how she had come to be in this place with this man. Too often, as now, all she could say was, "I don't understand."

"This year we supply the Unita rebel forces with arms. Next year they might be in power, and then we'll supply their enemy, the government forces, with training and arms. It's an open field. All the rich Western nations are major players in this game. Your America, Britain, France—they all have arms for sale to the highest bidder. And believe me, the army who controls diamond fields like these—" his arms swept forward in a huge circle—"is the army who can afford to pay. Angola has more oil than Nigeria and probably more diamonds than any other country on this continent. The government finances its army with the oil, and at present, diamonds from the mines farther east in the area of Camafuca, near Lucapa and Catoca. Of course, no one can tell what will happen in just a few years. Now Unita buys arms with diamonds. But soon, I think, there will be a joint venture with Russians—myself and some comrades—to develop the kimberlite pipe of rich diamond deposits in Catoca. And then we will be dealing in government-controlled areas. Here one must be very generous with dos Santos and his government men."

Yury continued, "The stones you hold in your palm every day, they are not called blood diamonds—conflict diamonds—for nothing. Of course, it's all about power. Western countries' quest for diamonds, gold, and power has prolonged conflicts in Africa. The wars in Africa are fought largely because wealthy countries seek *more* wealth, *more* power."

He made the words sound like a chant, a song of longing. Miriam nodded. What else could she do? As usual, Yury was an enigma to her. Now he leaned forward and stared at her across the fallen log, one end burning, the other sticking out like a dividing line between them.

"I have news of your son," he said.

Miriam caught her breath, then watched her hands begin to shake, thankful that the pressing darkness cloaked their betrayal. She knew he was watching her. She told herself surely this was yet another one of his bluffs, his way of playing cat and mouse with her—this time a cut above his usual cruelty. Still, the words were so wonderful that she looked up, met his eyes. The cold blue was there waiting for her. Even in her dreams these eyes followed her, watched her.

"He is alive."

"How do you know this?" she asked, knowing full well it was just more of his precious power he sought—a sick, manipulative power over her. Still, she responded, fighting to keep her voice steady, waiting for some sign that he spoke truth. In the meantime, the voices in her mind screamed out in hope and fear. *Could it be? Martin? Martin!*

"I received word today from the plane that landed. I'm sure you saw the new men enter the camp." She had, but now she wondered why it was so important to him that she know these things. This was what the last weeks had been like. A blind woman in a dark room, Miriam felt her way step-by-step—part of her numb, the other part acutely aware of the terror in and around her.

Now, again, he played his trick of changing the subject. The empty laugh, cut short by a question. And she *would* answer him—that much was clear in his tone. He blinked. "Tell me again about cutting the diamonds. Tell me the words in English."

"Martin?" The name a sigh, a gasp for air.

"Tell me," he insisted, his voice grating like gravel.

She would not be allowed to bring up Martin. In the past, whenever she had tried to obtain specific information during their conversations, Yury had always managed to turn it around so she ended up doing his bidding, often repeating the words he so loved hearing. It was nothing but an explanation, a repeat of lectures explaining the technical definitions of clarity and carat, simple information about the cutting of the stones. The "words in English" he requested were words of violence, but Miriam had noticed that, as with so much that attracted Yury, including herself, such words cast a spell of calm over the man. Even now, as she began the litany yet again, trying to keep her voice even, Yury sighed and threw his head upward with an addict's relief and satisfaction.

Miriam recited in monotone, "A diamond is first cleaved, then sawed, and finally bruted. It is purified by cleaving after a split has been made. When one diamond is used to brute the other, a bruting machine is used to shape them into a rough outline, removing the edges yet retaining as much as possible of the original rough diamond. The result is a bruted diamond. . . ." Her voice faded away. She stood and walked away from Yury, away from the fire, away. To make her hope, even for a few seconds, to resurrect the grief and pain of her loss, had been incisive torture. And Yury visibly enjoyed every minute of it.

The next morning, yet another planeload of strange men arrived in the camp. They spoke Portuguese, but that was all they had in common with the Angolans. *"Da América do Sul,"* she heard one of her courier boys say as the big men walked past her table and stared openly at her chestnut-colored hair. She wore it tied back and up in a bun, under a hat, but she still attracted too much attention.

From South America.

The sense of power shifting behind the scenes haunted Miriam. On the same day she heard that both Unita and Angolan government forces, opposing sides, had met in the camp. And there were different Russians. Yury's original bodyguards—except for Joseph—had disappeared into the bush on some sort of mission, replaced by others. Was Yury playing two mafia factions against one another? She had noticed men from the Middle East in deep discussion with him. And who were these Brazilians?

In this impossible situation, dealing with cutthroat criminals, all Miriam wanted, all her heart cried out for in this hollow half-life, was some truth, something she could trust, a word of comfort. She thought incessantly of Owen and Martin, their presence somewhere in a parallel world to this one. Miriam reached out to them in thought and words and then wondered if this could be called prayer. She had heard Owen speak often of the comfort he found in his prayers.

There came a night when Miriam, wanting to connect somehow with Owen, finally decided to whisper into the darkness, "God, help me. Please. Help them. Save my son, my husband. . . ." But her words rang empty in the hollow of her heart.

Chapter 34

It is many years since these things have happened.
The Lord is with us—Emmanuel! I am writing in
English from a place I could only dream about
before. With my words I go from heaven to hell.
So now my desire is to be a storyteller to children.
Perhaps I will become a writer of books, a teller
of stories. For as this story has healed me in the
telling of it, so I wish to heal others and let them
know they are not alone.

I once asked you, "How can God forgive me?" The
answer is through His Son, Jesus. I see that now.
But I could not see it at first. It is as if both hell
and heaven are here on earth. I lived and went to
hell. You have taught me to say, "These things
happened to me. I was forced to do them." Only a
small part of me believes this. I can admit that here.

So these are not such easy things to write about,

but you knew that when you asked me to do this thing. Why must I relive this, revisit hell? Because now I may do so with Jesus at my side. His holy presence will protect me in a way I could not see then but do now. This, then, is healing—the path in a journey that takes us through the darkness and into the light. Mama Edith taught me to accept the evil and violence I am capable of, we are all capable of, receive Jesus' forgiveness, forgive myself, pray for and forgive my enemies, and be healed. This thing, I think maybe it is not easy, which is why I am not the one to do it. In this healing, only God can make me whole.

In God's holy Word, Paul wrote to the Corinthians: "Blessed be God, even the Father of our Lord Jesus Christ, the Father of mercies, and the God of all comfort; who comforteth us in all our tribulation, that we may be able to comfort them which are in any trouble, by the comfort wherewith we ourselves are comforted of God."

Jesus is with us in the dark places, especially in the darkest places.

What is His name? He is "God of All Comfort." His name means "I am."

"I am what?" a child like me asks. And this is what makes my heart smile. Listen, God is all. He says, "I am. . . ." Even I can fill in this empty place with any good word I wish, and God fits. Loving. Caring. Seeing. Understanding. Emmanuel— "God Is with Us." These are all God's names.

Me, I was Temporary Thing, Sold Person, One Who Moves a Lot, Child of Sorrow, the Caller, and God Is Merciful to Me.

The prophet Isaiah wrote these words from God for an orphan like me: "As one whom his mother comforteth, so will I comfort you; and ye shall be comforted."

In this place now, even sleeping on a soft mattress, my skin cool from the touch of smooth fabrics wrapped around me, I still sometimes wake myself, crying out at night. For I do not even know who my mother is. The images I see of another war on television, somewhere else, the children, rip me open, and I find myself crying in bed like a small, small boy. My heart is breaking, Lord. I do not even know whether my mother and father are dead or alive.

A home, a mother, a name, and if God chooses to answer my prayer and bless me indeed, then to go to school. He has blessed me indeed. The blood of Christ binds us together—mother, son, father, brother. This is my family, my home, who I am.

I believe the promises of the Bible hang like fruit in the air. When we pray, we reach up and take this promise, that one there. Many of these promises need a lot of prayer, and when we stop praying because we are tired of waiting, the promises are just left hanging there. They could have been ours if we only had been willing to pray a little longer.

If I could remember now my name, my first name, the name my first mother gave me, it would be in the place my first brother told me of, the place where "I am" God is. There it is never dark, and there is no fear. In this place I can hear my mother calling for me. I recognize her voice, my name.

I have found favor. Now, where I am here, there is one name only.

I am Daw.

In the Arabic of Sudan, this name means "Light." Now God is not the only one who calls me by my name.

Chapter 35

Owen prayed in the darkness for his wife, that she would be kept safe, that God's hand would be on her, guiding her words and actions until he would bring her to a place of safety. It was an old prayer, a prayer of nearly a month—four weeks, the twenty-eight days since he last saw Miriam.

Owen saw his son every day, however, and loathed every visit. It had started with that initial contact in the dark and grown into a macabre pantomime directed by this Yury Falin.

Today Owen watched the group approach his cage with dread pulling at him more powerfully than his hunger. It struck Owen every time how small Martin's eyes appeared without his glasses. Martin had transformed before Owen's eyes, growing daily more subdued, less his old self, increasingly docile and obedient. Now he marched behind Falin, his strides exaggerated to match the men beside him. Owen grimaced as Martin tripped over a root, then looked up and squinted, turning his face from right to left, as if he expected someone to say they had put it there on purpose.

"Time to feed the enemy," Falin said. Owen scowled. It was a well-used trick, but it worked eventually. Reduce him to no-name, nonhuman status, and in time the inhumane treatment was easier to justify.

It had become a daily ritual, the litany of lies at Martin's expense. Yesterday, when Martin failed to clean and reassemble his rifle within the time Falin allotted him, there had been no food for Owen. And Martin's face had shown he understood the lesson perfectly. His father's starving state was his fault.

"You want to feed the enemy, Martin?" Falin asked. He handed old crusts and gamy meat to Martin, who stood and waited for Falin's nod.

Instead, Falin nodded at the two guards and had his men drag Owen out of his cage, with its accursed low roof, into the sunlight. Owen could only hear his son's voice, begging, "Stop it. You said you'd let him go."

It was a form of torture Owen knew no defense against. He had anticipated that whatever it was he was supposed to do would be forced out of him by using Miriam against him. But to use Martin in this way was to engage in a level of brutality Owen had rarely encountered. Not to mention that in the hostage situations he had been involved with, Owen had always been on the outside—a crucial difference. Owen had no answer to the savage control Falin so enjoyed wielding. Falin seemed a master at it. Owen had seen few better, for Falin used Martin to break Owen's will and Owen to break Martin's.

"You're letting me go?" Owen asked now, since to act like a victim would only serve as an invitation to more abuse.

"Of course," Falin said, his mouth mocking.

"No, please. I'll do anything. Don't take my dad away." Owen noted that this sudden outburst from Martin took Falin as much by surprise as it did Owen.

Falin looked sideways at Martin. "Now, Martin, that is what I want you to teach the enemy—a willingness to do anything. You have learned that well. Martin, tell the enemy what you said this morning."

Martin grimaced. "This is my fault. If I am good, I may give the enemy food. If I am bad, the enemy is hurt."

Falin smirked. "Of course, the next step is, I'll kill this enemy if he doesn't do what I ask."

Owen suddenly saw Falin's own enjoyment of the anguish he caused, the power he exercised over them, as a weapon Owen could turn against him.

"And where is my wife?" Owen asked, trying to throw Falin off balance.

"You have no wife." Falin did not even blink.

Owen grabbed hold of this idea to use Falin's love of torment. Perhaps he could tempt Falin into giving away more than he intended with the promise of further pain. "Why me?" It was a question that had plagued Owen all this time. There were still so many unanswered questions. He saw brief hesitation in Falin's eyes—perhaps he was closer to finding out.

Falin tipped his head from side to side, pursing his lips. "Shall I tell you where you are going? Sudan."

Had the ruse worked, or was Falin lying? Owen's thoughts flew back and forth, calling up the facts. Northern Sudan's Arab Muslim government had been waging war against southern Sudan's Christian populations for decades. Since 1983, the civil war had taken a particularly ugly turn. The stakes? Owen said the word out loud. "Oil."

Falin flashed a cold grin.

"Why me?" Owen asked again. Out of the corner of his eye, he saw Martin fingering the meat. He would not even look at Owen. Owen tried to stand straighter.

"It has nothing to do with you. Perhaps I could say only, by allying themselves with northern Sudan, Western governments would just be continuing their support for the groups they sent arms and money to in Afghanistan in their war against Russia."

Something in Falin's voice caused Owen to listen more closely. The pitch had changed. It was not hard for Owen to make the connection. A mercenary Falin's age—yes, it all fit. He said, "You would have been trained in that war."

Falin's cruel kick in his side was all the answer Owen needed. Even as he nursed the new pain, he smiled deep inside himself. Finally, he had found his enemy's weak spot.

Miriam's reputation as the Western woman who read a diamond's true worth spread through the bush. A small group of French-speaking smugglers from Zaïre joined her regulars from Angola. They, however, asked a pair of English-speaking Liberians to tell her that many thought her too sharp in her assessments. "Just a warning, madam." They smiled at her.

Miriam frowned. So although Yury bragged to the Angolans that she had the sharpest eye, some of the locals resented her for not being open to their bribes.

That, she thought, was the least of her problems. Miriam could not seem to shake off the lethargy that had kept her as much a prisoner as Yury's own orders. She knew only by the increase in rain that at least one season had passed. Yet, despite the increasing spells of fever and chills, she found herself thinking clearly enough to wonder certain things about Yury and his business dealings. She fantasized about forcing his hand, beating him at his own game of lies and extortion. After all, in another life, Owen had told her she could bluff with the best of them.

Then she realized her metaphors were all wrong. This game of life and death Yury forced her to play did not resemble poker. Inwardly she relaxed slightly. Chess, she could play. If Yury sought a check-mate, she would just have to outmaneuver him. So he thought of her as a pawn? A pawn could change into a queen if it reached the other side.

Miriam tried outwardly to pay attention, as Owen had taught her, to apply the focus she had learned in her diamond assessment and the strategy she had practiced in her chess. But inwardly she spent all her energy hoping for her son, longing for her husband. Every day her heart sought them, wishing safety for them both. She often thought it was as if a strand of thought connected them still, its gossamer thread of hope almost indistinct from the web entangling her in this place.

A week after the Brazilians arrived in the camp, Miriam was busy with an unusually large packet of stones when she heard a familiar voice speak at her table. "Madam remembers me this time?"

She looked up and smiled, nodding gently. "Yes." She turned to her interpreter and asked for something to drink. When he had gone, she looked closely to make sure this was indeed the same boy who had approached her a week earlier. "You still have not told me your name."

The boy flashed her a smile, then looked down and mumbled something.

"I can't hear you," Miriam said.

Then he said in a tone so low she hardly heard it, "Can you show me how you read the stones?"

So Miriam took a piece of white paper from her pocket. She folded it several times and dropped an uncut diamond into the trough. "See, what color do you find reflected against the white?"

The boy leaned forward. His fingers took the paper and he said, "It is clear. This is yellow."

"Now try this one," Miriam said as she exchanged the stone for another.

"Ah yes. I see now. This one is blue. A blue light shines from it when the sun strikes it here between the paper. You have helped me see. This is a fair trade. Listen, madam." He brought a knife out of his pocket and started opening and closing it. "I have heard there is a boy being held hostage in one of the camps near here."

Miriam reached out and grasped his shoulder. He dropped the knife in the mud and said something in Portuguese. "You must tell me more," Miriam ordered.

"I only know this thing. Also, that this boy does not see. He stumbles. And he speaks like you do." The boy stooped to pick up his knife and glanced away from her.

Miriam followed his gaze and saw Yury watching them from where he stood with a group of men. A terrible thought occurred to her. Was this boy part of Yury's tangle of lies—had he been asked by Yury to say these things in another attempt to manipulate her? But how had he known a detail like Martin's poor eyesight? How could anyone here know such a thing if Martin *wasn't* here?

The boy said hurriedly, "You know what I say now? I know of this Western child. If I tell you more, will you pay me more for my diamonds?" Once again Miriam wondered if he just toyed with her.

She opened her mouth to ask how he even knew she searched for a child, when at the same moment, the boy moved away from her, the frightened glance in Yury's direction his only good-bye. She heard the clicking sound of his knife even after he disappeared among the trees.

Chapter 36

Miriam determined that night she would try out her theory. She would trade concessions for information, give him the satisfaction of appearing to take the bait. "Yury." She moved over from her side of the fire to his and stood beside him. "I need the truth about my son."

He reached up without looking at her and took her hand in his. His fingers stroked hers as he said, "You fear I am only playing with you. But I am not, Miriam. Come, dance with me. Did you know it is Christmas Eve?"

She had not known, and now the two words felt absurdly out of place, stripped of their usual meanings. No crisp air, no carols, no warmth, and no family here. She heard music from somewhere in the camp; a man sang. She allowed Yury to draw her into his arms, but her body remained stiff. His touch repulsed her, but she forced the thought out of her mind. *What about Martin?* she wanted to say.

Yury's voice: "You would give me a dance, maybe a kiss, and who knows what else, just for information about this boy. Your son, Martin." Again, his tone made it clear this was a statement.

She took a deep breath. He could know the name from what she had let slip earlier. She said, "What you really want from me, only I can give, and it must be given—you cannot forcefully take it. Am I right?"

Yury's hand tightened around her waist. He liked the feel of her close like this. It had been a long wait, but finally now he could enjoy her willingness. He answered her question. "You know this well, Miriam. There are certain things in this life that lose their sweetness if not given freely. You have tasted enough bitterness, am I right? And now you want to know for certain if this is true. You are thinking maybe you should not believe this. Maybe Martin is not alive. Maybe this is just a cruel joke I am playing."

Yury breathed in the scent of her hair. *You are wondering, do I care?* He hated admitting it to himself, but he did, and far too much. "Listen, I promise you I can get you into the group that controls Martin. I have even seen the boy. This is a rival faction that holds him, but I—"

She tried to pull away from him. "Rival faction? They are Russians, then?" But her voice sounded mocking.

He nodded. "You will not believe me?" Yury wanted desperately to give her a sign that he could be trusted. A sudden thought occurred to him. "I *know* what it is for a boy to miss his mother." He swallowed. His voice flat, he said, "My parents both died. Both killed themselves. I was raised in a state orphanage." He peered at her. "What? What are you thinking?"

"I'm remembering images from orphanages in Romania they were showing on our television when the Eastern bloc opened up. The extreme poverty, the state those children were in . . ." Her voice trailed off, but Yury had heard enough. And seen enough—the expression on her face.

Her skin now burned to his touch. He backed away from her. "You!" he accused. He had let down his guard for a single instant, and this was his reward. "Do not *pity* me," he hissed. "I learned to fight as a child, and this was more than enough to get me out of there at a young age. I *know* who I am and what the extent of my wealth and power is. No one can threaten that."

He turned away from her gaze, his head splitting open, his gut heaving with shame that he would have become so vulnerable. But it was too late. Yury had seen her witness his weakness. If she felt sorry for him, he would never forgive her.

Never mind that she could not even understand the word she had used. *Poverty*. Never mind that out of hunger, as a child, he had sucked on pebbles. What did she know of Stalin's Soviet Union of the fifties, when poverty and pain swept across his country in pogroms that became obsolete as people disappeared by the millions?

During the next few days, Miriam had fleeting thoughts of trying to get a letter out by means of one of the couriers, but she realized none of them could help her in this shadow dimension. Again and again she repeated Owen's words of warning: *"Every little thing should be bargained for. Never give away anything. Only make a concession in return for something else."* But she had lost track of what she *could* bargain for. How far did she have to go to reach the end of the playing board?

She heard children calling in the night. She tormented herself with the fantasy that Martin was alive somewhere, somewhere near. This image had taken the place of her old fantasy, that tourists had picked him up. She wondered why Yury's words held such sway over her imagination.

Miriam had met many children involved as couriers as she set values on their diamonds. She had made a point of learning at least twenty new words of Portuguese each day, and now, after a month, she knew enough to ask these couriers if they had heard of a child, a Western child, being held prisoner somewhere.

She asked her questions softly, out of the hearing of Yury and his men. But the answers were just as often a shy shake of the head, a sideways glance, and sometimes, from the bold ones, a request to view the stones through her loupe. Miriam had picked up the Portuguese quickly, but even when she recognized the same children coming back, she did not ask them for their names or ages or where they were from.

She did not see the boy with the knife again, the one she had shown the secret of the white paper to.

Yury's strange admission to her about his childhood had changed something between them in a way Miriam couldn't understand. Now, for the most part, he treated her with disdain. More than ever, Miriam had the sense that he was playing with her, for now every time they saw each other, he told her Martin lived. It was as if he knew this was all she thought about, dreamed about.

And now he discovered yet another way of terrorizing her. Whenever he reissued the claim that Martin was alive, he threatened that any attempt on her part to escape would mean he would maim her son.

"I thought you didn't have access to him?" she asked, but he refused to answer.

In recent days, ever since she met the boy with the knife, Miriam had been waking at night to the echo of a child crying in her dreams. *Martin.* Then, when one of her regular couriers, a little girl, said to her, "Madam, I pray for you," the concern was too much for Miriam. She felt her control slipping away slowly toward panic.

That evening Miriam paced in her tent and realized with a start that she had no idea what day it was. Yury had said something about Christmas Eve a few days earlier. Had the new year begun already? Surely, she thought, it must still be the last week of the year. Sick and confused, Miriam felt like she finally had run out of options.

That same night, at the fire, in what she perceived as a desperate ploy to hold her attention, Yury said to her in that bitter tone he now used, "I have good news, *Miriam.*" He fairly spat her name out, his contempt so obvious. "My brothers have allowed your Owen to go free."

She could not believe him, refused to, told herself, *It's a lie. Everything out of his mouth is a lie.*

But Yury was ready for her disbelief. "Don't you want to know why? Or how close or far from you he was being held?"

"I don't believe you," Miriam said.

"Well, you may or may not believe me. But yet again, I speak the truth. You have seen the North Africans in the camp."

Miriam tried to clear her mind. She had seen them discussing something heatedly with Yury, but in Arabic. There were just too many missing pieces.

Yury said, "They have asked me to continue holding you as hostage, to make sure Owen throws the deal."

"What deal? Which deal?" she asked.

Yury only laughed.

As she lay on her cot later, Miriam wracked her brain to remember how many days and weeks had passed since they took Owen from her. It must be more than a month—or not? Then she thought of the moon. It had been full when she arrived here, and it was full again now. This provided meager solace, though, as she felt her own grip on reality slipping. Miriam could no longer remember how many rooms her house in San Francisco held. Nor could she remember a night when she did not wake up soaked in her own sweat. Whatever was causing her fevers had intensified. Thoughts haunted her of malaria or a stomach parasite, feeding on her weakness, but her fear for Owen and Martin overruled all else. This she hardly dared to acknowledge, its dimensions loomed so monstrous.

Miriam woke with a start and reached for the lantern. Then she thought again how her only moments of privacy were inside her tent. Yet even there, when she turned on the lantern, her silhouette could be seen by anyone passing outside.

The next morning Yury stood waiting outside her tent. As logically as if she had told him why she tossed and turned, he asked her, "How many days have gone by since I brought you here?"

She could not answer him, and it only added to her pain that this, too, had slipped from her grasp. *What happened to my focus, my resolve? Owen?*

Sleep-deprived, sick, and unstable, Miriam felt as if she swam in a tank with smooth sides, as if every time she attempted to climb out, she slipped further into the deep. Was it the fever? Or were Yury's mind games finally having their desired effect? Miriam would try to force herself to think of things in terms of home, to remember what she read in the guidebook, to measure her experience in non-African contexts. But instead, she would catch herself watching the trees for a sign of color, or watching for a bird she might not have seen before. And then, just as suddenly, her point of convergence would shift and she'd see in a painfully clear light how the trauma of losing both her child and her husband and being held prisoner for endless weeks was threatening her very sanity.

At those moments, she would also become aware of something else. And that was Yury's growing cruelty as he became impatient with her reticence.

That evening at Yury's campfire, Miriam met a rough South African who bragged to her in a drunken slur, "Now, take Tanzania. Gold and diamonds are big business in Tanzania. That country's been suffering from over twenty years of socialism, which really means everyone's skimming off the top. That's life. A gold nugget weighing four and a half carats was found in my mines last week. Never even entered the books. Local police and security took their cut. Company management got the rest."

He leaned on the back of her chair, his breath on her face. "I bid on a 9.2 carat diamond. I bid a hundred twenty thousand dollars. Was outbid by a Lebanese who paid a hundred fifty thousand." He cursed. "The Lebanese mafia are who really control the diamond smuggling on this continent. You can tell your boyfriend he's got his work cut out for him."

Your boyfriend. Miriam glanced across the fire to Yury, to see if he'd heard. She couldn't tell.

After the South African left, Yury came to her side of the fire and stood before her. He had been drinking with the miner, but only now did Miriam realize how much. "Your Martin is safe," he said.

The words still cut through the scar tissue their repeated use had caused. Miriam rose to her feet, unable to silence the insistent voice that screamed *she* was the prisoner here, *she* was the one kidnapped, *she* could not leave.

Yury took her motion as one of acquiescence. He moved quickly and touched her for the first time since the night he had talked about his parents, placing his hand on her lower back and forcing her to take that last step in his direction. "Perhaps he is near. Perhaps I will take you to see him someday. Would you like that?"

Miriam squeezed her eyes shut against the images he baited her with.

"But first, I want to celebrate tonight. You know it is New Year's Eve? Our South African brother was right about the Lebanese but wrong about me. I get what I want. And now there are, thanks to me, less Lebanese to get in the way. You understand? Tonight we celebrate a major victory!" He threw back his head and laughed. Empty, a sound only.

Miriam resisted, but he only pulled closer. One hand touched the side of her neck, then moved to her throat and downward. Miriam held her breath. He flattened his palm and pressed so hard against her collarbone, he forced her to take a step back into his other hand, positioned at the small of her back.

"Ah," Yury said with a sharp intake of breath. "What is this? Hidden treasure?"

Too late, Miriam realized what he meant as his fingers pulled at the leather string and the black-stoned engagement ring rose to his summoning.

He looked at her, then back at the ring, forcing Miriam to look upward as he held the bootlace taut and tilted the ring toward the light of the fire. "A black diamond? And a large one. *His* ring. Why do you keep this thing near your heart? Don't you know it was *he* who brought you here?"

Miriam's own hands flew to his to stop him from yanking the ring. *No, Yury,* she thought to herself, *that was you.* She watched his face closely, but Yury did nothing. He only looked at her and back at the ring, his eyes confused. "Please," Miriam said, "it means nothing to you."

"And everything to you. Is that it?" He coughed and spoke in a steadier tone, releasing her ring and rubbing his temple with that hand instead. He reached in his pocket for a bottle of pills and quickly swallowed three. Then he said, "Is it what our Brazilian brothers would call a *carbonado*, perhaps?"

Miriam hesitated. The carbonados were black diamonds from Brazil, harder than ordinary diamonds and used in industrial diamond tools. She knew, and Yury probably did as soon as he viewed her ring against the flames, that hers was different—a pure black diamond, a diamond saturated with bits of graphite inside the diamond.

Yury said, "Most black diamonds are worth half their white counterparts, just boart, a cheap quality diamond. A dead stone is one without any life, any brilliance. Life is the brilliance of a stone."

"Yes." Miriam hoped his distracted state would last long enough for him to decide he didn't want her ring. She heard him groan as he rubbed his head. Miriam took advantage of the moment to stuff the ring back inside her shirt.

Then he straightened up and focused. "Say the words again—*our* words." Yury breathed her name as if tasting the sounds, his lips pursed after the second syllable. "How I have often thought of this moment. *Say* them."

Miriam felt something give way in her will. She didn't know how, but Yury had transformed the act of recitation into one of violation. She looked at him, trembling inside, but refused to open her mouth. He halted their shuffled two-step around the fire and tightened his grip on her waist, now adding the second hand. Then he hissed, *"Say* it with me."

As Yury began to speak, exactly mimicking her own accent, Miriam felt the shame betray her, deep color crawling up her neck and cheeks. He hissed in her face, "A diamond is first *cleaved,* then *sawed,* finally *bruted*. It is purified by *cleaving*." He paused. Miriam could feel his chest rise and fall, his heart beating through the shirt. "The result is a *bruted* diamond. Is that what you see here, Miriam? To you, am I nothing but a *brute?*" Yury tipped her chin up, forcing her to face him.

As he lowered his mouth onto hers, Miriam shoved him off balance and broke free from his clasp. She stepped away, all but spitting out her disgust of him. *"Don't.* Don't *touch* me again." Miriam knew he must see the distaste etched on her face. After all this time, she had finally lost control of her mask and let him see what she really thought of him.

Rage flashed across his face, the high cheekbones flushed, his eyes narrow slits of lightning. And then, as he wagged his face right and left, noticing the eyes of his men watching them, noticing the South African who had emerged from his tent when he heard their voices raised in anger, Miriam saw another emotion take control of Yury. This emotion Miriam had seen before. And she had learned to fear his shame even more than his anger.

She backed away another step, but his hand lashed out and grabbed her arm, twirling her toward him in a macabre dance. Then with the back of his other hand he struck her in the face. Still holding her fast, Yury looked up and met the gaze of all who still dared to watch. Then for her ears only, he leaned close and whispered, "I have waited long enough. I will force you to love me."

Desperate with daring, Miriam gagged on her words. "Would *you* love me then?"

She left her words hanging between them as he let her arm fall and she ran toward her tent. She ducked under the flap, letting it fall closed. Fear, abandonment, lies, all followed her inside.

Chapter 37

Me, I walk now tightly holding on to Jesus' hand, my eyes clenched closed. "God is with me; God is with me," I tell myself over and over. This place I will tell you about, it is the place you sent me back to. But now Emmanuel, "God with Us," is blessing this place so I will never have to return again.

There came a day in our camp in Uganda when soldiers came and burned down the camp. We had no protection. When the rebels came into our camp, this is what I heard. I remember because these are the same voices I hear at night, even now, when I wake up wet and shamed. At night I still don't want to see any torch flashes. They remind me of the night I was abducted the second time. Even when I am not asleep, sometimes I get bad dreams. I hear rebel soldiers threatening to kill me.

Anne de Graaf

I see a long line of frightened children tied with ropes—we are older now—and hear men yelling orders to kill the children. This is what I hear:

"Don't just kill, but capture them."

"Shoot them; shoot them."

"Kneel down! Now get up."

"Oh! My children!"

"Don't shoot, just capture, and we will kill them under that mango tree."

"Very few have died. You people there—I want to kill more."

"These were killed in the church, approximately two hundred. Young ones were beaten against the tree."

"Taste the bitterness of war!"

These voices have followed me from Uganda to Zaïre to Tanzania to here. They have followed me from hell into heaven, from the past to the present. Will I ever stop hearing them? I wonder.

Now I come to those things that I think you do not really want me to write about. If you knew the pain these words summon, you would not ask this of me. And I know what I tell now will only hurt. These soldiers treated us not as children, not even as goats or cattle. We had no names in that place. My only sign of hope was my brother later, for I came to know my brother there. But before that, we children, the ones just captured from the camp, were tied together and made to carry burdens. We ate weeds and berries. It was a very difficult thing, being so thirsty. I drank things I would rather not tell you about.

The soldiers used the girls as wives. And some of us younger boys were also used in this way. I was terrified all the time. Looking back, yes, the night is what held such terror—my fear of the soldiers who drank too much. They were out of their minds with craziness and beat us in anger, although they sometimes were laughing as they let the blows fall.

In this place with the rebel soldiers, I was even more alone. I listened and tried not to talk to anyone. They told stories of how anyone from Sudan would be sold as a slave. This I did not want. But a small, small voice in me said, "You are already a slave."

I prayed very often during this time. Who knows how long? Weeks? Months? "God, save me. God, save Your child, please."

The rebels told us we were safe after they gave us strange things to eat and drink that made my mind go in circles and see things from the treetops. They said we could not be killed. The first time I saw a big boy blown up, I knew they lied. At first I carried water and food; then they gave me a weapon. I wanted that very much because it made me feel safe. I learned to take it apart and clean it better than most. During the fighting though, I let it drop. All the noise around me—people yelling, explosions!

So then I had to carry bags of millet. The bags were so heavy I trembled and fell three times. I was warned that if I fell again, I would be beaten. Sometimes we marched all night. In the morning one time I refused to eat, asking the rebels where they were taking us. I was warned that if I continued refusing to eat and complaining or asking questions, I would be beaten to death.

In that place, I killed for the first time. This boy, he could not keep walking, so they told me to shoot him. His eyes pleaded with me to hurry and finish it. His eyes follow me still. In that place, killing became easy and normal. It seems strange now, looking back, that I shot my gun and people died. Even though you tell me I was given no choice, still I wonder, and I see some of the faces. His face. His eyes.

This has been a difficult thing, to focus on something different. Thanks be to God that there is another reality now that the wars in my life are over. Why? The soldiers told us they were our family. They promised us food, clothing, money even. The gun meant food and survival. One boy told me, the gun is god. Listen to the voice of god. Obey him. And when you kill, you are making them neighbors of god.

So I listened and killed the enemy, or else he would kill me, the soldiers said. Where would I have gone? I had no support, no protection. Those who tried unsuccessfully to escape were beaten and hacked to death, often by other children. They told us, "The smaller the child, the smaller the sin."

God sent my brother to my side. I first saw him standing in a place where many dead bodies lay. Here the bones were not dry, but stinking very much. My brother, he watched as the rebels made two other boys eat parts of the dead bodies. He watched, and then he turned and looked straight at me. This is when my heart recognized him. These soldiers, they were telling these children that this eating would give them the strength of those who had died, that they would be protected from bullets.

Me, I did not believe them, and this was being said by my eyes when my brother saw me. His name is Simba mkali. Fierce Lion.

Simba mkali has a lion's heart because he feels what others feel, can see and understand. This also makes him a very good leader. I saw him and knew this about him. And this is how the idea entered my head, by looking at his face at that moment.

It was my idea that we run away.

After some days of watching him closely, I whispered it to him, and he said he should beat me for it. "I am very much in need of a big boy who can hunt and track and hide in the forest, and you have those skills," I told him. "Plus, we would listen to you. And when I saw you watching some of the little ones, I saw in your eyes that you would most likely not turn me in."

He said, "You are too clever, too brave. It will cost you someday."

I ignored him. "It is easy," I told him and made up a little bit of a story. "I have run away before, from soldiers in Sudan, and from a camp in Kenya." So I told him my plan.

In this way, one night I created a diversion. I put on a show by imitating different people in the camp. I drew the attention of the guards. My brother, he knows where everything is and steals supplies and takes the newest children. He is gathering them when he is discovered and he disappears into the forest with just a few. He is very

good at tracking, so also very good at covering
his tracks.

I had these soldiers laughing very hard. I mimicked one man I knew the others did not like, and
they enjoyed that. Then I walked and talked like
another. They laughed some more. I hoped they
would laugh long enough for my brother to get the
others free, but they discovered the missing food.
My brother is fierce, mkali, and he fled, but only
a few children got away.

I did not.

The first soldier, the one who nobody liked, he
grabbed me and told the others it was a ploy. I
was the distraction. Then they tied me to stakes
on the ground and began to whip me. My hands
and legs spread very far apart. I have never felt
so much pain as at that time. And then I stopped
feeling the pain but could still hear the blows.

At this point I thought, I am very close to going
there.

Rope on skin does not sound like anything you
have ever heard before. And then I felt insects
on my face. And then I do not remember anything
else.

I was crying like a girl. I was being bounced up
and down, and I was weeping and whining like a
woman. When I opened my eyes, I saw the ground
moving under me. Someone carried me like a sack
of cassava flour over his shoulder. I moved my
head and my neck cried out that I had hurt it.

It was my brother. He carried me. He had
watched all this, had watched what they did to
me, and he came back for me when it was very

dark. They thought I would die that night—that is what the soldiers said. What use is a small boy? They laughed and walked away. This my brother told me later, for my brother was watching, and he came back for me.

He asked, "What is your name?"

I said, "Brother, me, I am Simba mdogo."

Here, in this place, my name is Little Lion.

Chapter 38

Miriam dreamt of many mirrors. Each showed her a fearful face, her own. But when she reached up to touch her skin, all she felt was the smooth surfaces of the glass reflecting her movement.

She sat up in the dark, her voice ringing in her ears, and heard the scuffle outside the tent.

"Joseph?" No answer. Where were the other askaris?

The groans outside Miriam's tent welled into shouts and thuds of heavy boots running past. Miriam felt the ground shake. A split second later an explosion rocked the tent. She saw fire through the tent flap and, against the light, a body being thrown through the air toward the campfire. Then the camp and her tent fell into blackness.

Miriam crawled blindly, groping for the cot. As she frantically pulled on her boots, she heard men pushing and hustling, imagined them ducking and dashing into the darkness. She heard grunts and moans, then gunshots. Miriam felt her way to the back of the tent and slipped under the canvas opposite the door. She didn't know where Yury was and she didn't care, but she was getting out of there as fast as she could.

She stooped low and backed out but had no sooner stood up when another explosion sent her to her knees. She covered her ears and heard the cries of someone lost in all the noise and chaos. This sound would not leave her, even as she scrambled to her feet and began to run. She had heard it before.

Miriam lost all sense of the camp's layout. Her legs carried her left, right, behind, between. She crouched and hovered until yet another burst of gunfire drove her on. At first she ran along the periphery, crawled toward what she thought must be the river, the airstrip. But nothing looked familiar.

Salvos pummeled the ground. Miriam stood, whirled, ran away into the night, but looked back once when she thought she heard a child yelling. When yet another blast tossed bodies upward like a sacrifice, Miriam turned again and fled finally into the jungle, unable to escape her own screams.

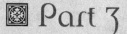 # Part 3

I tried to isolate an answer from among the sea of questions. My story began in Africa. That much I knew. But as to what had happened to me and why, I could only guess. Who I was, where I came from—did any of it matter in the face of all I searched for now? All I had lost?

These were the questions that kept me awake at night. What did I not know?

Those nights I could not stop screaming as the darkness fell over me yet again, like a bad dream revisited. I woke up crying out loud, a wail. Was I keening for the woman I left behind when I crawled to that place, a grief so deep it sounded in the animal parts of me? Or was my weeping the cry for a child lost?

How do I search for a child that cannot be found? This question hounded me as I plunged into the never-ending night of fear and loss and pain.

There was no hiding from it.

I was lost.

Chapter 39

A hand rests on her shoulder. The screaming has stopped. Then another voice, and she lets him steady her as she stands. The hand is gone. She hears a rifle being cocked. A child giggles.

The woman wakes up in a strange tree room, but she is lying on the ground. Branches piled against each other form the walls, and branches of huge leaves arranged above her provide shade. She hears a groan and turns over. Because her eyes are open, the first thing she sees is the boy.

The woman sits up. Her head throbs. She touches her forehead and feels a welt, a soft scab. Her hand comes away with sweat covering the palm. She looks at her arms and sees tiny beads of moisture all up and down their sides. She is shaking.

Another groan comes from the makeshift hammock with arms hanging downward—a body belly down, with its face turned away from her. The hammock is stiff and straight like a table, stretched on poles, unhewn wood, more tree branches, preventing the boy's back from arching the wrong way. She looks more closely as now the head rises up, turns toward her, and red-rimmed eyes look into her own.

It is a boy, maybe ten. He blinks and asks, *"Madame. Pouvez-vous . . . s'il vous plaît?"*

The woman shakes her head. "I don't speak French." She still hears a ringing in her ears, and when she begins to stand, this worsens. Her hands fly up to her forehead, trying to keep the skull from splitting.

"Ah, English then." The boy begins to cough, and the woman watches him spit in the dust beneath him. A stream of dark blood forms a tiny puddle underneath his face. She tries to stand again, one palm pressed against her left ear to dam the pain, the other hand holding on to a nearby pole for support. As she straightens, she sees the boy is covered in leaves, like those above and around her. Flies have swarmed over the leaves. She walks toward him and waves the flies away.

"Ah, thank you, madam." He gasps and says something in a language she does not recognize.

"I do not understand," she says wearily.

Then, in clear English but with the stress often on the wrong syllable, he says, "Your hair is the wrong color and your nose the wrong shape."

The woman doesn't respond. She is too unsure of where she is, what has happened.

He says with a small sigh, "I thought I was *there*. They told me I have a mother now." Then his eyes close, and the woman soon hears the boy snoring softly.

▨ ▨ ▨

The woman ventures out of the tree-branch shelter she shares with the boy and sees a camp of similar shelters arranged around a fire pit. A group of children look up and come toward her. They are dressed in torn and faded T-shirts. The trousers fall short on bare legs, hems unraveled. Four boys stop just opposite the woman, their faces sullen. One of them holds a rifle casually in two hands, its tip pointed toward her feet. The youngest steps forward and reaches toward the woman's hair. She bends lower and he touches it. Then he laughs and says something to the others, but they become angry and shout at him. Instantly, the little boy looks as if he has been hit and, without a sound, runs away into the bush.

Now the woman is left confronting the three teenage boys. She tries to focus on their faces but sees nothing but the angry eyes. She looks for adults and sees none. She says, "Who are you? Where am I?"

They do not reply. One of them returns to the fire pit and brings her a banana leaf with some kind of paste on it. He offers it to her, then takes a bite himself, using his fingers to bring the food into his mouth. The woman understands and reaches for the leaf, when another one of the boys yells at the one offering it to her. An argument erupts, but she cannot understand anything they are saying. The first boy puts the leaf on the ground and backs away from the woman as if he dares not turn his back on her. The woman steps forward, picks up the food, and nods her thanks.

In the evening she hears voices in the bush, a group approaching the camp. The five newcomers are nothing but teenagers, all between the ages of thirteen and sixteen. The same boy who brought her the food that afternoon now comes to where she is standing with an odd-shaped gourd container and, holding it upside down, mimes the action of drinking. Again she thanks him, and the woman takes out the plug and drinks. Only when the water hits her throat does she realize how thirsty she is. And that she literally cannot remember the last time she drank anything at all.

The tallest boy from the group that has just arrived approaches her. She notices that the others watch him as if their lives depend on it. She lowers the water and waits. He begins to speak to her, and she recognizes a few of the words as Portuguese. When did she learn those words? she wonders. She can pick out only bits and pieces of what he says. "Slower, please," she says in the same language, again surprising herself.

He does not smile but nods and repeats himself. She thinks he is saying, "We found you in the night. You had stumbled and fallen." Here he points at her legs and forehead. Then he straightens up, waiting.

The woman bends and runs her hands over her legs, surprised to feel such bruises through the fabric of her pants. Where did these clothes come from? Why is she dressed in battle fatigues? Dried red mud encrusts the sides of her boots. She straightens and looks more closely at the boy. The others are staring at them.

He holds their respect, that much is clear. He is tall, with long arms, wearing no shoes, baggy pants, and a pale blue, cotton T-shirt with some sort of logo that has long since become illegible. He has a round face and flat nose, fine lips, small ears. He holds himself ramrod straight and walks with shoulders thrown back, in sharp contrast to the other boys, who swagger and slouch.

"Welcome," he says in Portuguese. She can understand this much. "What is your name?"

The woman says, *"Chamo-me . . .* I am . . . Mi—" Her voice stops as she wonders how to finish the word. She shakes her head. The drumbeat in her ear is worse.

"Your name?" the boy asks, lowering his chin in a sudden movement of disbelief. Then he nods. *"Sim, compreendo. 'Minha senhora.'* Yes, I understand. 'Madam.'"

"Estou doente. I am sick," she says, reaching out her hand. What else can she do? *"Obrigada.* Thank you."

But when she touches the boy's arm, he jumps to one side as if she has burned him and keeps staring at the spot where her fingers rested for only a split second. The woman does not understand. The other eight children gather around them now and are chattering excitedly in another language.

The woman watches them and wonders where they come from. They look so different from one another; they could not all be from the same tribe. And where are their parents? She tries again to ask them this in Portuguese.

Instead of answering, one of the boys asks her about herself, and now she does not know what to answer. "Where are you from? Where is your husband? Your children?" She can only shake her head in confusion. She is not even sure what he is asking.

She knows there is something wrong with her. What does she remember? Night, running, panic, explosions, fever. Then darkness. Again she shakes her head. She remembers nothing of how she came here, nothing of her life before meeting these children in the jungle. She twists the wedding ring round and round her finger, wondering if it will fall off, as she listens to the children mimic her accent.

Chapter 40

Since the only one who seems able to speak any English is the boy in her shelter, the woman waits the next morning for him to wake. As she waits, the leader comes inside, ducking his head at the low entrance. He carries a roughly carved wooden bowl and in it is something smelly and wet. He nods at her and begins to remove the leaves covering the sick boy's back. The woman stands across the hammock from him and bends to help.

"Who is he?" the woman asks in Portuguese.

He stops and says, "Madam, this is my little brother."

"What is his name? What is your name? You didn't tell me." But the boy shakes his head and makes an odd clicking sound. The woman follows his gaze and gasps.

He has begun to remove the bottom layer of banana leaves and now exposes a patch of skin. The woman sees dark blood encrusted around swollen flesh. In some places, the dried crust has acted like glue so that the leaves must be pulled, tearing open the wounds on the boy's back. Only now does he make a sound. As his older brother gently coaxes the green away from the skin, the younger boy begins to breathe hard but does not cry out.

The woman swallows at the sight.

The boy's entire back is a mass of purple pulp. Welts rise up in a jagged random jigsaw, the sections of his back and all up and down his legs cut into broken mounds of flesh—so many pieces.

The woman backs away, her hand over her mouth. Then she runs from the little lean-to and bends over behind a tree to throw up the little bit of cereal she had managed to eat earlier.

It is another morning, and the woman feels the individual tears running over her cheeks sideways onto her nose. The boy in the hammock says, "Me, I am getting better."

The woman opens her eyes. "Who are you? Who are all of you?"

"You have not been awake for three days. I watch and hear you as you move your leg like you want to jump or run. My brother, he says you want to be called *minha senhora*. That is 'madam.' This I would have called you anyway."

The woman watches him chatter, feeling the words of a familiar language, her English, cascade over her mind in a cool stream of comfort. Even being called madam sounds good. She senses her weakness. She is very thirsty, but her stomach is knotted and sore.

"We are soldiers who have run away. A small group joined up with another smaller group to make a larger group, when we found you, madam."

The older brother shows her how to dress the wounds of the younger. She sits beside him for hours, day after day, keeping the flies from laying eggs under his skin and allowing the air to help harden the scabs. She dresses his wounds with fat from an animal the boys have killed, whose meat they eat over a fire. She does not ask what kind of animal.

The woman sees some of the children shivering. They shuffle from place to place, then fall to the ground, their hands shaking. They complain of being cold, then hot. She asks her patient, "Are they all sick?"

He says, "No. And yes. Sick different than you. The soldiers were giving us magic bubbles and said it would keep us from being shot. When you stop taking them, you still can get shot and you are sick."

The woman wonders about what he is not telling her. She wants to reach out to them, is drawn to the children instinctively, but a part of her recognizes that she is even more lost than they.

She is not sure how much time has passed since the children found her and brought her to this place. The one in the hammock has told her they are waiting for him to recover enough from his wounds to be moved again.

"Where do you come from?" she asks the leader. "Where are we?"

"Angola."

The woman nods. This feels familiar. Later she wonders which of her questions he was answering.

In the mornings there is a set routine as the leader calls the boys together. The woman watches the ritual and thinks at first it is some sort of pledge to remain loyal. When she asks the leader about it, she catches the mumbled word *Deus* and realizes the boys are praying.

When the woman tells her patient, he explains that his brother is leading the boys in daily prayers for forgiveness, even though "God can never forgive what *we* have done."

"What is that?" she asks. When he does not answer, the woman says, "I cannot believe you pray." The words are out before she can stop them.

"How can we not when God has led us here? Don't you?" he asks.

The woman shakes her head. *I have lost my memory. If there is a God, he has abandoned me.* She does not say out loud what her next thought is, that the desperate plight of these children only reinforces the woman's bitter sense of betrayal by any God there might be in this dark place of jungle and dirt and death.

During the next morning session, when the boys are confessing their guilt, the woman sees them standing there hungry, alone, scabs and flies on their legs, sores covering their feet. The leader narrows his eyes, then closes them and repeats the incantation.

The woman wants to stop him. She has no way of knowing what they have endured, but she knows one thing for certain. The thought is crystal clear despite the confusion that will not leave her alone in this place.

None of this is your fault.

She grabs on to this in anger and rebellion. And then she wonders why she cares so much, why it even matters when she hears the children praying.

◈ ◈ ◈

"What do you like doing?" the woman asks the boy in the hammock. She is pleased that he seems to have less pain and is talking more than ever, asking her the English words for a bizarre variety of things. It is the day he has said he will try to stand.

"Music. It makes us very happy. Me, I can dance better than anyone. And I am very brave." As he speaks, he starts to roll out of the hammock. The woman helps him to his feet and can feel his muscles tensing in pain. He is still weak but determined. He soon leans forward, his hands on his knees, then slowly straightens up at her side, a great grin shining on his face.

The woman laughs, startled by the sound from her throat. She sees this boy for the first time upright and is struck by his long face. The familiar scarring on his back and arms and legs only highlights, in the woman's mind, the front of him now visible—smooth-skinned, close-cropped hair, a high forehead on the heart-shaped face, long neck, square shoulders, small nose, bright eyes, brown with the whites shaded a light pink like the sunrise.

She had thought he was around ten, but when she observes the build of his muscles, the Adam's apple in his throat, she wonders if he isn't twelve or thirteen. He is a handsome boy in all respects, but especially because of his disarming smile, that gap between the two top front teeth only accentuating the straight teeth and making him that much more charming. She shakes her head at his confidence.

Then she sees something dangling from a string she noticed around his neck earlier. Since he has never stood facing her before, she could not see it until now. His eyes follow hers, and he says, "This is my pen for when I go to school. You may touch it."

The woman leans forward and fingers it. She can smell the salve on his back. The pen is a red ballpoint, the cheap, plastic kind where you can see the staff of ink inside. It is almost empty.

The boy nods at her neck. "You have a pen too?" he asks.

She straightens and feels the strip of leather he has noticed. She knows a ring with a black stone dangles from it next to her skin, but she does not know why it is there. She found it when she first woke here in a coherent state. In the dark she rubs the ring, and it makes her feel less alone. Now the woman thinks it might be better not to show this to these boys. So she leaves it inside her shirt and hesitates.

The boy adds, "It is good to have something you hope for and dream about. It is good to keep these things close to our hearts."

Again the woman does not know how to respond, but he calls out in a loud voice, "Brother! I am standing!" He turns to her, drops his voice, and says as if sharing a great secret, "Me, I am always hungry."

Now that the group is moving, the woman becomes weaker. She is the second to last one in line as they trudge through the jungle. They hike along muddy paths, going from clearing to clearing. In some places plant life rises fifteen feet above them. Branches grope in all directions, leaves the size of a human head always facing the sun. Many times the woman feels like she cannot breathe as they walk stooped through the tunnels created by the bigger boys and their pangas.

Their only water supply is stagnant, smelly stuff that the woman is afraid to drink. But she is forced to when she can think of nothing but her thirst. Her arms and legs are cut by rough brush. Monkeys chatter as they move. Her back is always aching as she crouches and walks, day after day, hour after hour.

She hears a phrase often among the children: *"Eyali djamba. Njamba, eyaliboyé."* She asks the boy she cared for, who seems never to leave her side, "What does it mean?"

"This is the language of the place we are in now, so me, I am not sure."

"You *know* where we are?"

"My brother says this is Zaïre. And the one who looks like the youngest, but isn't—he is from a Pygmy tribe. That is Etoka, and it is his language."

The woman asks, "What do you think it means?"

"Something like 'This is the way it is in the forest.'"

The two brothers are a strange pair. The older one sits solemn-faced with wide eyes and rarely smiles. As he leads their ragtag gang through the rain forest, he radiates a quiet authority.

One night the two boys sit beside each other, and the woman sees the older one is whittling a small rhino out of the rubbery wood of the trees all around them. He hands this to his brother, and the younger boy closes his eyes and bows his head in thanks. The woman is deeply moved by the act of small kindness from this teenager who, she has noticed, sleeps with his gun and panga on either side of him.

This elder boy looks up and catches her staring at them. She expects him to become angry, as he did earlier that day when her hand brushed his arm again unintentionally. Now he says of his brother, "He is the child I was not."

"Why won't you tell me your names?" she asks. It has become a routine with them. And she is forgetting how often she has asked this.

The boys exchange glances. The younger one says, "My back is better because of her care."

His brother nods acquiescence but then stands to turn his back on her.

The younger boy says, "My brother, he is called Simba mkali. Fierce Lion in English. Me, I am his brother, so I am also Simba. Simba mdogo. You call me Little Lion."

Chapter 41

At night, the woman tries to sleep on the ground like the children do, but ants keep her awake and thoughts of snakes torment her. One evening she can no longer wave her arms to ward off the mosquitoes that emerge as soon as the sun goes down.

Little Lion crawls over to the woman and says, "Me, I see your skin. Here, sit up and I will help you indeed." He smears mud on her face that hardens into a protective shell. Simba mkali sees this. The woman catches the jealous light in his eyes as Little Lion gently strokes the mud into place around her eyes. She looks over the younger brother's shoulder at the elder one and knows she has broken some unwritten rule.

After Simba mkali walks away, the woman says, "Little Lion, you have gentle hands. And you're a good boy to help me like this. Simba mkali's not pleased, though. Why?"

"He is afraid for me. It is the same reason he was angry when you touched him." The woman has been puzzled about this, that no one will allow her to touch them. She hears the children's cries at night and yearns to help them, but every attempt she makes to hold them in the dark meets with fear and hostility. Her heart is broken by their anguish and her own confusion. She wants to give back.

"Why? Little Lion, why won't any of them let me closer?"

"You are a woman. The soldiers taught them that when a woman touches them, they become sick with slim."

The woman says, "What?"

"The slimming sickness. You get thin and die. This is a sad thing. Me, I don't believe anything these soldiers told us. My brother let you touch me when I was beaten, and your hands brought healing just as his did. But he will not remember this now."

Simba mkali appears and stands over them. He says something in harsh tones to Little Lion, but the woman does not understand. After Simba mkali leaves again, she asks, "What did he say?"

Frowning, Little Lion says, "My brother, he says I talk too much. I am not normal."

His face is crestfallen. As he stands to go, the woman reaches out to take his hand, but Little Lion pulls away. She insists. When he hesitates, the woman turns his hand over and places her palm on his. She is at a loss for words, then says, "Do you see your long fingers, Little Lion? In my culture, you would be good at playing the piano." Her words ring hollow in this place. The boy's blank expression mirrors her own empty recognition. She tries again. "Tell your brother I don't have slim. Tell him I only want to help."

During the day, the woman stumbles with fatigue. She only eats a few of the berries and none of the grasses the children share with her, but she does join them when they stoop to cup the stagnant water of the swamp. Sometimes they sleep during the day, walk a few hours, sleep some more. It is the only retreat from hunger, this sleep.

Flies buzzing, cicadas calling, Little Lion hisses, "Look to the right, madam."

They are skirting a hill. The woman looks into a clearing below and sees a black form hunched over a fallen tree trunk. It rises up, and she is astounded at its bulk. "Gorilla," she says, more to herself than to Little Lion.

The children creep past, and now the woman understands why Simba mkali has led them on such a circular route. He is careful to keep them downwind from the black beasts. The woman stands still and watches a smaller gorilla emerge from the brush and sit beside the larger one. The two do not touch but stare in the same direction.

She is trying to think of new ways to reach out to her young guards. Simba mkali still will not let her close. Then one night she asks the boys, "Do you know how to read?"

The littlest one brings out a tattered book. He is the one from Zaïre, the one called Etoka. She has no idea where he has been keeping it, then realizes he must carry it close to his body, tucked into his shabby shirt. He hands it to her and bows. She opens the cover, but sweat and rain and sunlight have wiped away any trace of the written words. All she can make out are an occasional capital letter and a few barely discernible illustrations.

She does not know how to respond. The book is worthless. Etoka points at the book proudly and asks her something in French. The woman turns to Little Lion for a translation. "He wants to know if he may read it for you," Little Lion says.

The woman blinks. The expectation in the faces of the children around her tells her there is only one answer. *"Mais oui."* She hands the book back to him.

Etoka coughs importantly. The others gather round, squatting in a circle, quiet, attentive. Etoka begins to speak in French. He moves his finger along the blank page in a horizontal pattern, its tip tracing invisible lines of text. His voice rises and falls. She hears an intonation change as he switches into dialogue—a deep voice, then a high-pitched one.

The children laugh.

The woman hears this sound for the first time. She sees their smiles, a gang of eight-year-olds in young men's bodies, and Little Lion leans toward her, smiling. "You understand? This, it is a very funny story."

Again, at night, the woman is listening to the sounds around her. "Little Lion?"

"Yes, madam."

She cannot see him, but she sees something else.

He asks, "Do you see the angels?"

The woman squints. There is no moon. It is very dark, except for these tiny lights flitting back and forth.

Another day, the woman asks Little Lion, "How does Simba mkali know where to take us? Where are we going?"

Little Lion says, "God is leading him."

The woman feels the hard knot of cynicism in her tighten. "I don't think so. Little Lion, please don't tell me we've been wandering in circles."

But she has offended him, and for the first time, he turns his back on her. That afternoon, the group is sleeping when the woman wakes up to Simba mkali's hand over her mouth. The fact that he touches her tells her something extremely important must be happening.

The woman opens her eyes wide. He motions that she must be quiet. She nods. Then he takes his hand away and points toward the bush. She sees Little Lion and the others crouching behind large trees. She looks around her and sees nothing in the cleared area, hears nothing. But Simba mkali is hissing at her to follow, and she obeys. He lies down and she does the same; then he reaches over and covers them both with branches and large leaves. She sees Etoka scramble up a tree and lie flat on a branch above them.

Men's voices enter the jungle. The woman is shocked at the sound and sight of grown men. These big men pass by the clearing. She can see them walking just a few meters away. She does not move, hardly breathes. They are soldiers wearing the same uniform and carrying identical packs, heavily loaded. Whatever army they belong to, they are well supplied, the woman thinks. She counts twenty-three men, then lowers her head and watches the insects crawl onto her arm.

The woman waits for Simba mkali to signal it is safe so they can move on. Instead, once the soldiers have passed, he and three of the older boys start arguing. She assumes they are angry at him for leading them into danger. And then Little Lion comes up behind her and says, "It is you they are fighting about."

"Me?"

"The other boys think you are a danger. They did not believe me when I said you cannot make us sick. You are a threat, they say. They think the soldiers might have been looking for you. They say if the soldiers find us and you are here, then. . . ." He does not finish speaking. Little Lion picks up a rock and throws it hard. A monkey chatters at him angrily.

She looks at the group arguing. Observing his tone and outstretched hands, the woman understands that Simba mkali is defending her. Eventually, the other boys throw one last look in her direction. She wilts under their gazes. Simba mkali gives the sign they are to move on through the bush.

As they walk, Little Lion tells her, "We children have run away because we never want to be anyone's prisoner again. My brother, he was telling them you are someone important. He tells the others to leave you alone, but you are worth feeding, since he will use you to keep us free no matter what."

At nightfall, she thinks they are all asleep when she dozes off. But then the woman wakes. This time she hears crying. Two of the boys are weeping, and Etoka and Simba mkali are holding them, rocking them back and forth. She hears Simba mkali comfort the others by saying the same words over and over. He repeats the tone she has heard in the morning ritual. She only recognizes one of the two words, *noite*. Night.

The woman looks away. Little Lion is lying near her. His eyes are wide open, and tears run over his cheeks. His mouth shapes the same two words.

"What is it?" the woman asks. "A prayer?"

"No, a place. Nevernight."

He's right, she thinks. *This* is *a never-ending night we all seem caught in.* She asks, "What has upset them? And you?"

He does not answer. So she asks, "The soldiers? You are afraid again of the soldiers? Is that it?"

Little Lion sniffs and turns over, still not answering. But the woman sees his shoulders shaking with silent sobs.

Chapter 42

The woman hears the crack of thornbush branches. She whirls, and from where she stands she sees a quick movement out of the corner of her eye, nothing but a shadow.

"What is it?" she calls to Little Lion. He shakes his head. Ahead and below, they can see Simba mkali hacking his way through the underbrush. The woman does not take her eyes off the spot and answers her own question without looking at him. "I'm not sure, probably just my imagination." The woman stops to push the hair out of her eyes. Then she hears a grunt. Just one. A panting grunt. She *knows* that sound.

"Leopard!" she hisses.

She feels the attack, senses the pending attack and turns her head. A movement, a swift shade of movement so fast the woman can hardly focus on it, then the leopard rushes. She freezes, knowing she should *do* something. *"Leopard!"*

A shot rings out, and the birds in the trees around them rise as one, a cloud of noise. "Simba mkali!" the woman screams, and together she and Little Lion tumble down the hill. There is no answer, only the silence that follows any explosion in the bush, as every living thing holds its breath. The woman scrambles down the rest of the way and careens around the corner of the cleared-out area. The boys are waiting for them. They stand in a semicircle, still, looking down.

At their feet lies an enormous leopard stretched full length, so close that Little Lion almost trips over the corpse before coming to a halt.

And beneath it, the body of Simba mkali.

The woman sees Little Lion start backward. Terror crawls over his features, and his face looking up at her is filled with such loss that she must step away at the pain she sees. She tears her gaze from Little Lion and forces herself to look down.

Simba mkali's arm lies outstretched, the rifle a meter away. His fingers curl upward, palm empty. She can see one shoulder and one leg, scrawny and scabbed, but the rest, including his face, is buried under the leopard.

She bends down and puts her hands beneath the animal's belly. "Help me," she says to the boys. The two taller ones lean down beside her, and together they heave as the deadweight pulls against them. They manage to shove the corpse off his chest enough to see an enormous puddle of blood soaking through Simba mkali's blue shirt.

"No. *No!*" In a rage, she braces her back against the tree behind her and shoves the leopard's body completely off the boy with both her feet. Then she drops to her knees beside him and lifts up the cotton fabric, threadbare and torn, searching for the wound.

The leopard's claws have shredded his right shoulder, and the fabric falls apart in her fingers.

Her own hands are the only ones touching him as the rest of the group backs away at the sight of his blood. This covers her palms, her knees, her arms. The stench of it causes her to turn and gag. But when the woman faces Simba mkali again, his eyes open.

Little Lion cries out. A warmth runs up the woman's spine as a wellspring of gratitude rises inside her. She cannot even speak as, automatically, her hands continue searching his side for the source of so much blood loss.

He croaks something she cannot understand. Little Lion shouts out, "The blood, it is the animal's. It just took his breath away. The blood is from the leopard. Heh." The woman sees Little Lion turn around and raise his face to the sky. She is crying and shaking at the toll such an effort has taken. Simba mkali rolls onto his side as a fit of coughing seizes him. The other boys begin to talk all at once, yelling with relief and excitement as they reenact the killing scene.

But the woman is looking at Simba mkali, and he grins from ear to ear at her as Little Lion dances around them both.

That night the boys cannot sit still. Their hollow-eyed suspicion has fled. Many times in the past weeks the woman has tried to draw out their stories, only to have her attempts met with cold contempt. She is not African, not a child. Even worse, as far as the boys are concerned, she is a woman. Little Lion, of course, is different. And sometimes, unbidden, a confession will spring forth from the others, as on the night she woke to their weeping. But for the most part, over the weeks they have remained to her a closed book, unwilling or unable to share about their pasts, each tidbit of information a rare jewel.

On this night, Little Lion entertains them all with his story about a lion. "It is in the time before I was kidnapped a second time. My friend walking beside me had a wooden leg. You know the kind?" He walks with a limp, perfectly imitating the posture and gestures. The children laugh and clap.

"So this friend, he is standing when the lion runs at us. We wave our arms like this and shout, 'Agh! Agh!' " He moves his body like a tree in the wind, and the boys grow quiet. They have all known a terror of wild beasts as they traipse through the jungle. Now the woman shares this with them.

"But the lion, he does not listen. 'Quick,' I say to my friend. 'We must climb this tree.'

" 'Me, how can I climb a tree? Look at my leg,' my friend says. I do not think this is such a good time to explain everything in detail. I am in a hurry indeed. So I grab him, and because I am so brave and strong—"

The other boys interrupt him with a hoot of laughter, covering their mouths with one hand and pointing at him with the other.

". . . and big—"

Again they erupt, holding their sides. The woman is smiling with them and clapping to encourage Little Lion, who now stands with one foot raised and an arm holding on to the imaginary tree branch just above his head. He is losing his balance and swaying back and forth as he waits for the laughter to die down.

"This, I do not understand. Look at me—am I not like a stork in the water? No. I am a boy climbing a tree very fast." He mimes the movement of shinnying upward. The woman can all but see the tree trunk as he scrambles up it. "But my friend, he is still on the ground. So back I go." Again the funny movements, but now downward, and he lands on his back, rolling in a backward somersault.

"I pick up my friend and heave him upward. Oh yes! My friend, he reaches for the branch and pulls himself onto it. I join him, and together we make our way up the tree to a very high place.

"Now you must not forget that what we did happened much more quickly than my telling about it here. For the lion, he is coming! This lion, he reaches our tree and walks around in circles, looking for us."

The woman watches, amazed, as the boy drops to all fours and saunters around the spot where the tree should be, his body a model of feline grace.

"Then this lion, he throws his entire body up the tree. We watch this and are suffering greatly. The lion comes very close with his first lunge. And then . . ."

Little Lion stops and looks them all in the eye, going around the circle slowly. He says, "You feel our fear, yes? What do we smell?"

One of the older boys answers, "The lion's musk."

The woman looks up, surprised. The expressions of terror on their faces show they are there with the two boys in the tree, feeling the bark beneath them, smelling that lion.

Now Little Lion opens both his hands wide, pale palms turned outward. He swivels on the balls of his feet like a dancer. "This danger is very great. The lion leaps a mighty leap, full of strength. My friend cannot climb higher. He yells, 'Agh!' I yell, 'Agh!' The lion growls, 'Agh!'

"And what happens? I fall out of the tree. The lion, he fights with me, but I get away and climb back up again. Then the lion jumps again, and now he has something in his mouth. My friend, he has lost his leg, but it is the wooden peg, and the lion runs off thinking he has his dinner, and we are left in the tree, very happy to be still alive."

He ends the story by lifting his shirt to show the scars, his still-red welts. "See, he did this to me!"

The woman sees the rapt faces, eyes sparkling in the firelight, and wonders if Little Lion knows how great the gift is that he has just given them. He took them somewhere else for a few moments, away from the fear, away from the fatigue.

The woman does not ask where Little Lion's friend is now or why the scars on his back do not look like those a claw would make.

Chapter 43

They finally emerge from the forest and find themselves on an open plain. The woman looks up and sees a night sky shining in starlight. She turns in a circle, and Little Lion says, "Madam is dancing with the stars."

"No, I . . . it's just so strange. I know their names, but not my own."

"You can call to the stars by name?"

The woman says, "Well, in a way. Look—" she points to the left— "those three stars in a row—can you see them? That is the belt of a great hunter called Orion. See, above and below him are two stars spread out, like his hands and feet would be. And that smudge is actually many stars together, called the Milky Way. Now where . . . ?"

The woman turns in the opposite direction, over her left shoulder and then points. "Ah, there it is."

"What?"

"This is hard with so many stars, but try to focus only on the brightest ones. Squint your eyes."

"Make them small?" Little Lion asks.

"Yes. Now, do you see six bright stars shaped like an arrow, sort of? And there, it looks like an arrow pointing upward. The top of the arrow is four stars. The tail is made up of two stars called Pointers. They point to those four stars at the arrowhead. That bit is called the Southern Cross. That is south." She rotates, pointing three more times. "And that is north, west, and east."

Little Lion is jumping from one foot to the other. "You must tell this to my brother." He is off. A few moments later he returns with Simba mkali. "I have told him you know how to listen to the stars." He turns his face toward his brother, and the woman is struck again by the adoring gaze.

Simba mkali says a string of sentences so fast, the only word the woman hears is *noite*. Little Lion sees she has not understood and interprets. "He says he knew a commander who learned from the night like you. This commander was a great soldier, killed very many people, and was never afraid. He led them in night marches and always brought them where they should be. My brother asks if you can teach him. Please."

The woman tries not to think about the implication—that they have been wandering aimlessly all these many weeks. *Or has it been months?* She glances up at the sky again and can remember at least two full moons. She must ask the question, but it comes out sounding more like an accusation, her voice on edge. "Ask your brother where he thinks he has been leading us."

"I know that," Little Lion says. "We have been following the forest, and now the forest has ended. We look for a river, and that will bring us to a lake. We cross the lake, and we find a camp of refuge. I know of these camps. I have been in one or two before the soldiers came. These are good places, where there are schools. All my brother and I want is to study. So he is bringing us there. East."

The woman fights the panic, senses she is peering over a precipice. Not only has she lost herself; she has lost her way. *These boys have no idea where they are,* she realizes. A lake, the edge of trees, some river—how could anyone use these as guideposts?

"Tell him, teach him where east is," Little Lion tells her.

She stares at the boys. "You really don't know?"

Simba mkali answers, and Little Lion translates, "He says he has heard the soldiers talk of these places, but that it changed. Sometimes the enemy came from the north, and sometimes from the west. But he has known all along that if he could find east and head there, he would find refuge."

So the woman takes a deep breath and repeats her explanation of the constellations as Little Lion translates. Despite her despair at discovering the boys truly have no idea which direction they are heading, she is grateful for their quick understanding. She can see it dawning on their faces as she points out more and more shapes in the sky. "Look, to the right and down a bit from Orion."

"The great hunter?" Little Lion says.

His eagerness calms her slightly. "Yes. Now this is for both of you. That is a lion, but he's sitting upside down."

The younger boy claps his hands, but Simba mkali has eyes only for the Southern Cross. The woman points out another group of stars slightly behind them. "That group looks like a cross as well. That's why it's called the False Cross. Look for the Pointers. Then you'll have the right one."

The boys start talking excitedly, and the woman cannot follow them. "It is not a story. You see," Little Lion says. "You see, I told you God is leading us. Each day we pray which way, and God shows us where to walk. He will bring us to a place of safety. We pray for our brother and follow him, for God is guiding him toward the light. With his cross. Now you are helping show us that when we follow the right cross, not the false one, he will lead us. Indeed, God is our refuge."

The woman stares at the boy. "Where did you learn to talk that way?" she asks.

When he does not answer, the woman sees only a small form, weary with wishing, haggard in hope. She turns to the older brother and, on a whim, asks him if *he* has a story. She knows from watching him that he cannot be as open as Little Lion. Now she is hoping their closeness here under the stars will encourage him to share something with her.

He answers her slowly, so she can understand the Portuguese. "I am a man. In many things, he is still a boy."

"What kinds of things?" the woman asks.

"He can trust."

"And you can't?" she asks, wondering more than ever what his life has been like to yield such eyes.

"I trust God alone."

"But who taught you both to talk this way, so religious—like pastors, ministers in a church?"

Again the blank stares.

"You know what a church is? A big stone building . . ." Her voice trails off. *What's the use?* She thinks of something else. "You trust Simba mdogo, don't you?"

"Yes," the older boy says.

"And yourself? You trust yourself, yes?"

But Simba mkali will not answer her a second time. He turns away.

Little Lion has watched them stumble through this dialogue. He strokes her arm. "My brother, he does not say so, but we are both wondering, do *you* trust God?"

The woman answers by looking upward, the starlight a mocking map of lands long forgotten. "How?" she asks, unable to mask her dismay at not even knowing all she has lost. "How can I possibly?"

The woman cannot get away from the fear. She knows she is fighting a raging fever. She retreats into herself—sick, unstable, weak. The knowledge that they have had no sense of direction has thrown her into despondency. She can only think she will die and be left behind by these children. She sees the same landmarks over and over and is convinced they are walking in circles.

When they stop to rest, Little Lion often comes to sit beside her. He is sometimes happy to talk about his adventures, and the woman never quite knows which versions are true, since there are so many heroic tales. "How many times were you kidnapped?" she asks.

"Five times," he says.

Another time he tells her a story and starts it by saying, "Me, I was never kidnapped." He is talking to her as she lies on the ground and does not care anymore about the dust and insects. He tells her stories, and the woman knows that it is his voice that keeps her from taking the last step, of saying she will not get up and walk anymore.

He asks her, "What do you see?"

The woman answers, "Only darkness."

"Come out of that place," he tells her, but the woman can only close her eyes.

Little Lion explains the significance of the gift she has given his older brother. "A wise man knows where he is headed. Now he can lead us to the lake, and on the other side we will be protected."

The woman sees water and waves. She is in a boat, has just crossed a lake as wide as a sea, and does not know what to do when they land.

"Go forward—go and ask," a child's voice urges her.

A woman is reaching for her, pulling her out of the boat. People making so much noise all around. Then she hears the children's voices, her children. They are crying out. The woman looks behind her. Little Lion is shouting and struggling as a huge soldier pulls him away from the arms of Simba mkali.

"No!" the woman yells. She staggers and falls. The other woman catches her, but these are the same soldiers they hid from in the bush. Same uniforms, same weapons. Desperate, the woman can do nothing now that these huge men with machine guns have captured them, taken them all prisoner.

She sees her boys kicking the soldiers. The woman goes hysterical, screaming, "Don't take my child! Don't kill my boy!"

The last thing she hears is Little Lion calling out, "She does not know where she has been."

The last thing she sees are her boys running away again, disappearing into the bush.

Chapter 44

It is a voice.

"Yes, I believe she actually saw the troops through the children's eyes after traveling with them so long. Over."

A pause, then, "You must understand, she is physically *and mentally* ill. Such questions would only confuse her further. No, I don't know how long she has been like this. When we found her, she covered her ears and screamed, screamed like a child. When David and I finally got her to calm down, she stood up and fainted. Then David picked her up; she lay in his arms, lifeless, hot with fever, but with her eyes opened. She has been like that ever since. Comatose, with eyes open. Over."

The voice approaches, and the woman sees it comes from another woman holding a walkie-talkie against her mouth. She is reading a handful of papers, looking up, she says, "Yes, I know. . . . No. Listen, I have to go. . . . Just see what you can find out about any Western woman gone missing in Zaïre. . . . Yes, an American accent. I've heard her calling out. . . . I know. Check all the embassies. . . . Over. Roger, Whiskey Mike out."

The woman hears the voice, but there is a loud hum in her ears, and it is hard to concentrate on what this woman is saying.

Yet the other woman is waiting for her when she opens her eyes again. The other woman smiles kindly and has broth for her to drink. Sweet, lukewarm soup.

"My name is Edith."

A sudden fear settles on the woman, causing her to shake involuntarily.

"You are very sick, you know. Here, drink this, then go back to sleep."

The woman likes Edith's touch, soft. She tries to focus on the face and sees again her smile and the gentle eyes. When she straightens, this woman called Edith carries herself like a queen, turning lightly on the balls of her feet. A purple ribbon gathers fifty braids at the base of her neck.

She returns and the woman sees Edith's round face, full cheeks, the outline of fine cheekbones, a straight nose, tiny ears. But Edith's greatest beauty is in her hands, long and graceful. Her cool fingers brush the woman's hair, gently working out the snags.

The woman says, "I remember traveling many weeks—maybe it was months—with children. My boys . . ."

"What else?"

The woman stops talking.

In the days that follow, the woman knows only that she is weak, feverish, sweating. The effort to sit or stand sometimes exhausts her. Her gut is a knot of cramps; she suffers from nausea even after the fever and chills abate.

Edith is talking with someone from her office in the same building as the bed where the woman sleeps.

A man's voice says, "She should stay here with you for another reason. Your training. You know how to help people like her who . . . have lost more than just their way in the physical sense. She is lost mentally, searching in her spirit. You have no idea what she's been through. But I'm afraid. . . ."

"Afraid of what, Emmanuel?"

"I'm afraid she has lost a great deal—her identity, her mind, who knows what else?"

Edith answers, "Yes, I see it in the way her eyes will not come to rest on anything. The fear, like an animal's when it thinks the hunter is near. Here, in this place, she is safe."

The woman rests on top of a bed and watches the mosquito netting spin like a knotted cocoon, its ends in twisted butterfly wings. She watches the dark corners of the ceiling, searching for small bats' heads, mice, the lizards frozen onto the wall. A baobab nut thuds onto the wrought-iron roof.

And then she is outside, sitting under that same tree. Edith's idea. Edith says she doesn't eat enough. Edith thinks the fresh air will give her back her appetite.

So the woman sits on a wooden bench under the baobab tree, the one with the owl's nest. The woman sees him coming over the meadow—low, dark, wide wingspan. The night before, he slammed into her door, hunting for the bats in the roof or maybe the rats.

Soft wind rustles the dried leaves of autumn. In the days since she arrived, the baobab leaves have spiraled downward—she watched this from her window—until the tree now stands bare-branched and beckoning, the bench at its base. The baobab, with its rootlike branches, looks upside down to the woman.

She hears the two women behind her in the devotions building. They talk and sweep—their voices soft and serving. She hears the radio operator say, over and over, "Arusha." A broom falls. Wood bounces against stone. Men's and women's voices. A crow, the generator in the background, a baby's cry. A lizard scuttles under the leaves.

The dust is everywhere. This brick-red dust dyes everything it touches. It cakes her shoes and ankles, sifts like rusty powdered sugar onto every surface. It blows around her when the wind picks up.

This, the woman thinks, *is a place of wind and dust.*

When Edith joins her on the bench, the woman asks, "Where am I?"

"This place? It's called Inside the Drum." Edith takes the woman's hand and holds it with both of hers. "Only the maker knows what a drum is made of, what its inside looks like, what its purpose is."

The woman smiles. By now she is used to Edith speaking in poetry. And now she has thought of a way to make Edith laugh.

Edith asks, "Why are you smiling?"

"Because I meant, *what country* am I in?"

Edith's laughter refreshes, a spring of bubbling sounds, and the woman cannot get enough of it. She watches Edith's graceful form almost fall off the bench as she shakes up and down with delight. "You, you know this. You heard the radio operator? And what language are the women sweeping behind you speaking? It is Kiswahili."

The woman nods. "You're right. I haven't heard Portuguese spoken since I came here."

"That's right, my sister. *Karibu Tanzania.* You are welcome here."

"And Inside the Drum is. . . ."

"The name the local villagers give this compound."

As if on cue, a group of village children run up to the fence and wave at them. "Mama Edith, *shikamoo!* Greetings!"

"Marahaba!" Edith calls back to them, waving.

Edith begins each of their sessions together by blessing the woman. When Edith prays, she covers her face with one open hand. The other runs up and down the woman's arm, stroking away whatever she sees and the woman cannot. She blesses the woman's will.

Part of the woman resists this, but she does not want Edith to know her true feelings. *She* does not know her true feelings. She surprises herself by feeling ashamed to admit, in the face of Edith's goodness, that she may have turned her back on God somewhere in the darkness, that endless "never night" that her boys talked about. She may be a bad person. So she pretends and allows Edith to continue blessing her, day after day.

After her prayers, Edith listens and looks at the woman as the woman tells her about the children. Edith has asked her to work backward, and in the course of several weeks, the woman manages to get as far as the explosion the night Simba mkali and the rest of her boys found her and brought her to the place where Little Lion was recovering from his beating. And then, the woman can go no further.

"What happened before the explosion that night?" Edith asks.

The woman stares off into space and can no longer hear her voice until Edith says, "Please, can you wiggle your toes for me?" Then she is back under the baobab, and she and Edith are smiling at each other.

▦ ▦ ▦

"Have you had any trouble with the pit?" Edith asks the woman. They are walking together toward the walled-off toilet corner of the compound reserved for the women.

The woman laughs. "You should have seen what I had to do in the jungle," she says. "My needs are simple."

Edith nods. "So often most of our energy goes into trying to tame what is around us, reconciling our surroundings with our needs. The simpler our needs, the more reconciled we become."

One morning the water truck doesn't arrive, so Julie and Excellence gather water from the river. Back and forth they walk, the full plastic buckets balanced perfectly on their heads, chins high, hands at their sides. Soft breezes rustle; tree-leaf shadows dance. Always in the background: the generator, the chickens, children running somewhere.

▦ ▦ ▦

Edith has invited her to sit in on an art class of children meeting in the devotions building, a round, thatch-roofed structure with tree-trunk poles as supports and glassless windows opening onto the compound yard. It is the heart of Inside the Drum. The woman walks up the concrete steps and crosses the threshold. The children are bent over paper, some with paints and charcoal, most using crayons.

She is not sure if they have been this quiet when they met without her, when she might have been listening from her bench under the baobab. She looks around and greets them: *"Habari."* The children say and do nothing. She sits in a corner and hears Edith talking, but the children will not stop staring at her. The woman stands up and leaves.

"I will not force her to go back to places she is not ready to visit."
Edith's voice outside the woman's window. "When she heard me say
that my children have also lost everything, she only looked up, as if
her body could recognize her own plight but not her mind. Her movements tell me she has not lost her mind as you say, but her *self,* her
sense of where she belongs. She lives in a nonworld."

"You are a healer," says another voice. "You help your children distinguish between their fantasy escape worlds and reality."

Edith sighs. "I know, Emmanuel. And this *is* her predicament. What
else can I do?"

"In this land, on this continent, there may be a way for her to find
herself again. Perhaps God will reach down from his heavy sky and
touch her through the beauty of his wild creation. Take her to a place
where she can hear the music of the stars. Let us continue to pray for
her healing.

"Lord, if anyone can find themselves again, it is in this vast plain of
beauty. I wish this for her, that she would hear the stars sing and know
again who she is, *what* she is. I see this. Her running away with those
children, struggling to make peace with herself, haunted by a specter.
Let this walkabout through Africa grow to be a search for identity, a
search for healing and a reason why. And ultimately, a search for you,
dear God."

"Will you reveal yourself to her, please, Lord?" Edith's voice.

Edith reaches toward her, and the woman can feel the muscled arms
squeezing her tight. They are the same height. Edith says, "What
comes from the heart must not be hidden. You will tell me when you
understand this?"

The woman nods but thinks, *This is all happening somewhere else.*

Chapter 45

"We are going on safari," Edith tells the woman one day.

She looks at Edith, puzzled.

"It will be good for you," Edith says. "We will meet up with my little brother, who at this point is between clients, and he will go with us. This word *safari*—it means 'journey.'"

"His or mine?" the woman asks. "Am I ready?"

"We will do this slowly," Edith says, "introducing you back to the real world—'outside,' as you call it. And we will discover if there is anyone out there who can help us learn more about your own story."

They fly north in a small plane to the nearest city, Mwanza. The woman looks on the map and sees it is in the northwestern corner of Tanzania, on the southernmost shore of the great Lake Victoria, the source of the Nile. Lake Victoria borders Kenya, Uganda, and Tanzania.

Looking out the plane's window brings the woman a vague feeling of familiarity. But hidden behind that knowledge lurks a fear of the unknown, a fear of what she does not know and should, a fear of the open space. In the forest she could hide and pretend to see where peril threatened. Now she cannot even recognize its face.

Edith leans forward from her seat behind the woman and tells her their connecting flight will not leave until early the next morning.

Then they will fly east to Arusha, a small city in northeastern Tanzania and the jumping-off point for most safaris into the Serengeti National Park. The woman asks Edith why she kept hearing their radio operator at the compound trying to hail Arusha, and Edith says it was because her organization has an office there.

When the woman sees Lake Victoria from the plane, she says, "It's even larger than Lake Tanganyika." She drinks in the sight of the gigantic body of water after so many weeks in the compound of nothing but dry dust. "Do you think we could go swimming in it?"

Edith says, "I'm afraid that's not possible. Do you see anyone in the water? That's because of bilharzia. Tiny worms transmit the disease by entering through the skin and attaching themselves to a human host's intestines or bladder. Weeks later, a rash and high fever develop. But not until several months to years after exposure does the real damage show up—irreversible destruction of the internal organs. The worms infest most streams and lakes in this area."

The woman nods and shivers.

Edith says, "Don't worry. It's one of the first things we treated you for—that and other parasites. You're fine now."

Once in Mwanza, the woman approaches the waterfront. "It should smell different," she says more to herself than to Edith. "A large body of water should smell damp and briny."

"Like salt?"

"Yes."

"Ah. You've lived by the sea," Edith says. "The change of scenery is already shaking clues loose."

They enter the city center on foot. It is the first time since she was found that the woman has been in a large group of people. Edith keeps looking at her, but the woman is determined to prove she has made progress. She glances at their shopping list of supplies as they walk through the market area. "Canned food, fresh fruit, rope," she says out loud.

Edith says, "Let me do the shopping. Why don't you just look around? Shall we meet back here in an hour if we don't see each other before then? Here, take my watch." When the woman starts to object, Edith says, "Don't you know what we say about watches here? People in the West have watches; we have the time." She chuckles softly. Then Edith unstraps a simple lady's watch with a plastic band and hands it to her. "Come on, it is just a cheap one, I promise."

"Thank you." The woman is embarrassed by the unexpected gift but even more surprised that Edith will leave her alone in the crowd. She does not mind, though. She wanders through the main shopping district, going in and out of shops, checking out the street stalls, listening to the people around her argue about prices.

The woman stops to admire a stall with pink-and-purple-striped baskets. The woman who comes forward to meet her says, "I make them myself."

"You do very fine work," the woman says.

"You would like to buy some maybe?"

At that moment, the woman realizes she has no money. She goes through the motion of searching her pockets, then shakes her head, confused.

The stall keeper says, "Ah, your husband. You are afraid to spend too much money because your husband would not approve. I must tell you, sister, in my family *I* am the one who tells my husband what to spend." She reaches for the woman's hand and softly slaps the palm, laughing out loud.

The woman looks down. Her touch is like velvet. She joins in the laughter as the stall keeper continues holding her hand in a limp embrace. "Maybe next time you will buy something from me, eh? God bless you, my sister." Her other hand comes up to stroke the woman's arm once. Then she releases her and returns to her chair at the back of the stall.

The woman stands staring after her, listening for something, but not knowing what. Then she says, "Yes. *Asante sane.* Thank you so much." It was one of the first Kiswahili phrases Little Lion had taught her.

The woman turns at the sound of a honking horn on the other side of the street. A truck stands caught between a herd of goats and two old taxis. A man steps out and yells at the goatherds. Inside the truck the woman sees a man with deeply tanned face and hands. He opens his door and stands up in the opening. One arm on the roof, he shades his eyes, looking for someone over the crowd's heads. Instinctively the woman ducks into a doorway as he growls in an undertone at his driver. She waits until they pull away before returning to the street.

Why did I do that? How did I know that wasn't a friend, perhaps even someone searching for me? The woman asks the question and knows immediately that the answer lies in the desperate fear, the sense of what she *should* know, that will not leave her alone. She feels watched. She feels followed. But who is stalking her? Or is she just being paranoid? Edith warned her it was a common enough occurrence, given her circumstances. Yet her instincts just moved her into a place of hiding. Well, how much did she dare trust a forgotten self? *I can't even make out my own identity, let alone that of an enemy.*

No. She shakes her head. This is something she now knows for sure. Somewhere out there, someone is tracking her. *But when Edith asks me how I know, I won't be able to answer.*

The woman forces herself to walk past the rest of the stalls, then stops at the end of the row and takes a deep breath. She looks around. There stands a teenage boy beside a blanket covered with carved, jade-colored soapstone. She picks up one showing the arms of two abstract figures interlocked, as one pulls the other upright, and the one below upholds the one on top.

The young man comes over to stand beside her. "You are very lucky today, madam."

"Why is that?" She turns the piece over in her hands, its touch alone calming her further.

"Because I am your best friend."

She smiles at him.

His eyes dance as he brings out an orange rag, gently takes the carving from her, and begins to polish it vigorously. "See, now the sun itself shines out of the stone," he says.

The woman nods. "Is it—?"

"Yes, madam?"

"Did you carve this yourself?"

"I did."

"Where did you learn the design?"

"At a special school for stone carvers. My teacher was from Zimbabwe." He steps even closer to her, and the woman glimpses blue-purple tones as his skin catches the sunlight.

She says, "I . . . have seen this kind of art before. I think Zimbabwean art must be famous."

"Yes. Art and AIDS—we call this disease 'slim.' This is what the rest of the world knows about Africa. It is like the weather, always with us. What is your name, madam?"

The woman swallows. "I . . ."

He laughs very loudly, then says, "Very well, madam. I am Heaven. *Karibu.* You are welcome."

The woman sees Edith watching her from across the street. She quickly thanks the boy and joins Edith, Heaven's welcome ringing in her ears.

That night the woman dreams again of a child crying. She seeks comfort in the thought that they will be leaving Mwanza at dawn. A sense of urgency has grown with each hour they remained. *We're running out of time. But time for what?* She cannot shake the incessant sense of dread, of stumbling blind in dangerous territory. Or the voices in her head that insist she must keep going. *The only true danger is to stand still, for then I'll surely be caught and killed, and all I ever loved will be destroyed and thrown into the pit on top of me.*

Just after sunrise the next day, as they bump their way over the road back toward the airstrip, the woman catches one more glimpse of the gigantic Lake Victoria. The deafening voices of the night before stay silent as gray light on water holds her gaze.

The woman catches herself wishing she had reached out to touch Heaven's arm.

In Arusha they pick up a four-wheel-drive Toyota Hilux truck. By noon Edith is driving them through Masailand, where the woman sees round huts, men in bright red-plaid blankets, sticks in hand, moving through the dry dust. Edith tutors her in Kiswahili, teaching her more words, and they laugh at the woman's mumbling as she memorizes vocabulary. The shortwave radio hanging from the roof between them hums and chatters.

All day they drive over the dusty, potholed road. They make one stop in Masailand and pass teenage boys and girls with white paint on their faces.

Edith teaches her the Masai phrase *Sih-day.* "Peace be with you." She explains in sober tones that the white-faced Masai children are celebrating a recent circumcision. Both boys and girls.

They stop in a traditional village set up for tourists. At the witch doctor's hut, the crumpled old man with red eyes will not speak to the woman. "A power greater than any I serve protects you. I can see that, even if you cannot." He turns away and continues his "drumming to heal." That is what the sign in front of his hut says.

In this village a group of children follows them from hut to hut. One teenage girl catches the woman watching her nurse a newborn. The girl approaches the woman when she is finished and hands the baby to her. The woman puts him over her shoulder, and he lets out a resounding burp. Everyone laughs.

"You know, you have borne children," Edith says.

The woman looks at her over the soft head of the baby.

"Look at you. Your hand cups his neck, supporting the head, fingers spread. Only a mother does that without being told."

"Yes, and I know what it feels like to nurse. That's what I was thinking as I watched her." The woman hands the baby back to his mother.

"Your body has told me you carried a heavy baby."

"How . . . ?" The woman begins to speak, then realizes the answer the same moment Edith replies.

"When you were ill, I noticed your stretch marks."

"It's true." The woman cannot shrug off the confusion descending on her. She knows it's true because a growing conviction that there is a child out there somewhere—her child—has stoked the fire of panic deep within her. Somewhere her child waits to be rescued. The woman knows, more surely than she knows herself even, that if she waits too long, her child may die.

Edith's voice brings her back to herself. Edith has squatted down and asks the circle of children around them, "What do you need?"

One boy who could be eight says, "I mostly need a bicycle so I can ride to school."

"I need a television. I want some shoes and clothes," says the boy in a white shirt.

His little brother is holding on to one hand. He says, "I need some toys . . . a soft drink. A nice place to live."

The woman asks him, "How old are you?"

"I am three, madam."

The other children laugh and cover their faces with their right hands, peeking out between the fingers. Edith points at them in turn. Around the circle she goes as they recite:

"I need some clothes, and I want a house."

"I need a fridge to freeze drinks in plastic bags to sell."

"I need a house and a stove to bake things I can sell."

"I need a watch and a pair of shoes. I want a bicycle so I can get to school on time, because the bus is always late."

Until the last child, very small, another younger brother of some-one else, says, "I need a toy car. I want a gun and a bicycle."

Edith thanks them, straightens up, and starts to leave, when a little girl runs up to the woman and asks for pens and paper for school. The woman gasps at her touch, then turns away, back to the truck.

There she is surprised to find tears running down her cheeks.

They spend the night near a mountaintop at the edge of the Serengeti Plain. Edith says this ridge is actually very near the Ngorongoro Crater. She points, and the woman thinks she sees water in the dis-tance. It is chilly and foggy on the mountaintop. They sleep in tents set up on grass, and it feels too soft to be the ground.

In the middle of the night the woman wakes up on her side, feeling the familiar warmth of another body along the back of hers, being held. She rolls over, not surprised to find the tent empty. What takes her breath away is the assurance that the heat felt so familiar.

She is used to sharing her bed.

The next morning they drive the rest of the way up the mountain. Surrounded by such thick fog, the woman cannot see farther than a few trees ahead. Then, as they maneuver the switchbacks down the other side, the fog lifts to reveal a canvas of vast savanna plains full of flowing grass, game dotting the horizon, and acacias pushing up the sky with their flat treetops.

Chapter 46

Edith's brother, Paul, meets them at the gate of the park. According to Edith, he is a professional safari guide. And for some reason they will not tell the woman, the three of them are going game-driving. As they enter the Serengeti, they grow quiet. The place is incredibly beautiful—dry air, breezes with the scent of grass, and granite *kopjes,* or little rock islands rising up out of the grasslands. Before them, as far as the eye can see, a broad horizon of grass and game. . . .

With two vehicles, they game-drive all day, and this is what they see: Lions. More lions than even Paul thought possible. Prides of eighteen and twelve and twenty-two. More than a hundred. The woman sees them hunting. She sees cubs. A cheetah struts across their trail in the thin, golden light, turns and looks straight at her. She hangs out the window of the truck and breathes it all in—the African sights and sounds. Twice she sees leopards draped across a high branch, legs and tails dangling, fat bellies hanging over the wood.

When they stop to eat, the woman tells Paul the story of Simba mkali and the last time she saw a leopard. *My boys,* she thinks, *they are never far.* Edith says nothing, but the woman can tell Edith already knows how much she has been missing them, worrying about them, everywhere looking for them, even back in Mwanza, searching. . . .

At night she hears sounds all around, baboons barking. And again the reminders of her time in the bush. *It's strange,* she thinks. *My time with the boys is really my only memory, and even that seems like a dream now—the dirt and hunger and fear. Am I then left with no past? No. I have a past; I just don't know what's in it. Are there children? Do I have more than one? Is there a man who loves me, who is looking for me? Who else is pursuing me?*

At that time, with the questions whirling all around the woman, one image appears; one voice rises above the rest. More clearly than ever she can see Little Lion's back, still hear his stories, still understand his searching heart. And it is almost more than she can bear to think of them all still out there, still exposed, still in danger. Is it their pending doom, her boys' fate, that keeps her in the grip of panic? Or someone else's? The woman ponders these things over and over.

Halfway through that night, she looks out the flap to see Edith's flashlight on inside her tent. Edith's silhouette on the canvas wall tells the woman that she's sitting up and holding a book on her lap. The woman lies back down and falls asleep to the sound of Edith's voice reading aloud.

They are up at dawn. Red sun. Gold, yellow, copper-top tinted grass. Nineteen lions line up to hunt, moving closer, the little one staying behind. Colors all around, cool savanna grass, soft, dry breeze.

If only I could capture those colors, the woman thinks, *the sky heavy on umbrella acacias, as if the weight of so much beauty pushes down on everything living and we cannot bear the burden.*

The woman asks, "So, Paul, can *you* tell me exactly what it is your sister is doing?"

Edith's little brother is more than six feet tall. He speaks in flawless British English, and his eyes glow like dark coals. The woman's eyes rivet onto his hands. Like her own, they never stop moving.

"They're calling it the largest repatriation effort ever. For thirty years the conflict in Mozambique has dragged on. More than one-third of the population of seventeen million people has had to flee the country. I mean, they are everywhere. Refugees from Mozambique live in Tanzania, Malawi, Zimbabwe, Swaziland, even South Africa."

His long fingers tick off the countries as he says their names. "But the peace agreement signed last year has set off a chain reaction of people returning home. And this is the most amazing part."

The woman is puzzled for a moment and does not know why. Then she realizes his answer seems to have nothing to do with her question. Still, she nods. "Paul, you speak as if you've studied this in depth."

He laughs. "Too much depth and not enough breadth perhaps."

Edith says, "He doesn't like to tarnish his reputation as a Rambo in the jungle, but Paul here has a master's degree in political science from Cambridge and a doctorate in international studies from Harvard."

"It's my sisters' fault."

"Edith?" The woman wonders what he means as she tries to digest Edith's description.

"Well, her and my other sisters. We are a large family of nine children. And in Tanzania, the continued education of children is a responsibility of the entire family. My uncles and elder siblings all insisted I study abroad. They helped pay the exorbitant fees. If parents cannot afford their children's school fees, then the rest of the family has an obligation to pay. Now that I'm an adult, I am responsible for helping put my nieces and nephews through school."

"What do your other brothers and sisters do?" the woman asks.

"They're involved in various aid groups and NGOs."

"That's nongovernmental organizations," Edith says. "For example, our eldest sister works in Botswana with the United Nations Children's Fund, UNICEF."

"And Edith?" The woman wonders if now she will get an answer to the question she asked earlier. It is something she has often asked herself, but not Edith.

"Edith? She's a child psychologist. Her specialty is providing trauma therapy. Anyway, I'm the baby, and as my sister the psychologist would say, that's probably why I rebelled."

Edith laughs, and Paul looks from one woman to the other. They have left the other vehicle back at camp for the morning and are driving cross-country. The steering wheel jerks in his hands as he tries to keep on the track. "What? Don't tell me. . . . Why didn't you tell her these things? You mean . . . she doesn't *know* what we're doing?" he asks his sister.

"She didn't ask."

The woman groans. "So now I'm asking. Edith, I saw you with the children. Now we're out here. What's going on?"

"Yes, so now that you ask, I will tell you. The truth is, we came out here to collect my brother because we are going on safari."

"I know that. We're doing it now."

"No, I mean more safari, a longer journey. What Paul was talking about. I wanted to give you a taste of the Serengeti, and Paul had to return his vehicle to a lodge on the other side of the park, so we thought we would combine the two opportunities. As he said, there is something very exciting happening right now in a certain country bordering Tanzania. Paul and I need to go there."

"To Mozambique?" The word rings through the woman.

"To Mozambique, where there is an emergency need for workers during the mass repatriation program."

"But why did you bring me along?"

"Because I thought this safari would do you good. And because we are so extremely shorthanded. And because this way I can remain with you. Did you have someplace else you were planning to go?"

"But why . . . ?"

"My sister, it is very simple. You can help me. You may not know this yet about yourself, but you yearn to help children."

After Paul delivers his vehicle, they continue on the loop around the park, taking three days to head back toward the entrance they came through. On what Paul warns is their second-to-last night in the park, they manage to set up their tents just before sunset. Then darkness falls, sudden and complete. The woman notices that even the game holds sacred the moments before the stars rise and after the sun has disappeared.

She waits, wondering what the first sound will be. Edith and Paul have both turned in early after dinner, but the woman is not tired, despite getting up before dawn each morning to see the animals.

She feels her way back to the truck and the pile of dried brush and branches they gathered when setting up camp. As she looks down at her feet, a light shines from behind her—a soft light, a muffled light from far away. She turns and stands still for several moments as the moon begins to rise. It glows orange, then yellow—a moon on its back. Edith has told her that in Asia they see a rabbit running. The woman looks for the man in the moon. Now both man and beast have been knocked sideways. Idly she wonders what she should see in the moon here in Africa.

Paul's snoring rings from his tent and, in a curious way, the sound reassures the woman. His near presence gives her a sense of safety. She stoops down and begins the job of moving the wood and scrub over to a midway point in the camp between the tents.

Her lighting the fire acts as a signal sounding in the bush around her. Crickets begin their chorus; the hippos on the other side of the river start to splash and snort and croon to one another. The woman hears the elephants they have passed farther down the road salute one another. She smiles, remembering Edith's words: *"In Africa you are never alone."*

The woman makes the fire without thinking. She did it so often with the boys, it is a part of her unconscious routine. She feels strong, awake, alert. She arranges the fuel as her boys used to, with a large stump sticking out of the campfire. That way, as it burns, she can shove the stump farther into the fire. Thankful for the light from the sky and the fire, the woman secures the site, checking to make sure the truck doors are locked, that she has the keys in her pocket, that no food has fallen out accidentally or made its way into the tent. Then the woman sits down by the fire in one of the collapsible camp chairs.

She watches the flames and can feel her mind and muscles relaxing. The bush rings with sound now, and the woman loses her thoughts among the noise. Edith was right to bring her here. In the days they have been on safari, she *has* grown stronger. She was already healthier after what Edith assured her were really two months at the compound. But now she could actually feel the changes in her body—no more fever or chills, her appetite back, the nausea withdrawn. Any malaria she might have caught must have receded with the fevers.

The woman does not know how much time has passed, but she wakes up because her neck hurts. She has fallen asleep by the fire. She stands and stretches high, her arms pointing to the stars. Their brilliance never fails to catch her by surprise. With the constellation Scorpio wagging its tail at her, the woman makes for bed. The last thing she does is take her boots off and bring them inside; then she zips her tent flap closed, leaving only a small triangle of the opening bare to the mosquito netting.

First the smell wakes her, then the sound. The woman does not know what she was dreaming, but when she wakes, she feels heavy-tired and knows it is still deep night. She glances at the watch Edith gave her, its iridescent face glowing on her wrist. *Three in the morning. That smell, what is it?*

The sound comes from behind her head. When she hears it, the woman sits up in fright, hugging her knees, as whatever it is comes closer and the stink rises around the tent in a cloud of foul rot. The animals around the woman's tent cackle to one another, their calls mixed with snorts and growls.

Hyenas.

The woman saw plenty of them during her time with Little Lion and Simba mkali and the other boys. The children passed their terror of the ugly beasts on to her. She has watched the hyenas often enough, tearing at a corpse with powerful jaws that can crack bones. She knows they smell and sound as awful as they look.

The woman strains to hear Paul or Edith but cannot make out any sounds other than the animals'. There are at least two. She crawls over to the unzipped corner window and peers outside the tent. The glowing tree trunk from her campfire sheds no light on the devastation she can hear happening all around her, and the lack of flames has made the animals bold. The hyenas are digging and turning over the branches she has dragged into camp.

The woman suddenly has an image of a hyena snout shoved into her face. She feels something move against her feet, which rest against the side of the tent. She stifles a scream and backs away from the opening. She wonders how Edith and Paul can sleep through this. She cannot see anything; they must have smelled her.

Thankful that her tent contains no food they would try and steal, the woman sits huddled in the very center, hugging her knees, breathing heavily through her mouth to avoid gagging on the overpowering stench. And realizing that when she was with her boys, everything was different. Then there was the very real danger that the hyenas would sense their vulnerability and attack them, sniffing out the weakest, little Etoka. Her heart wrenches as she thinks of them all still out there. Still vulnerable.

And then the hyenas are gone. One cicada sounds the retreat, another answers, somewhere an owl hoots, and so the normal sounds of the African night return. The woman crawls back into her sleeping bag and curls up in a tight ball, wondering when the night will ever end. *Another three hours and I can finally get up.*

Again she wakes, but now the sleep pulls at her with a force that tells her she has only just barely fallen asleep. And yet it is nearly light.

A moan, a groan. The woman hears a low rumble. An answering rumble, another groan, a guttural pant. She opens her eyes, aiming them at her wrist again, and at the same moment, hears the flap of her tent rip open.

Chapter 47

A giant claw tears at the tiny flap. The woman watches, petrified, as the flimsy fabric gives way. The fur-covered hand with nail-tipped blades moves down as if in slow motion, down from the wall of her tent onto the ground, taking half the material with it.

Through the gap shakes the mane of a lion, a male—an enormous, drooling, openmouthed lion. His musk overpowers the woman, and fear keeps her pinned to the ground, her body rigid inside the sleeping bag. She does not move. She does not breathe. She dares not even blink. The lion grunts and takes a step forward.

She thinks, *He's not looking at me, but he must smell me.*

The lion takes another step and now he stands, filling her tent. From the ground, where the woman has never felt so big and noticeable, she watches the small insects crawling across the fur on his belly. She can hear him panting. Each time he exhales, he grunts, a low laugh.

The muscles in his back leg ripple just once. In a single, sudden movement, he springs at the back wall, clearing her bag without even brushing against it. His tail whips across her face as he falls into the back of the tent, pulling it all down around her.

She waits long enough to take a deep breath. Then, in a mad scramble of panic, the woman scratches the fallen fabric off her face and sees that the lion has escaped the cloak of his own making. In one motion, she kicks off the sleeping bag, leans forward, feeling for her boots, slips them on without tying them, and dashes for the truck. Out of the corner of her eye she sees a second lion, a female this time. She wonders if these two are alone, mating—or will an entire pride follow? Her hand shakes uncontrollably as she turns the key in the door, throws her body onto the seat, and shoves the key into the ignition. The motor roars and shatters the predawn peace.

Slowly, as if she has thought a long while about doing such a thing, the lioness turns to look straight at the woman, her eyes drilling through the windshield and focusing on the center of the woman's very soul.

What? What is it? In less time than it takes to breathe in and out, the woman catches herself thinking with the lion. Then she jams the truck into first gear and roars the few meters toward Edith's and Paul's tents, honking the horn full blast as she spins the tires.

She chances a backward glance to where the lioness still stands, staring after her. She knows the great cat can cover the ground between them in a fraction of a second. What the male has not seen, the lioness now recognizes.

The woman rolls down the window. "Lions!" she screams. "Edith, Paul, get out here!" He bursts through the tent, rifle hanging in his hand. "In the car, hurry!" she gasps, leaning forward and throwing the passenger door open from the inside.

Paul doesn't ask questions. He carries one boot in his other hand and hops to the open door, then heaves himself across the seat just as Edith emerges from her tent and stumbles into the backseat. The woman releases her foot off the brake and floors the gas pedal. The clutch jumps as she shifts into second.

The truck flies over the thornbush, onto the sand track, away from the river. The woman concentrates all her attention on the driving. Only at the watering hole does she slow down, the dawn now showing in the tint at the horizon's edge. She brakes but leaves the motor running, then turns to Edith and Paul.

He is still sitting with one boot on his lap. A huge grin stretches across his face. "Well, did you see them?" the woman asks impatiently.

Paul chuckles. "Rough night, huh?"

"Don't laugh at me. Did you see them?"

"*Them?* No, I saw the lioness in the mirror. She looked like she had something to say to you. I take it we're safe, no damage done?"

"I saw them both," Edith says. Her many braids cover her shoulders like a mantle. "What happened?"

"How can you both stay so cool? No, the only *damage* is my tent. And it could have been me too, for that matter. Her mate walked right over me. Well, he jumped over me." The woman tries to calm her voice and wonders, *Why do they keep smiling at me like that?*

The woman grimaces. As she starts to turn the truck around, Paul puts out a hand to stop her. "Wait, let's stay put just for a few moments. This is the best time to see the game."

Edith says, "Sorry. My brother is paid to be in tune with nature. He may sleep deep, but his timing is uncanny."

The woman leans back in the seat to watch the sun burst in a blaze of color over the edge of the eastern sky, the acacia trees around them bowing low in homage. Reds and golds wash across the expanse.

In the outside mirror, a movement catches her eye. The lion pair lumber down the sand track after them. She says nothing, just turns off the motor and rolls up her window as they watch the lions saunter up to the water's edge and lower their heads as one into the water.

That night, the stars call to the woman, her face warm beneath their rich blanket. She wanders a short ways from the camp, head thrown backward, taking a few steps at a time. Dizzy with the sheer mass of light above her, stars from one horizon to the next, she remembers her boys. She remembers the names of the stars, remembers the boys' challenge to her on that magic night in another dimension, when Simba mkali finally opened himself up to her.

She looks down at her arm, wishing she could still feel Little Lion's touch there, even as she hears his words: *"My brother, he does not say so, but we are both wondering, do you trust God?"*

Now the woman senses a shift, hears a whisper. What was it Little Lion once told her about God showing the way? She listens for the boy's voice, her ache of missing him all the greater. Even this orphaned, wild boy knew how to distinguish the ones who did not follow God because they were lost.

I am lost. I am lost and in the dark and now have even lost those children.

The words come to her softly. She misses the anger, gropes for the bitterness. *"And your ears will hear a word behind you, 'This is the way, walk in it,' whenever you turn to the right or to the left."*

The woman does not know the source of the words beating in her heart. And yet she longs to follow their call as hope filters through the barren spaces of her soul.

Could this possibly be how—the way to trust? For the first time, she opens herself up to seeking.

She wills herself to turn from darkness to light and immediately knows she never did walk alone. *"Come unto me."* She takes one step and then another, toward the low horns trumpeting, a single beat sounding, their resonance filling her now.

The woman chooses to trust, chooses to be willing to be found, chooses to believe.

She thinks of Little Lion—his smile, the rich cadence of his voice, how he once confessed his longing to know his real name. She looks up at the stars, a cover of caring, their call to her a wish, a sigh, a prophecy. She has her eyes wide open when a desert wind wraps its arms around her and she hears it breathe her name.

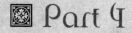 Part 4

That night I felt. I felt. In the quiet caress and murmur of a night wind, I re-
membered who I was. The shock of the lion, the peace of the landscape's
pressed-down and overflowing horizon—these things helped bring me to a
place of knowing. The lions shook something loose in me. All that day I
kept turning around, aware of the long-shadowed light, as if its presence
followed me.

Not in the thunder of the lion's roar, but in that gentle breeze as the stars
hummed a hymn, I began to find myself again.

Chapter 48

This wind began in the far reaches of the land and swept over the mountains, across the desert, to meet Miriam in that dark place, her mind the wilderness.

Miriam returned to camp and said, "I know . . . my name."

Paul stood up quickly and peered into the darkness. Edith looked at her carefully.

"Me. My name. It's Miriam. Miriam Vree."

"*Karibu nyumbani.* Welcome home. Your homecoming, my sister Miriam. You have come home to yourself!"

In Edith's arms, Miriam did indeed feel as if she'd come home. "There's more," she said.

Paul waited, then stared into her eyes. As he listened to Miriam's story, his face stretched in amazement.

"What is it?" she asked, laughing.

"I'm just astonished that our prayers were answered so quickly. What I mean is, I suppose we could have known that God would meet you in this way. It is a wonder your face doesn't glow, or your thigh is not out of joint. Instead it's in the way of Elijah that God came to you. Not in booming thunder or fire falling from heaven, but in the soft touch of a wind. A southerly wind, no doubt," he added.

"Excuse me?" Miriam brushed her hair out of her face and stared hard at him.

Paul said, *"Hamlet.* 'I am but mad north-north-west: when the wind is southerly I know a hawk from a handsaw.' Hamlet's curse, a lost mind when the wind blows wrong."

"Hamlet? Isn't that . . . ?"

"Shakespeare. Do you remember him too?"

Miriam turned to Edith. "So our safari guide can quote Shakespeare? What kind of brother do you have, Edith?"

"A very special one, Miriam. Ah, I do like the sound of your name."

That night, as Miriam listened to Edith's steady breathing in the tent they now shared, she stroked the ring around her neck, running the sharp edges along the inside of her palm, turning it over and over. *I know my name now, but who gave me this? Does he know I'm here? How long have I loved him? What is* his *name?*

Early the next morning, after leaving the park to return to Arusha, they climbed the same mountain as a few days earlier. They drove up the winding switchbacks in four-wheel drive, then turned a corner. Miriam looked down, and what had been covered in cloud before now shone in otherworldly beauty.

She gasped.

Edith turned around from where she sat beside Paul and said, "Oh, Miriam, you didn't know, did you?"

"I . . . had no idea."

Paul said, "Ngorongoro Crater is like a chunk of heaven God forgot to take back with him. Inside this volcano crater is a paradise of water, grass, and game. Herds of zebra, buffalo, and impala graze clear across a cool, verdant valley in the middle of all this dryness. The rhinos here never leave. The elephants sometimes migrate by road, and the giraffes take a trail up the side, but most of the game is born here and dies here."

The truck stayed on the dirt road and lumbered over the edge and down into the crater. Miriam wondered how mere fog could possibly have kept her from knowing about all this when she and Edith drove alongside the valley a few days earlier.

They crisscrossed a valley floor covered with game. Miriam saw fla-mingos, hundreds and hundreds, coloring the lakeshore bright pink. They witnessed another lion hunt. This time one of the lionesses chased, then climbed up the back of a buffalo calf, pulling it down with claws Miriam could see so clearly through the binoculars, she felt a shiver of recognition. It was over in a flash, and the lionesses were al-ready feeding, their necks red with blood.

Watching the lions, Miriam caught herself thinking, *I know how the prey feels.* Then she squared her shoulders and scolded herself. *Look at me, recovering more and more every day. Besides, if anything happens, Edith and Paul can protect me.* This unshakable conviction that someone chased her was surely only a silly fear.

That afternoon they left the park and headed back to Arusha to catch a plane to Mozambique. Miriam sat in the backseat of the truck, her mind going over all that had happened to her on this safari. She could not believe so much could change in such a short time. "Who-ever your friend Emmanuel is, he was right," Miriam mumbled.

But Edith did not hear her.

They flew into Maputo, then caught a small connecting flight to the north. Edith and Paul had been told to head for Mozambique's coastal border region, just inside the Mozambican border in the Cabo Delgado area. From the airstrip, it wasn't easy to locate the exact camp, but thanks to Paul's determined efforts and yet another hidden talent as a helicopter pilot, Miriam soon found herself running under the blades, across a windy meadow, into a vast sea of blue plastic tents.

The camp was purely transitional, a stop-off point for people return-ing from camps in other countries and headed to their homes else-where in Mozambique. So no permanent buildings, no stone compounds stood on the open space. Blue tarps with the UNHCR (United Nations High Commissioner for Refugees) insignia served as walls and roof in all the tent shelters.

The staff of UNHCR had taken over managing the task of reintegrat-ing the returning refugees. The sheer number of people they were try-ing to help far outweighed the capabilities of the trained aid workers,

Anne de Graaf

even with an influx of volunteers from all over the world like Miriam, Edith, and Paul.

That first night, after getting settled in her tent, Miriam found Edith standing in a circle of children, the deep burgundy and gold fabric of her gown and headdress billowing around her. "You look like an African queen," Miriam said.

Edith led the group in songs and soon had them clapping their hands and dancing with her. Miriam took a closer look at the children sitting on the ground and saw that several were missing their legs. Most of the older girls had babies strapped to their backs in bright-colored cloths.

In the days to come, Miriam quickly became caught up in the frenzy of helping people head back to their homes. Every day, more and more refugee buses arrived, and the aid workers had to make sure each family received enough food for the rest of their journey home, a supply of the blue plastic tarps, and tools and seeds to plant crops during what already promised to be a bountiful rainy season.

The UNHCR had put together a program for equipping the returning refugees with these bare necessities for returning to their villages while also trying to scratch together some preliminary programs for rebuilding homes, schools, and roads. Both the aid workers and the returnees were aware that after three decades of war, the homes most people were going back to had long since been burnt to the ground.

The camp itself was laid out in neighborhoods. Streets ran through at right angles, and on both sides of the streets stood the tents. Administration and training tents rose higher than the rest. Individual NGOs took care of their separate responsibilities—water, food, social services, and medical services. A Red Cross tent served as a small hospital, but only for emergencies. Here and there tall trees gave some shade, but most of the terrain contained only the hundreds of blue tents. Nothing gave the impression of permanence. This was a transitional camp, and when the repatriation program was over, the tents would be rolled up and shipped to the next location.

During her brief training, Miriam heard one senior program officer say, "We're working eighty-five hours a week, but it's a wonderful experience watching these people. Their homes have been destroyed, the roads are ruined, and some limp home on one leg. But they are *happy*."

It was true. An almost tangible hope permeated the camp. Miriam sensed its presence in the aid workers, who were relieved at working somewhere *without* a disaster, but especially in the Mozambicans, who could not contain their joy at finally coming home.

She soon discovered that although many people spoke some Kiswahili, her sketchy Portuguese was in great demand. One of the aid workers explained that most of the people in East Africa speak at least three languages fluently: their own tribal language; Kiswahili, the language of East Africa that bridges Uganda, Rwanda, Burundi, Zaïre, Kenya, Tanzania, southern Somalia, and northern coastal Mozambique; and then either English, French, or Portuguese, depending on the colonial history of their particular homeland. For Mozambicans, this language was Portuguese.

The first time Miriam witnessed a busload of returning refugees arrive at the repatriation post, a man jumped out and started shouting. He turned to everyone still on the bus, calling out, "God has granted us the miracle of peace. Let us give thanks!"

Men and women spilled out of the overloaded, fifties-model bus. Many of them knelt down on the spot and kissed the dirt. They carried children and bundles. Miriam knew that all their worldly possessions were most probably in those bundles. She watched the women hoist the loads onto their heads and walk away, hands at their sides. She saw a young man hopping out of the bus on one leg, a hand-whittled wooden crutch under each arm.

Miriam approached a teenage girl with a toddler, a baby on her hip, and one on her back. She offered to carry the baby as they walked back to the registration area. The girl kept thanking her as if Miriam were responsible for the peace. "I swore if I were ever allowed to return home, the first thing I would do is get down on my knees and thank God for bringing me back, together with my children."

"They are lovely," Miriam said. The baby had already discovered Miriam's hair and was entwining his pudgy fingers in her curls, pulling it out of the short ponytail she had braided that morning.

"All three were born outside their country. But our name is no longer *Wakimbizi*, 'Those Who Run Away.' We are no longer refugees. Now my children are *home.*" Her voice shook with emotion as she said the last word.

Miriam looked at the girl sharply, surprised by her own sensation of envy. *What of my home? Where are my loved ones?* The familiar desperation rose in her. Miriam tried to quench it with the thought that surely her situation was different, but it ravaged any hope she managed to salvage with denial.

You will never find them. It is already too late.

Each day at the relocation camp, Miriam rose at first light and returned to her tent long after dark. Although she usually fell asleep within seconds of collapsing onto her cot, her nights were often broken by jagged dreams about the young victims of land-mine accidents she saw limping around every day.

Then one night something came to her like a flash of memory, cutting into her consciousness.

I am looking down at an orange plastic bucket with minnows. I carry the bucket, light reflecting off the water, with another. A child's hand holds the handle beside my hand, our skin touching. My other hand is held in the grip of a man's hand. I see our three pairs of bare feet walking side by side in the sand.

Miriam woke with her fingers pressed into her shoulders and blood in her mouth from chewing the inside of her cheeks.

She and Edith shared a tent with two Swedish women and an Irish nun. But Edith rarely spent any time there. Miriam's only chance to see Edith without the constant swarm of children hovering around her was at the weekly staff meetings.

At her second such briefing, Miriam heard that already more than a million Mozambicans had made their way back. In an overwhelming response to the news of peace, they were hurrying home, streaming into the country through at least ten different entry points. "We are in the midst of something very special here," the UN deputy representative told them. "Unprecedented. Highly unusual."

Afterward Miriam went over to where Edith stood deep in conversation with a colleague. She overheard Edith confess, "What I struggle with most is the sight of so many children who have lost an arm or leg because of the land mines. I don't know how to keep my own emotions in check."

Miriam stood at Edith's side, surprised and relieved to hear she wasn't the only one losing sleep over these images.

The man standing opposite them, a Nigerian working for UNICEF, said, "At least here we have relatively few orphans because families remained together or were quickly reunited after they fled the country." Then he called out to someone on the other side of the meeting tent and left them.

"Didn't really comment on what you said, did he?" Miriam asked.

Edith looked at her and said, "No. But perhaps there is no answer. I think we're all disturbed to see so many with lost limbs. Some deal with it differently than others. I haven't figured out how, my way, not yet. Why do you think they're *flying* aid workers to posts within Mozambique? And these people must now travel over mine-infested roads to get back to their home areas."

She sighed then and turned to Miriam. "What about you? Are you sorry I brought you here? You know I'm here for you if you need me." Edith linked arms with Miriam and steered her outside the tent.

Miriam looked at her friend. She wore blue jeans and a blouse with a bright purple-and-silver starburst embroidered across its front. Edith had wrapped her braids in a circle on top of her head like a crown, making herself a few inches taller then usual.

Miriam wondered if now would be a good time to bring up the image she'd remembered. *But how can I even be sure it was a memory and not a dream?* Miriam laughed uncomfortably. "Am I sorry to be here? No, not at all. But I'm feeling the same things you are. I thought it was because I couldn't distance myself from it all because of my own . . . condition. But it turns out we both feel the same way. And that helps."

Edith brushed a cool finger against Miriam's temple. "Still nothing but your name? No hint of a past?"

Miriam thought of the smell of the lake, the echo of a touch on her back in the tent, and the image of the orange bucket. Even if her senses had granted her these pieces of her past, they weren't enough to solve the puzzle of what had happened to her.

She shook her head and turned the conversation to something real. "These children . . . well, my lost boys—I think of them all the time. And so when I see these other children, it's like they're all around me, but I can't reach them." She paused. "So I told myself that was the reason the kids here are getting to me. My boys, plus the fact that I'm still confused, and I'm not a professional."

"Well, now you see that even us so-called professionals have trouble coping with tragedy. You know why I don't sleep much these days?

Because I dream of the children I see here so happy being blown up within sight of their promised land."

Edith fell quiet, then added, "And then there are the child-soldiers. I have them in Tanzania too. These are the ones who break my heart—damaged inside and out. Like your boys, I think. Do you want to know what one girl said to me yesterday when I tried to convince her that their raping her and forcing her to kill others was not her fault? She said, 'God has been angry with us for starting the war, and he has punished us.' Ah, Miriam," she sighed. "The children's voices haunt me."

That night Miriam woke herself up, kicking her heel against her shin.

I dash toward the shadow. Sun on my back. Straining to catch up to the woman who is always one step in front while staying ahead of the hunter one step behind.

The explosions that night six months ago had thrown Owen to the ground. Now he stood and leaned against the wooden bars of the cage where he had lived since they brought him to this place. He remembered well the night of all those terrible bombs, when he had thought he would burn alive in his cage. But he remembered even better the last time he had seen Martin, ten days before that attack on the camp, when Yury Falin had kicked Owen for bringing up Afghanistan. The price Owen had paid since then had proven far too high.

Owen had been over and over the sequence of events in his mind. And he still did not know if he had been targeted for the kidnapping, and if so, why. He had been here a few weeks; then he'd seen Martin; then Falin had used Martin against him for another few weeks. After that day when Falin had told him the deal had to do with Sudan, there had been nothing. Except the bombs, of course. But no contact with Falin anymore and worse, not a word about Martin.

For all Owen knew, Martin could have been killed during that bombardment. He tried not to torture himself with such thoughts, but the long days and longer nights had preyed on his fears, flushing a plethora of scenarios as the weeks and months dragged on and on.

Owen had to admit that Falin was good. He had contained the damage Owen could do by very simply shutting him down. Zero communication. Each day Owen tried to get news from the guards, but no one answered his questions. Owen understood this was Falin's way of punishing him for gleaning the information about Sudan and about Falin's background, the rare glimpse of his potential weakness. Owen did not want to think about why Falin had removed Martin from him. Certainly it had to do with lessening Owen's influence over the boy and increasing Falin's.

But this was all speculation. Maybe Falin was dead. The guards who brought him his food and water said nothing. So for six appalling months, Owen had talked only to himself and paced his cage.

They had built it so it came just a foot short of his own height. He could see everyone around him, and they could see him. It never failed that as soon as his shoulders no longer hurt from the stooping, they let him out to walk around, so his shoulders hurt again when he returned to the cage. He had tried to come up with an escape plan but had found no way out of his trap. When they did let him out, three men stood guard. His belt no longer fit him. His hands shook when he watched them move.

Owen counted the scratches he'd made in the thickest wooden pole. Yes, seven months in total—six months since the explosions and the last time he saw Martin. And this would be June. He told himself it was important to keep track, which was why he kept going over the dates.

He paced, stooping, until his neck and shoulders began to hurt; then he dropped to the ground and did push-ups—fewer every day, he noticed. Seven months, or two hundred and eleven days, he had lived, survived, endured. He watched the insects and listened to the birds, grateful now even for the cage, rather than a closed cell or a hole in the ground. Here at least he could breathe fresh air.

Owen had learned the discipline of fixing his thoughts on Martin and Miriam. He challenged himself each day to remember their list of characteristics, moments, memories, and then to add one more. One a day.

Woven between it all he laced a tapestry of prayer. *Keep them safe. Bring us together. Protect them from harm. Send people to get me out of here.*

This initiated his set daily routine. The next steps included running his hand through his beard until the tangles were out, then calisthenics, reciting out loud every piece of poetry and Scripture and play he could remember.

And then he would return to the book he was writing in his head. Every word and phrase and sentence was fixed in his memory. Owen would recite it all out loud, chapter by chapter, before he began to write a new paragraph—sometimes two a day.

The book was about coming alongside others, serving, learning to love in small acts that later grow into the great acts necessary for conflict resolution. He based its premise on a phrase warning against racial superiority: "Let us gird ourselves with the towel of fellowship."

"In today's world," he now recited to himself, "it is not enough to simply negotiate an end to conflict. Look also at how it is possible to work for conditions that *give* peace a chance. I am referring to an infrastructure of peace that undergirds the political decision making—provisions like transition packages and election arrangements. For a lasting peace, there must be ethical behavior. . . ."

Chapter 49

The next morning, seven busloads of children were all due to arrive at the same time. The children had been sent on ahead of their parents. The UNHCR office called upon all the NGOs to make available as many aid workers as possible to receive and process the children as they waited for their parents.

Miriam arrived at the road out of breath and saw Edith and Paul on the other side of the field. She waved and started toward them just as the buses rolled in.

The next moment a cascade of color and laughter, shouts and smiles erupted out of the worn vehicles. Miriam stood still as the children ran toward her. Hundreds of them, all ages, all born during the war, in another country—not theirs, not this one, not home. Now, coming home for the first time in their lives, they shrieked with happiness.

These former refugee children wore T-shirts, cast-off T-shirts from all over the world. Some bore slogans from nonexistent sports teams like "Giants American Football." Words in French and English emblazoned across their chests called out yesterday's slogans, past battles fought, dreams hoped for, products advertised, cities visited, things thrown away. One boy leaped high in the air, arms spread wide, and whooped. His shirt said, STRESS.

Anne de Graaf

The children raced across the field, a cloud of sound and excitement erupting as even the adult aid workers could not resist laughing and smiling and joining in the chorus of *"Karibu! Karibu!* Welcome, welcome!" Everywhere, like a wide field of wildflowers bobbing in the wind, spread the bright grins, the sparkling eyes, and the children's cheers of triumph.

Miriam stood very still, taking it all in: older siblings holding on to the little ones, bare chests and skinny faces, stragglers struggling on crutches, dust everywhere, hands touching and waving, small bundles of possessions. More than one child wore three layers of tattered shirts with collars frayed, loose shorts, no shoes. The young girls wore cotton cloths wrapped around their waists, babies strapped to their backs. A little boy with stars on his shorts and a yellow long-sleeved shirt galloped right up to Miriam and hugged her legs.

With his touch, the tidal wave of emotion hit Miriam full force. She staggered back, listening to their voices:

"Come, brother, we are home!"

"See, I told you it was green and beautiful."

"No more refugee camps!"

"This is a good day—I think the best I have ever had!"

"Look, show them what we practiced."

And singing. They sang and chanted and laughed and smiled and joked and cheered and ran and played and even danced until Miriam could stand it no longer. She ran her hand along the cheeks of the child at her feet and, when she felt his tears, stooped down in the dust to put her arms around him. He was laughing and crying, his chubby hand shaking like a leaf as he brought it up to her own face, then showed her the tear.

Other children careened into them, embracing her, thanking her, not even knowing who she was or what she had or had not done. Miriam lost her balance and fell over backward. The boy brought his right hand up to his face and chortled so hard, he doubled over and held his tummy with the other hand.

More children joined them. Miriam fell into their laughter, let it engulf her until she heard her own throat making the sounds. Tears coursed down her cheeks. Children touched her, held her, ran their hands up and down her back, over her shoulders, through her hair. Some began to dance in a circle around her and the children on her lap, at her side. They moved their hips and stomachs to an unseen rhythm they all could feel. Others joined in song and clapped their hands. "Going home! Going home! *Deus obrigado!* Thank the Lord!"

In this way the children brought their boundless gratitude to Miriam and offered it as sacrifice for all the pain and dismay, theirs and hers, wiping every bit of it away in tears, theirs and hers, a baptism of pure joy. She soaked it in as if she were sitting in the surf on some tropical beach, the warm water of these children's voices melting away her winter of tight fear.

"Miriam, Miriam!"

Miriam was following the children. She searched among them, their laughter and singing and stories engulfing her, even as she allowed their hope to bolster her own.

"Miriam!" When Edith caught up with her, she asked, "Is something wrong? Why are you wandering like this? I saw you go down. What is it? Who are you looking for?"

Miriam looked at her for a moment, then said hesitantly, the words coming to her at the same instant as the ragged memories, "I had a child, my own child. I remember I'm looking for a child. I lost a son. I'm supposed to be looking for him."

"And your husband, then?" Edith asked.

Miriam shook her head, still uncertain. "Yes, a husband. I can see my son on a man's broad back, walking toward me on a white beach, the sun in my eyes. But I don't see his face. His name?" She looked around her and saw the crowd of children, still all smiling and excited. Miriam said, "It has something to do with Mozambique, with this place, these children's smiles. . . ."

The little boy wearing star shorts ran back to Miriam, shouting, "Thank you for the peace! Thank you for the peace!"

"But I didn't—," Miriam started to say to him.

"Who did then? I want to shake his hand and say thank you, sir!" The boy ran off again.

Miriam stood watching him, his question shaking loose the scales over her mind's eye.

Miriam sat beside Edith, the two women alone now under a tree. "Owen," she repeated. "So, my husband's name is Owen. Owen O'Neill." Miriam looked over at the crowd of children, now calmer but just as triumphant as two hours earlier. The aid workers were organizing them into smaller groups and trying to keep siblings and cousins together. "What just happened?" Miriam asked Edith.

Edith said, "If I understand all that you just told me, I think it might be a combination of several factors. There's the children, the same ones your husband described to you as being so special, Mozambican children. And there's the peace, the same one he helped forge, and your being in the same country he last worked in. Add to all that the emotional impact of the children's laughter and their joyous homecoming—I think it just washed over you like the newfound memory it is. The combination triggered your memory of who *did* make the peace possible. It all came together in just the right way and set you free to find yourself. This is a process that has been under way since the lion in your tent 'shook something loose,' as you put it. That incident acted as a catalyst, the shock and adrenaline jarring your mind. Regaining your physical health and remembering your name were just initial steps." Edith took her hand. "Are you ready for this?"

Miriam nodded.

"Then will you pray with me, Miriam?"

Miriam was glad to bow her head, Edith's familiar blessing taking on a deeper meaning now.

"Lord, please bless Miriam's will. Lord, please bless my sister Miriam. Bless her indeed. Carry her in your palm as she retraces her steps, walks again the path that brought her here."

Edith paused and Miriam waited. "Miriam, something has occurred to me. Keep your eyes closed now. I know you have decided to follow Jesus. But have you received his gift?"

"Gift?" Miriam mumbled. Her mind felt numb.

"You have been brought to this place to receive something from God. Before we can ask for his healing, I must ask, have you ever received the gift of his forgiveness?"

"No." A silence followed, and Miriam slowly began to weep. "I can't even forgive myself for losing those poor boys who have nothing, nobody, and not fighting harder to find out who I am, to find my husband, Owen, and a son whose name I don't even remember—can you imagine? And other things I've doubtless done wrong in my life. If I can't even forgive myself for losing it all, losing them all. . . ." She opened her eyes. "How can he forgive me?"

Edith turned to face her, one hand stroking Miriam's arm. "That is the point. You have it the wrong way around. It is not possible to forgive ourselves until we receive from God *his* forgiveness. Repentance is a gift of God, as are those tears. You've taken the first steps on this safari. Now take a few more."

Miriam said, "I don't see how he can. . . ." She felt Edith squeeze her shoulder, as if to prompt her. She closed her eyes again. "You know. I'm so sorry . . . thank you. . . ." More tears choked her voice.

With Edith's arms around her, Miriam heard her friend promise, "Someday soon you will find you can forgive yourself, and then you'll even find yourself wanting to pray for and forgive your enemies. But long before that, the regeneration that is God's own healing will already be well under way. That is my promise to you, dear sister. Now, are you *sure* you are ready for this?"

Miriam nodded again, and Edith raised her voice. "Great God in heaven, heal Miriam, keep her safe, protect her from evil as you show her the past. Walk beside her, hold her hand, and reveal the rest of her story. In your most holy name we pray. Amen."

Miriam opened her eyes and saw deep anguish carved onto Edith's face. "What's next?" Miriam asked.

"We'll work backward. Can you tell me what happened just before Simba mkali found you? who you were with? why you were alone in the bush like that?

"Who were you running away from?"

Yury counted the months. It had been half a year since he lost her, his greatest jewel yet. He blamed the Liberians and the Lebanese and the Libyans.

The Liberians had acted as catalyst in the catastrophe. Their complaining of the assessments Miriam performed, their insistence that she did not give a generous enough description of their stones—this had set the entire disaster in motion.

The Liberians had gone to his rivals in that area, the Lebanese. Yury and his men had only recently established their presence around those particular diamond fields. So the Lebanese, who held traditional rights to the illegal trade, had been only too glad to resume work with the couriers.

And the Libyans were just plain demented. Their terrorist insanity was what first had brought him into contact with Miriam, his wish for her love now a curse. Recently he had been wondering if the Libyans' presence had brought *their* enemy to his territory.

After the attack on the camp, Yury had told the men under his command to scour the bush. Every man. All other operations were put on hold. They had spent weeks looking for clues but had found nothing, not one chestnut-colored hair.

Miriam Vree had disappeared from his world as mysteriously as she had entered his heart.

The job was so well done, so utterly complete, that Yury was starting to think it had been handled by the Mossad, Israeli Intelligence. But what on earth could be the connection? Unless it was revenge on Libya . . . ? No, it must be something else. But he did not know what. And this distraction was destroying him. He was off his game, missing strokes, allowing others to make advances into his business ventures.

Now he had probably held on too long. Well, he was glad to finally deliver this particular package. The Libyan could have him and his tiresome references to Afghanistan. Yury had done the preliminary work; now El-Fatih could finish the job. El-Fatih did not need to know about Yury's loss of the woman. The boy remained as Yury's only consolation for this loss.

With every passing week, Yury had hoped he could forget her, put out of his mind the echo of her voice, and force out of his heart the touch of her hands, the smell of her hair, the gnawing longing for the love he never knew.

With every passing week, he had failed.

Chapter 50

Miriam still heard a child crying in her dreams. She had assumed her nightmares about children being maimed had to do with the returnees she worked with every day or with Simba mkali's group. She had said nothing to Edith about the flashes of memory because she didn't want to acknowledge that the danger might be true.

With the full restoration of her memory, though, Miriam realized the real source of the images—a fear for her son. Yury's threat that he would maim her son if she tried to run away—that was why she could not breathe at night. This fear made regaining her memory a bittersweet victory. The more she remembered, the more the panic seemed to close in on her, claiming her as its own.

Miriam told it all to Edith as she remembered it. "He was in the jeep—the crash knocked him out. I was hoping the soldiers wouldn't see him. But then we were taken—we left him there, alone. Now I hear him crying for me in the night.

"His name . . . his name is Martin."

There. She had said the name out loud. In doing so Miriam longed to gain a firmer grip on the hope, a wish, a cry in the dark. "I think my Martin must be alive," she said.

And then, in the very act of facing that memory, the doubt reinforced in strength. It became so overwhelming that Miriam felt more like someone wrestling with the wind as she wondered, stepped forward, then fell back against the buffeting of her newfound belief.

Miriam hardly knew how to pray about her tremendous loss, even worse than she had feared—her husband and son, both gone. But she knew who she was, she reminded herself. It brought scant comfort. The weight of all she now knew she must forgive herself for crushed any featherweight hope that day's session with Edith had released. For starters, there was her lack of love and support for Owen when they were safe at home, not to mention losing and even forgetting her very own son.

That night she dreamed specifically about Martin. She dreamed as she had in Angola, hearing his cries, smelling his hair, then waking up soaked with sweat. *I am mother-haunted.*

But even as she dreaded a return to sleep and the child's cries that had haunted her so interminably, she realized she now also heard a new sound: the laughter and the voices of the children who had awakened her memory that day and brought her back to herself. The children's hope had touched her heart. Dare she also hope, in the midst of such a realization of loss?

The next morning, Miriam knew only one thing for certain. She must get her family back—find her son, find Owen. "I had a husband. I had a child." She repeated the claim to Edith as if the words themselves could cast away the uncertainty.

"When you first arrived at the border post on the shore of Lake Tanganyika, I noticed you spoke like an American," Edith said. "You need to give yourself time, though, to adjust to all the changes you're experiencing. It's not easy, what you're doing, Miriam. And perhaps this is no longer such a good place for you to be. You know, it is perfectly natural that you feel angry. Something was stolen from you—"

"Edith, don't. I know what you're trying to do. I don't need any more of your blessings or prayers for healing. I need to take some concrete action and find my family. I've been up all night thinking about this. Why, all this time Martin could have been living with strangers. That Yury was probably just lying to me. Martin must be safe, if some tourists found him." The old dream brought little comfort now that Miriam realized seven months had passed since their kidnapping.

"You can still seek a greater knowledge of God. That will bring you comfort."

This was too much for Miriam. "God?" She fairly spat the word out. *"God* allowed evil men to kidnap us. *God* landed me with those animals in Angola."

Even though a part of her meant them, Miriam regretted the words as soon as she had said them, especially when she saw Edith swallow and look to the left, then back to her with a completely different expression, one Miriam could not read.

"Miriam, I know you are still deeply troubled by your losses."

The words fell between them like dead lumps of clay. Miriam's disappointment pulled on her like quicksand. Now it was she who turned her gaze away from Edith. *But why should the world look any different just because I've changed?* She hurt so badly inside, she could not imagine anyone understanding. She felt like she might suffocate in her disappointment.

Edith said nothing for a few moments. Then, "I notified the embassy in Dar es Salaam, but no one has reported missing a woman fitting your description. As soon as you knew your name, Paul and I radioed the same authorities, but there still was no response. Perhaps that is because the name you remembered was your maiden name and the embassy might be looking for a family by the name of O'Neill. I think the best thing is to go in person to the U.S. embassy. Let me go with you to Dar, though. Because you are a patient under my care, I cannot let you travel alone. Surely you understand that."

Miriam had not missed the distance in Edith's voice, distance Miriam herself had put there. But she also had not expected Edith to still want to remain at her side. This meant more to Miriam than any words about seeking or faith or prayer.

Now Edith even smiled at her. "Besides," she said, "I need to check in at the head office and pick up some cooking pots and escort a photocopier back home."

"To the compound in western Tanzania?" Miriam referred to it as a common ground they both shared. "But you're not finished here yet," she objected.

"I insist, Miriam. I have spent enough time away from my children in the camp. A new wave of refugee children is arriving there, and the need is great. They are my first priority."

Paul carried Miriam's bag to the jeep that would take her to the closest airstrip, where Edith already waited. His voice rolled the Rs and assumed the cadence of a university professor as he talked about what they had seen. ". . . but sometimes there are massive breakthroughs. It's as if barriers no one ever expected to crumble . . . do, and seemingly rigid conditions like dictatorships evaporate into thin air." He put her bag into the back of the vehicle, brought up his closed fists to chest height, then opened both hands wide, spreading his fingers as if he had just performed a magic trick.

"Like the Berlin Wall, or the Soviet Union?" Miriam asked.

"Yes, and like now, here in Mozambique. This one will keep historians dumbfounded for decades. After so many years of war, such vast shifts in population, to witness the miracle of reconciliation—it is almost beyond belief. When you see something of this scale, something so improbable, surely it is of the Lord. But there is more to it as well.

"You see, I believe it is the willingness that God looks for. Just say, 'Send me,' and see what miracles he can work through you. The motivation is everything. There is a connection between this people being willing, our own willingness, and the miracles such as true reconciliation."

"Are you speaking from personal experience, Paul?" Miriam looked at him more closely. He wore the green military uniform of Tanzania and looked very official. She could not read the insignia on his collar but knew he must be an officer of some sort.

"Yes. No. My sisters, other people—they've talked this way. And I've found it to be true. Ah, well. Have a safe journey. Travel in dignity, Miriam. You have come so far already."

Miriam blinked back her tears as the jeep drove past the new arrivals' camp. A cloud of dust enveloped the faces watching her—a girl with a baby; three children waving; a barefoot boy running fast, small legs pumping, chasing after them, pale palms turning this way and that.

They left Mozambique and flew along the Indian Ocean coast to Dar es Salaam, the capital of Tanzania. Edith explained that the name meant "Harbor of Peace." Miriam sensed the North African presence as the chant of the imam rang out on the streets, calling the city to prayer.

Women walked outside in loose-fitting swirls of dark fabric, arms and legs, necks and torsos carefully covered. This bustling harbor city, sweltering and humid, shone colorful with stands and markets, the streets crowded with people from all parts of Africa and the Middle East. Cars from previous decades rattled down pockmarked streets, rocking in and out of the craters. The sounds of music and shouting engulfed Miriam as she sat in the taxi on the way to the embassy, her window rolled down to take it all in.

When they stopped at a stoplight, a child asked if she wanted to buy a newspaper, while another offered to wash the windows. But the driver shooed them away.

At the embassy Miriam told her story to a sympathetic foreign service worker from somewhere in the American South.

"We have no record of your being reported missing, I'm afraid."

"What about my inquiry when she arrived at the border?" Edith asked.

The man said, "I'll check with the consul. One moment, please." He left the office.

Another official returned five minutes later. He introduced himself, then said, "I'm sorry, ladies. There's nothing here about anything Ms. Vree has been talking about. No missing person's report, nothing on her husband or this so-called kidnapping."

He looked between the two of them. "My colleague did say you were undergoing psychiatric care and had been uncertain about recent events. Perhaps . . ."

Miriam stood up, ignoring Edith's calming hand on her arm. "You have no right to assume such things. All right, where are the forms? I'm filing a formal report of my husband's kidnapping. I can't believe the State Department hasn't already done this. He was, we were, on holiday when Angolan rebels—oh, never mind. I'll write it all down."

It was obvious this was the first anyone at the embassy had heard of the events, and obvious the women would get no information that day. Miriam applied for a new passport and was told the processing would take some time. She had to borrow money from Edith to pay for it. Miriam believed Edith really had called in the report when Miriam appeared at the border. What could possibly have gone so wrong that Edith's request for information about a woman under her care could have gone missing?

"May I at least make a phone call to people we know at home, in San Francisco?" Miriam asked. "My husband is an employee of the State Department."

"I'm afraid not, ma'am. You can make calls at the post office. And we can't advance you any money, either, I'm afraid."

Miriam did not leave the embassy until she had dropped every name she could think of from the foreign service and the State Department— Owen's colleagues and superiors—but no doors opened for her.

At the post office she found herself shouting into a phone while standing in a booth watching lice crawl up the glass door. Static. No connection. "Try again tomorrow," said the lady behind the counter.

"Welcome back to civilization, huh?" Miriam said to Edith.

Their next stop was the head office of the organization Edith worked for, an NGO called World Mission. The taxi let them off in front of a row of stores. Edith led Miriam around to the back of the building and up yellow-painted stairs. When they opened the door, the secretary stood and welcomed them both with hugs. She wore a purple, blue, and pink turban and a dress of the same fabric. She barely came to Miriam's shoulder, but her presence could be felt in the bubbly way she did everything from taking their bags to answering the phone.

Edith beamed as a tall man with hair that went in several directions came out of a back office. "Ah, Edith! So good to see you again. It has been too long! Happiness, some coffee for our guests!" As the secretary left to get the coffee, Miriam found herself meeting Frank, the director of World Mission's Dar office. His smile warmed the entire room, and he was only too glad to welcome Miriam into their "family," as he referred to the staff.

"Edith prefers the field, but I like the city," he laughed, as if it were some great joke.

Once the introductions were over, they followed Frank into his office. It contained a bare desk and a table with a shortwave radio on it. "Sit down. Yes, sit down. There. Are you comfortable? Yes? Milk for your coffee? Sugar? Some water? No? Ah, fine. Now, Edith. I'm afraid we have to talk business. Miriam, you do not mind? Yes, I can confirm what we radioed you in Mozambique. I have news today that a great influx of children has arrived at our camp. I am receiving desperate cries daily for your return. What is the situation?"

Edith glanced at Miriam. "This is why I am here. I can leave tomorrow."

"And take the cooking pots with you?"

"And the photocopier, provided there is room on the plane."

"Ah." Frank leaned back in his chair and smiled straight at Miriam.

Miriam had no choice but to smile back. "What?" she asked. "Why are you both looking at me that way? What has she told you about me?" Miriam looked accusingly at Edith.

Frank said, "Only that you have a gift for children. But how can we help *you*, Miriam? I have been following your case quite closely. Edith is certain things are not as they seem. Did you receive any assistance at the embassy?"

"None whatsoever. It was like hitting my head against a wall. I'm still trying to sort everything out. And I couldn't even make a phone call, not even at the post office."

"Of course, of course. Yes, this happens." He stopped and grinned at Miriam again. "If you give me the numbers you are trying to reach, I will ask Happiness to try them when the phone lines are operational again."

"Oh yes, please," Miriam said. She took the paper and pen he offered and started writing down the information, part of her quietly pleased that she knew Sue's number by heart. "But this is in America, and I have no money. . . ."

"This is not a problem."

Once Happiness had come and taken the paper away, Edith said, "Miriam, you know I need to return to our compound and conduct my workshops. What will you do now?"

Miriam felt at a loss. Her earlier energy had dissipated, and in its place she felt only emptiness. "What do you think I should do?"

"Well, certainly, you should focus on looking for your family. What is more important, you should go home, back to the States. Don't you think so?"

Miriam nodded. She had been thinking the same. But now she caught herself saying, "I can't leave Africa while Martin and Owen could still be here. I must find them. But there's also. . . ." She caught sight of a World Mission poster hanging on Frank's office wall: "Giving Hope to Children."

"What?" Edith asked.

"Nothing," Miriam said, but she was thinking of her boys, who had brought her to the border. And she was remembering Owen's coaching—*"What do you know for certain? Act on that"*—his words a familiar blanket of comfort. She blinked.

Frank cast a glance at Edith, then said but did not ask, "You have more to say."

"Yes," Miriam said. "Yes," as if just now hearing her own voice. "I won't leave Africa until I know more about Martin and Owen. I can't go looking for them on my own. I could go to Nairobi and wait there. But where would I go? I know no one."

Yury had paid his informant well. This was what bothered him most. Yury had been making regular deposits into a certain account in Luxembourg in this man's name, actually to the same establishment where Yury banked, but to no avail.

The Americans might think they were the leading capitalists in the world, but they still had a thing or two to learn about supply and demand, he thought.

This Marine soldier stationed at the embassy in Nairobi was young and green and greedy. When Joseph had approached him with an offer to sluice information from embassy missing-persons files he could access and photograph at night while on guard duty, the young man had been only too happy to accept the bribe, with its promise of tax-free funds. When Joseph told Yury what the Marine received as salary, Yury thought that only a foolish government would pay those who guard their embassies so little. It was asking for trouble.

His was a neat arrangement, Yury thought. But it had yielded nothing in return, not one single morsel of information on Miriam's whereabouts.

Perhaps, he thought, he should set up a similar arrangement at the embassy in Dar. But that city was clear on the coast, a long ways from where she had disappeared, in the center of Africa. And the U.S. had no diplomatic relations with Zaïre or Angola. No, if Miriam surfaced anywhere in East Africa, it was logical the news would get to Nairobi.

When she did, Yury would know about it.

Chapter 51

Edith agreed. "Nairobi is a dangerous city."

"Well, only sometimes, in certain places." Frank paused, then asked, "Do you wish to continue staying at our compound and live where you were before, near the refugee camp?"

Both Miriam and Edith looked at him. "It is very simple, ladies. Such a thing can easily be arranged. Of course, we are always looking for good field staff, and you would have Edith close at hand if you needed her." His eyes danced as he brought his fingertips together.

"Oh, Frank, this is a fine idea," said Edith, "except that Miriam needs to find her family. We all agree that is her top priority. But you could do this, Miriam, even if you *did* return with me. You are so much better now; you could learn how to help with the children."

Edith was clearly taken with the idea, her enthusiasm growing. "We have such a mixed bag at my camp—children of different ages, different nationalities, different backgrounds, and then there are those classified as Unaccompanied Minors, or UAMs.

"I would teach you, step by step, and there are others who will help you learn. Oh yes! I watched you in Mozambique, Miriam, and the children respond to you. You *see* them. It's like a second sight, a talent, a gift. No one can teach you that."

Edith paused. "Now, what I want to know is, is this what *you* want to do? Will you come back with me?"

Miriam remembered this had always been Owen's question of her—what did *she* want to do? While listening to Edith, Miriam had intended to say no to the invitation. She didn't have the skills, her own emotional state was too raw, it would be much better to. . . . But midway through that train of thought she heard herself say, "With all my heart." She wondered if perhaps her answer tied in with this new resolve she felt taking root inside her.

She told Edith, "I see them; you're right. I really do see them. I want to be trained to help the children. At least let me be useful while I try and set the wheels in motion to find my family, and wait." Her voice sounded like someone else's.

At that moment Happiness appeared in the doorway. "Your phone call has gone through. Come quickly."

Miriam ran from the office and grabbed the phone on the desk. "Yes? . . . Sue?" She shouted louder. "Yes, it's me, Miriam. . . . No . . . A long story . . . I'm safe, yes. Tell me, though—have you heard anything, anything at all from Owen? . . . No. I . . . what? . . . Yes, please get ahold of his boss. . . . What? . . . I know. Listen, Sue, Martin—hello? Hello?"

Tears of frustration ran down Miriam's face as she returned to the office. Edith stood without a word and crossed the room, enveloping Miriam in her arms. "There is no sign of Owen in San Francisco," Miriam told them. "My friend said none of our friends or colleagues had heard anything about either of us all this time. Someone in the State Department told them we went missing, but no one claimed responsibility for a kidnapping. I don't understand."

She hesitated. "I can't go home without him . . . them." The idea of returning to the U.S. without her husband and son seemed as terrifying to her as the kidnapping she had endured. Miriam knew the uncertainty would drive her over the edge. Again. Back home all she would do was grieve for the loss of her dream that at least Martin might be safe. Here, she might still have a chance of finding them both.

"I . . . need to stay put," Miriam said slowly. "If I have to wait somewhere, I'd rather it be with you." She managed a feeble smile. "Besides, I can't bear the thought of us saying good-bye yet."

And there was something else, something Miriam would not admit to out loud. Not yet. She kept seeing the children's faces that gave her such joy. She wanted more of that. The Mozambican children's joy had challenged her to hope, to be willing. Now she found she really wanted to make a difference. It was this willingness that finally shoved the fear aside.

Miriam told herself she felt good about making a decision. She might not have found many answers, but at least she knew which direction she would go. She held on to this certainty, the next step, trying not to listen too closely to the dire voice inside warning about a choice that just didn't seem logical. She left all her names and numbers with Happiness, and with the people at the embassy, about where she was and how she could be reached.

The next day Miriam and Edith boarded a Red Cross chartered flight. With cooking pots shoved under their legs and the precious photocopier jammed onto the seat behind Miriam, they flew out of Dar es Salaam and four hours west, back toward the heart of Africa.

When Miriam returned with Edith to be trained for working with refugee children, she saw the old compound in western Tanzania with new eyes. During her first week many things felt strangely familiar. Nehemiah, one of the camp officers, with gray-peppered hair on his head and arms, had always been a figure in the background. Now he became a mentor, her interpreter. She noticed for the first time that he was missing two of his front teeth. She guessed his age at anywhere between fifty and seventy. He walked with a slight stoop, one leg dragging behind the other.

Thanks to Nehemiah's explanation, Miriam now understood what it meant that the villagers—some Muslim, some Christian—called the area where the compound was *Kalimungoma,* or Inside the Drum. "Only the maker knows what a drum is made of, what its inside looks like, what its purpose is." She remembered these words that Edith had told her as if she had dreamed them somewhere else.

There was the same pit toilet hidden behind a UNHCR blue plastic tarp, a STOP sign on the wood, lizards on walls, flies everywhere, wind, dry leaves in a July winter. The same village children waited for Miriam as she emerged from the toilet corner, cheering when she appeared. Did they recognize her?

"Habari mama!"

"Habari!" she replied.

"Nzuri," they said, then burst into peals of laughter and ran along the fence paralleling her own path. She smiled as the wind chased their laughter away.

"Why do the children call me 'mama'?" she asked Nehemiah.

"It's what they call any woman old enough to have children."

Miriam learned not to let her mosquito net touch the ground at night because of the ants. She shared her old room with a bat, the ants, a mouse, the mosquitoes, and the rats who came at night to look for food.

There was no phone connection in the compound near the refugee camp. All communication with the outside world happened via Motorola walkie-talkies or the giant shortwave radio. "Arusha, Arusha." She remembered hearing that call when she was there the first time, but she had not really understood then what happened around her. Now she discovered that many of the calls came in from their office in Arusha. And "Whiskey Mike" were the call letters for the World Mission field office. Their compound was located near a village a few kilometers down the road from the refugee camp, and the nearest phone was in a town whose name she could not pronounce, a good three hours away by car, where the airstrip was.

Miriam grew aware of the daily rhythm of the compound. Up at dawn, to bed after dark, when the generator hummed and clattered, providing electricity only at night between eight and eleven. All their laundry and cooking and dishes were taken care of by the various World Mission staff. The water was heated and the cooking was done over open fires.

In the mornings an Isuzu pickup truck rolled in, reggae with an African twang booming from the cab, as some of the staff from the local village arrived for work. Then the twenty or so workers joined the eight staff members for devotions in the round, thatch-roofed building at the center of the compound. In this open meeting place, feeling cool morning breezes and looking out at the ancient baobab tree, Miriam heard children from the nearby village cry and call out while men's deep voices laughed and spoke in a rhythm she now heard as Africa's heartbeat. The cadence of Kiswahili prayers, songs of praise. She thought, *One God, his Word in another tongue*. The Scripture readings made her think of Owen with a sharp pang of longing.

On the first day of her second week in the compound, Miriam listened as Nehemiah translated for her. "Today's message is that the evil in this world cannot be ignored. It is here. To deny this is to cheapen the price Christ paid. Once you accept the evil, you can live in Christ, turn to him every moment, since now you know what it is you turn away from."

Miriam nodded, listening to the chorus of amens around her, but wondered how she could ever turn to Christ every moment.

As she learned the names of the other staff members, Miriam grew curious. She gladly placed herself under the authority of the Tanzanians around her, all men and women who had at some point in their lives found the courage to help refugees. And now, despite diverse backgrounds, they found themselves in this compound, alongside this particular refugee camp, doing the task at hand.

The refugee camp had been set up several years earlier by the Tanzanian government and now resembled a small city in its own right, with a population of more than fifty thousand. The village a few kilometers away housed compounds for the various organizations helping run the camp, including World Mission, which managed the camp, administering the other organizations' efforts. Many of the NGOs and UN organizations also had larger compounds in the town three hours away, where the phone and the airstrip were.

Miriam asked Nehemiah one day, "Why are you here? Don't you have a family?"

"Yes," he said, "and the salary I earn goes back to them. But you know it is not that much. My family lives four hundred kilometers north of here. Here in Africa, it happens often that men work far away from their families—in the cities, in the mines—and then send home the money for school fees, et cetera. I never did this kind of aid work before. I was listening to a BBC interview with a former child-soldier, who said, 'I was ten when the soldiers came into our village and took me into the forest. For four years they fed me and gave me something to drink. Better to stay with them than die.' "

Nehemiah continued, "Children will do anything—trust and believe and obey. When this child was asked at the end of the interview, 'What are your plans?' he said he wanted to go home and be a soldier so he could protect his village and defend his home against anyone who would try to separate him from his family again.

"I see myself in this camp. I see my youngest son, who is nine years old, with these children. I see my family lined up with these people. In the next war, *I* could be the one without a home.

"Here, you learn how much a person needs the love of another. Just one other. Not love in general, but love from just one other person. You are alone and afraid and have nothing. A refugee has run away from home in fear. Then one person says, 'I will help you.' It means everything!

"You asked earlier what I have learned here. Well, I have learned to serve. Yes, it is a calling. I serve the Lord. I am here to comfort the refugees, to comfort as God comforts. Some of these people only look over toward the other side of the lake and say, 'There is our land.' My job is to walk beside them and try to help them think of other things."

The more Miriam learned about her fellow workers in the compound, the more she thought of the community as a religious brotherhood, even a priesthood. Each of the Tanzanians she worked alongside had left his or her family to live here, close to the camp, to care for the refugees. They saw their families sometimes only once a month.

Moses, the camp manager, had kind eyes and gray hair. He was their *mzee,* which means "respected elder" or "chief." Miriam learned to pronounce the Kiswahili word correctly: "em-*zay*-ay."

Miriam knew she would never forget how Moses had welcomed her back when she returned to the compound from Mozambique with Edith. His warm smile as he held both her hands in his melted the cold uncertainty that had plagued her the whole flight back.

Owen had tried to stay alert the entire trip. In the back of trucks, then on a plane, landing somewhere very hot and dry, always blindfolded. The dust and sand felt different here. Days and nights later, he heard voices speaking Arabic and felt hands untying the filthy rag covering his eyes.

They had come for him during the third week of June. But now he did not know the exact date since he did not know how long the trip had taken. Owen knew only that when the moment came to leave his cage, he had looked back before they blindfolded him and wondered why he felt safer inside than outside.

Now he knew. As soon as the cloth was removed, someone struck him full in the face.

Owen looked up, blood stinging his eyes. Through the haze he saw two figures approaching, the sun bright behind them and blinding him to their features. Heat tremors shook the mountains of sand around him. The sun beat down; he tasted salt on his lips. Owen raised his chin.

All during the long trip he had tried to keep his emotions in check, to listen and feel what was happening to him. Alongside every thought lurked his worry for Miriam and Martin. *Let them still be alive. Let them be safe.* He had also primed himself for what he felt sure would be a key encounter, reviewing the few facts he knew about Sudan, the oil deals there, outlining the suggestions Falin had let slip before his communication blackout a half year earlier.

Owen squinted at the men striding toward him, trying to summon to mind all these thoughts and plans. Two additional men flanked him. His assailant appeared from Owen's left and slammed his fist into Owen's gut. Owen crumpled. The men on both sides dragged him to his feet.

He opened his eyes as the two who were walking stopped before him. One was dressed in black and carried a heavy pack. The other stood with legs spread, barking in Arabic at the two men who held Owen and the one who had struck him. Owen blinked the sweat out of his eyes. He saw crimson robes dancing in the hot breeze, a turban of a slightly darker hue, a full beard partially hiding thin lips, eyes narrowed to slits.

The man opened his eyes wide, and Owen saw the sheerest shade of green. "I see you recognize me."

"El-Fatih," Owen said, his heart sinking. He had to gather his strength not to surrender all hope of surviving this ordeal.

Owen had met the man only once before, a year ago, in London, while seeking a connection with the supply of IRA arms. El-Fatih, a Libyan arms dealer among his other roles in many parts of the world, had stood in the background during the meeting with contacts from the suppliers. That initial meeting had been a preamble for the talks that later broke down.

Owen had operated at the time under the assumption that stopping the flow of arms from Libya and America, the two main sources for Irish terrorists, would bring peace to his homeland. What he discovered then was that the IRA would agree to everything but surrendering their arms. Even without his personal complications in the case, this would have been enough to break the deal. But the combination of his family history and the sheer power of the man now standing before him had proven doubly destructive to the cause of peace.

Owen's mind raced. If El-Fatih was the one pulling Falin's strings, then this situation involved much more than just a few mercenaries training a few other mercenaries. When the Irish talks failed last year, Owen had shut down the negotiations, walked away, and prevented any deal whatsoever. He wanted no part in the power shifts going on behind the scenes, was unwilling to trade his integrity even for lasting peace. His refusal to compromise had cost him, but he had insisted that no good could come of traveling a trail that branched off into the illegal weapons market and illegal profits from war, diamonds, and oil.

And Owen knew this was exactly what this man standing before him represented. He knew because the man himself had told him when he attempted to bribe Owen.

Owen struggled with the implications. How could he use his knowledge of Falin's loosely formed conglomerate of Russian mafia factions, an umbrella syndicate with connections among both the Angolan rebels and government people? How did it all link up with Libyan terrorist trainers of the IRA? *So I was targeted.* He coughed and said, "I thought this was all about Sudan. Tell me what you want."

"Is that what Yury told you? Perhaps it was for the benefit of someone who might be listening. It does not matter. No, I arranged for your cooperation specifically, after our brief encounter in the Irish question."

Owen strained at the possibilities, lunging at conclusions. Because he had turned down the bribe? "This is about Ireland?"

"Now you disappoint me. Of course not. I need a man known for his honesty. And yes, if you do well, we may use you for future jobs. Perhaps Sudan would be one of them, but for the moment, the war there continues to serve its purpose very nicely indeed. The oil wells provide a handsome revenue to everyone involved in prolonging the conflict."

Owen's mind latched on to three words of precious information: *the war there.* So they had not brought him to Sudan after all. Or had they? El-Fatih had a reputation for ruthless lies and the manipulation of power. Owen braced himself against the sheer danger of the man, against believing anything, against taking anything for granted.

"Where am I?" he asked.

El-Fatih said, "Please accept my apologies for such an inhospitable welcome. It is not what my people are known for. If you would turn around . . ."

As Owen felt himself released by the strong hands on both arms, he followed El-Fatih's gaze beyond his shoulder. He began to turn in the sand as El-Fatih's voice continued, "You will see that things are not as they seem. Not everything here is dust and desert."

Owen wondered what he meant and raised his eyes. Not thirty meters away rose a stone wall; beyond it, some sort of fort with a mosque and minarets, a massive structure surrounded by palm trees, their tops barely visible beyond the top of the wall. Through the open gate he caught sight of a fountain, a small lake. Between Owen and the walls stood the truck that had brought him here.

Owen shook his head. "An oasis."

"My oasis," said El-Fatih.

Chapter 52

Miriam awoke every morning in the compound to the sounds of roosters, a bell clanging, something that sounded like an outdoor organ, the voices of women going for water, children crying.

She took her showers at night before going to bed, in a far corner of the compound near the toilet area. Lanterns hung on the outside walls. Sometimes she heard a child crying the whole time. Whitewashed brick, dirt, and clay formed her shower cell. She wore rubber sandals and showered with warm water from a plastic bucket standing on a bar above her head. At the bottom of the bucket were some holes poked out with a ballpoint. There was a plug, and when she turned a valve in the plug, this acted as a shower spout. When the bucket was empty, her shower was over.

Each day Nehemiah continued to work with her, teaching her many things she needed to know—the basics of Kiswahili, the camp hierarchy, the histories of the peoples represented in the refugee camp, cultural cues, body language, ways to listen, and how a camp with fifty thousand people functioned. After her training with Nehemiah, she could begin taking Edith's workshops on helping the children.

It took two weeks of instruction before Nehemiah told her more about why he was there. They were sharing a meal of *chapati,* a kind of flat, round bread. They sat tearing off pieces of *chapati* to pick up the other foods on their plates. Miriam was careful to use her right hand only.

In answer to another one of Miriam's questions about his background, Nehemiah coughed. Then, without looking at her, he said, "I worked in the air force ten years as a transport officer. We brought soldiers to and from Uganda during the war against Idi Amin. The effects of wars now seem nastier than back then. In Uganda the soldiers could kill and come home, drink, be paid more than most people, receive their bonus, and forget until it was time to go to the next war. You know, Edith's brother, Paul, also served in the army. Special forces. Actually, I believe he's still in the reserve forces. So his uniform is much flashier than anything I ever wore." Nehemiah broke out in a deep, expansive laugh.

Miriam smiled with him, still wanting the rest of the story. She waited, saying nothing.

Finally, Nehemiah continued, "Now I think every soldier should visit a refugee camp. Here you realize that for every person killed there is a foster child, a single-parent family, an unaccompanied minor, an orphan, a widow. Here you see the true price of war."

He paused and only then looked up at her, but sideways, confessing. "I am not young. Maybe I want to try and make right the things I did in that war by helping the refugees here."

A little later Moses and some other staff entered the dining area. Miriam watched as the younger men fetched Moses' food and bottle of Coke for him. The first thing everyone always did before a meal was thoroughly wash his or her hands with water heated over the fire, and soap. Bent over a basin, they turned open the flow of water from an old coffee percolator.

Miriam saw Edith's form block the light in the doorway. "You would think we would run into each other more often in such a small place." Edith laughed as she took a seat beside Miriam. The fact was, they saw each other only a few times a week, sometimes at meals. While Miriam was undergoing her cultural training with Nehemiah, Edith's skills were in high demand elsewhere.

"I'm the only psychologist on-site," she said, "and unfortunately that means I spend most of my time giving workshops for the other field workers."

"And you'd rather be . . . ?"

"With the children, of course. I'll find a balance soon, but it's hard. On the one hand, there are people—well, like you, Miriam—who come from all sorts of backgrounds and just know they want to help. So they need to be trained. If they're not from East Africa, they are first given cultural sensitivity training, like what you've been getting from Nehemiah. Then they come to me. When I train others, more children are helped than I could help if I were alone. I have to realize this more often. But at the same time, I miss my kids."

Miriam nodded. "So do I. I feel like I'm split in two—or three even. One part is focused on my training, but the other is always wondering about Owen and Martin, and the third part is thinking of my kids, the boys who saved me in the bush. I don't know what to do with myself sometimes."

"Look what you've endured," Edith said. "This is all psychologically valid, Miriam. You switched into coping mechanism and became ill and lived as a different person after you were separated from Owen. These last two weeks are the first time in what I suspect is several months that the world—the real world—has opened up to you again."

Miriam recalled that she perceived more details now, like the bluish weeds bobbing in the wind. They must have been there before, but she hadn't noticed them. "Well, my kids—I don't know if I'll ever see them again, but I think of them, pray for their safety every day. And I feel like Owen and Martin are with me; I just can't see them. Oh, I don't know. I *long* to find them again. Sometimes I don't think I can stand to be separated from them one more day. The uncertainty . . . All right, you said you want to be nearer the children. What about those children you taught in that art class? I remember . . . in the devotions building, you had a class."

"Yes." Edith was watching her closely. "They're not here anymore. They were shipped off to another camp. This is one of the reasons I could go to Mozambique when I did. So, have you been thinking about that morning you visited the class?"

"Yes, I remember everything, but there are some things I don't understand. You know, those children—I've always wondered why they said and did nothing when I was there."

Edith replied, "This often happens when strangers visit my classes. With this particular group, I saw their noise as an indication of their trust in me—trust I had built up with them. They were the loudest group I ever had. Then you came in. And it wasn't just you, because after you left, I tried it again with Nehemiah here. The children just froze. It proves they were still traumatized."

They ate together in silence until the meal was finished. Miriam had learned to leave some food behind as a sign to the cook that she had been satisfied. Edith gestured to the remnant on Miriam's plate. "In the West it is the other way, I've heard. Children are taught to clean their plates—is that right?"

"Well, in some places, yes. But there are so many things different from here. For instance, in the country where my parents came from, Holland, they have a problem with too much water."

One of the men at their table said, "What? How is that possible?"

Another one spoke up. "She is right. I studied in Holland for one year and saw it was true. They are afraid of flooding, and they even use canals as fences for the livestock."

"Don't the cows just swim to the other side?"

"No," he said. "Every now and then you hear about a cow who falls in the water. But while I was there, I never heard of any who swam across."

"Then they have dumb cows. African cows can swim across whole rivers. When we have water."

They all laughed very loudly at this, and then Moses asked Miriam to tell them something of what she had been learning. "Let us see how well Nehemiah has done his job."

Miriam looked around the table at the warm smiles and swallowed. "Well, I've learned that the *kanga* is a traditional printed cloth bearing a proverb. Women wear the kangas in pairs. One kanga is usually worn over a dress or skirt to protect the clothing, and the second may either cover her head or be used as a sling to carry a baby on her back."

"Yes," said Moses, "this is very important. Every woman knows about kangas. Very good. And your Kiswahili?"

She laughed again. "Talking during a meal is usually viewed as *tabia ya kizungu,* a European habit. Tonight we ate *chakula kitamu*, delicious food. We are all here for the *watoto*, the children. *Tunajitegemea* means 'We depend on ourselves.' *Nimechoka* means 'I'm tired.' *Kwa nini unasafiri peke yako?* means 'Why are you traveling alone?' Tonight we ate *ugali*, corn or cassava flour mixed in hot water until it becomes stiff like bread. And *karibu chakula* means 'bon appétit.'"

Miriam glanced at Nehemiah, and he gave her one of his sidelong smiles of approval while the others all laughed with her and clapped. Miriam felt relieved when the conversation returned to administrative issues concerning the camp. As she poured boiled water from the thermos jug into a mug and added the powdered instant coffee, Miriam thought about some of the marvelous things she had learned about these people that she *hadn't* said out loud.

She saw these Tanzanians as people of joy and grace. At any moment of the day she could look up from wherever she was and see them walking, men with men and women with women, holding hands, laughing, smiling, sometimes slapping each other on the shoulder or lingering in the three-part African handshake. When they greeted each other, the encounter took a long time. Many things were said. "Hello, good day, greetings. . . . How are you? . . . Do you have news? . . . How is your health? . . . Your family's health? . . . Your crops?" And whenever anyone said something funny, people responded with a soft slapping of fingers onto the other person's palm. The only times she had heard Tanzanians shout was when they were joking. These were the images Miriam treasured most.

She had also learned that the Kiswahili word for "stranger," *mgeni*, was also the word for "guest." And this was in keeping with the generous history of Tanzania, a subject she had been reading about in the books Nehemiah loaned her. She had learned that although Tanzania was a poor country, refugee camps had been there for twenty years. Ever since independence in 1961, Tanzania had demonstrated an overwhelming willingness to take in large numbers of refugees. Hundreds of thousands of people from Mozambique, South Africa, Rwanda, Burundi, and Zaïre had found safe haven in Tanzania during the seventies and eighties.

Miriam had read a lot about Tanzania's first president, Julius Nyerere. He had gone to extraordinary lengths to provide refugees a dignified existence, sometimes even offering them land and housing. During the eighties, Tanzania had the largest refugee concentration of any East African country. President Nyerere had even granted citizenship to all the Burundian refugees who came to Tanzania in 1972. Most Tanzanians revered their former president and considered him a valuable elder statesman. Although he had come under criticism for some of his socialist policies and for the invasion of Uganda in 1979, which drained government resources, his wish to depose Idi Amin was also viewed as an act of courage, as was his longstanding opposition to apartheid.

"Well, Miriam, what do you say?"

She looked up at them all, their eyes an invitation. She knew they knew she hadn't been listening. She waited as they chuckled and nodded. Then Moses said, "I was saying that perhaps tomorrow would be a good day for you to visit the refugee camp for the first time and start working with the children."

Yury looked at the boy. "Tell him to do it again. And if he can't aim any better, he receives no food. Will he never learn?"

Joseph returned to the shooting range. Yury saw the boy drop the half-opened weapon into the dust. Now he would have a time cleaning it. *And he'll get every grain of sand out if it takes him all day.* Yury watched approvingly as Joseph cuffed the boy, sending him flying.

The boy began to say something back to Joseph. Yury walked out to the range. "What did you say?"

The boy saluted. Well, that was something at least. "I can't . . . see."

"What?"

"I used to have glasses, and I can't see far away without them."

Joseph moved down the line to the other boys, correcting their posture and how they held their guns.

Yury sighed. He went up to Martin. "You need glasses? Is that why you're so bad at shooting?"

"Yes, Commandant."

"Well, it's no excuse for dropping your gun in the dust."

"No, Commandant."

Yury heard the other boys snickering at Martin. He whirled. "You want food?" he barked at the boy standing nearest. Silence fell in that direction.

Then he turned back to Martin. "Do you see anywhere I can get you glasses? I think if you try a little harder you can do better. Your parents spoiled you. Now do it right!" he ordered.

Martin stared at him. "Yes, Commandant." The next time he aimed and fired, he hit the target.

Yury snorted. "Finally."

Starve them, beat them, feed them. Yury knew it was the only way to get the best out of boys like this.

It was good enough for me.

Chapter 53

The next morning, with Moses' words ringing in her ears, Miriam climbed into the old white Land Rover for her first trip to the refugee camp. Before driving off, Nehemiah and the driver bowed their heads and prayed. Miriam did the same. After the prayer, Nehemiah translated. "We prayed for safety and that we would say and do what Jesus wants us to this day."

Less than an hour down the road, they passed through a checkpoint at the gate to the camp. Miriam's first reaction to the camp was one of surprise since she had expected something similar to what she had seen in Mozambique. But this camp was a much more permanent establishment. The main buildings were made of stone, and many of the refugees had built homes for themselves using red-clay brick and plaster. Still visible were the edges of the blue plastic UNHCR tarps, which served as an underlayer for thatched roofs.

Miriam also saw some huts made of tree branches and other homes with walls made of bundles of grass tied together. All of these less permanent dwellings were covered with the familiar blue tarps. The houses were lined up along streets, and the camp went on almost as far as she could see.

As they drove slowly along, being careful for the many people and potholes, Nehemiah confirmed that the camp spread out over an area much larger than either the local village or the nearest town. In fact, it would take almost an hour to drive from one end of the camp to the other. He said that, of the fifty thousand refugees living in the camp, more than half were children. He added in an apologetic tone that there was not enough food to go around. Nehemiah pointed out the layout of the neighborhoods and explained that the camp had its own government, with one year a woman, the next year a man serving as camp president.

Everywhere children stood watching and waving at them as they drove past. Though separate NGOs were responsible for the various aspects of the camp's operation, World Mission coordinated the different efforts and helped maintain the roads as well as taking care of food distribution. It was obvious just from looking around that resources were strained. The people needed more food, and the roads needed more attention.

Miriam rolled down the window, despite the dust, and watched one young girl carrying a tall bucket full of water, the sunlight shining through the orange plastic. The girl held one hand at her forehead, the palm against her face, fingers cupped upward against the bucket, like a one-handed prayer of supplication.

When they stopped in front of one of the stone buildings and finally got out of the Land Rover, Nehemiah introduced Miriam to the Unaccompanied Minors coordinator. Jonah, himself a refugee, devoted his time and energy to tracing the parents of lost children, seeking to reunite families. Jonah coordinated his efforts with UNICEF and Red Cross/Red Crescent personnel. They went inside and sat at a table on undersized wooden chairs.

In soft tones Jonah spoke of the war as if it waited for them just outside the open windows of the building they met in. "War separated these children from their parents. Many came home from school one day and found their parents dead or missing. They ran away into the forest, in terror from the war. Some families were separated when running away. At night, or in panic, the parents went one way and the child went another.

"The children, if they are lucky, find someone in the forest who says they may join their group. This small group finds another small group, and they become a larger group. The war is following them, hunting them. After months of hiding and running on foot in the most terrifying conditions, without water or food, not knowing what direction to run and in a constant state of desperate fear, sometimes they reach the border and can be offered protection in a camp like this one."

Miriam listened, her heart pounding in her chest. *I have been there*, she thought. Although she was the newcomer, she knew firsthand the very conditions Jonah described. Here in the camp, surrounded by children who were victims of war, that other place, that other dimension, her other existence, suddenly seemed much closer. *How is it possible that I ever survived?*

"Why do you do this?" Miriam interjected, trying to mask her own memories. "How can you stand to hear their stories?"

Jonah shook his head as if she had misunderstood. "Because there are also the stories of children being reunited with their parents. And stories of children going to school for the first time. And children finding foster homes.

"A child who has lost her parents will have only one wish, and that is to find her parents again. Each time a child is reunited, I feel reborn, as if I have just found my own parents. This job teaches me about love. We try to find foster families for the children who arrive without parents. When this is possible, we try to teach each of the foster parents that they must imagine how they would want their *own* children to be treated should they ever become lost. It puts things into perspective." He paused. "Of course, we try to get all unaccompanied minors assigned to foster families, but many of the child-soldiers go unwanted."

After an awkward silence, Miriam asked, "And your own children? May I ask where they are?"

From his shirt pocket Jonah withdrew a piece of paper, unfolded it, and revealed a color photo. Miriam recognized the trees in the camp, and Jonah told her the names of his children. "I have three children of my own. One was born in this camp. I have lived here four years."

"Four years! Don't you miss your home?" The words were out before she could stop them.

"I'm not homeless," he said as if expecting this to be her meaning. "I have a home—*my* house, in *my* country. And yes, I miss my own home, my own land. Yet I know it will be a long time before peace comes."

Nehemiah, sitting beside her, nodded solemnly. "We can pray for God's miracle, his intervention."

Miriam looked at the two men and wondered at their vision, their courage in light of their own losses and the tremendous needs surrounding them.

Nehemiah had told Miriam she would probably be assigned to Jonah's UAM department. She would need to undergo Edith's training before actually working with the children, but she was welcome now to meet some of the other staff in the department and get a feel for the camp itself.

For the next hour or so, Miriam walked around shaking hands, listening to stories, and trying to remember names. Rachel, a former child-soldier, now worked with the next generation, while Grace, a former au pair from England, helped as a hospital supply worker. Grace mentioned that they often had shortages of medicines and other basic medical supplies.

At the community-services office, Miriam met a man who said he was a Buddhist from Switzerland. He told her that the woman from New Zealand who usually taught the prenatal nutrition classes was on furlough, back in her own country for a year.

The last place Nehemiah brought her was an area set aside for classrooms. These buildings were more like open-air pavilions, with frames and supporting columns made from tree trunks and with roofs of thatch covering the ever-present blue plastic sheeting. Low wooden walls ended in open spaces, windows without glass. In these airy schoolrooms, classes of fifty children in the morning and fifty in the afternoon sat on half logs coated with red dust. Without notebooks, without pens, the children listened to their teachers and wrote on slates with chalk. With a pang, Miriam thought of the red pen hanging from Little Lion's neck and how very much he had wanted to go to school.

As they crossed the area leading up to the largest of the school buildings, Nehemiah told Miriam, "Only the primary-aged children go to school for free. Their teachers are themselves refugees in the camp and receive only a small stipend. All secondary-education classes are taught by volunteers. Some of them are university professors who hold doctorates but had to flee when war broke out."

When Miriam looked at him in surprise, he went on. "Yes, most of the refugees here are well-educated people who speak several languages. Many had their own businesses, even nice cars, and sometimes a second home in the mountains. It is not unusual for the intellectuals in a society to be the first targets of a harsh regime. Educated people do pose the greatest threat with their understanding of the larger world and their ability to organize opposition.

"In any case, here they are paid nothing and there is no money for books, so a small amount of tuition is asked of each student, but even this amount often causes hardship. All the younger children receive classes in different languages, including sign language, and they learn math, science, history, and social studies. The attitude of these people is that they want to make good use of their time here and teach as much as they can to their children so that when there is peace and they go back home, an educated generation can run the country. Ah, here we are. See, this is what we call our 'school under the trees.'"

Miriam had heard the children before she and Nehemiah reached the building. A man stood outside waiting for them. Nehemiah introduced him as one of the teachers.

"This is a good day for you to visit," the teacher told them. "The children are rehearsing a play they have written themselves. They hope to go to Dar and perform it there for World Refugee Day. Will you come and join us?"

Miriam bowed her head under the tree-bough doorway and entered the children's world. She watched their faces, heard their songs and laughter. Light from the window filtered through fine red dust. A young girl drummed in the sun's spotlight.

A teacher offered Miriam and Nehemiah two of the four white plastic chairs in the room. When Miriam crossed her legs, the two girls sitting on the other side of the room watching her did the same. Every motion Miriam made, the girls imitated, down to the way she held her hands. Finally, Miriam smiled at them. They smiled back.

"These children are very bright, and they love having an audience," Nehemiah whispered to her.

Miriam thought again of Little Lion. "Yes, I've seen that."

The children danced in a circle, kangas tied low around their hips. A young boy and a young girl, followed by a teenage boy and a teenage girl, moved their shoulders, shuffling forward step by step, then swaying hips against each other from the back and from the side.

Miriam sat for an hour, listening to the children sing and dance, act out scenes, and recite poetry. The theme of all their creative effort was peace. A young girl said with arms outstretched, "Yesterday, today, division, democracy, equality, justice! War never brings peace. We are all the same. There must be no more war!"

Another child stood to speak. "Children! Children of the world, listen and help us! War separates families. War makes children into soldiers. War kills people. War made us run away. War never brings peace. Children of other countries, band together to end war in our countries!"

Although the performances went on, a silence seemed to descend on the teachers, the children performing, the parents watching, and the many other faces peering in through the open windows, sunlight and dappled tree shadows framing their faces. One boy cradled his baby brother in his arms. Miriam caught herself saying under her breath, "There must be something I can do here, some way I can help."

After the program, Miriam and Nehemiah thanked the teachers and the children. "You should be very proud," Miriam said.

Back outside, a group of children hurried past her, kicking a ball between them. When Miriam looked more closely, she saw bare feet kicking a bundle of rags glued together.

Owen's eyes drank in the sight of the lush oasis. El-Fatih had pointedly ignored his question about where they were. He growled at the men around Owen, and they bowed and jogged back to the vehicle, leaving them alone. "You must pardon them. They are used to another type of prisoner. Please follow me."

Owen looked behind him at the vast mountains of sand—red, orange, darker red, on into the distance, as far as he could see. To the left and right, more sand. Before him, this place of green, water, life. He could be anywhere in North Africa—Libya, Mauritania, northern Sudan. "Where else would I go?" he mumbled.

"Indeed," responded El-Fatih.

Owen found he had trouble walking more than a few steps without stopping to rest. His neck and shoulders ached from his new freedom to stand upright. By the time he reached the gate he was panting, waves of sound rushing through his ears.

El-Fatih waited for him and nodded. "I understand Yury has kept you these many months in less than agreeable accommodation. I hope you will find my home somewhat more comfortable. I have never understood how he could live in the jungle like that. He insists he prefers the field. However, I have business to attend to now, so you will excuse me."

El-Fatih swept away. Two young men approached Owen and nodded. He followed them into a palatial part of the fort. Mosaic floors, marble columns, high ceilings, cool air, dark passageways—Owen tried to take it all in, but the murmur in his ears had grown to a roar. Just when he thought he could not take another step, his escorts swung open a pair of huge oak doors and stood at either side. Owen entered a suite with wooden slats over the windows in a diagonal design. Cushions and carpets warmed the corners of the space, while in the center bubbled a light green pool. On a table stood bowls of fruit and hummus and flatbread, beside them plastic bottles of water, their sides dripping with condensation.

Owen stumbled, and the young men caught him before his head could hit the stone floor. After so very long, the sight of so much luxury overwhelmed him, focused his weakness. He did not know whether to cry or laugh.

Two hours later, however, Owen felt reborn. For the first time in over half a year he had bathed, shaven, and eaten something more than scraps. His stomach was not happy with the fruit, though; he realized he would have to take it slow. He still battled the dizziness, but as he descended the stairs, he found he could straighten his shoulders almost all the way. He followed the young man who had brought him the cotton robes he wore, the same one who had helped him shave when his own hands would not hold steady.

Now he entered a vast room, a ballroom, and found El-Fatih alone, sitting on the floor surrounded by piles of papers, a laptop resting on a pillow to his right. He reached over and clicked closed its lid, then stood as Owen approached. A door shut softly at the far end of the hall.

"You feel better, I hope."

"Yes, thank you. I am grateful for the water and food and the cool, dry air. And for your hospitality."

El-Fatih smiled slightly and motioned for Owen to sit, then did the same. "I am sure you have been trying to sort out the various connections."

Owen nodded. He had been doing little else. "This is not about Sudan," he said. "This is not about Ireland."

El-Fatih pulled at his beard. His eyes danced.

Owen sighed and switched tacks. "How is your youngest son?"

The man sitting opposite him acquiesced, bowing low.

Owen thought, *First round, mine.*

El-Fatih said, "This is what I enjoy, talking as one civilized man to another. My son is well, thank you. He will have his MBA next week, in fact. I will not be able to attend the matriculation ceremonies, however, as there is a meeting on a certain Greek yacht that calls for my attention."

Owen had searched his brain while in the bath for any personal details he could remember about El-Fatih. The only one that had come to mind was this son studying in. . . . "He's in Boston, isn't that right?"

"No, in Philadelphia. The Jesuits, you know."

"What about the rules of Islam?" Owen asked.

"They still apply. But he is there to learn discipline and obedience. The Jesuits teach these things better than any imam I know. My other two sons studied in London and Moscow. This way they get a good education, and I keep the markets covered as they develop business networks for the future. Several friends of the two elder boys are already being groomed for ministerial positions in their respective countries. A few are CEOs in their own right."

Another pause followed. Owen wondered how much small talk would be required before they reached the reason for this meeting, but El-Fatih surprised him. "Now, Mr. O'Neill, you are familiar with the Bicesse Accord?"

Owen's mind fastened onto the first mention of actual details. *Of course! The Bicesse Accord of Angola!* So he had been very close when he hinted at this possibility to Miriam. Why hadn't he thought of it since then? His mind must be very dulled to not have reached that one logical conclusion. When was it again? Recently . . . yes, two years earlier—what had he read? He tried to force his mind back into the situation he had been asked to assess. There had been some similarities to the Mozambique agreement and one huge difference. The similarities had to do with a post–Cold War shuffling of allies. The difference was that no real peace had been made.

He answered El-Fatih with the truth. If he spoke openly now, he could later draw against that deposit of trust. Besides, El-Fatih would already know everything Owen was telling him, and Owen's words would just confirm his goodwill. "Yes. I received a memo from a colleague asking for my input as a consultant. I passed."

"Not so willing to switch sides?"

"No, too busy with the Mozambique deal."

"Well, you're not too busy now, are you?" El-Fatih stood and started pacing.

Owen said nothing. If Angola was the sphere of influence, then diamonds and oil were the stakes. But who . . . ?

"I am not the source." El-Fatih stopped walking and spoke with his back turned so Owen could read nothing from his body language. "Yury is my man in the field, and I gave him the job of obtaining your services. But I am here in the capacity of someone who was wronged by the very sort of politics you oppose so outspokenly. Which is why I have brought you here. What do you know of this Angolan agreement?"

Owen said slowly, "I think it is more a question of what I do *not* know. I know the Bicesse Accord was an attempt to end the conflict between the Angolan government and the rebels. I'll be honest with you; because I was involved in our little Irish fiasco, I wasn't exactly reading every article about Angola. I have no idea what happened after the treaty was signed or even how the talks ended."

"They ended surprisingly. Yes, there are certain parallels with your own recent success in Mozambique, which was yet another reason for inviting you here."

"So what have you given me so far? Besides the fact that I hate switchovers, couldn't be bribed, have a reputation for honesty, and booked success in Mozambique, why am I really here?"

El-Fatih said, "Let me just say this is because you will know how to achieve results with the parties involved."

Owen hesitated, then said slowly, "You want me to take a job outside the State Department?"

"No. We want you to take one inside."

Chapter 54

During the next week, Miriam accompanied Nehemiah to the refugee camp almost every day. There she spent time helping out the various people she had met the first day. At the end of those seven days, it was time to begin her formal training. Moses told Miriam she would be attending Edith's weeklong lecture series starting in town the next day.

The more time Miriam spent with the children in the refugee camp, the more sure she became that this was where she wanted to be as she worked and waited for news of Owen and Martin. So far, everything she had been learning seemed geared toward helping her come alongside the children and meet their needs effectively. Edith's workshop promised to expand those skills while giving Miriam an even more focused view of what she would be doing.

Early Monday morning, then, Miriam took a vehicle that had to be dropped off in town for a World Mission arrival from the airstrip, threw onto the backseat a bag full of letters and packages to be mailed, and drove in the opposite direction from the camp, toward town.

Just the night before, Moses had warned her that there would be quite a crowd and she should get there on time. "Our Edith always has a full house." When Miriam looked at him questioningly, Moses had smiled. "You didn't know? She has published three books about children in armed conflict. She's an expert in her field. I believe there will even be some visitors from the former Yugoslavia who want to help children traumatized by the conflict there." He paused. "But knowing Edith, I suppose she wouldn't have told you all that."

Miriam thought about this during the three-hour drive, about how effectively Edith had helped her. *Is it just by chance that I ended up with exactly the right person, a psychologist with the expertise and wisdom to know how to help me? Is it by chance that I was rescued by a group of children with enough survival skills to get me to this place of safety? Is it by chance that Owen and I were kidnapped?* Her mind wandered, thinking of the implications.

Once in town, Miriam ran the errands Moses had asked of her, just as she had a few times earlier with Nehemiah. At the post office, when she picked up the mail, an envelope with a U.S. stamp and her name on it caught Miriam's attention. She recognized the handwriting and tore it open.

The letter from Sue contained words of comfort. It bridged Miriam's two worlds. Sue was offering to fly out and join Miriam, to do whatever it took to help find Martin and Owen.

Miriam glanced at the envelope again. Sue had written in care of the World Mission office, which meant Happiness *had* passed on Miriam's details to the list of people she had given her before flying out of Dar. At least *someone* was following through on an offer of help, unlike what she had experienced at the embassy.

Miriam did not wait. She ripped some paper out of her notebook and wrote Sue back with a list of people to contact and offices to call, pleading with her to be Miriam's eyes and ears back in the States. She told her to stay put. Together they *would* find Owen and Martin. They *had* to. When she had finished, Miriam read over the letter and wished she really believed her own words. Then she bought an envelope and the stamps and mailed the letter before leaving the post office. It would go out with the afternoon plane said the woman behind the counter.

Now Miriam tried to shift mental gears, to come back to her present reality. On the way to the World Mission office, she rumbled past the offices of several aid organizations for refugees and children. Here all the offices together formed a separate, newly built part of town. She noted the satellite dishes on the roofs, something she had forgotten about during her month "in the field," as town-based people referred to any outlying locations. New-looking four-wheel-drive vehicles sat in front of many of the new buildings. She couldn't help noting contrasts with her own compound, where the staff chose to drive second-hand vehicles and use walkie-talkies with weak batteries so they could have more resources to meet the needs of the refugees.

When Miriam reached the World Mission office, she dropped off Moses' envelopes and packages and made sure they had a guest room left for her. All this took much longer than Miriam had planned. So despite Moses' warning, Miriam arrived late for Edith's first lecture. As she pulled up to the community center, Miriam noted the insignias on other vehicles. It appeared that representatives from several international organizations were there, in addition to the social workers, teachers, and refugee workers Moses had said she would meet. Frustrated and out of breath, Miriam hurried down the hallway and slipped into a seat at the back.

Edith was already speaking. About fifty men and women sat in the white plastic chairs and took notes. Edith was answering a question someone had asked. "I've heard this story before," she said. "Independent of one another, the children's groups who make it here often say angels led them or that God showed them the way. When I ask what the angels looked like, they say light. When I ask how they knew it was God leading them, one boy said, 'Madam, surely when you hear the voice of God you know who it is.' "

A murmur of laughter ran through the group, and Miriam smiled.

Edith continued, "So yes, I believe them, though I have never been privileged to be in such a dark place that this light shone bright enough for me to discern it. You have to keep in mind that these children, especially the former child-soldiers, have a hard time discerning the real world from other worlds. And we cannot force them to remember anything that is too painful for them. We must always remember that these are children.

"It is very hard for these children to know how they should cope with the horrors they have survived. We use art, dance, and theater to help them work though their trauma. And whenever possible, we try to get them to tell their stories, to share what happened to them. This helps them face their fear and their guilt and begin to move on.

"When children arrive, we ask those who can to write about the day they came to the camp. They can write about anything that happened before that, but they usually find it easiest to start with the recent past.

Those who cannot write are given clay and paints, or we try to get them to describe out loud what happened. Always remember that when we listen to someone's story, we give back the gifts of dignity and integrity to the teller. So, one of the things we'll be working on here is our listening skills.

"We've found that if children can tell the truth once, there is hope. Then we set the story aside and move on. Repeated tellings, as requested by some of the journalists who come through the camps, is very bad for the children. Once is enough. And even once is not easy for many children. Their experiences differ. And they differ from tribe to tribe, country to country. Congolese children, for example, are much more communicative than, say, Ethiopian children, who will see everything but remain shy. Many children say what they think others want them to say, desperate for approval.

"At the same time, be prepared to hear them say your questions are ignorant. Did they see dead people? 'Who didn't?' they will answer. Did it hurt them to leave everyone behind? They will say something like they did not think of their hurt; they had to run away. The real challenge is getting them to talk about their own emotions, how they *feel*. Do that and again; there is hope for recovery.

"Now," she said, "I want to shift the focus back to child-soldiers. Let us be clear about what we are discussing. Adult soldiers manipulate and force children, sometimes as young as six, with brutality, so they in turn will torture and kill others. Keep in mind that, worldwide, nearly thirty major conflicts involve children as combatants, porters, spies, cooks, and sex slaves for older soldiers. Some children want to learn how to handle the lightweight AK-47, believing it will improve their own safety in war zones. These lighter weapons mean children as young as eight can be armed.

"Children blindly obey whomever they fear, even if given the most evil orders. This is their desperate way of winning adults' approval and affection. Many see the army as a surrogate parent. The army has fed, clothed, and given them shelter. To gain the approval they need, the children might surpass the barbarity of their original instructions.

"I know a commander who said he would rather face an armed adult soldier than an armed child-soldier. A child is unpredictable. Many of them have been made addicts or alcoholics, which compounds their instability. Add to that the hormonal changes of adolescence and you have a formula for disaster. Also, children have more stamina, are better at surviving in the bush, do not complain, and follow directions."

A hand went up and a voice with a German accent asked, "Is there no protection for the children from international quarters?"

Edith answered, "There is the 1989 UN Convention on the Rights of the Child. Larger countries can set sanctions or place pressure on those who have agreed to it, but not all countries have signed this, including the U.S."

She paused. "Listen, our focus here is not on political solutions but on helping the individual children who have managed to escape. The good news is we've found that children are extremely resilient. With support and guidance, they can learn to cope. And they must learn in order to survive. The children you will be working with are the survivors, obviously. And it stands to reason that many of those who made it are quite gifted. They have courage, optimism, fortitude—the very qualities we must cultivate in ourselves. Our jobs are to help these children as they come to terms with what has happened to them, what they have seen, and what they have been forced to do. They retain their hopes and a passion. And they still have a future. We must remember this.

"More than anything," Edith said, "the former child-soldiers want peace and the chance to go to school. Many of the girls dream of becoming nurses. Some of the boys want to become ministers. I have seen children here take on full responsibility for younger siblings and other children as well. With the tidal wave of AIDS orphans, child-headed households are becoming more and more common. The testimony coming through the lives of these children speaks to our best instincts. They soften our hearts."

Chapter 55

Miriam spent the next week feeling like she was back in law school. Between the lectures and reading material, not to mention small-group discussions, her mind spun with statistics and theories and reports.

Edith's final lecture before taking them in small groups to observe her work with children in the field took place Friday morning.

As Miriam sat in the now familiar room letting the words wash over her, she couldn't help but feel that Edith meant them for her, spoke directly to the bemused and split parts Miriam still juggled during each day, but especially at night. The part of her that waited—for news about Owen and Martin. The part that wondered—whether her boys still survived somewhere in the bush. And the part that was willing—to help, no matter what.

Edith's last words lodged firmly in her mind and heart: *"Remember, every child has a name and a story."*

In many ways Miriam felt she stood at a crossroads. That afternoon, as she drove back to the compound with Edith at her side, Miriam brought this up. "I know you must be exhausted—," she started to say.

"No, I always have a great deal of energy after these sessions," Edith said. "Why do you say that? How did all this affect you?"

"Well, I'm haunted by the knowledge that what I went through—I mean, after the kidnapping. Well actually, during that too. Anyway, I can't get over the fact that my experience with the Simba brothers was merely an average occurrence for hundreds of thousands of children around the world. I mean, how do you or I—or anyone—cope against such overwhelming odds?"

"By 'cope' you mean not give up helping? It is a common enough reaction, even for people who did not endure what you did," Edith said. "I have it too sometimes. This has a name: compassion fatigue.

"Miriam, I don't want you to underestimate what I was talking about on our last day in Mozambique. About the need for forgiveness and divine healing. Some of the organizations represented in these seminars are not Christian by definition, but I have never received criticism for my teaching that Jesus heals. They don't dare. I have too much field experience and too many success stories. But even if they were to object, I would keep on teaching this because it makes all the difference both for the children and the workers.

"I think our greatest fear is that what we do is useless, that the things Jesus stood for—love and justice and forgiveness and kindness among men—will count for nothing. This is why I blessed you, why I bless the children I work with, why I teach that Jesus is alive and healing and still a very real part of all our stories. It takes a very long time for any of us to accept the evil and violence we are capable of, to receive Jesus' forgiveness, forgive ourselves, pray for and forgive our enemies, and be healed. But when it happens, it is the greatest miracle of all. It is like the prophet Malachi told us: 'Unto you that fear my name shall the Sun of righteousness arise with healing in his wings.'"

They rode in silence for a few moments. Then Miriam said, "I felt the power of those children's stories, the case studies you gave us. They're still with me."

"Well, have you considered this then? At some point perhaps you should write down everything you remember about the kidnapping and your time with the children in the bush. Do you also need to tell your story in order to heal?" Edith asked this in a tone that told Miriam she needn't answer out loud.

Miriam recognized her own boys' faith in the stories of the children Edith had given her. If those boys could believe and feel God's presence, couldn't she also? She remembered that day out in the Serengeti, when she caught herself yearning for the tender touches of God, as Little Lion called the soft breeze. She was yearning for something Little Lion had wanted to give her.

But her own story? Could Miriam ask of herself what Edith had now taught her to ask of the children—to go back into the dark places of her own remembering? Her own kidnapping was surely a place of darkness, but there was another as well, the memories of her parents' disagreements, the polite estrangement, the lonely pain that had permeated her home as a child. So in that bouncing car, as the afternoon sun arched lower and lower, Miriam asked for God's help, as Edith had taught her, to face those particular memories and move through the painful feelings they raised. It was a place to start.

Miriam let her memory take her back and then back some more until she fully experienced the pain she had felt as a young girl. Suddenly she realized that the tension between her parents had helped make her who she was. The uncertainty of her childhood home had given her a sensitivity to children in conflict, whether physical or emotional. She might never find out the secrets behind the whispers weaving through her childhood, but she could empathize with children who felt torn. At the same time, Miriam certainly felt grateful for her parents' willingness to at least keep trying to love one another.

Miriam remembered the few times she had asked her father to tell her about when he was younger. He had described the ice skating on canals, but as soon as he began to talk about the late1940s, her mom had nervously interrupted them, cutting short the conversation. Miriam knew both her parents had suffered as children during the war years in The Netherlands. Had they been, like the children in these camps, like Miriam herself, shaped and shadowed by trauma they feared to face?

This left Miriam with one more question: *Could a story untold be just as powerful?*

The long trip seemed to be over in minutes. As they pulled into the compound, Edith spoke as if to no one in particular, her eyes on the potholes. "Miriam, you have come so very far and have even found much of what you lost. Stories heal those who tell them and those with ears to hear. If you can ever reach the point where you can face the details enough to allow Jesus to walk by your side as you go back to your kidnapping and all that happened afterward, I have no doubt you will find that telling your story will open up a new place of hope and healing inside of you. It is the greatest gift you can give yourself.

"Maybe you really should try to write it all down. Then someday— when you hold up the pile of pages in your hands, tap the bottom edges on the table, and straighten the stack until the edges align smoothly—then you can say you have mastered these words, captured them on paper so they can be seen and felt and heard, given them a shape so they can no longer haunt you, no longer harm in unseen ways."

"Is this really the power of words?" Miriam asked.

"It is the power of story."

Inside the compound, Miriam made sure her weekly dispatch was sent to the embassies in Dar and Nairobi, asking for follow-up. Their answers still made no mention of Owen or a missing child named Martin.

All day Saturday Miriam felt torn. She took Edith's advice and tried to write down her feelings, but only got as far as "Which child is worth more? The one with AIDS or the one without? My Martin or . . . ?"

On Sunday, Nehemiah, dressed in a suit, invited her to one of the more than fifty church services being held in the refugee camp. They left the compound and drove to the camp, then up and down the dirt tracks until they arrived in an area Miriam had not yet visited. The church building, like the classrooms, had glassless windows and walls and roof supports made of wood, narrow trunks hewn from trees around the camp.

Nehemiah translated the sermon theme for Miriam since it was being given in a native language: "Why does the hope of Africa shine the brightest? Where does light shine most brightly? In the darkest places. Africa is plagued with war, famine, drought, poor leadership, and AIDS. There is no darker or more desperate area in the world. Western journalists call ours 'The Hopeless Continent.' The *only* hope is that in Christ. That is why the hope of Africa shines the brightest."

There was no need to translate the music or the joy of the worship-ers. The youth group played on guitars made of jerry cans. The choir clapped one hand on top of the other, turned them over, stepped forward, stepped back, waited a beat, clapped again, then began singing together.

The minister looked directly at Miriam and said, "Your country is at peace. Ours is not. When you see the sores on our children's feet, know that at home, they did not have this. Pray with us for peace." Then he and the rest of the congregation spoke words of blessings and welcome.

During the offertory Miriam watched women come forward and drop handfuls of corn and cassava flour into the plastic tubs. She marveled at their generosity, knowing their food rations consisted of a bare few hundred grams per day. Miriam could look around the open-air room and see the effects of a vitamin-deficient diet, although the children also received powdered milk and high-protein biscuits. It was the lack of fruit and vegetables that caused sores on their arms and wounds on their feet, forcing some to limp.

As Miriam put some of the small stipend she now received from World Mission into the green plastic basin, she gave with the right hand, two left fingers touching the inside of her elbow. The sign of respect.

After the service Miriam asked the teenagers in the choir a question Edith had taught as one of the best icebreakers, no matter the culture. "What do you want to be when you grow up?"

One girl with a yellow scarf said, "A food shop owner."

The boy who had made the guitars out of jerry cans said, "A guitar maker."

Most of the children said they wanted to become pastors.

"These people don't care about politics," Nehemiah said as they headed back to the jeep. "They simply want to go home."

Owen stared at El-Fatih. His heart raced. They would hold Martin and Miriam until he swayed some negotiation, threw some deal. Some future deal. Something to do with Angola.

El-Fatih invited Owen to join him for a meal. He brought a bowl of water, and the two men washed their hands in silence, then sat on plush cushions before the low table. Owen knew no business could be discussed as they ate. The two young men who had brought Owen to his room now served him and El-Fatih plates of rice and lamb with a yogurt sauce.

Owen ate a few bites of each dish. He waited until the servant boys left the room. Then he heard another door close somewhere else. "We are being watched?" he asked El-Fatih.

"Of course."

"By the women?"

El-Fatih raised his shoulders. "But you will not see them. We are alone."

"And the boys? The servants?"

"This will shock you, perhaps, but these are slaves I acquired."

Owen said nothing more until the meal was cleared away. El-Fatih thanked him for sharing it with him.

Owen said, "I don't know if you know the story of the Norwegian foreign minister who managed to get the Palestinians and Israelis to finally talk by inviting them to his farm, where his wife cooked them a meal."

"Yes, there is power in sharing a meal," El-Fatih replied.

An awkward silence followed, which Owen allowed to stretch until El-Fatih coughed and went back to their discussion. "Very well. I do not know if you know the story of Angola. During the seventies and eighties, the U.S. and pro-apartheid South Africa on the one side supplied General Savimbi's Unita rebels with cash, missiles, and reinforcements. On the other side was the communist government of dos Santos, with support from the Soviet Union and Cuba."

Back in Angola, Owen had surmised that Yury was playing both sides, the government forces and Savimbi's Unita rebel forces.

"You may be aware," El-Fatih went on, "that while the Bicesse Accord was being negotiated, the United States placed on the table an offer of fifteen million dollars in new weapons technology."

Owen whistled softly. "No, I didn't know that. I doubt if it was made public knowledge. This was given to America's ally Savimbi?"

"No. And now you have finally uncovered the answer to your own question of why you sit here across from me. The U.S. gave these funds to General Savimbi's *enemy*, dos Santos. It seems there has been a reversal in foreign policy in your government. And my client, the man I offer my services to in an advisory capacity, has requested that I persuade the Americans to honor their previous allegiance."

"Savimbi is the one behind all this? *He* is the one you work for? But why the American switchover?"

"I don't work for him. I offer him my services," corrected El-Fatih. "But you should know the answer to your own question. You witnessed similar dynamics at work in Mozambique. In a post-Soviet world, communism has become less of a threat. And dos Santos has renounced Marxism, which makes him less objectionable to your government. With the fall of apartheid, South Africa pulled out as an ally. But the deal clincher, as you would call it, is the discovery of oil in government-held areas in Angola. As we speak, the U.S. has promised to become the largest trading partner and to supply the most sophisticated arms possible—on the level of what's given to the Israelis—but to their former enemy, the Angolan government. For the oil."

"And the elections last September?" Owen thought he remembered that his and Miriam's kidnapping had happened just two months after the Angolan elections.

"The elections ended in chaos. Savimbi was furious at losing his U.S. support. He controls the diamond fields. Last year he gained control of some oil fields as well. But this year the Americans have officially recognized dos Santos's Angolan government so Chevron and Texaco can move in."

"So, was it your idea to kidnap me?"

El-Fatih nodded. "The Bicesse Accord has proven a farce. There is no lasting peace."

"Savimbi wants his money and arms. It has nothing to do with peace."

"As you say."

Owen stood up and began to pace the perimeter of the hall. He paused by a window that looked down on a courtyard. Nothing moved in the afternoon heat. He let his eyes wander over the walls. He searched the palm fronds and listened to the birds nearby. A child laughed somewhere. Another door closed. *What am I not seeing?*

"What do you want me to do?" Owen finally asked. "The deal is done. If the American oil companies have gotten the U.S. Administration to make an agreement like this, nothing I can do will reverse the policy. Savimbi will just have to accept his losses and find another sponsor."

"I am to tell you that you must go back to your government and change their minds."

"No one would believe me. They'd know I was targeted. Compromised."

"Ah, but this kidnapping can be explained away. You were not targeted. Rebels were reported that far south by other tourists traveling in the Caprivi Strip. You were just an innocent victim of the switchover in 1991. I masterminded the idea. Savimbi approved it. Yury executed it."

Owen asked himself what motivated El-Fatih. *Profits.* So what could he offer him? His mind searched their previous conversations until he found the nugget. He turned and faced El-Fatih. "I will offer you American interests in *Sudanese* oil fields."

Once again, El-Fatih bowed low.

So, Owen had been right. Savimbi's rebels in the jungle did not rate higher than El-Fatih's own personal interests. El-Fatih controlled oil in northern Sudan, and he wanted more. *He wants the same deal dos Santos got.*

"If the U.S wants oil in Angola, they will want it in Sudan," Owen said, thinking fast. "Keep me alive, free my family, and I will convince the U.S. government to support northern Sudan against the south so they can bring in their oil companies."

"The north is Arab and Muslim. They say we make slaves of the Christians." El-Fatih's tone mocked him.

Owen winced inwardly at the words, knowing they were true, knowing that making this offer to El-Fatih went against everything Owen believed in, everything he had fought against for so long. Here he was, working to promote behind-the-scenes switchovers, trying to play one party against the other. And lying as well—because he had no intention of actually doing what El-Fatih asked of him.

Owen's one indisputable benefit from this deal? It could free his family.

Chapter 56

On Monday Miriam went to the camp with Edith to observe how she worked with the children.

"You begin by coming to the children's level," Edith explained. "When I worked with street children in Dar es Salaam, I often just sat down on the sidewalk beside some kid who was begging in a traffic jam. Meeting them where they are is crucial. Spend time with them. Show commitment. Demonstrate that you are there for them and will not abandon them as so many other adults in their lives probably have. Do not meet in formal surroundings, but instead play a sport or share candy or a soda with them. Listen well, ask questions, repeat what they say."

Their first stop was at an art class for older children. Miriam asked one boy about his picture and was amazed at the flood of images he described as he pointed to separate figures.

"My name is Solomon. This is a picture of a church. People were in the church until the destruction and killing of people by the rebels. I was in a refugee camp when they came. They arrested people at random. If you were a man with a shirt on, it would be used for tying another person. They gathered all the people under a big tree and separated women and children from the men. Women and children were asked to sit down. The men were all told to lie down. The rebels surrounded the people, and three of them started killing the people with pangas and a gun. One of the killers used a hoe. The one with the gun is the one who killed most of the people."

Another boy explained his drawing of people running. "That I escaped was an accident—well, like an accident. We were playing when strangers came to my village. They were soldiers. We just ran. We ran, not thinking where to. My brother helped me run. We didn't say good-bye to our mother and father; we just ran. When there is shooting, I can only think of running to save my life. I heard the shooting and screaming and the bombing. We ran without anything, nothing—no food, no clothes—nothing."

Edith and Miriam went next to a clay-modeling class. Two girls sat giggling behind their hands. Miriam sat down across the table and asked, "What's the joke?" They did not answer. She saw they had made two figures, both holding guns. "Are these soldiers?" Miriam asked. The girls grew silent. They sat on the rough wooden bench in their tattered dresses, scratches and scars visible on their arms. They did not smile. Then Miriam asked, "What are your names?"

The one on the left said, "Janet, and I am sixteen." Then she blurted out, "I was so scared because I had heard that they do bad things to girls who are abducted. I tried to protest and beseeched them for mercy, but instead they beat and threatened me."

Miriam sat quiet and still. Janet had reached across to stroke her hand, and Miriam did not dare to move. It was one of those sacred moments Edith had told her of. A moment only to listen.

Then the other girl began to speak, her voice a whisper like the breeze over a field of grass. "They abducted me but still went ahead to kill my mother and father that night."

Miriam looked at each of the girls. Neither showed the least sign of emotion; stone-faced, they stared beyond her. "And your name?" she finally asked the second girl.

"Constance."

The teacher said it was almost time to end the class. She asked the children to go around the circle and name one thing they liked about their lives.

When it was Janet's turn she said, "I am happy at the counseling center because the people here are kind and listen to our problems."

Constance whispered, "I like having someone caring for me."

Afterward the teacher told Miriam, "The only way you will see them excited is when the subject is school. School is their anchor. These girls see school as the only way to take control of their lives. What I hear from the few girls who make it to us is complaining about the responsibility for younger children weighing heavier and heavier each year. One girl told me, 'I dreamed of someone someday taking care of me. I am relieved that I don't have to marry and have children yet. That I still may be a child.'

"We offer these children a new way of looking at themselves. This can happen through school, through teaching them a trade. But most important is that they learn to see themselves not as victims but simply as children."

Owen noticed that El-Fatih matched his shuffling pace as they climbed the path to the top of the castle wall. After this long day, his mind and body were weary with too many complications, too many loose ends. He still could not fully visualize the map of options El-Fatih kept unrolling before him.

El-Fatih was talking again. ". . . these commodity wars, hostilities fought not for big ideological or political causes, as in the past, but over control of diamond fields, petroleum concessions, coca leaves, and poppies that yield narcotics. Market-driven warfare is part and parcel of globalization, and it seems to be at least as brutal and unrelenting as ideological warfare ever was."

They stood on a parapet beneath the night sky. Owen tried to catch his breath. He stared at the sliver of new moon lying on its back, with Venus pulsing above its belly. El-Fatih's lecturing tone could actually mean a desire for a closer connection. Owen said, "When I first met you, it was in the financial district of London. Do you find it hard to leave this desert?" Both men gazed out over the fading hills of sand, a thousand shades of red waves in the wind.

El-Fatih exhaled loudly. "It is true. I am in other countries two hundred days of the year. When I come home, I camp in the desert for a few nights. It is what I was doing when you arrived here. It is what I long for. My wife understands. I have sand in my blood."

Owen changed the subject again, hoping now to glean perhaps a few more morsels of information. "Falin, he is working both sides, isn't he—dos Santos *and* Savimbi?"

"Yury Falin does what I tell him. He has been a weak man since I first met him."

"In Afghanistan? The poppies you were referring to? The Soviet invasion?"

"All factors to be taken into consideration," El-Fatih said. "Yury is the man in the field for the highest bidder, a supplier of mercenaries. Nothing more. When Savimbi insisted on taking action, I suggested we obtain your services. This appeased the general."

"Long enough for you to gain control of the diamond fields Falin is accessing?"

"Perhaps. But that is neither here nor there. What we want you to do is lie about a threat so your government will reverse its policy and resume support of Savimbi."

"You know that's impossible. No one would believe me."

"It was done before. Kissinger lied in 1975 about the presence of Cuban troops in Angola. I once spoke to the CIA chief, who said the conflict was the *result* of U.S. intervention, not the cause. This is the reason you were chosen—a U.S. negotiator who has opposed Kissinger's causes in the past. And here you were in Africa; it was too sweet a deal to pass up. I am aware of your past. You are doomed to failure because you cannot gain the distance necessary to see the creative solutions. You have not done well in Ireland, and as a result you lost your sister, your only living family. Am I correct? Except for your wife and son, of course."

Owen felt the sharp upward twists of El-Fatih's words cut any response right out of him.

El-Fatih pressed on. "I reject your previous offer and raise the stakes. You will do as I have asked and work from within your State Department to secure Savimbi's support once again."

Owen thought it was as if he had not even mentioned the Sudanese oil. Why the reversal in El-Fatih's behavior?

Owen heard a rock dislodge from the trail below. He peered down the path they had just taken, then froze. El-Fatih raised his eyebrows at him.

Two tall guards approached, wearing uniforms similar to those Owen had seen in Yury's camp. "He is here," the tallest said. Owen could feel the man's disdain in his unwillingness to make eye contact.

They returned to the palace. A big man in battle fatigues and a black beret paced the hall. He turned quickly at the sound of their approach. Owen saw a line of five bodyguards walk toward them. They searched Owen and El-Fatih, and Owen noted El-Fatih's frown. Then a photographer appeared. The general stood beside Owen, and their picture was taken.

Owen waited to be spoken to, but no one said a word. He heard only the sound of men breathing. Then one of the young men El-Fatih had said was a slave appeared and nodded at him. Owen followed him to his suite and heard the door lock after it had closed without a sound.

Chapter 57

Miriam knew her heart was following two different paths at once.

In the camp, working with the children, she had found a place of peace, of belonging, a home. She would never forget the soft, soft sky, bright with stars. The damp air at predawn, the only time you could inhale deeply with no fear of dust. The spectacular flowering violet-blue jacaranda trees. The oleander blossoms scattered at her feet. The noble baobabs with their small knotted, nutlike clusters, the red leaves unfolding in early spring. The cooking fire with its great pot of water, ever steaming. The large red-coated plastic buckets lined up in a row.

And the children. Each day she sat among the little ones and held them on her lap, stroking their dusty heads and tense backs. She knew they were the reason she was here, that caring for them was something she wanted to do.

And yet she was never without the ache that reminded her that Owen was still missing. Martin was still missing. That there had been no word from either of them. One night Miriam realized it had been five weeks since she had filed the missing persons reports at the embassy in Dar. After all that time working in the camp and still no word, Miriam could no longer ignore the thought that perhaps it would have been better to stay in Dar or go to Nairobi or even return to the States. With each passing day her conviction grew that she had made a terrible mistake and should leave the compound. After all, the embassy had misplaced Edith's initial request for information. Maybe they had lost Miriam's documents as well.

The next day when Miriam arrived at the refugee camp, she went looking for Edith and found her talking to Jonah at the UAM office. As Miriam walked up to them, she heard Jonah say, "I'll take care of it right away." Then he ran past Miriam, flashing his smile but not saying a word.

"Was I interrupting?" Miriam asked.

Edith laughed. "Not at all. You know Jonah."

"Well, not really," Miriam said. "I guess I don't."

"What is it, Miriam? You came looking for me for a reason."

"Yes." She swallowed. "Edith, I've decided I can't wait for news any longer. I'm going crazy here. I *have* to find Martin and Owen, but I just don't know what to do. Should I return home? Maybe. There still hasn't been any word, not even from the embassy?"

Edith shook her head. "You know I added Martin's description to the Unaccompanied Minors files. It is an extraordinary case. And we've been radioing the embassies in Nairobi and Dar every week. As soon as anyone knows anything, they will contact us. Stay here, Miriam. Just for a little longer."

"Why?" Miriam asked.

Edith said, "Well, for one thing, it looks like I'm not the only one who needs you."

At that moment the children's voices caused Miriam to turn in recognition. Little Lion collided into her, hugging Miriam so hard her knees bent. Miriam crumpled and held him close, her sobs muffled in his neck. She felt his own chest rise and fall.

Then, just as suddenly, even as Miriam realized how extraordinary his show of emotion was, Little Lion backed off. He seemed ashamed of his hug and was looking over Miriam's shoulder. She turned around and saw Jonah in the distance, walking toward her and grinning. But a meter away stood Fierce Lion, his face very serious. As she stood, he stepped forward and gave her his hand to shake three times, the African way; then he backed away. Out of the corner of her eye Miriam saw a small crowd beginning to gather around them. She brushed her tears away impatiently. "Where are the others?"

"Back there." Little Lion motioned as he took up his post beside his brother. "They gave us our own plot to build a hut on. I was on my way to ask for more blankets. I can sell them and get more food. We learned that already. We tell them we don't want to sleep all together. They'll believe us. Especially when *I* ask," Little Lion said, grinning.

"I'll bet they do," Miriam said. Together they laughed.

Miriam felt a familiar touch on her shoulder and watched Little Lion's grin melt as a mask of indifference covered both boys' faces. She turned as Edith said, "So these are your young guards? I had a feeling; that's why I sent Jonah to fetch them. Well, stranger things have happened in this place. How rare, that you finally found them."

Little Lion pushed his chest out. "Actually, this finding, it is something that happens often to us now."

Miriam spoke to Edith about taking on the counseling of her group of boys. Edith agreed that because Miriam had shared their escape to the border, she might have a better rapport with them. "But I should warn you," Edith said. "These kinds of children are extremely difficult to get close to. Working with them will mean a commitment on your part. Which means that if you start this, you cannot leave soon, as you were planning to. You cannot go back to the States in the middle of the process. Once the boys start opening up, abandoning them at the wrong time could hurt them badly."

Miriam said, "I have more faith in them than in myself. All right, I'll stay. Going back to the States probably wouldn't help, anyway. What could I do there? I know Martin and Owen are here. They have to be. They have to be alive. They *have* to. These boys, they're the closest I have to family until I get my real one back. If they can find me, perhaps I can find Martin and Owen. You know, I've even been praying, and I think this is the right thing to do. I mean, the boys arriving like this—it's a sign, isn't it?"

Edith gave her a hug. "We'll keep the calls going in. And you're right—the miracle of these boys finding you demonstrates how God can surely reunite you with your family."

The first time Miriam went to visit her boys, she found herself in a part of camp she hadn't seen before. Here, tents took the place of the brick homes. Hostile teenage stares watched her vehicle churn up dust alongside the dirt road. Tall boys hung around the fronts of these tents in pairs. Some squatted along the roadside, while others walked in groups. Their saunter and sullen stares reminded Miriam of the gangs she used to catch glimpses of in East Oakland. Here lived the former child-soldiers, unwanted by any foster parents.

Miriam remembered something else Jonah had told her when he described the foster-parent program. "Many children are ashamed of their crimes. The fear they knew while fighting makes way for fear of never being normal again. They don't even know what a normal family life is anymore. The children have lost their families or are no longer welcome at home. They have lost their own childhood. Indeed, they are utterly lost."

In the days to follow, however, Miriam caught bare whispers of humor among these boys, the beginning of restoration. Although they often spent whole days just sleeping, there were also periods when they played soccer outside. Miriam spent her time watching them kick a wad of rags around like a soccer ball, mending clothes for them, helping fetch water, trying to bring some kind of regular rhythm to their lives.

The first reference Little Lion made to their time together in the bush was when he said to her, "You look different, not so sick."

Miriam smiled. "That's because I'm not sick anymore. Mama Edith has helped me, like I want to help you."

"So you thank her?"

"Yes. But I also wanted to thank you, you and Fierce Lion. If it weren't for you two, I would have died in the bush. You saved my life, and I will always be grateful." Both boys stood solemnly before Miriam. Her voice cracked. They nodded, looked at each other, and turned away.

Miriam sat beside the fire in front of the boys' tents, stirring a stew she had made for them. Both Little Lion and Fierce Lion squatted beside her, whittling some wood. The three of them were alone. Miriam was lost in thought about how they probably never would find foster families for these swaggering child-men. What kind of future did they have?

It had been almost two weeks since they arrived, and only rarely did she feel she was making any headway. No one else in the camp spent time with them, and many of the other refugees feared adolescents such as these. Even Little Lion let her only so close. He never talked about his past, and she learned that his grin at their reunion had been a rare gift.

Miriam decided to try something different today. "You know, I think your brother is a very strong leader. Very wise," she said to Little Lion. "And he must have been a good fighter, wasn't he?"

Now Little Lion opened his mouth, smiling and gesturing, as if Miriam had found the key to all his dreams. "Oh yes. He is very fierce. You know, that is his name too. Simba mkali."

Fierce Lion looked shy, but a little smile crossed his lips.

"Yes, Fierce Lion," Miriam translated. "You know, because I was so sick when I traveled with you both, I don't know so well anymore what you told me about your past."

Now Fierce Lion spoke. "Well, you know I am his brother. We share the same name." He paused, and Miriam was careful not to say anything. She nodded and threw some sticks onto the fire. And she waited as the elder boy continued.

"Simba mdogo comes from Sudan. I come from Angola. We have been brothers since we saved each other's lives. We chose these names to frighten all our enemies who would chase us and force us back to where we were. But now Simba mdogo and I know no other names. We are family." He paused, clearly unsure about whether he had said too much. "That was a long time ago."

Miriam turned to Little Lion again. "Do you remember the night after the soldiers came so close? It was like a night that never ended, and you said you like to go somewhere to hide, then—a place to go whenever you're afraid and have bad dreams."

Little Lion said, "For a long time, I dreamed of running away to a place where there was no war, where I could go to school again, where there was food, and where the bombs could not hurt the goats. In this place it is never dark or scary. It is never like night there. It is a place we tell stories about to each other to make us feel brave. It is with us always."

With that conversation as a breakthrough, Miriam was able to deepen her relationship with the boys. They slowly opened up to her, as she did to them, until during one session, she asked them to talk about the first time they had killed someone.

Fierce Lion looked on, unsure whether or not to participate. When no one in the group responded, he finally said, "This cannot be a good thing, going back to these places in our minds."

But little Etoka raised his hand and began to speak as Little Lion translated for him. "My first killing was hacking someone with a panga." Miriam knew the curved machete, had seen plenty of them in Yury's camp. The children all laughed, some covering their mouths with their hands, then stopped suddenly as Fierce Lion stood.

Fierce Lion coughed uncomfortably. He said, "This man was a civilian, an adult around thirty years old. He was abducted, then he tried to escape, so they made me kill him. I did it. I was disturbed in my mind about him; I was not feeling well; I was just shivering that first time. But after I got used to it, I could do it normally.

"It is part of our military training that if you overrun an army detachment, you charge in and kill the wounded. There were so many, I cannot remember every person I killed. Over one hundred. When I was still in the bush, I was actively participating in this. It did not trouble me. I just did it."

Fierce Lion's openness served as a signal to the others that it was all right to share. Miriam felt grateful for his leadership—still wise, still choosing the best for the children in his charge. The others took his lead almost eagerly, as his words seemed to open a floodgate of confessions.

"This is what happened. Capturing old people and children below eight years, then they stab and cut their hands."

"Many people were captured, and when one failed to walk, he was killed."

"I have bad memories of war. I witnessed continuous killings."

"I am fifteen. When the rebels came I went out from our home, trembling with my heart in my mouth, fearing that I would be killed any minute. Some children who were too weak to walk were just chopped up with pangas and left to die on the way. This scared me so much. In the bush I was allocated to a man to be his second wife. If you refused to show respect, you were beaten thoroughly. . . ."

"I know these people they killed. This one, when I would come home from school and be hungry, he would give me food. Now I remember. Those men who killed my friend, they should be killed."

Miriam wondered at how eagerly the boys spoke, as if glad to get the memories off their chests.

"When I go to the front, I smoke so much that I'm not afraid of anything anymore. If you refuse to take drugs, they call it 'technical sabotage' and you're killed."

Another teenager spoke up about taking drugs. "I am a rebel. I fought off the trouble. I took in the bubble. I said double trouble. I'm a man who's not stable."

"I was already killing at the age of eight. We had to kill everyone we saw. Any child who didn't help kill was beaten hard."

"This boy could not walk, and he was shot. The abducted children carry heavy loads. But I thank God for his mercy on me, for I escaped."

That night, back in the compound, as Miriam tried to sleep, her boys' low voices thundered over her like a summer storm. The horror of their words startled and chilled her anew.

They came for Owen the next morning. The tall African guards who had searched him the previous evening dragged him half-naked from the cushions on the floor. They threw him down the same stairs he had ascended as a guest only hours before.

They brought Owen to a hangar outside the fort. On the way he saw again the vast sand dunes, crimson and rippling in the desert wind and heat. The servant boys and El-Fatih—all the images of comfort from the previous day—had vanished. The soldiers tied Owen's arms and legs and knocked him to the ground. He waited for their next assault, but it didn't come. They left him there in the red sand, letting the sun bake him until Owen began to hear Miriam's soft voice as he prayed for her, his Irish complexion tender and raw beneath the fiery midday rays.

Suddenly the men were back. They dragged him inside and dumped him in a tub of ice-cold water, submerging his body within meters of the generator working to create even more ice. Owen did not know how long they left him there. He regained consciousness at the sound of shouting voices, but when he opened his eyes and focused, Owen saw only El-Fatih watching him. They were alone.

Owen croaked one word. "Why?"

El-Fatih swiped at a fly. "I have, as you said, priorities. And when General Savimbi, the man who controls a major share of my diamond trade, comes in person to my home, when he tells me we really must convince a certain negotiator to convince a certain government that they should not turn their back on former allies, then I will not put any personal interests before those priorities."

Translation: You were being watched, Owen thought. He said, "And to give me a taste of what sudden reversal feels like."

El-Fatih smiled. "Perhaps. Yes."

Owen heard himself ask again, "You knew Falin from Afghanistan?"

"He and I met over ten years ago. I looked then much as I do now." He ran the back of his hand along the flowing robes and a turban. Owen noticed his mind was picking up only on certain details. He tried to focus better as El-Fatih said, "He was a much more cooperative prisoner than you."

"Tell me why my family is involved."

"They're Americans. And Americans killed the young daughter of our leader."

Owen's mind reeled. *Savimbi or . . . Qaddafi?* No, an attack on the Libyan leader's family might be a reason they would give to the world if necessary, but what was the real truth? Owen wondered if El-Fatih had lied about everything he told Owen. *Keep him talking. God help me.*

"Perhaps I have not been persuasive enough," El-Fatih said. "We will hold your family, and if you do not cooperate during talks that will be announced in the coming months, we will kill them. Do you agree now?"

"What you're asking is impossible. I could never convince the State Department to reverse their policy. If they want that oil . . ."

"I'm sure you will find a way." El-Fatih looked away.

Owen's teeth chattered so loudly he couldn't think. He clutched at his chest, the burning sensation clawing at his heart.

He pitched forward, one hand over his heart, the other trying to grasp the edge of the tank. Water filled Owen's nostrils as the terrible pain claimed him for its own.

Is this the day?

Chapter 58

Two weeks after her reunion with the Simba brothers, Miriam and Nehemiah returned from the camp to find a bright blue Land Rover parked at the World Mission compound.

"This is Paul's vehicle," Nehemiah said. "You have met Edith's brother?"

"Oh yes." Miriam pushed her hair out of her eyes. It had been a long session with the boys that day. "He's quite a character, the safari guide who knows Shakespeare. Oh, wait, doesn't he also have a doctorate in international studies from Harvard?"

"Then you don't know everything. He has a *second* doctorate in divinity, served as a missionary to the West, was a pastor in New York City. Now he works to raise money as a safari guide to pay for the pizza restaurant in Mwanza he bought for former child-soldiers. And on top of everything else, he's a reservist in the National Guard."

Miriam stood open-mouthed as Nehemiah began his usual routine of wiping the red dust off the upholstery inside the jeep. "Really?" It was all she could say.

Miriam hurried off to Edith's room, where she found Paul bent over Edith's desk, talking to his sister in serious tones.

He stopped as soon as Miriam entered, straightened up, and said,

"Ah, there you are. I hear only good things about you." He enveloped her in a hug.

Miriam laughed. "Paul, Nehemiah was just extolling your virtues and telling me all about your different ventures. I see you in a new light, I must admit."

"I hope he didn't tell you everything," he said, glancing at Edith. Miriam caught the look but did not know what it meant.

"Miriam, come. Let's go for a walk while the sun goes down," Paul said. "I've been sitting all day, driving on bumpy roads."

Miriam looked at Edith again.

Edith just shrugged her shoulders and gestured for them to go. "At least then I can get some work done."

"Tell me about your boys," Paul said as they walked down the concrete steps. They strolled under the trees and past the oleander bushes, out of the compound gate, and toward the village.

Miriam shared with him about the boys' recent progress, then said, "Nehemiah also told me you have a restaurant. Tell me, do many of the boys who have been through what mine have ever truly recover?"

"It depends on if they have ever experienced stability before they were kidnapped. If a child has had even four years in which to bond with anybody, then he *might* bond later."

"Sometimes I wonder how they can possibly heal after all they've been through."

"How can any of us? You know what Edith would say: If a person can tell their story, if they make it that far, they might be one of the few who can heal and live a normal life."

"But what do *you* say?" Miriam looked up at Paul as they walked in the lessening light, the sky cut open and bleeding red and purple across the horizon.

"I've seen it with the boys in the restaurant, after therapy, the kind you're doing. Which is so crucial, Miriam—don't underestimate that cleaning-out process. After that, there is a small chance they will be motivated enough to study."

"What if I could help sponsor their education?" Miriam asked. "I'm going to have to go back someday, but I promised Edith it wouldn't be until I finished counseling the boys."

"Well, that's just it. Boys like that are never finished with counseling. But there does come a time when they are more stable, relatively speaking. Yes, certainly, paying their school fees would help. High school is more than most get."

"And if they want to go to university?"

Paul paused. "Yes, Edith told me your Little Lion is gifted."

"Well, he's not really mine."

There was an awkward pause, then Paul said, "Edith also told me you have an extraordinary talent, that you're good with the children and you're a natural problem solver, a peacemaker." When Miriam started to protest, he added, "No, I'm serious. I've heard you're getting quite a reputation in the camp for settling differences. What was it you set up this morning?"

Miriam laughed a little self-consciously. "It wasn't that big a deal. It's just that I've been spending hours each day when I'm with the boys waiting in line for water. There are only so many pumps, and everyone in the camp wants water for cooking and washing—well, you know how it goes. So I wait in line with them to talk and pass the time of day. It's a huge waste of time. Many people just leave their buckets in the line and go do other things. But sometimes, among the teenagers living on their own, this isn't honored so well, and people cut in line or change the position of their buckets when they think no one is looking. And especially with the boys, this means there are fights."

Paul made a wry face. "Yes, I would imagine that's what it means."

"Anyway, all I did was go around to the different households in that neighborhood and set up a roster and times, three times a day, when it's each household's time to go fetch water. So, no more waiting in line and no more fights."

Paul nodded. "That's what I mean. Edith said you've even been coaching the judges, the elderly people in the camp who have been voted into positions of settling differences." They walked down to the riverbed, dry and rocky beneath the bridge, and were silent until Paul said, "I've been praying for you, and I see God has been opening doors. You know, the time is coming when you will look to your talents, your dreams, your training, and ask yourself, 'What is my heart's desire, planted there by God?'"

When Paul said this, Miriam felt sure she wasn't ready to answer such a question. But as he finished, something inside her leapt at his words. To cover up the rush of hope, Miriam asked, "Paul, on top of everything else, are you a prophet?"

"I've been called worse."

The next day at the camp, Miriam met the boys and went to church with them. Afterward, as they walked back to their huts, Fierce Lion came up and stood in front of Miriam, forcing her to stop and look at him.

He began to speak Portuguese so quickly that Miriam couldn't follow. Little Lion sidled up to them and interpreted. "My brother is telling you he is changing his name one last time. Hearing God's holy Word read again like he did today reminded him of something his mind used to know. He talks of a child who leads them in the place of peace where the children are safe. This was said in God's holy book by a man named Isaiah."

Fierce Lion's voice rose into a chant, a recitation, and his younger brother mimicked him. "There is a place where 'the wolf will live with the lamb, the leopard will lie down with the goat, the calf and the lion and the yearling together; and a little child will lead them.' My brother says *he* wants to be that child in that place, the place of no war. He says we should call him *Filho*. This word, it means 'child.'"

She repeated *"feel-yoo"* after him—his new name, child, *Filho*.

"He says he has forgotten all his other names, including his fighting one. If he cannot be the lion, then he wants to be the child who leads them. He says. . . . " Little Lion paused, then smiled as he continued. "He says that he saw this in the future back when I first asked him to be our leader."

Miriam knew at this moment that once again she faced her own choice about whether to learn from the boys and grow in faith. She could look at the children's hope and see it as a bitter thing, assuming they were only going to be disappointed. But Miriam's decision to love them and learn from them had, in itself, become an act of faith. She saw herself reflected in Filho's courage to trust as she heard him say, "I want to share this place with you, Madam Miriam. I will go there and wait for you."

Miriam's voice shook. "Yes, of course . . . together . . . Filho." She saw that this imaginary place where he wore a new name had become more real for him than the cruel reality he had lived in for so long.

The tall boy started to leave, then turned back to Miriam and called her, *"Mae."* Mother. Before she could react, he added, "I have had different mothers and fathers in different places, but Little Lion is my brother forever." Then he walked off, ahead of the rest.

Miriam turned to Little Lion, her heart beating fast over what certainly marked yet another breakthrough. "It was right that I called him Filho, wasn't it?" He nodded, but Miriam didn't like the troubled expression on his face as he gazed after Filho. She asked him what was the problem.

He asked, "Can God call me by name if I do not know my name? Will I hear him?"

Miriam wished she had understood more of the sermon, wished Paul were here and could give one of his wise answers. She could see the intensity in Little Lion's eyes, his trembling hands, the throbbing vein in his neck. She realized, *This means everything to him.*

"Yes, you will hear him," Miriam began. "Listen, you taught *me* to hear God; did you know that? You taught me to hear his voice. Not that I hear him all the time, but at least now I'm learning how to listen. You will know your name—you already hear God's call."

Little Lion nodded slowly, his lips pursed. "This, it makes sense. I know God knows my real name. He calls me, and when he does, I will know who I am.

"Me, his own treasure of darkness."

That night, because it was Sunday and the curfew was not enforced, Miriam sat with the boys, staring into the firelight, sharing their silence.

"You want to ask us another question?" Little Lion said.

Miriam smiled. "I was thinking about our journey together, and what happened to you after you left me here, and why you came back."

"It was not good with the soldiers," he said. "We felt safer in the jungle, but then we were too hungry and tried again, and it was better this time. We followed Filho."

Then Miriam thought of something else. "Little Lion, when we traveled here through the jungle, we followed Filho then, too, remember?"

"Of course."

"Well, how did Filho know which way to go?"

"He followed God." Little Lion nodded. "He followed the light."

"The morning light?" Miriam wondered if what she had thought was just aimless wandering had in fact been a deliberate trek toward the east, the rising sun. She turned to discover that Filho had come up behind them and now stood listening to the conversation.

She looked at the older boy. "Can you explain how you knew which way to go every day?"

"I have felt God's hand on me, saying go this way, go that way, and we prayed for this every morning."

Little Lion said, "This is not such a difficult thing, to follow Jesus."

Miriam realized he literally followed. "How?"

The boys shook their heads, until finally, Little Lion's face brightened. "Listen, during the journey, did you not learn how to follow? Soldiers never know where they are going, but they know how to follow."

Filho said, "His holy presence was with me as I took this journey, blessing my steps, even when I could not see."

A little later Little Lion stood up and said, "There are questions burning in my mind now. You are not African, yet you stay with us. You ask what we hope for. But what is it *you* hope for?"

Immediately Miriam thought of finding Owen and Martin, but another answer sprang into her mind unbidden. She would never forget the impact of true peace she had witnessed in Mozambique. Miriam realized that to find this peace for herself, hidden in places of conflict—this too was something she truly hoped for. The very idea of it made her heart sing and ache with longing at the same time.

She looked into the future and thought, *To be a peacemaker—that's what I want.* Then she realized, *And becoming a negotiator like Owen is a means to this end.*

She looked into the present, around the small circle, and her eyes came to rest on the two brothers, their faces still sharing one emotion. She thought of how she longed to help them and others like them.

Then she looked into the past and stumbled upon a gift, a pearl worthy of her audience. "I have a story to tell you," she said. "All this time I have been asking you to tell me your stories, and now it is time for me to tell you mine. You, who have given me so much, now may hear my story-gift to you.

"You're right; I'm not African. I come from a city on the water with a bridge the color of gold. . . ."

Now, for the first time, Miriam told them what had happened to her, where she had been, what she had lost and found. In the telling, she wove their hearts together in time.

The night had grown very still by the time Miriam finished. She sighed. "You see, I too have been in dark places . . . lost until you found me. And then a whispering wind brought me back to myself. *Upepo mpole.*" She even knew the Kiswahili for it.

Another silence descended on them until Little Lion asked, "What is it? You are thinking of your son and husband?"

"Always." She sighed again. "I look for them in my heart and reach out to them wherever they are. Will I ever see them? Will I ever find them again?"

"Did you know me before you found me?" Little Lion asked, his eyes bright in the firelight.

But Filho had gotten up and started pacing back and forth. Finally he stopped in front of Miriam and Little Lion, hands on his hips, feet spread apart. "This thing," he said in Portuguese, "it can happen."

She looked up at him, blinking in the moonlight that shone behind his face. She could not read his features well, but Little Lion seemed to read her thoughts as he asked, "How is this possible, Elder Brother?"

When he did not respond, Miriam whispered, "You *know* where my family is?"

"We did not know this was your family, or we would have spoken up earlier. We did not even know you missed your family. But now . . . when you told us of your son and his father, a big man, we thought yes, these were the names spoken by the commandant. *Owen. Martin.* A small, weak-eyed boy. They are where you came from."

Miriam hurried on, her understanding outrunning the words now. She nodded, speaking to herself, "So Yury had them all along." Then she stood and saw her own hope reflected in the eyes of Little Lion. His brother stood still at his side. She reached for their hands, but they both drew away, in step, away from her touch, dancers to a tune she still could not hear. "It's all right. You . . . you have given me a great gift tonight. Thank you."

No smiles. The same passive faces, but now a slight twitching in Little Lion's lower lip. That was all, a passing grimace.

Filho said, "I can find our way back to the camp where we found you, where the explosion happened. I can find this place."

The two boys stood shoulder to shoulder. Little Lion stared at his brother with eyes brimming over with trust and pride and confidence.

Filho nodded slowly. "I remember the way. If I go back as I came, with the sun at my back in the morning instead of in my face, and find the river and follow it, we should find this camp."

Miriam blinked back tears. "I would never ask that of you." She had opened her mouth to say they would find another way when Filho reached out and took her hand. She stared at their hands, fingers entwined, speechless at his touch.

"We will do this thing." Then he turned and walked away from Miriam, Little Lion trotting in his wake.

Miriam's worry about Owen and Martin eclipsed all other concerns that might have troubled her. She knew only one thing now. The thought burned bright as a beacon.

I know where you are.

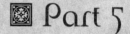 # Part 5

I remember thinking: Miriam, you have no way of going back.

I said to myself, I don't know where they are. I don't even know if they're alive.

Those words wrapped themselves around me like a thick and vicious vine, choking the breath out of me, forcing me to stumble and fall.

But then I looked up from where the words had tripped me, peered closely—and I could make out hope.

It was hope handed to me by a child—for my child, from my child, to my child.

Chapter 59

When Owen came to himself again, he lay in his cage back in the Angolan jungle. His first impulse was to think he had dreamed it all—the red sand, the oasis, the torture. Two signs convinced him otherwise. He opened his eyes and saw his arm, a swollen purple bruise inside the elbow. A jagged path of track marks testified to the awful fact that needles had entered his body. The pounding in his head told him he'd been drugged for the trip back to Angola from . . . wherever he had been, somewhere in North Africa.

He decided that nothing El-Fatih had told him could be trusted. Chances were he had fed Owen a mélange of truth and lies—the most lethal cocktail, since misinformation often did more harm than false information.

Owen shuddered at the thought of the needles. His mind reeled at new dangers looming as he shifted his weight, straining to sit up. Then he noticed the tingling sensation in his right leg. He busied himself with assessing the physical damage of what he thought might have been another heart attack, while another part of him tried not to face a different kind of attack to the heart.

As if eavesdropping on his own troubled thoughts, he heard the words, *Have I now become my worst enemy? I swore never to let this happen*

*again—compromise my own ideals just to get the job done. Instead of nego-
tiating, I simply lied. I lacked the distance to negotiate properly—that was
the problem. I lost all perspective because this was a personal enemy. So far
every attempt I have made in this direction has ended in disaster, with my
family paying the highest price—*

He stopped at the precipice of that deadly thought, using precious
energy to step back from the edge, forcing his thoughts instead to an-
alyze.

*This is what happens when I do what I hate, negotiate for an enemy,
switch sides, betray, negotiate for personal reasons.*

In a corner of the cage near the door, Owen saw the second sign,
physical proof that he had left one place of torment only to return to
another: a small pile of red desert sand. Back in this place of dread,
Owen shook his head as more grains fell before his eyes.

Miriam rushed back to the compound. It had been very late when she
left the refugee camp, and it was just past midnight by the time she
pulled into the compound. The generator had long been turned off,
and everything was still. She crossed the parking area and dropped the
keys into the motor pool drop slot beside the office door. She knew Paul
and Edith would be up at dawn, so she told herself she only had to survive one short night of not knowing—knowing and not knowing.

She slept in fits, imagining the scenarios, praying that Yury still had
Martin and Owen, trying to slay the dragon of doubt. It had been so
long—eight months now since the night of explosions when she ran
away from that camp. Could they really still be there?

Miriam woke with a start. It was already light. She could hear people
walking by her window. She brushed the mosquito netting out of the
way, quickly dressed and pulled on her boots, then hurried to find
Edith. One of the laundry girls told her, "She and Paul went to the
village for an early morning meeting with some of the other child-
service NGOs. It was only supposed to last an hour. They should be

back soon." Miriam glanced at the empty parking lot, longing for the bright blue shape of Paul's Land Rover.

Miriam went to the radio operator and asked him to patch a call through to the American embassy in Dar es Salaam. It took a half hour, but Miriam knew it was worth it when the radio operator surrendered the headset to her and she heard the voice on the other end say, "American embassy, hello?"

Miriam took a deep breath. "The consul's office, please."

"Yes, he's just come in. One moment please."

The connection sounded scratchy, but she could still make out the voice of the man she had spoken with two months earlier. "Yes?"

"Hello. This is Miriam Vree." She sat straighter, impatient with the buzzing in the background, with the man on the other end, with his apathetic voice repeating her name. She reminded him of who she was and of their meeting, then told him why she was calling.

He contradicted her twice, telling her she was misinformed.

"You don't understand," Miriam insisted. "I have *confirmation* that my husband and son are there. Two witnesses who saw them last December." She wasn't going to mention that these were two refugee boys, former child-soldiers. So obsessed was Miriam with her mission, she hardly gave the boys a thought.

"What do you want from us?"

"I want helicopters, Marines. I want to storm the camp and get my husband and son out of that place. It's been over nine months since we were kidnapped!"

"Mrs. Vree, what you are asking for is impossible."

"Why? This is an official of the U.S. State Department. Owen even had bodyguards in the past. Why not now? What? What has happened?"

He sighed. "Let me take this in another room. Just a moment." She heard a hum; then his voice came in a little more clearly. "We've received word that your husband has terrorist ties. . . ." He hastened to add as Miriam started to interrupt, "I have your file before me now."

"And who exactly are you?"

"Mrs. Vree, I am the intelligence officer for this embassy, and we are now speaking on a scrambled frequency. Nonetheless, I don't really think it's appropriate for me to spell out any of this. There is a certain country, Great Britain, an ally, with vast diamond interests throughout the world. This same country is the target of terrorist attacks from a group training in Libya."

It took all of Miriam's self-control to listen carefully and not interrupt.

"There was also some question of your husband being sighted in Libya by one of our operatives, although this has not been confirmed. However, if this and your husband's ties established during the Irish talks had not been enough to place him under suspicion, we have since received a photograph of him with Savimbi, the head of the Angolan rebel faction. Judging by your husband's appearance, he was not being held against his will." He said this as if it was the last thing he needed to say.

" 'A certain country . . . the target of terrorist attacks'—you said Britain." Miriam paused. "And the terrorists—that's the IRA." She did not say the name of De Beers, the British company that controlled diamond interests all over the world. "But the Irish talks were more than a year ago. And Owen has no ties with terrorist groups—what do you mean? Savimbi in Angola? Is that who you said he was with? But you think someone saw him in Libya? He looked all right?"

He ignored her. "I have the memo here in front of me. The State Department must have anticipated some questions in this case. They see your husband as working for Angolan rebels now, and they don't want to jeopardize recent oil treaties. He is consorting with the enemy."

"The enemy?" Miriam asked weakly.

"Yes, as of last year the Unita rebels are our enemy."

She thought, *That was probably more information than you meant to give out.* It was certainly more than Miriam could process. Savimbi? The Unita leader? She did remember Yury talking about government-controlled areas and the Unita rebels. That must be the conflict. *How had this happened?* "Did the embassy really lose the inquiries about us, or were they just ignored?"

Only silence answered her question.

"Listen, I need *proof.*" Miriam nearly choked on the words. "Do you have patrols flying over that area? You said you thought he was sighted in Libya? Is he there now? What do you base these . . . these *accusations* on?" Her mind leapt at possibilities. "Satellite photos?"

"That is classified information, but, yes, sporadically we do have shots of Angola."

"So he *is* in Angola. You've seen him on these photos? How can you tell it's my husband? Is he being held there against his will?"

She heard the timber of his voice shift, then realized he must have opened a window as sounds of traffic and callers at the street market below came across the line.

"Yes, he is there. We have positive identification. We just have no way of going in there, even if the situation called for such action."

Miriam swallowed the words, *I'll bet you can't*. She steeled herself against the implication of his words. "And my son? *My son?*" she hissed.

"I cannot tell you. I honestly do not know. I have a son myself, you know, so I have an idea of what you must be going through."

Then the connection was broken. Had the man hung up? Miriam stared at the phone, opening and closing her mouth, the crawling weight of lies all around her now.

Miriam paced the courtyard, waiting for Edith and Paul to return, then finally decided to go look for them on the road to the village. She spent a frantic half hour walking up and down side tracks leading to the other agencies' compounds and finally returned, only to discover Paul's vehicle in the parking lot.

Miriam found Edith and Paul talking in the compound kitchen. She burst in on them and said, out of breath, "Cuango. They're in Cuango! In Yury's north Angolan camp, where he held me. They were there all along, Martin and Owen."

When Paul and Edith turned to look at her, their faces mirrored none of Miriam's excitement.

"What?" she asked. "What is it?"

Paul stepped forward and took her hands in his. She looked down at them. Then she looked up into his warm eyes, deep and dark. "Miriam, we know this. It's why I came here. We've known for some time that what you described as one camp is, in fact, a massive network of training camps and clandestine mining operations in that area." He paused. "You deserve to know that lately a great deal of unrest has erupted there. Evidently the warlords are fighting it out, and it actually looks as if someone is planning an elimination campaign."

" 'Elimination campaign?' What is that? But why . . . why? I mean, *how* did you find out? Why didn't you come and tell me?"

"But I am telling you. I just thought it would be best to check with Edith first."

To see if I could handle it, Miriam thought, but she said, "Because you weren't sure how much you could talk about times and people in my recent past. So she cautioned you not to take me back to places I didn't want to go, and to be gentle. Am I right?"

Paul looked from one woman to the other. He nodded and hesitated, then said, showing her he had not understood, "Well, of course there's no possibility of your going back there. No, Edith and I were just talking about the ramifications."

"Ramifications? I come here and tell you I *know* where Martin and Owen are, and you talk to me of 'ramifications'?" Miriam noticed Edith's silence. She pulled her hands away from Paul's and crossed the room to be closer to her. "Edith?"

Edith turned toward her and grasped Miriam's shoulders. "Please forgive me, Miriam."

Realization fell upon Miriam like a giant boulder, crushing the trust between them. "You knew before today? You knew where they were. How long? You *both* knew? *How?*"

Paul said, "I guessed from satellite photos, and I only told Edith after we all returned from Mozambique."

Miriam squinted at Paul. "Who are you? *What* are you that you have access to things like satellite photos? I just got off the phone with the embassy, and they said they had seen Owen in photos like that. Do you work for them, in between being a safari guide or something?"

"No. Well, I was, am. But you're right. In addition to all that, actually in between the missionary and guide jobs, I was . . . am . . . part of a special-forces unit designed to help crack down on poachers . . . and smugglers."

"Diamond smugglers?" Miriam watched him nod.

Paul crossed the kitchen in two strides and looked to the right and left, checking that no one stood near the open windows and could overhear. He lowered his voice. "Actually I got tired of preaching about the wrongs in the world and decided to *do* something about the evil." He scratched his chin. "I trained the men myself, but we all come from the anti-poaching defense league. First we fought the poachers after the rhinos, then the smugglers and their diamonds. Smaller game, but higher stakes."

But Miriam wasn't interested in rhino poachers. Her mind spun around her single point of focus. *What about Owen and Martin?*

Paul continued, "That Yury Falin you were with is a big fish, but he is swimming among the sharks. The Lebanese have controlled the diamond mafia on this continent for half a century, probably longer. They won't give up their hold on the government-controlled areas easily. And the Unita rebels are taking and losing new ground every year. But I'm sure the new breed of post-communist Russian mafia like Falin are not the only ones trying to swim on both sides of the river. Competition is fierce among all those trying to rise to the surface in that infested part of Angola. And the interests backing every party involved have endless supplies of money and arms at their disposal."

His words triggered a memory. Miriam said slowly, the words summoning the image as she spoke, "I know. I remember. I remember on that last night, Yury said he had eliminated a Lebanese smuggler. And there was a South African . . . and Brazilians." She looked up, blinking.

Paul nodded. "We know this. The Brazilians are putting together a joint venture with the Russians for control of the diamond fields in government-held areas in the far north of Angola. Both the government forces and the rebels are getting their arms and training financed by outside sources. The whole world wants those diamonds."

"Yes, Yury talked about a place called Catoca." The name came to her mind as a single, clear gong. "He was going to do something there."

Paul pursed his lips, then said, "Right," as if settling an unspoken argument. He reached into the breast pocket of his safari vest, pulled out an oilskin map, and laid it on the counter in front of them. He traced his finger to the left. "Look, smack in the middle of the target area, northeast Angola and southwest Zaïre. This stretch, nearly fifty-five hectares—that's the largest kimberlite pipe in the world, with some say an estimated production of about one million carats. So you saw the Brazilians?"

Edith moved in to stand beside Miriam. "What's a kimberlite pipe?"

Miriam stared at the map, realizing for the first time that her lost three months traveling with the boys had been spent covering a thousand kilometers of equatorial forest. She stared at the blankness of the territory and let her words wander from what really pulled at her mind. She said in a dull voice, "Kimberlite is the mother ore of diamonds. A kimberlite pipe is a giant vein of kimberlite running through the geological strata, like a vein of gold, but containing diamonds."

Miriam could not shake the weight of feeling trapped, as if all those layers of rock threatened now to crush her. *Forget the kimberlite!* she wanted to yell at them. *Forget the Brazilians!*

"What about Martin and Owen?" she finally managed to rasp.

Miriam tried to move away from the many questions clamoring to be asked and search for some answers instead. "Please . . ." Her voice broke. "We have to rescue them. What about this 'elimination program'? You mean bombs, don't you? Whose bombs? The government-controlled forces'? The rebels'? They're all just terrorists, no better than these mafias."

Only one thing was clear to her now. She knew her family's whereabouts. She knew Owen and Martin needed to be rescued *now*, before some "elimination program" got into gear, injuring or killing them in a cross fire. And for whatever reason, Paul and Edith seemed unwilling to help her. Maybe there was no one she could trust to help.

A plan, based on something Paul had suggested, began forming in the back of her mind, gradually pushing other considerations aside.

Miriam allowed Edith to put her arms around her, then felt a look of devastation creep across her features. "They've started bombing already, haven't they?" Miriam heard her voice rise, felt the ground shift and reality retreat a step.

Paul reached across the counter, but Miriam backed up, pushing Edith away. The buildup of tension through the previous night now threatened to break her mind in two. "Get away from me. Both of you! I can't believe you're letting them remain in such danger. Get out. Get out!" She heard herself scream, the sound a familiar one, as another part of her watched her friends back away.

Paul retreated from the room, his hands held palms outward. He glanced at Edith, who said, "Why don't we let Miriam calm down a bit. We're not here to provoke you, Miriam. We'll be in my office when you're ready to talk."

Miriam turned her back on them and held on to the edge of the counter, her breath coming in jagged gasps. By the time she heard the door close behind them, her plan had taken shape. She grabbed the map and keys Paul had left behind. Her thoughts were racing. *Get food. Pack supplies. Take money. Water.*

She crossed the empty courtyard, went to her room for what little money she had saved from her small salary, put together a kit, and ran for Paul's Land Rover in the car lot. She waved at the askari on duty, and he opened the compound gate as she drove past the other buildings. In her rearview mirror, she saw him close the gate behind her. She turned left and headed for the main road toward town.

At the intersection with the road going to the refugee camp and back to the village, Miriam almost crashed into a large tree branch stretched across the road. The wind the night before must have knocked it down. Leaving the motor running, she got out to haul the branch aside. It moved easily enough. She returned to the vehicle and drove on.

Miriam navigated around the biggest potholes in the road but bounced in and out of others, arriving at town in record time. She avoided the new-neighborhood cluster of aid-agency offices. She didn't want to take any chances that Paul and Edith had radioed ahead about her theft of the car. She hoped they just thought she had gone to drive off some steam and get away by herself somewhere.

Either way, she knew she didn't have much time.

Chapter 60

Miriam veered around the last corner before the clearing, then skidded to a stop. Red dust enveloped the Land Rover. Edith had told her this dry season seemed even drier than usual. Miriam pushed the words away and looked upward, shading her eyes as she concentrated on a pinpoint of darkness within the lightest of gray cloud cover. She listened a few more moments, then could hear the whine of the approaching Cessna.

On the other side of the airstrip a fuel truck arrived with a smaller truck to take the plane's cargo back to town. The flight from Mwanza came in every Monday and Wednesday. Sometimes it delivered medical supplies or mattresses, and sometimes it carried people. Miriam watched the plane land, waited until it was being refueled and unloaded, then approached the pilot. He stood a short distance from the plane, smoking a cigarette.

The pilot flashed a smile at Miriam. "You going to give me a lift into town, or are they?"

She smiled back. "So you're not flying back today?"

He shook his head. "No cargo. But I've got some diplomat I have to take back tomorrow. Why? You know somewhere I can stay besides the one hotel in town?"

She ignored the hint and his grin. "Actually, I was thinking more of making you a business proposition. I need a pilot."

He raised his eyebrows and spat into the dry dirt. "Can't. Against company policy."

"I'll pay you." Miriam straightened her shoulders and fingered the leather bootlace that still hung around her neck. Slowly she brought out her engagement ring and held it up in the sunlight. Its darkness gleamed.

The pilot coughed. "I see. Where to?" The truck crew honked the horn at that moment, and the pilot raised a hand to wave them off. Only after they had disappeared among the trees did he repeat the question. "Where to?"

"Northern Angola."

"No way. I'll just get my bag and lock up, so you can drive me into town." He turned his back and started walking toward the plane.

Miriam quickly undid the knot and slid the ring off the leather. She did not chase after him, but simply waited. He would come back. She had heard enough gossip in the compound and while running errands in town to know this was a man who could be bribed into doing just about anything. She waited as he disappeared into the plane.

Five minutes later she knew she had the right man when he reappeared and walked toward her carrying flight charts instead of an overnight bag. "Look, I'll take you as far as here—" his finger punched one of the maps—"to southern Zaïre, but no farther. That's dicey enough as it is. Why would a woman like you even want to go to Angola? Never mind." He eyed her up and down.

Miriam led him into the shade of the trees, away from the plane. She took his hand and opened the palm, placing the ring at its center, then lifted the upturned hand toward the sky. He held it up to the light again. "What is this? A black diamond?"

"Yes. And an unusually large one. Very rare. Very valuable. See how it picks up the light? This will more than cover the fuel, your time, and a little extra cooperation. So, how about a compromise? You take me to the Angolan border."

The pilot stood with his face pointed toward the sky, one eye closed. He peered at the stone. As Miriam watched his mesmerized expression, she knew, as sure as the diamond's very brilliance gave it a life of its own, that the deal was done.

The plane ride lasted most of the afternoon. As they headed west, flying into the sun, Miriam fought the realization of what exactly she had done. Now she had nothing, absolutely nothing of value with which to bargain for the release of her son and husband or for anything else she might need.

Miriam could not shake the dread, the conviction that her instability had plunged her into further chaos. She thought of the last case she had worked on before the kidnapping, before the madness began, the life insurance case where she researched the point of diminishing returns. What is a life worth? When is the price for any given life too high to pay? What price had she just paid for this chance at life? No less than her last link with Owen. What if she never saw him again? *What if he's dead?*

No, she couldn't afford such thoughts here. Miriam heaved them from her mind. She looked out the window and saw only treetops, broken by the occasional ribbon of water snaking its way through the forest. The dark, winding thread reflected the trees all around. Unbroken green, a thousand different shades, surrounded the surface below the plane. Miriam opened her small backpack and tried to reassure herself with the kit she had packed: the solid presence of a map, a compass, three bottles of water, some bread, a packet of cheese, and a length of mosquito netting. She probably should have packed a knife, but she didn't have one.

Where am I? Old words haunted her now. *What new territory is this?*

She suddenly remembered the title of a book by Joseph Conrad that Sue once gave her, a book about this very area, the middle of Africa. Where was she? In that same *Heart of Darkness*.

The pilot turned his head a bit and looked at her doubtfully. "See those lights? That's Tshikapa. That's where I wanted to drop you off. Offer still holds."

Miriam did not reply. Instead she unfolded the flight charts he had placed on the floor between them. It took a few moments for her to find what she was looking for. Then she counted the rivers out loud. "Here's Tshikapa. Now I count one, two, three rivers as we continue heading west. The fourth river is the Cuango. It marks the border.

You'll find an airstrip just east of the river, right on the border. Set me down there, please."

The pilot looked at her in surprise. She knew he now realized her so-called compromise was exactly the destination she had wanted all along. He said, "You've been here before." Then he asked, "Someone meeting you?"

Miriam did not answer. She looked straight ahead. It wasn't long before she sighted clouds of smoke coming from the trees along one of the rivers.

"That's the Cuango," the pilot said.

Miriam said nothing, paralyzed by the fear of what she was about to do.

As they approached the area, the puffs of smoke ceased. The plane landed without incident, the pilot complaining that although he barely had enough daylight to get back, he would have to stop first to refuel. Miriam told him she was sure he would manage somehow. She thanked him and walked away from the plane, purposely ignoring the shrubbery to the left that covered Yury's fleet of helicopters. She had taken a good look when they approached the airstrip and had felt a surge of relief when she saw the mound of branches still intact. *He's still here.*

She walked in the opposite direction, pretending to know where she was going as a path opened up before her. Then she heard footsteps running after her. She whirled and saw the pilot rushing to her side, waving a handful of red flares. "Look, take these. And some matches. It's the least I can do. I must be out of my mind, leaving a woman alone out here."

His speech was cut short by an explosion from the direction of the river. Miriam dove for the ground. The pilot yelled, "My plane—I've got to get out of here!" Head ducked low, he doubled back the way he had come. Miriam stayed on the ground until she heard the Cessna take off. It banked sharply and flew east.

Miriam tucked the flares in her kit and retraced her steps until she could see the airstrip again. She skirted its edges, heading for the helicopters. Just behind them was the real path she wanted, the one leading back to the old camp and, if Paul and the consul were right, back to Owen and Martin.

Her hand flew to her neck, searching for a reassuring shape, but found only the rapid beating of her heart. *All gone.*

Martin waited where the commandant had told him to. He watched the fireworks and knew they meant trouble. Commandant would be mad, and Martin had determined he would do his best not to make him madder.

He took apart the Kalashnikov and cleaned it again and again, practicing as Joseph had shown him. It was easier now. He wanted to break his record the next time they used the stopwatch with him. He was good at doing things close-up.

Yury fought for control. Everything he had worked for threatened to go up in smoke if he didn't act fast. His precious Mi-24 combat helicopters had proven helpless against the antiaircraft missiles the other factions used. Where had they bought those? His mind spun. Too modern for Soviet makes. Now all five camps would have to be dismantled. Yury ran for cover as another rocket soared into part of his precious cache of air fuel. Then he ducked and ran in a zigzag pattern to the command tent.

Joseph stood just inside the flap, watching him approach. "We have allowed ourselves to be pinned down. A regrettable error in tactics."

Yury said, "What will be regrettable is if they've hit the combat helicopters. I just received a communiqué that we're holding the rebels at the riverbank. I'm headed for the airstrip and will be back as soon as I'm satisfied the helis are still safe."

Once in the vehicle, Yury's walkie-talkie crackled. He held it up to his ear as he drove with one hand, shifting and steering faultlessly at the highest speed the dirt track would allow. His head pounded worse than the rain of explosives falling on his camps.

"Right . . . What . . . ? The airstrip? Repeat, I do not copy."

Miriam heard the Land Rover before she saw it. She hid behind a clump of vines and caught a quick glimpse of the driver. *Yury.* She would not have to wander for days in the jungle, trying to find his location after all. He had come to her.

She watched to make sure Yury did not climb into any of the helicopters. No, he only seemed interested in checking something, then returning quickly the way he had come. Miriam willed her feet to take her onto the dirt track. She stood beside his Land Rover. Waiting. Then he saw her. His look of utter amazement gave her the first advantage in the most crucial negotiation she had ever attempted.

Yury had no regrets about talking El-Fatih into shipping the hostage back to him after the man broke down. Yury claimed him and gave only the excuse that he wanted to keep him alive for personal reasons. Perhaps El-Fatih knew Yury might succeed where he had failed. Both the general and El-Fatih would owe him. Yury simply had more means at his disposal. Yury told himself he had no regrets. Damaged goods might still yield a profit.

If this were true, though, why didn't he feel that way?

He knew the answer but resisted its implications. *She* had ruined his taste for this particular business venture. Miriam, his longing for her, had distracted him, delayed his plan to use the boy as the means to break the father into submission. But the man had gone and broken himself first. And now Yury needed the boy as bait for Miriam.

Yury climbed out of the Land Rover, walked out to the airstrip, and surveyed the afternoon's damage. When he had finished, he felt for his walkie-talkie to radio that he was on his way back to the camp but remembered he had left it in the vehicle. As he headed back that direction, he glanced at the low sun. Only a few hours until the night bombardment would resume. Still, they had made good progress today. Tonight they might even push back the enemy to where he belonged, Yury thought with a slight smile.

His eyes blinked at the sunlight pouring in from an open patch between the trees. He reached for the sunglasses in his breast pocket. As he bent forward slightly to put them on, Yury heard her voice.

He thought he must have imagined it, must have summoned the sound through his thoughts of a few moments ago. He waited for an almost inconceivable amount of time, trying to sense what it was that had given him such a sensation of her nearness. Then Yury looked up.

"I've come back," Miriam said. She struggled to hide the trembling in her voice, in her hands, in her heart. She told herself there was no other way but direct confrontation. Yes, this was what had to be done.

She watched Yury almost drop his sunglasses, then fail to put them on. His gaze rose to meet her own. His eyes clouded, the shade of pale blue ice shifting slightly, but only for a second. Then he closed the distance between them, reached for her hand, and brought it to his lips.

His voice covered her, but she could not discern the truth from the lie. She expected a curse, but instead the words blessed her, their sounds a prophecy, as Miriam's surprise rooted her to the spot.

"You come back to me now out of your own will. This, you will not regret."

Chapter 61

In the days to come Owen could not be sure if the pounding was his own weak heart that had betrayed him, his head from hunger, or the shelling that seemed never to let up. He wondered who Falin was trying to bomb now, Savimbi or the government forces? No matter. He could go nowhere. Not in the real world, anyway.

Once again Owen forced his thoughts back from the chasm to the treatise he was writing in his mind. *Page 54. The heartbeat of God. Something about dark places. I have seen the children in this dark place and know these—the meek, the poor, the downtrodden, the brokenhearted, the persecuted. We are all his children. The Beatitudes, Isaiah 60—they describe the same reality, the heartbeat of God, the quiet pulse discernible even in darkness. The darker the place, the more secure the hope of those for whom the only source of light is our Savior. We are bound by the blood of Christ. . . .*

He rubbed his neck, unable to tie up the threads before they unraveled further. Was there no one act he could complete?

Let me stand, I pray.

It had grown into his own private act of worship—to struggle out of the fog his mind and body subjected him to and force himself to stand up. Owen grabbed the bars with both hands, and with sheer upper-body strength he pulled himself upright. He panted, head bent to miss the roof. Since the heart attack—he assumed it was a heart attack—brought on by the heat and ice, his leg muscles did not always obey the messages from his brain. They took longer to warm up, and he had to ease them into service carefully. When his muscles spasmed, Owen lost full control of his legs. Then he had to wait for the attack to pass, watching them shake like separate entities.

Let me stand became Owen's prayer every day. And every day again, eventually, he could feel the strength running up his spine, into his arms, down his legs. *Your strength, I pray.*

"Why do you think I came back?" Miriam asked, afraid Yury could see how his words embarrassed her.

"Show me your eyes, and I will tell you. I have dreamed of this moment. People always come back if they want something badly enough."

Now Miriam understood. *He thinks I have come back for him.* She was willing to use this as an opening gambit, a means of initiating the dialogue. Had the power of love, even an illusion of love, somehow eclipsed Yury's other self?

Yury leaned toward her. "Miriam, will you forgive me?"

Miriam forced herself to remain calm. Surely, in his eyes, *she* was the one who should be asking forgiveness. Had he forgiven her then for running away, the previous betrayal? Did he even remember? Or was he just playing with her now? Miriam swallowed, but the lie came easily. Too much was at stake. She looked up at him and said the one word she thought he must be looking for: "Yes."

She shook herself mentally. *Stay sharp.* She reminded herself to define the objectives clearly. "What do you want, Yury?" She knew the answer, feared it even, but also knew he needed the chance to hear his own voice, hear how he controlled her.

But Yury did not answer. Instead, he turned away from Miriam and coughed. "Come," he said gruffly.

In the Land Rover, winding through the bush, late-afternoon shadows piercing the undergrowth, Miriam went over and over her options. She did not have many. Tell the truth or continue the lie? If she played along with his assumption, she stood a chance. He had fallen for it the first time. Why not use herself as the bargaining chip?

Miriam glanced at him and wondered why he kept rubbing his head. She realized her acquiescence had moved Yury deeply. After all, he did not know that she knew Martin and Owen were there. Perhaps it was enough that he believed she came back for him. All she needed was to buy a little time. She had no getaway plan; she would think of that once she had her family again. No, she must concentrate first on finding them. Now that she was so close, she did not intend to leave without them. Not again. *Never.*

She watched him swing the wheel to the left and shift into gear, tearing up the terrain. Yury took her down a road freshly hewn from the bush. She noticed the fresh panga cuts in the trees on both sides. He stopped in a clearing. The hum of insects and the movement of monkeys in the trees caused her to look up. Two tents were tucked between a circle of tall trees.

The sight of her neck stretched upward like that drove Yury crazy. Her beauty still as dazzling as a frozen lake in winter, tranquil and deep, like the flecks of blue in her dark eyes. He had missed her so much, the yearning had grown into a tumored pain, an ache always within him. Through the fighting, the deals, Yury had longed for her alone.

How could he show her what this meant, her act of coming back to him? And her forgiveness for his impatience with her? She had asked him what he wanted, but the real question was, what did *she* want? It must be something they both could share. Yury suddenly realized an unexpected gift he could give her that would bind her to him forever.

"Where are we?" Miriam asked.

"West of where you stayed the last time you were here. At that time I had three camps close together. Two were training camps for the mercenaries I send out around the world. What? You are surprised? And the third, as you well know, was the diamond post, but that is now destroyed thanks to the troops on the other side of the river who represent a different group of Western interests. They know the worth of my mines, but I have made a deal I cannot back out of." It was good to have someone to share his business interests with.

"When did the attacks begin?" Miriam asked.

"The night you left me." Yury decided he would not ask her where she went that night or why. He surprised himself in his capacity to love, this urge to give because of love. *It goes against everything I have deemed worth pursuing in my life.* Yury saw himself how breathtaking the change could be. Why was it that sometimes he could see with such jagged clarity? They could share a lifetime together . . . as a family. The thought calmed a part of him he never even knew had needed taming. He breathed deeply, trying to ease the headache working up in force against his left temple.

Yes, an unexpected gift.

Miriam heard the voice say, "You're back!" She leaned her head out the window and listened to the sound a split second before she saw the boy. Her ears recognized this child's voice, but her eyes did not see him.

Then Miriam's hand flew to her mouth, and she swallowed her own cry of dismay. Yury did not hear her. He already walked toward the little boy standing in front of the tent.

Her seven-year-old, now turned eight, more than nine months and another lifetime older than the last time she saw him—left him behind, she reminded herself, alone in their vacation jeep—there he stood. No glasses on, he squinted in her direction. Worse, he held his little body in a wide stance, the same arrogant posture Yury had assumed. He had not yet seen her inside the vehicle.

"Martin." She said his name softly, feeling the word between her lips. The boy looked up as she swung open the door and got out. A look of disbelief flashed across his face, then recognition. He took three steps toward her.

"Freeze." Yury spoke the one word in an even tone, showing no signs of emotion, and Martin stopped moving. He didn't just stop walking. He stopped breathing.

"Martin?" she asked, but the boy did not even blink. Miriam could not control herself. She ran forward to kneel at his side and tried to take him into her arms. But Martin refused to yield to her touch.

Miriam stood, fury burying all her previous resolve. She looked at Yury. "How could you? You, after what you went through as a child, how could you inflict the same pain on another child? What have you done to him?"

But Yury only shook his head and raised his hand slightly, as if a fly buzzed near his head. "At ease." He used the same hollow voice, but something in it was different, harsher.

Startled, Miriam saw Martin spread his feet farther apart, place his hands together behind his back, and raise his chin. He did not even look at Miriam.

"You want to know what I did to him?" Yury mimicked her tone as he came up beside Miriam and took her arm in an iron grip, forcing her to stand behind Martin. "I stole him from you." This last he hissed into her ear, twisting her arm so she had to lean toward him. "You still do not understand, do you? Your son belongs to me, will always be my possession, no matter where I am or where he is. I own his soul."

Yury's sudden reversal in personality and his bearing toward her shocked Miriam even more than what had become of her son. She shuddered in surprise at the words, puzzled as well as upset over Martin. Her gaze fell on the back of Martin's head. She saw the cowlick he had worn every morning since he started sleeping on his back as a baby. This small sight tugged at her more painfully than any of the changes in his behavior.

"Remain at your post until further notice," Yury commanded Martin.

At the sound of the order, Martin's back straightened. "Yes, sir."

Martin obeyed automatically. Hear, obey, be rewarded; don't hear, disobey, be punished—this had been hammered into his little soul. Miriam saw this in an instant, recognizing the behavioral pattern from her boys and other former child-soldiers she had met. It was what had kept Martin alive, how he had endured. She understood that his capture by Yury would demand a terrible price from them all. Martin's retreat into safe behavior showed that he was paying that price even now. Hope had been sacrificed on the altar of fear. As Miriam saw and understood, her mother-heart broke for yet another lost boy, this time her own.

Yury repeated, "It was I who kept him alive. I am his hero. You can have him back in exchange for coming with me, on my terms—do you understand now? Save your son, Miriam. Children are so pliable, so trusting, don't you agree? They will believe anything, do everything. . . ."

"Stop it," she gasped. *Martin, what must you have endured to be so transformed?* Then Miriam realized she could not lose sight of the reason for this meeting. For Martin's sake. She must focus on Yury.

Miriam thought as fast as she could. She had spent only a month with Yury the last time she was here. But now, with Edith's words of healing as a prism to see through, Miriam identified a pattern to his instability. Too late she realized that she should not have mentioned Yury's childhood. It had triggered the tremors in his personality, and then she recognized the fault line. Edith had taught her what to look for. Thinking back, she could see the same pattern in his behavior toward her the first time.

Anytime Yury is reminded of his childhood, he lashes out. He fears abandonment, powerlessness. Yes, it was logical. His parents had abandoned him by committing suicide. His whole life had been a reaction against poverty and helplessness.

She had inadvertently hit this raw nerve when she saw Martin's brainwashed state. Was he then so afraid of loving because it caused the very powerlessness he so hated? *And the forgiveness?* The only way Miriam could see forgiveness fitting into Yury's profile was if he somehow blamed himself for all that had happened to him. Edith had told her many times that children see the bad events in their lives as connected to their own behavior. "It's not your fault" often released in a child a floodgate of guilt.

"You will come with me now," Yury said.

She looked at the vein throbbing in his cheek. *First I must calm him.* She had to summon back the softer Yury.

She straightened. "Listen, I'm sorry," she said carefully. "I was just . . . overwhelmed at seeing my son. But you're right. You did save his life, and I am grateful."

He was pulling her back to the vehicle. She did not resist, though her thoughts continued to bounce back and forth. Yury was one problem, but how to end the suffering for Martin? She glanced at the little form standing alone in the sunlight now, waiting to be relieved of duty. Miriam watched Yury warily as he held the Land Rover door for her. As she reentered his car, his world, his warped universe, Miriam felt the finality of all her decisions come slamming down upon her like a blue door to some dark and dusty dungeon, making her a prisoner to past and present.

"Martin, it'll be okay. I'll be back," Miriam said, but there came no reply. She turned to Yury, wary of his volatility, steeling herself to keep the accusation out of her voice. "I'm here now," she said. "You have me. Surely now you can let him go. . . ."

"But you still don't understand the terms properly. This is your gift. Something we both share."

"You want us to—" she hardly dared to say the words, their implication so outrageous—"you want us to *share* my son?"

"You must be willing, dear Miriam. Are you willing to come with me, to love me as I love you? You said you forgive me, that you have truly come back to me. But I want to hear it, I want to see it, I want to feel it."

Martin was shaking. He did not let the commandant see this. He remembered too well the beating he had received when he wet his pants in fear—that time when there was a lot of noise all around, blasts and bombs. No, this time he held his ground and his water. But still, he shook.

His mother. He remembered her. He remembered her smell and her soft touch and her voice. When he heard her speak his name, it felt like warm seawater washing over him on the beach. He remembered a distant shore, a place with white sand, remembered riding high up on his father's shoulders with the sun in his face as his mother called his name.

Martin stared into the sun now. The light was too bright. He could say to the commandant this was why his eyes watered. It happened every time he looked into the sun.

Chapter 62

Yury took her to the guest tent. The irony amused him. He did not say another word to her but nodded at Joseph, whose only response to the new arrival was raised eyebrows. The last thing Yury heard before wheeling the Land Rover around and roaring out of the camp again was Joseph's voice ordering one of the boys to get their guest some water and food. He enjoyed the desperate expression on Miriam's face.

He drove back the way he'd just come. Since the attacks on his camps, Yury had taken to moving his personal tent to a different location every week, and with it the tent he made Martin stay in after the cabins were blown up. He blocked out the explosions, the ragged gunfire coming from the direction of the river. Tonight they might make more progress than they had in previous weeks. Lately the conflict had ground down to a stalemate, but Yury knew it would continue indefinitely until one side's supply of ammo ran out.

He felt gratified to see Martin still holding his post, and in the sun. Yes, the boy had learned a great deal. He invited him to his own tent, and together they sat down. He handed the boy a Coke from the ice chest Joseph brought there every afternoon and poured himself a vodka. He should be conferring with his battalion leaders. There must be a way to break this impasse. But first, he had to deal with the boy's mother.

"How did you feel, seeing her again?" Yury asked Martin.

Martin's hand began to shake, and Yury nodded. He knew enough. Without waiting for the boy to answer, he said, "I have a special assignment for you, a mission. I want you to go to her just before sundown and offer to take her wherever she wants to go, even if she asks to see the prisoner. You remember where he is?"

Yury needed her to take this test. This way he would find out whether she was really here for him or not.

Martin nodded. "Yes, sir."

"It is not so far, a half click from the main camp. If she is interested, walk there with her, but pretend that this is against the rules. Then report back to me about her response. Do you understand?"

"Yes, Commandant."

Miriam paced back and forth in the tent, and it felt as though she had taken herself back to the place of her nightmares and now could not wake up. She was right back where she had started during that month with Yury, lost all over again.

She heard a slight knock on the tent post by the door. "Yes?" Her heart leapt as Martin stuck his head into the tent. "Oh, Martin! You're here. Come here, sweetie! Talk to me."

His face remained impassive, but she sensed his fear in the way his eyes flicked from one side of the tent to the other, as if he expected to see someone else there. How she longed to sweep him away, away from this place and time, back to San Francisco and the soccer practices of a year ago. He remained in the entrance. She moved toward him and again wrapped her arms around him. Again he would not move.

"He sent you, didn't he?" Miriam whispered into his ear. His little-boy smell, the scent of sweat that had hung over his clothes whenever she washed them, rose to meet her.

Martin nodded. "Do you want me to take you somewhere?" he asked in a loud voice.

Miriam stared at him. "Like where did you have in mind?" she said slowly.

Martin looked at his feet for a few moments. When he didn't answer, Miriam ventured, "Do you mean to see *someone?* Martin, do you mean your father? Dad?"

Martin still refused to meet her gaze. He only nodded. She watched him swallow several times. *All right,* she thought, drawing away. *If he can't meet me in my world, I'll come alongside him in his.* She had learned well enough how to do that these past months.

"Yes," she told him. "Please. Will you take me there? Are you allowed to?"

Martin looked relieved and motioned for her to follow. "We must be quiet, though. If the commandant finds out, I'll be punished."

Miriam didn't know how to respond, but she grabbed her pack and allowed Martin to lead her out of the camp. No one seemed to take notice as they slipped into the jungle. She glanced sideways at the amber blaze of setting sun and figured they must be heading back toward the airstrip. Finally they came to a large open area. She saw the charred remains of trees and structures—a few rows of bricks left, twisted corrugated iron hidden among the long shadows. She glanced at Martin to see if he was sure of his bearings and realized he knew exactly where he was going. He looked intently to the left and right, stopping every few steps to listen.

Miriam shadowed his steps as Simba mkali—no, Filho—had taught her to so long ago during another journey. She had learned how to make a minimum of noise. Now, when Martin crouched low, Miriam did the same. He raised his little arm in a fist, the signal to halt and be still. Miriam cringed at seeing how well her son assumed the posture and movements of a soldier.

Martin motioned for her to come up beside him. "There," he whispered. "He's in that cage."

Miriam swallowed her gasp. She saw Owen's body lying facedown in the dirt, surrounded by wooden poles set upright and tied together with leather bands. Palm fronds formed a partial roof, protecting him from the sun. She couldn't see his face but could tell he was painfully thin.

Miriam opened her mouth to ask Martin how often he had visited his father, to ask much more, when Martin said, "The commandant has ordered me to cease contact with the prisoner."

"Your father," Miriam corrected him.

"He is a subversive. But I can tell you they leave him alone except at sunrise, when he receives food and water. More than he deserves."

Miriam could not help herself. She shook Martin's shoulders and hissed. "Remember who you are, Martin. This is your *father*. And I am your mother."

Immediately his eyes glazed over, and he stood staring blindly.

Miriam grabbed at him again, wanting to hug him, wanting to hold him, wanting to make the last nine months disappear and go back to that place where he was her son and they lived in safety. But Martin raised his arm to stop her. He warded her hand off with a block, then ducked and ran back the way they had just come, into the jungle. Miriam watched him, shaken by his transformation, torn between the urge to chase after him and the desperate ache to see to her husband. But Martin had already disappeared, and Owen was just a few meters away.

Holding her breath, she stood, ducked, and hurried into the clearing. Miriam heard only her own rapid breathing, birds in the treetops, cicadas chirping, her footfalls in the dry dust. The sun dropped away with a sudden movement, and the jungle grew quiet. She knelt at the door to the cage and ran her fingers up and down the hinges of shrunken leather. The massive padlock looked out of place, too modern for the rough-hewn wood cage it held together.

She needed a knife. Miriam wriggled her hand and arm between the bars, then leaned forward to try and touch Owen. He lay so still, she thought for a moment he might already be dead. But once she quieted her own fear, Miriam could hear his uneven breathing. Up close now, she saw his beard looked long and ragged and gray. And she could see one side of his face, slack and hanging in jowls, but she could not reach him.

"Owen, Owen!" she called to him, glancing to the right and left, listening for a patrol. "Owen!"

He did not move. Miriam moaned. She was close, so close, but still could not free him. She had nothing with her, nothing sharp. She clawed at the leather thongs but to no avail. Then her gaze fell on the ground inside the cage. Even in the fading light she could see the scratches on one of the thicker poles—little marks carved into the wood, every five a bundle. She followed their winding line, appalled that she could not count them all.

"Owen! Owen!" She shook the wooden poles, but the cage stood solid. Miriam stood and walked around the cage, thinking there must be a way in, a way out, somehow. She smelled, then saw the corner he used as a latrine. *How dare they do this to him!* She felt rage rise up in her, even more than when she had seen the damage to her son. She hated Yury for the cruel game he had played with her, for tormenting her child and reducing her husband to this state.

Miriam's recent recognition of Yury's unstable state, her understanding of the forces that had shaped him, no longer mattered to her. The depth of his cruelty dwarfed any compassion she might have felt earlier.

"Owen!" Miriam forced herself to concentrate, to really look at the cage. *There must be a way inside.* "Owen, answer me! Owen, are you all right?"

Miriam's mind played tricks on her. *Maybe he's dead.* She waited and saw the slight movement of his rib cage. Yes, she could see him breathing, but she couldn't touch him, couldn't feel him. Miriam paced back and forth beside the bars, cursing this false proximity.

"Owen, please! Owen!" Miriam peered through the twilight, staring at his head. He looked so gaunt, so old. She fell to her knees, leaning her head against the wooden bars, fighting despair. She had come here thinking what? That she could rescue Owen single-handedly? And Martin? How would she ever reach him, let alone break the spell of authority Yury had cast over her son?

Oh, God, help us please! When will this nightmare be over?

Yury had to be sure. That was why he left her alone. He left her alone with the boy after ordering the boy to take her wherever she asked to be taken. When he spotted the two of them heading east, he knew with a sinking heart why she had really come back. His suspicion had proven true.

He had been willing to forgive her, to start over. He had even nurtured a fantasy of their somehow forming a family. But this had all been stolen from him like the wooden top he once owned in the orphanage. Stung by her betrayal, Yury knew what he had to do. He waited for the boy to return and give his report.

"I did as you ordered, Commandant." The boy saluted him.

At least the child will not lie to me.

When Martin had finished, Yury rewarded him by giving him the pistol he had been wanting. "Here. It is small but very fine. You may have it. I am pleased."

Martin stood a little straighter as he accepted the new weapon. "Thank you, Commandant. This old man . . . ," he began.

Yury was halfway out of the tent when he heard Martin's words. He turned. "The prisoner, you mean?"

"The prisoner. Is he alive? I mean, he looked like those others I saw."

"He looked dead." Yury said the words for him and exited, ignoring the boy's question so he would feel his displeasure. He almost ran into Joseph, who stood just outside the entrance. "What is it?"

"I've just come from the west lookout tower, and the night bombardment has started early."

"I heard." He hadn't, but he would not admit he could not focus this evening. "Give orders to move the munitions dump. Now that it's dark, get our fuel and ammo back to the new campsite."

"We're retreating from the river?"

"We're regrouping. I can't make any money if I'm being bombed all the time. How are the helis?"

"Still intact."

"Right. Tell the others. Start moving everything back to the new position, and fast. I want it all repositioned and camouflaged by sunrise. I'll join you at the airstrip in an hour."

Yury walked away from Joseph, advancing toward the clearing. He stood alone, listening to the shelling and trying to gauge the damage. What on earth had they gotten hold of? His arms dealers had let him down, not making the shipments on time, and he was in a tight spot. But from the sounds of the attacks, weaker with each passing night, Yury had assumed his assailants suffered even worse depletions. He had thought tonight would mark the turning point, but now he heard only too well that a new shipment of arms must have been supplied. The explosions' force, proximity, and increased regularity all pointed to an undeniable fact: Yury was outgunned.

It had taken him years to grab the mines in this area, and he wasn't about to give them up without a fight. Yet they had forced him into a retreat; he had to act carefully and not waste what ammunition and fuel he still had. But first . . . he raised his eyes and saw her kneeling by the side of the cage.

Yury looked forward to venting his frustration at the unseen, more powerful enemy assaulting him tonight. He tested his own emotions. *I feel nothing for her.* The storm had cleared. He was back to his old self. What had he been thinking?

He strode out of the bush, powered by the disappointment of a forced retreat. Yury grabbed Miriam by her hair, hauling her to her feet. *"Traitor.* I suspected as much. You will taste the fruit of your own lies. You claimed to want to stay with me. I thought you could not know he was here. But you did somehow—I don't care how. And you wanted to go to him. Well, I am not such a fool. You want him? Then you shall have him."

He grabbed her arm and twisted it so far back around the shoulder straps of her backpack that she had to kneel again. He did this with one hand and enjoyed the feeling of power coursing up his spine. With his other hand, he fished out the key to the padlock and opened the cage. He had learned firsthand of this kind of enclosure during his time in Afghanistan and had imported its shape, especially designed to break a man's back after repeated periods of standing. He threw the woman inside and jammed the padlock shut.

Yury walked away, laughing to himself. *Let her rot. Let them both rot and die in each other's arms.* He would leave them there tonight, and with a little bit of luck his enemies would bomb them both. He might even move an empty fuel tank to the clearing to make the target more appealing.

Chapter 63

Owen struggled to move, to change position, but his legs were still too stiff. They would remain that way until halfway through the day, only moving well if he found the strength to exercise properly. He thought this might be the result of his heart attack from the ice water, perhaps also from the prolonged confinement and the drugs they'd given him in Libya. But it might also be due to his malnutrition and dehydration.

One thing Owen knew for certain, and that was the location of El-Fatih's fort. He had gone over and over their words, his conversations with both of those beasts, El-Fatih and Falin, and there had been just too many references that pointed to Libya. Yes. He was sure of that.

Yesterday—or was it the day before?—he had not even bothered with his exercises. He would decide how much time had passed when he woke up again. He wondered why he no longer felt hungry. Nor did he feel pain. But just the thought of sitting up seemed an overwhelming venture, so he stayed down.

Owen calmed his breathing. He heard a movement very close. *Not alone.* He sensed it.

His eyes fluttered open, and he saw stars on a moonless night, the stripes of his enclosure outlined against the starlight.

"Owen?" He heard Miriam's voice, but not for the first time. He had heard her then too, in the blazing sun outside El-Fatih's oasis.

"Owen?" He felt the pressure of her hand on his face and realized it must be a rat. He turned his head with a groan to focus on this latest ghost. He mumbled her name, but it came out garbled. This illusion—was it a sign that his mind had finally surrendered to his surroundings?

Her hair, her touch, her voice, her tears showered down on Owen, so real, so close, he believed she really did crouch beside him. He knew this place. He had memorized every corner of the cage, every discoloration in the loose bark. The moon rose suddenly and shed light into the clearing. His eyes saw the shadow of a person leaning over him.

Someone has entered the cage.

While one part of him thought this, another part experienced the sensation of her proximity. His mind had played tricks on him before, but none as vivid as this. He could even smell her sweet scent, like the jungle after rain.

"Owen, look at me. It's me, Miriam. It's really me. Owen, stay with me, Owen!" Her voice faded, and Owen struggled to hold on to its soft ringing in his ears.

Someone shook him, and he came to again. This time the moon lit her face fully. "Miriam," his mind mumbled, but his mouth would not make the sounds properly. The mirage of Miriam smiled.

"It really is me, Owen. I'm here, at your side. I'm not leaving you again. I'm here."

The realization pierced his mental fog finally, and Owen's eyes widened. He summoned the strength he reserved for standing and propped himself up with one hand, forcing his body into the sitting position.

Once he leaned against the tree posts, he could reach out and touch her, feel her, listen to her laughing softly. *Yes, my Miriam.* His hand touched his mouth and felt the half smile. Her face mirrored a concern he could tell she did not want to show, but he saw anyway. He ached to communicate, but his mouth could only groan. Owen's fingers traced the path of Miriam's tears on dust-caked cheeks framed in pale light.

He leaned over and wrote with the same finger, shaking so hard he could hardly control the forms it made in the dust.

Adamas.

The word calmed Miriam's rising panic.

Ever since Yury had caught her, since his violence and raging rejection of what she had hoped they could still somehow discuss, Miriam had given in to the voices screeching that she would die in this place. Once she realized the extent of Owen's shattered health, Miriam heard them shriek that her husband would now die here. *Because of me.* It was all her fault for taking matters into her own hands.

But *adamas.* The word introduced a new sound into their prison, one whose tenor silenced these hissing taunts. It was her father's diamond word, the word they had shared. *Untamable.* By scribbling this in the dust, Owen gave Miriam a sign that the man she knew survived. *Indomitable.* Somewhere in his half-paralyzed shell of a body, fading in and out of consciousness, her Owen, the Owen of *then,* was with her now. He might not be able to communicate fully with her, but with what little strength he still had, Owen had passed on a word of hope.

Miriam took the understanding inside herself and believed that yes, they both would be all right. The thought came to her and settled on Miriam's heart and mind, the choice to believe a promise all her own.

She faced the fear, accepting that although she might be back in a prison of Yury's making, back in the everlasting night, she also was back at Owen's side. And Martin was near. There must be a way out.

Adamas. Please, God, give me the faith to believe.

All night Miriam watched the stars reel overhead as the shelling continued in the distance like thunder, growing. She slipped Owen mouthfuls of water and bits of the bread and cheese she had brought with her in the small pack, grateful that Yury hadn't taken it away when he threw her inside the cage.

Owen slept, his head on her lap, sometimes seeming to be in an even deeper state of unconsciousness. He awoke or came to several times that long night, and although he appeared not to see her, not to recognize her, except for that one time, he did accept the nourishment.

What she wanted was to share everything with him, to tell him about her journey, her losing herself and finding Edith, finding God, finding him.

There would be time enough for that. Had to be. For now, it was enough to know he lived. But though he was alive, she could tell he had suffered in devastating ways.

Toward dawn, Miriam heard a stick break, then soft voices. She caught sight of the figures only after the stars began to fade, and she lowered her gaze to ground level. Then Miriam thought she saw two forms approach the cage, running from the cover of one tree to the next. They dodged the open spots, bent and rushed. Before she could react, two faces peered into the cage.

Miriam heard his voice before her eyes could focus on the speaker.

"Me, I knew this. You, who were lost, would be found. Now we have done this thing."

"Little Lion? Filho?" Miriam squinted as if emerging from a dream to stare at the intense, dancing eyes of the two boys. She shook her head. "But you can't be back here. How? Where?"

Filho whipped out a knife and began sawing on the sun-dried leather thongs holding the two feeblest of the tree branches. He said, "We are your rear guard. We could not leave you alone."

Miriam looked at him. "Filho?"

The older boy looked down at the dirt. "This thing, this place—this is not good."

Miriam knew what he referred to. "You know where we are?"

"Back there," Filho said. "It is where my little brother received his scars."

With his words, a sudden empathy fell upon Miriam. What must it have cost them to come back to this place, the place of their torture? What had they called it? Oh yes—"never night." She reached a hand out between the bars and grasped Little Lion's fingers.

Little Lion said, "But you would not leave us alone."

She said, "Please forgive me." Her words brought tears to her eyes. What she wanted to say was, *Forgive the world. Forgive us for not doing more to keep you with your family, to end the wars, to bring stability, to make your and your brother's lives worth as much as our own.* But all she said was what she had thought before: "You are back in your 'never night.'" It was the first time she had ever said their expression out loud.

"This place?" Little Lion laughed and spat into the dust. "Not here, *there*. Nevernight is somewhere very different from here, where there is no pain and no fear, where it is never dark, only light in Nevernight."

Understanding began to dawn on Miriam about this safe haven where they felt no fear, no horror, no pain, where it was never dark. She remembered their thousand-kilometer trek across Africa, how Simba mkali would comfort the boys by saying those words over and over, "Shhh . . . never night . . . never night."

In a flash of insight, she could see that these boys—though their lives had been shattered and their situation looked hopeless—had been full of faith and hope all along. They could look into the night sky and see heaven. She had been the one in darkness, looking for hope only in the here and now.

Nevernight. It was their name for heaven. How could she have missed it? Now she had another word to treasure. Just as *adamas* gave her a solid connection to the past, *Nevernight* opened her eyes to a life-filled future, regardless of what happened now to her and Owen and Martin and these bright-eyed boys.

She heard Owen groan, felt him move.

"Miriam?" he asked, struggling to prop himself up. "Who are they?"

Miriam's heart lifted. The food and water had made a difference. He recognized her. He could talk. He had taken note of the boys. He was even moving more easily.

"My boys," she answered him. "This is Filho and Little Lion. They . . . rescued me from here the last time. My boys." Again she groped for Little Lion's hand in the dark. His fingers wound around the pole, shaking it back and forth as Filho cut the leather. She grasped his hand in hers and shook to the same rhythm, sharing his strength.

"Tell me how you got here, Little Lion." She looked up into the darkness and watched the glow of explosions in the distance.

"This story, it needs a long time. And we are thinking more about opening this place and getting you out than the story. So me, I will just say that was no ordinary tree you cleared out of the road when you took Mama Edith's elder brother's Land Rover. That tree did not fall there on its own. And while you cleared it out of the way, well, the backside of the Land Rover took on two more passengers."

"And the airplane?"

Little Lion said, "In the same way, we climbed into the plane when you were talking to the pilot. An amazing thing, this flying."

Miriam glanced at Filho and saw a trace of a smile on his mouth and in his eyes.

Little Lion said, "The white plane did the same as the Land Rover, but behind the backseats. And when that same pilot ran after you in this place—here, I mean—then we left the plane. But, oh, we mounted up with wings like eagles, did we not, Elder Brother?"

Filho nodded. "He is right."

"So," Miriam said, "you were with me all along."

Both boys looked at her as if she should have realized this much sooner.

Chapter 64

Owen watched Miriam and the two boys who had appeared out of nowhere to free them. He still did not trust that she could be real. He reached over and touched Miriam's leg. When she turned to him, he sighed. "I must talk to you in case we're separated again."

He saw the devastation his words wrought on her features but held up a hand to ward off her objection. He and Miriam scooted over to the far side of the cage, and he dropped his voice so the boys would not overhear, hoping she could understand him. His ability to send messages to his mouth and speak them out had improved radically now that the nourishment she gave him had lifted the fog of hunger from his mind. The more he said, the clearer he spoke.

"Listen, you know the case I was working on last year?" he asked her.

"Ireland," Miriam said. "It ended badly."

He took a deep breath. "Yes, you know that. Well, there's a great deal you don't know because I didn't tell you. At some point I had sought contact with certain parties in Libya because that's where the terrorists targeting Britain were being armed and trained. Intelligence reports also hinted at the existence of a loosely formed conglomerate of Russian mafia factions, an umbrella syndicate with connections among both the Angolan rebels and these Libyan terrorist trainers of the IRA."

Owen began to cough. When the coughing fit had passed, he found himself breathing hard from the effort it cost him. But he also discovered if he spoke softly and slowly, he could now speak more easily.

"Listen, now. I was investigating the Libyan supply of arms to the IRA from 1972 through the mid-eighties. Qaddafi admitted in June 1972 that Libya supported fighting Britain in her own home. He told the IRA there were arms and support for the revolutionaries. You have to realize that for twenty years now, ever since 1973, Ireland has had unparalleled contact with clandestine arms suppliers. The three main sources were the U.S., the Middle East, and those who produced homemade weapons and explosives. Libya delivered a series of cargoes between 1985 and 1987 to Ireland by trawler.

"Then in 1986, the U.S. bombed Tripoli in reprisal for a bomb attack on U.S. soldiers in Berlin. And something important—Qaddafi's daughter, Hanna, was killed in that bomb attack. She was just sixteen months old."

It was more words than Owen had spoken to another human being in the last three months combined. He had been thinking about it so much; now it sounded good to hear out loud how it all added up. His mouth went dry. He took a sip from the bottle Miriam held to his lips. For a long moment they both said nothing. He reveled in his imminent freedom, as close as these boys' knife and their young strength. In another few moments he would be *outside*.

But he had to clear the slate with Miriam first. How could he do that and not reveal the total truth, since all of it could do more harm than half? He still had to protect her, but Owen felt a tremendous pressure from within to also share the reasons behind all that had happened to them. He would wait for her to start asking questions and see which he dared to answer. He owed her that much at least.

But Miriam did not ask questions. Instead, she moved closer to him, held him tighter, then whispered into his ear, "Owen, I trust you. I have never in my life met anyone with as much integrity as you. I think all these details are not really what you are trying to tell me. I hear what you haven't said. There's more than just the fact that our kidnapping was in some way retaliation for Qaddafi losing his little girl." She looked at him, and he nodded.

"So he ordered the kidnapping of the negotiator's family to force you to throw some deal or lift some sanctions or something. But I *know* you, and I know right now you are wrestling with the dilemma of how much to tell me and how much not to tell me, for my own safety. So stop it. You've paid a higher price than anyone ever could ask of you. All I really know for sure, all I *want* to know, is that you are alive and sane, and I thank God for answering my prayers. The rest . . . never mind the rest."

Owen shook his head. He wanted to confess the wrongs of his father, the terrorist commander, the sins visited on him by his family, the connections with Libya's El-Fatih and Angola's Savimbi and the ruthless Falin, Owen's own desperate lies and compromises. *Past and present.* But he also understood the unique gift Miriam had offered him. She who loved him enough to return to this abyss of abject misery, she who was God's own gift to him in this life—his Miriam knew better than he what they both could bear. He reached over and drew her to his chest. "Heart of my heart," he attempted, but the tears choked his voice.

Owen wanted desperately to get as far away as possible from the subject of what he might be asked to do someday. He had lied when he said he would do it, but that didn't mean they wouldn't ask him again. Or do more than ask. So instead he looked around for something else, something safe, something to lead her away from the minefield he held in safekeeping for them both now.

Owen looked over at the two boys who still worked diligently on his cage. "The older brother, as you call him. Filho—is that really his name?"

Miriam answered so quietly he could hardly hear her. "They don't know their own names. They're former child-soldiers. Oh, Owen, it's a long, long story, but these boys saved me, found me here twice now. And I've been learning about counseling children like them. There's a woman named Edith at a refugee camp in Tanzania, where I've been living while you were here. She's taught me so much. But most of all, God—he's met me in the dark places, especially in the dark places, like you said he would. And through these children."

Owen held her, unable to respond, drinking in the sound of her voice.

Miriam was astounded by Owen's improvement during the night. Perhaps with some more food and rest he might recover all the way. She thought a moment about this before summoning an explanation of the boys. "These two have healed more than most, although it's a fragile thing. They shouldn't be here, actually—back here."

"But their names?"

She wondered why he kept asking. "Well, that's just it. You see, they don't know their real names, so they've chosen new ones for themselves. They used to call themselves Simba mdogo—that's Little Lion—and Simba mkali, Fierce Lion. But recently Fierce Lion decided to take another name instead. Filho. The boys are very religious."

She noticed Owen raising a single eyebrow in that look he gave her whenever she had said something amusing. "Well, I mean, they have memorized lots of the Bible. There's a verse about a child lying down with the lion."

"It's the lamb that lies down with the lion, and the child leads them," Owen said.

"Anyway, he said this verse caused him to change his name again. I don't really understand how their minds work. They've led tortured lives, and now they're back in their place of torment. But I do know they've taught me to hope, and my faith means something now, Owen. Like you asked me, remember, back in the cell when we were together? God is real."

Again he held her tightly, tightly in his weak arms, and to Miriam it was the finest sensation in the world. She had come home, home to his arms.

Then he asked softly, "Don't you know what it means—*Filho?*"

"Sure, it means 'child.'" Little Lion had told her that.

"You're right," Owen said, "but it also means 'son.' *Filho* in Portuguese means both 'child' and 'son.'"

Miriam watched the two boys shaking the stakes, still sawing away at the leather, pouring their strength into freeing her and Owen. A bittersweet recognition settled over her, as softly as a blanket over a baby. *He told me to call him Filho. And then he called me Mae.*

Ragged gunfire burst through her thoughts as it erupted from the trees to the left. The night's bombardment, lulled into silence in the darkest hours before dawn, now increased in intensity as daylight broke. Explosions from both sides of the river came in flurries now. From the direction of the airstrip, smoke smudged the sky. Miriam heard helicopters in the distance. She said, "Yury's enemies seem to be closing in."

A few moments later, Filho and Little Lion managed to tear open one panel of the cage. The three of them helped Owen to his feet. He could stand but could hardly walk. Miriam shoved her shoulder under his arm, and they struggled out of the cage. Little Lion dashed off and a few moments later returned with a forked stick that Owen could use as a crutch. "Thank you," Owen said. "Both you boys are very clever. I wonder—"

A voice stopped him. Owen's head shot up, and Miriam read on his face recognition replaced by remorse. Miriam looked in the same direction.

"The Commandant said you would leave without me." Martin's voice.

Yury emerged from the underbrush, one hand on Martin's shoulder, the other holding a semiautomatic rifle.

Martin turned his head upward. "You were right, Commandant."

Filho moved so he flanked Owen, and Little Lion came to stand by Miriam. Yury walked straight for the little group and kicked the crutch out from under Owen without even breaking stride. Then he dragged Owen by the arm a few paces into the middle of the clearing and dropped him. Owen fell with a thud but did not cry out. He lay motionless.

Yury stepped over Owen, putting himself between Miriam and Owen. He stared defiantly at her. "You are *nothing* here," he sneered. His eyes passed right over the boys, and this gave Miriam the spark of an idea.

As she made a move toward Owen, Yury barked, "Don't." His walkie-talkie buzzed, and he removed it from his belt, then began shouting into it, a frantic edge to his voice. "No, *no,* I told you. Get back up there. . . . I don't care. . . . Right. Over."

Miriam held herself in check. She tried to swallow her hatred of Yury, knew it would only cloud her judgment. But her abhorrence still rose in the back of her throat. This man had caused so much pain in those she loved. He embodied all that was wrong and unjust.

"This man, he is our enemy," said Little Lion. She looked down into his face, his dark eyes so solemn.

"Yes."

"Then he is the man we must pray for."

Miriam stared at Little Lion, wanting to say, *No, what he has done is inexcusable.* Instead she took advantage of Yury's distracted state and whispered, "Now listen, you must go, go quickly, both you and your brother. Go, disappear, *now!*" She would not be responsible for their getting hurt.

Filho nodded and ran, but Little Lion hesitated, then tore away from her, dashed into the cage, ran back out, and followed Filho into the bush. Miriam knew that when Filho and Little Lion did not want to be seen or heard, they could vanish.

Martin had thought the commandant might be wrong. "Parents leave their children behind." That's what he had said. Then he had let Martin walk point as they returned to the place with the cage and the old man, the place he had brought *her*.

And she *was* going to leave him behind. They were getting ready to leave. Martin had seen it with his own eyes.

Mostly, Martin felt confused. So much was happening, it was hard for him to concentrate. The enemy pressed in. He had heard Commandant tell Joseph they needed to regroup. The shelling wouldn't stop. The sound of gunfire and helicopters grew closer.

And then *she* was here. And he kept remembering things. He felt mixed-up inside and couldn't decide which sound, which *person*, he should listen to. When Commandant ordered him to stay at his side, he remembered pain and rewards, and he obeyed. But he still felt like a part of him might be thinking something else.

Martin didn't feel pulled in two directions about those boys in the clearing, though. *They are the enemy. They freed the prisoner.*

Martin watched them run away while the commandant's voice rose and fell, giving orders through the walkie-talkie. Commandant hardly glanced at the boys as they escaped. Martin knew their sort, boys like he had trained with. No, he didn't feel any confusion about them like he felt about the old man and the woman. He didn't like it when the prisoner had to fall like that, but that was war.

Now Martin had an idea of something he could do that would please Commandant. These were bad boys, and Martin knew first-hand what should happen to disobedient boys. He was sorry when they ran like cowards and Commandant did nothing, but he was glad when he caught glimpses of them through the trees, circling back along the edges of the clearing.

⬚ ⬚ ⬚

Pain slammed against Owen's head and side as he toppled to the ground. He did not raise his head but lay still. He listened for a few moments, pushing aside the bellowing between his eyebrows. Rage roared up in Owen's throat at the thought of all that had been lost, the weeks and months of shame while being treated this way, his life worthless, and what might still happen to his wife and son at the hands of this man. But he swallowed it, forcing the power of his anger to take another form.

Owen poured all his strength into crawling toward Falin's back, only a few meters away. Then he reached up and pulled him down, tackling the man who had taken his family from him. Falin's rifle bounced beyond his grasp. Owen struggled to hold him with his weight, but Falin wriggled out of his grasp. He stood and laughed out loud, then began to kick Owen mercilessly. Owen felt his body caving in. From very far away, he heard explosions. And the sound of helicopters circling overhead. And his Miriam . . .

⬚ ⬚ ⬚

Miriam felt each blow from Yury's boots as if it struck her own side. She knew Owen could not survive such an onslaught. She screamed a war cry and hurled herself toward Yury.

"No, do not run toward him!"

Out of the corner of her eye, she saw red flames shoot upward and heard Filho shout that she must stop. She skidded to a halt and whirled just in time to see Filho throw his knife from the far side of the open space. It buzzed by her head and sank into the tree nearest Yury.

Then she looked to see Little Lion holding a flare up high as the red smoke and flames poured from his hand. In his other hand dangled her backpack. He met her eye for just a second. Then he heaved the flare at Yury.

It landed on Yury's shoulder, the flames licking his arm and face. Yury howled as the fire caught his sleeve. He watched his arm burning and hurled himself into the dust, slapping at the fire with his other hand.

Miriam sprinted for Owen. She gently touched his bruised side and placed two fingers at his neck, frantic for a pulse. Filho had followed her. She looked up at him, panting, "I told you to *go.*"

"We did."

"But you came back and—," she started to say.

"Don't move." It was Martin's voice.

Miriam pivoted and slowly rose to her feet.

Martin stood at a distance, but opposite her. He held a pistol securely in both hands. The weapon was pointed at Filho.

Chapter 65

Miriam's thoughts whirled like the helicopter approaching from somewhere nearby. What had happened? Her husband lay brutally beaten, crumpled at her feet. And there stood the brothers, her boys, who had risked so much for her. And Martin, on the other side of the clearing. With a gun.

For a split second it all froze, framed in African light. Miriam felt strangely distant from the scene. She held still and heard only her own breathing, her heart beating, heart bleeding. How had she possibly set at risk her Owen and the children she had learned to love?

"Martin." She took a step toward him, amazed at the steady sound of her voice. Then she wondered at the ease with which he drew on military knowledge he should have been too young to understand, let alone master.

In answer to her gesture, Martin fired a bullet in their direction.

Filho cried out. Then Little Lion dashed toward them from where he had thrown the flare and rammed Martin from behind. Martin hit the dirt and his pistol went flying into the brush. While Martin was down, Little Lion rolled three times, across the ground toward Filho. He pulled him upright, and both boys disappeared into the undergrowth. Miriam saw only the drops of blood trailing them in the dust.

She felt a heavy wind hit her back as the helicopter's roar filled her ears. She turned around, ducking from the cloud of dust rising toward the helicopter as it hovered over the clearing. She looked up, shading her eyes. Amazed at the close range, Miriam could even see the pilot's face. Then she recognized the features. "Paul!" She waved and yelled.

Paul set the helicopter down at the edge of the clearing, shut down the engine, got out, and ran toward her, talking all the way. "Miriam, we found my Land Rover and radioed the pilot, who gave us the coordinates of the place he brought you. We flew here this morning and have control of the airstrip, even stole a helicopter or two. The pilot told us he had given you flares. When we saw the red smoke just now, we thought it must be you."

Miriam grabbed his arm. "Owen—get Owen out of here! He's desperately weak, and just now was badly beaten. Whatever happens, you must save his life. Do you understand? *He* is the priority."

But when she looked up to point at Owen, what she saw was Yury.

He had managed to quench the fire on his arm, reclaim his rifle, and circle behind them. Now he seized Martin and headed for the helicopter.

Paul drew a gun, but Miriam yanked on his arm with both hands. "Don't shoot—my son—that's my son he has! No, please! Get Owen out of here. You *must* see to Owen." She thought to herself, *Only I can save Martin.*

Yury yanked the helicopter door open, climbed inside, and flipped a series of switches. He called out to Martin, who stood beside the helicopter, his head bowed under the accelerating blades.

Miriam glanced at Paul, who was struggling to raise and support Owen. She raced toward the helicopter. "Martin! No, not again!"

Yury jumped out without his rifle, shoved Martin inside, then climbed in and slammed the door just as Miriam reached the other side of the helicopter.

"No! Martin! Yury, you want me. Let Martin go. Let Owen go. He serves no purpose for you any longer. Please, let them both go." She was guessing, but it made sense, too, given the level of Owen's neglect. For a fleeting moment, she wondered why indeed Yury had kept Owen alive.

The answer descended on her with an old terror. *He kept him alive to lure me back.* Detonations all around her now, the roar of the helicopter—Miriam fought panic from the threat of losing her family, and herself, all over again. It took all of her self-control to focus.

Miriam wrenched open the other door and flung her body inside just as Yury lifted the helicopter a few feet off the ground. She managed to get only her upper body inside; her legs dangled.

Yury laughed. "What do you want?"

She looked up and saw him in the pilot's seat. Behind him she caught a glimpse of Martin, buckled into his seat, his features rigid with fear. The helicopter tipped dangerously, her weight pulling it out of balance. Miriam felt her feet hit the ground.

A car raced toward them, a red dust cloud behind and around it. Miriam recognized the same Tanzanian green uniform Paul wore. She had last seen combat fatigues like these in the refugee camp when a government minister came to visit. In her mind's eye she saw fleeting images of men and women, the children watching them, the dust a mist before her eyes. For a moment it seemed as if she saw the colors and sounds of the camp, and then fear jerked Miriam's own gut back to the present.

She heard a shouted warning. Gunshots coming closer. The jeep veered into the bush.

Yury continued punching buttons on the control board. The motor shrieked.

Miriam cried out, "Yury, please, take me instead. Leave Martin, please!" Had she come so far, so very far, just to have her son snatched from her like this at the last moment?

Yury raised the helicopter a few feet off the ground and turned it sharply. Miriam fell from the opening and struggled to stand, but the wind and flying dust drove her to her knees.

"You did not forgive me!" Yury hurled the words at her through the swaying door.

Miriam knew there was only one moment left and only one way she could possibly convince Yury. An opportunity was there—she could see it on his face—otherwise he would already have flown off. She knew that what he wanted was her, her love and her forgiveness. What she wanted was the safety of her son and husband at any cost. This much became clear to Miriam as she knelt in the dust, the scream of the blades in her ears.

She summoned all her strength and prayed, *Let me forgive him; let him believe me.* Miriam thought of Yury's instability, his spiraling in and out of manic moods. It wasn't a reason or an excuse. It was just how he had become.

The helicopter hovered, rotors cutting the air. How could she possibly keep it down when it kept trying to rise? How could she convince Yury to let Martin go? She knew deep in her heart that the only way she would ever save her son was if at that moment she found a way to truly forgive this man.

To rise.

To rise.

Not even all the strength her small frame could muster would prevent the great machined bird from soaring as it had been made to do. The rotors screeched affirmation in each strained rotation.

To rise.

The image and the verb merged, triggering something in Miriam's thoughts. *"To rise with healing in its wings."* The words cut through her fog, Edith's words from another place and time: *". . . accept the evil and violence we are capable of, receive . . ."*

Miriam wondered, if she could receive forgiveness, did she dare give it? All she had to do was be willing to pass on the gift. *But not to him!* Yet, what claim did she have to withhold it from another? *After all I've done wrong . . . ?*

"Yury, you were right!" She yelled as loudly as she could to make herself heard over the sound of the rotors. "I was lying when I said it before. But I'm not lying now. I do forgive you." She sobbed, then shouted feebly, "Please, will you bring my son back? It's not his fault!"

Martin, forgive me.

Miriam cried out once more, "Yury!" The helicopter tipped its nose downward. She saw Yury unbuckle Martin's harness. She half crawled, half scrambled toward them, struggling to clamber on board.

Bullets from the ground whizzed by her ear. She heard the clonk of a missile launcher, then an explosion to her right. Miriam fell to the ground, her hip aching. This place, she had been here before. The fear, searching in the dark, the sounds of explosions, men's voices, fighting voices, fire and mayhem all around her, caught in a cross fire. She had to fight through the terror to reach out for a different now.

Through the hail of bullets, she saw Paul cover Owen with his body. She heard Martin cry out. She saw the helicopter rise above the treetops, Martin's face pressed against the glass. She heard the scrape of metal, another explosion, then a sickening sound as one of the blades broke away and wound downward. The helicopter howled as Miriam watched it tip and spin, then collapse behind the trees.

Miriam ran toward the crash site.

She ran, and all her worlds unraveled as she saw the twisted heap smoking on the ground. Miriam beat her fists against the glass hull; it shattered into a cobweb of fractures. She ignored the blood on her hands and dug beneath the contorted frame.

Empty. Why wasn't Yury's body slumped against the controls? She frantically looked in the back.

Yury unbuckled Martin's harness. The memory brought her up short. Yury hadn't been wearing one either. They must have been thrown from the helicopter.

Miriam started to circle the crash site, stumbling over dead wood and vines. The sour reek of diesel filled her nostrils, turning her stomach. She grabbed a bare branch and swept back the brush, wielding it like a panga. Every few seconds she paused, turned, and headed in a different direction.

She did not know how much time passed before she heard a movement in the bush, a moan. She moved toward it and stumbled into an open patch where a tree had fallen, taking down several others with it.

On the other side, Miriam caught a glimpse through the undergrowth of a child walking toward her. She heard Little Lion's voice calling to her.

He appeared from among the trees, staggering under the weight in his arms as he came her way. Miriam saw pale arms, a pale face. She whispered, "Martin."

Little Lion laid him on the ground like a lamb. "He lives."

Miriam gathered Martin into her arms, her son's limp body hanging heavy against her chest. He breathed. She ran a finger over his face—drawn, no longer a child's, even when senseless.

Then she looked up. Through her tears of gratitude, Miriam saw Little Lion still standing. Miriam reached up her other hand and asked him, "Where is Filho, our Simba mkali?"

He answered, "My brother is going there now."

She heard the words and thought he meant to say, "My brother is coming here now." Then her eyes saw his, and her heart understood. This new loss etched onto his face could mean only one thing.

She wiped at her own tears as he knelt down beside her. The salty wetness trailed her fingers as they traced this new granite grief, its chiseled presence heavy and set in his old-man features.

Miriam pulled Little Lion close and raised his chin with her hand. Her tears pooled with his as he said again, his child's voice a chant, a prayer, a cry for peace, "My brother is going *there* now."

Epilogue

Owen walked beside Miriam toward the plane. Edith and Paul stood by the plane's open door talking in soft tones. The pilot stowed the last of the bags in the hatch under the wing. Owen saw Martin's head in the second window, staring straight ahead.

Owen felt a sudden urge to try one more time, to make it all right somehow. He longed to erase the last year, but the only way he knew to wipe a slate clean was through reconciliation. He had seen countries make peace. Why couldn't he do it in his own heart? If only he could forgive. But how could he forgive Falin, this . . . this animal? *As I wrestle with forgiveness, my heart closes in despair. God, why can't I draw on your love for this man?*

Then Owen had a thought, a glimpse of possibility. He caught himself saying, "I pity the man who loves you and cannot have you."

Miriam stopped. "Why would you say such a thing? Are you talking about Yury?"

Owen looked at her, hardly able to speak, so grateful was he for her presence at his side. Her dark, blue-flecked eyes, her chestnut hair, the soft tones of her voice all overwhelmed him. *You are truly an exceptional woman, Miriam.* "I . . . yes."

"What do you mean?"

"I'm just saying, I admit to some sympathy for Yury." *It's a start.* Owen went on. "I mean, he left me alive, didn't he? Why did he do that? It had nothing to do with me, once I was of no more use to his clients. I've been wracking my brain to understand why he didn't kill me. It wasn't to trade me for you—he had Martin for that. I think he kept me alive out of love for you. It was his gift to you, a token, even a subconscious sign of his true feelings. He might not even have been aware of that action as a manifestation of love."

"You're probably right," Miriam said. "Yury didn't even know the difference between cruelty and love." She was looking at him with tears in her eyes. "Owen . . ." Her voice trailed off as they reached Edith and Paul.

Paul extended his hand to Owen, then drew him into a hug. "Comrade-in-arms," he said.

Owen laughed. "Yes, that we are." *So many unanswered questions.* He paused, then led Paul a few steps away, where the women couldn't overhear. "Paul, I've been puzzling over how you managed to swoop into the heart of mafia-held territory and get us out with relative ease. Your old contacts wouldn't by any chance include the forces we heard attacking the camp, would they?"

Owen had known that Savimbi's Unita rebel forces in Angola had received aid and arms from South Africa and America in return for access to the diamond mines in rebel-controlled areas. And now he knew that dos Santos's government forces were receiving that aid instead. What he wondered now was if Paul had once fought in the anti-apartheid forces that opposed Unita, on the side of dos Santos. He knew Yury played both sides. Owen recognized the pattern. He was back to figuring out whose enemy was the enemy's enemy.

Paul smiled and shook his head to warn Owen away from a subject that was off-limits. "Angola has been a mess and always will be, as long as outside governments continue to interfere for the sake of diamond profits. Suffice it to say I called in some old debts. Don't worry, Owen. You and I are on the same side."

"And that would be . . . ?"

"The side of peace." Paul walked him back over to the women.

Owen nodded slightly to himself. Then he turned his attention to Edith and saw her slip Miriam a piece of paper.

"It has to be enough," Edith said.

Owen looked at the paper and read the names and addresses of several child-trauma experts in North America. "But they won't have your field experience."

"That's true," Edith said. "But, Miriam, I have taught you all I could."

"It's all right," Miriam replied. "There's nothing more you can do."

"Give him time," Edith said. "Look how much you have recovered in a short period, Owen."

Yet they all knew the trauma that ailed Martin was profound.

Edith gathered Miriam and Owen into her arms for a hug good-bye.

"Thank you." Owen and Miriam whispered the same words at the same time into the many scented braids.

When the engine's whine reached him, Yury raised his face to the sky, waiting. He had asked Joseph to drive him as close as they dared to the airstrip near the refugee camp; then they parked in the shadow of a giant baobab.

He looked up, hardly daring to breathe. The high-pitched roar came closer and then, there it was, a white bird ascending between the trees. The sun glanced off its wings, and Yury raised a hand to his eyes to reduce the glare.

"I think in the front window," Joseph said. "There. Can you see her?"

"Always," Yury whispered. *Always I will see you. Always I will seek you.* He rubbed his thumb over the black diamond ring turned inward on his smallest finger.

Martin refused to wear the new glasses they bought him. He didn't care that his bed was wet in the mornings. Served her right to have to clean up the mess. They asked him questions all the time, the two of them and that doctor with toys in his office. Couldn't they see all he wanted was to be left alone? That it was no use?

Martin sat on his desk chair, staring at his bedroom wall. Sometimes his lower lip quivered, but he had learned not to make a sound, not even a whisper. It was better this way—not hearing, not seeing, not understanding. Under his elbow the sketchpad, full and blank, lay beside an unopened package of colored pencils on top of unopened jars of paint.

He picked up a ballpoint, took it apart, spread the casing, tiny spring, and ink cartridge on the desk before him, then put it back together again.

Miriam took a deep breath and knocked on the door. "May I come in?"

As she opened the door, she saw Martin at his desk, fiddling with the pen again. He raised his eyebrows arrogantly, resigned, giving the message, *You will anyway, so who cares?* She sat down on the end of his bed, watching him sit ramrod straight in the chair.

"Martin, why do you hate it so much when I come in here?"

Before she could even draw a breath, he replied, "Because you always go away."

She felt hit in the chest; her heart doubled over. "But I'm still in the house—"

"If you come in, you have to go out. You both are always leaving. Again."

Miriam leaned forward, reminding herself of what the psychiatrist had said, that any interaction was progress. At least Martin was talking to her. She willed herself to hear the words yet again: *Miriam, accept.* She had to accept that she would never have the old Martin, never find him again. The best she could hope for, and it was more than good enough, was a physically healthy Martin, a new Martin, a different Martin, this stranger-Martin maybe a little more whole, in her own home.

She would fight him for that little bit of wholeness.

She tried again. "This being alone, you want to talk about it?" But she could see she'd gone too far too fast. Again. He frowned and stared past her shoulder.

Then she thought, how could she so dislike the company of her son? It was a terrible thought, and she blamed herself. But the tension in this room bore down on her like stone slabs of regret.

She heard Owen's key turn in the front door, and her hands stopped their clenching and unclenching, came to rest on her lap.

Owen called out, "I'm home. And I've got . . . it."

Miriam noticed Martin did not flinch, he didn't blink, he didn't even appear to be breathing. He gave no acknowledgment whatsoever of his father's arrival. Owen's stooped form filled the doorway. Miriam still could not get over how much taller he seemed now that he fit clothes three sizes smaller. Personally, she didn't like the scrawny look; she preferred the solid Owen. But as with Martin, what she had was enough. In fact, it was very good just to have him home.

"Your mother and I have something for you, Martin."

Miriam looked back over at Martin. There they were, all three in one room. Yet her son had never looked lonelier. Well, that might be about to change.

"I told you," Martin said, his voice barely a whisper. "I don't like it when you come in. . . ." He gasped.

Sliding across the floor, its four legs spread and the tiny toenails making scratching sounds as it slipped and scrambled across the parquet, a yellow Lab puppy careened around the bed and collided with Martin's legs. The animal quivered from the tip of its wet nose to its whipping tail. The two front paws tore at Martin's pants leg as it tried to jump onto his lap, missed, fell backward, gathered its paws together, and heaved itself upward yet again.

Miriam glanced at Owen. His face reflected her own hope mixed with apprehension. Their boy had to respond. If this worked, they might break through the barrier of indifference Martin had cemented himself behind. She watched Martin closely, wanting to give him time, give him space, give him love.

Owen coughed. "Well, what do you think? You like him? He's yours. You've always wanted a dog. Now you have one. It was your mother's idea, so you have her to thank."

Miriam quickly looked back at Owen. Why was he putting pressure on Martin? Hadn't they agreed not to do that? "Owen . . . ," she started to say, then caught the look of torment in her husband's eyes.

Of course. She had to remember that Martin's was not the only crippled spirit in her home. If you wait in a cage for more than half a year, the least you can expect is a normal, loving family. But they weren't normal. And Martin needed her attention more than Owen. There was only so much Miriam could do for them both. She could be there.

She could listen. She could use every tool Edith and the others had taught her. And she could pray for the miracle of restoration. But was it enough?

Torn now between her husband and her son, Miriam's heart went out to them both. She felt their brokenness in her own. She narrowed her eyes. *But Martin is a child.* Her child. Their child at home.

"Owen." Miriam stood and crossed the room to her husband. She laid a hand on his arm and could feel him shudder. "Owen, why don't I join you in the living room in a few minutes. Would that be okay?"

Her husband, in his wisdom, seemed to see what she did as she gazed at his ravaged face, twenty years older than a year ago. He nodded slowly. "You're right. I just upset him when I'm like this. It's all right, Miriam. I understand."

Owen left the room, reaching to close the door behind him. Miriam's gratitude that he had never asked her to choose between him and their son left her weak with relief.

She turned back to Martin, but he hadn't moved. His mouth still hung open in midgasp as he watched the puppy at his feet bounce up and down like an out-of-balance beach ball, throwing itself at Martin, straining for attention. As the door clicked behind Owen, though, something clicked inside Martin. Miriam saw him focus on the dog. His mouth closed.

"Martin? What do you . . . ?" Before Miriam could finish, Martin sprang into action.

He grabbed the puppy by the scruff of the neck and threw it across the room. It landed with a yelp of terror on the mattress, rebounded off the padded headrest, and tumbled onto the floor, disappearing under the bed. A trail of urine drops dotted the bedspread.

Miriam clamped her jaw shut and pressed her palms against her thighs. It took all her self-control to not reach for Martin, not yell, not shout, not give in to the fear and panic rising all around her. Was this what she was left with? A broken boy, a shattered husband, and . . .

She remembered Edith's words. *"You choose to ask for help, choose to be strong."*

Help me.

She tried to listen. What was Martin trying to say? Was it Owen's leaving the room that had upset him so much? Being left alone again? But she was there. Where was her Martin? Back in Africa? He had to still be in there somewhere. Would he ever forgive her enough to allow her to love him again?

All these questions pummeled Miriam, and yet she waited, saying nothing. Martin stood opposite her, panting with emotion. This was good, she told herself, better than the stone-cold mask of unconcern. Yes. Emotion was good.

Still Miriam waited. They could both hear the puppy whining under the bed. It made little yelping sounds that finally faded to a wheeze.

Martin looked at her, his eyes defiant yet focused on her own, no longer glazed over. He said, "It shouldn't jump up."

More silence.

"That's not allowed. Besides, it's probably covered with ticks and leeches."

"Why do you say that?" Miriam asked finally, her voice relatively under control.

"That's what Joseph said when I petted a dog. 'Don't touch them. They're covered with ticks and leeches.' "

Miriam sucked in her breath. This talking about Africa was also good. It meant he was facing his past instead of blocking it out. Still . . .

Believe.

"Martin? I believe that puppy needs a name."

Martin nodded. "Dog."

A response. A one-on-one response. A connection. A casting of lots, a bet on the future, an investment, a name to be used in safer times.

Miriam wanted to try again, but she still did not dare to move, afraid of breaking the spell. How to do this without arousing the guilt?

Martin squatted to the floor. Miriam took her cue and lowered herself with him, the top of the bed now at eye level. They both looked under the bed at the shivering bundle blinking in the darkness.

Miriam asked the question. "What do you think he's feeling . . . why doesn't he come out?"

Martin cast his glance at the soiled bedspread, caught her eyes, then looked down, reaching into the recess between them. "He's afraid."

In this new place, I pray for my brother. I pray for the killer of my brother. I pray for my enemy, but I do not pray for his sake; I pray for mine. This is a selfish thing I do, for when I obey this command of His. Jesus' healing power works inside of me.

Here I have found extreme favor in the eyes of the Lord God Almighty. Blessed be His name, for now when He calls me by mine, I hear. Many add their voices to His, using my new name, Daw, "Light." May they see His light, the light of His love, through this, my story.

In my culture, a story is a gift. You open yourself to the words and their power, you become one with the story, and it will change you. In this place, my gift to you is a truth I have run from. This truth has cost me dearly, but I pray it will set us free.

Now I have written this, a story-gift from the future. But this story, you may not want to read because it is so hard, sometimes it hurts.

This story, it has cost me more than any other story. It is the truth, my truth, the proof of God's own hand upon me.

Indeed, God has been so busy with my life, I wonder how He has had time for anyone else.

Miriam sat at her desk, the sun streaming through the open leaded-glass window as hushed voices gathered like a storm in her mind. She still could not know, would not know, how their voices had joined her own, now all wondering, whispering, waiting in this place of past raw fear, present raw hope.

What did she hear?

Miriam sighed, listening to seagulls and traffic and even a distant cable car, the sounds jarring her back to the present. She removed the last stack of paper from the printer and added it to the pile, holding all the pages upright and tapping them on the desk to align the edges.

The row of books on arbitration law lined up to her right. She reached to her left and gently closed the green journal. Its leather cover dropped onto the red-stained pages with a sigh of its own.

A single voice broke through these thoughts as easily as the light falling on her face and hands.

The screen door slammed, and Miriam heard the thud of a book-filled backpack landing on the floor.

"Me, Daw, I am home."

AUTHOR'S NOTE

I know two worlds. Here and there.

For my sisters here, know that I wrote this on a laptop, amidst comfort and plenty. If you have never balanced a burden on your head, then I know that you, like I, live in warmth from wool and oil but search, perhaps, for more.

For my sisters there, on the off chance that a copy of this book should find its way into your postal box, the mail brought in once a week by a neighbor going into town, know that I wrote this for you, inspired by your endurance, your dignity, your integrity. How I long to share you with our African-American sisters, to show them there is another place, another way, a place of even more beauty and color, where our fathers and mothers came from, a place remembered by the rhythm in our souls and the grace in our hearts.

Elise Potter, my one sister, was the first to show me that all the children are our children. She lives the compassion and justice for children I write about. Her son, Hing, gave me the ending for this novel; I owe him big time.

There the rules seem changed. The light is different. The unimaginable happens daily. I have written about these things and you have wondered. But remember, although the story of Miriam is fiction, all of the circumstances surrounding it are true, based on my own travels in these areas, interviews, and extensive research.

A few examples. I have had the privilege of learning from professional negotiators, drawing on their expertise and personal stories. The methodology I portray as Edith's trauma therapy is based on my interview with a leading Christian psychologist who has pioneered trauma treatment for victims of many types of abuse and particularly for child-soldier victims in Uganda. I visited the refugee camp in Tanzania and interviewed aid workers and refugees. I heard the children's voices, faithfully preserved in the voice of Little Lion. The poem at the beginning of chapter 20 was given to me by Vumilia Tchikala, a Congolese child in this camp.

Angolan rebels did attack the jeep of a French family on vacation, killing the parents and their three children along the Caprivi Strip in Namibia.

The peace of Mozambique continues to confound historians. It provides the model for other conflict-ridden areas in the world, a herald of hope.

Meanwhile, more than three hundred thousand boys and girls—some as young as six years old—are forced to serve as child-soldiers in armies around the world.

Groups of children traversing vast reaches of Africa amidst the worst of dangers do exist. In 1987, an estimated thirty thousand Christian children (known as The Lost Boys of Sudan) fled southern Sudan and the war, fearing kidnapping, forced enlistment, and slavery at the hands of the northern Sudanese, Arab-Muslim government forces. In 1991, after four years of safety, their Ethiopian protector, Mengistu Haile Mariam, was driven from power, and the children trekked back to Sudan. This time, more than ten thousand died from hunger, attacks from wild animals, exhaustion, drowning, and bullets.

A year later, the surviving twelve thousand children arrived in the Kakuma refugee camp of northern Kenya. For the last fourteen years these children, now young adults, have cared for each other. Refugee workers say they are remarkable in their compassion for one another and their unshakable faith. Some later left the camp and continued their wandering. In 1999, three thousand managed to emigrate to the U.S. and now live scattered across forty-four cities. Within the first year of their arrival, all were attending school; some have graduated from high school and continued to university. Social workers describe the boys' achievements as miraculous.

The Ediths are still there. Different wars, different power struggles, thirteen million orphans and one more genocide later, but they are there. I met one such Edith on a bus from Nairobi to Arusha, traveling through the heart of Masailand, a price on her head because she works for peace.

Anne de Graaf,
The Netherlands

ACKNOWLEDGMENTS

After a long journey, I am deeply grateful to so many who pointed me in the right direction:

- Nelson Mandela, Nobel Peace Prize laureate and founder of the Nelson Mandela Children's Fund, and his wife, Graça Machel, United Nations Secretary-General's expert on children in armed conflict

- Gary Haugen, director of the UN genocide investigation in Rwanda

- Lucy Reed, Brenda de Munck, and Teo van der Weele, whose personal stories inspire this story

- Anne Christian Buchanan and Dan Elliott, my editors, who not only saw the potential of this story but knew how to realize it

- Tyndale House acquisitions editors Becky Nesbitt and Jan Stob, who shared my vision

- My One-Heart, Aglow, and Chi Libris brothers and sisters, who prayed me through a three-year season of writing

- Friends in Nyarugusu refugee camp, Tanzania, who are still waiting for peace, and who helped me hear the children's voices, Rev. Mlanda Dunia, Wilondja-Kizai Tunza and Muzindikwa Basubi Job and the children in their classes, and Etoka Kiza-Miwade

- Rocky Mabuga, Abiyudi Msumeno, Agness Lyogello, Eric, Sylvester, Aristidi, Hillary, David and all the others of World Vision Makere, Tanzania, who made me feel at home, gave in so many ways, and taught me the greater meaning of "servant"

- Meriane Buhama and Jacob of World Vision Kasulu, Tanzania

- Dirk Booy, director; Wilson Lutainulwa; and Aggrey Assante of World Vision Tanzania

- Kai Nielsen, Deputy Representative of UNHCR Tanzania

- Joseph Kithama, a friend foremost, who helped open the doors I needed to pass through in order to reach the children

- Gerry Dyer and Erik Detiger of UNICEF Tanzania

- Oscar Pekelder, director of World Vision The Netherlands

Many thanks to St. John & St. Philip's Anglican Church in The Hague, including my brothers and sisters from Sudan, Tanzania, Kenya, Zimbabwe, Liberia, Ethiopia, and Nigeria, and Nigeria's ambassador to The Netherlands, Dr. Awolowo-Dosumu. Your voices resonate throughout the book in the descriptions of all that is beautiful in Africa.

Three girlfriends in particular deserve notice: Laurel Dukehart encouraged, Robin Jones Gunn believed, and Joyce Nyanyira fed me faith, helped point out cultural inaccuracies—my apology for any I missed—and declared me an honorary African.

Also, thank you, Florence. Your family's continued hope in a dark place is why I wrote this story.

Most of all, thank you to my family: Daniël, who cheered me on with every smile; Julia, for her young-wise insights; and Erik, my own true North.

I encourage you to contact local branch offices of these groups for information.

- World Vision is a Christian humanitarian organization serving the world's poorest children and families in nearly 100 countries. World Vision helps communities, families, and their children trapped in the vicious cycle of poverty to overcome difficult circumstances and achieve their dream of self-sufficiency. Whether through emergency relief or ongoing development, World Vision staff represent Jesus Christ's love and compassion for people impacted by wars, poverty, or disaster. World Vision's assistance extends to all people, regardless of religious beliefs, gender, or ethnic background.

- The United Nations Children's Fund (UNICEF) is mandated by the UN General Assembly to advocate for protection of children's rights, to help meet their basic needs, and to expand their opportunities to reach their full potential. UNICEF helps children get the care and stimulation they need in the early years of life and encourages families to educate girls as well as boys. It strives to reduce childhood death and illness and to protect children in the midst of war and natural disaster. UNICEF supports young people, wherever they are, in making informed decisions about their own lives, and strives to build a world in which all children live in dignity and security.

- The Office of the United Nations High Commissioner for Refugees (UNHCR) is mandated by the United Nations to lead and coordinate international action for the worldwide protection of refugees and the resolution of refugee problems. Its primary purpose is to safeguard the rights and well-being of refugees. It strives to ensure that everyone can exercise the right to seek asylum and find safe refuge in another State, with the option to return home voluntarily, integrate locally or to resettle in a third country.

ABOUT THE AUTHOR

Since 1987 Anne de Graaf has traveled extensively in Eastern Europe and sub-Saharan Africa, including Mozambique, Namibia, Zimbabwe, Botswana, and Tanzania, where she has interviewed villagers; UNICEF, UNHCR, and World Vision field personnel; and trauma therapists working with children. She stayed in a Tanzanian camp with more than 50,000 refugees, over half of whom were children. In writing The Children's Voices series she has interviewed international negotiators and collected quotes from children all over the world who are seeking hope after being traumatized by war.

Anne de Graaf has written more than eighty books, which have been translated into more than fifty languages and have sold more than 5 million copies worldwide. The novels in her Hidden Harvest series (Bethany House Publishers) are based on true stories of Christians in Poland, interviews, and intensive research. These books have sold in seven countries. The final book of the series, *Out of the Red Shadow*, won the Christy Award 2000 for International Historical Fiction. During the 1999 Frankfurt World Book Fair, she was awarded the East-European Christian Literature Award.

Anne de Graaf has also worked as a journalist for the Dutch national press agency and as an economics translator for the Dutch government. Born in San Francisco and a graduate of Stanford University, she has lived the past twenty years in Ireland and The Netherlands with her husband and their two children.